JUSTINE,
OR THE MISFORTUNES OF VIRTUE

DONATIEN-ALPHONSE-FRANÇOIS, MARQUIS DE SADE, was born in Paris in 1741 into an old patrician family. He was educated at the Jesuit college of Louis-le-Grand and at military school at Versailles. The end of the Seven Years War in 1763 dashed his hopes of a military career, and that same year he reluctantly made the good match his impoverished father forced on him by marrying Renée-Pélagie de Montreuil, daughter of a recently ennobled but wealthy lawyer. Serious sexual misdemeanours brought him to the attention of the police and he was jailed twice for his excesses. In 1772, for attempted murder and sodomy, he was sentenced to death and his effigy was burned in his absence. In 1777, after years spent in not uncomfortable hiding, mainly at his chateau at La Coste near Avignon, he was jailed and not released until 1790. During his prison years study was his therapy and writing his salvation. It was now that he developed a coherent system of atheistical materialism and wrote plays, novels, and the stories of *Les Crimes de l'amour* (*The Crimes of Love*), which he published in 1800. In the 1790s, having no love for the *ancien régime* which had deprived him of his freedom, he played a minor role in the revolution. Jailed as a political moderate, he escaped the guillotine in July 1794 by an administrative accident. Describing himself as 'a man of letters', he tried to make a living from the novels (*Justine*, 1791; *Aline et Valcour*, 1795; *La Nouvelle Justine* and *L'Histoire de Juliette*, both 1797) which justified their obscenities by reference to a comprehensive system of sexual *realpolitik*. In 1801 he was jailed as the author of *Justine*, and in 1803 was transferred to the lunatic asylum at Charenton, diagnosed as suffering from 'libertine dementia'. He continued to write and even helped to stage plays for the inmates. His applications for release were consistently rejected, and he remained a captive until his death in December 1814. Against his wishes, he was given a Christian funeral, but was buried in an unmarked grave.

JOHN PHILLIPS is Lecturer in French at Wadham College, University of Oxford, and Emeritus Professor of French, London Metropolitan University. He has written widely on Sade and his books include *Sade: The Libertine Novels* (2001), *The Marquis de Sade: A Very Short Introduction* (2005), and *How to Read Sade* (2005).

OXFORD WORLD'S CLASSICS

*For over 100 years Oxford World's Classics have brought
readers closer to the world's great literature. Now with over 700
titles—from the 4,000-year-old myths of Mesopotamia to the
twentieth century's greatest novels—the series makes available
lesser-known as well as celebrated writing.*

*The pocket-sized hardbacks of the early years contained
introductions by Virginia Woolf, T. S. Eliot, Graham Greene,
and other literary figures which enriched the experience of reading.
Today the series is recognized for its fine scholarship and
reliability in texts that span world literature, drama and poetry,
religion, philosophy, and politics. Each edition includes perceptive
commentary and essential background information to meet the
changing needs of readers.*

OXFORD WORLD'S CLASSICS

OXFORD WORLD'S CLASSICS

THE MARQUIS DE SADE

Justine,
or the Misfortunes of Virtue

Translated with an Introduction and Notes by
JOHN PHILLIPS

OXFORD
UNIVERSITY PRESS

OXFORD
UNIVERSITY PRESS

Great Clarendon Street, Oxford, OX2 6DP,
United Kingdom

Oxford University Press is a department of the University of Oxford.
It furthers the University's objective of excellence in research, scholarship,
and education by publishing worldwide. Oxford is a registered trade mark of
Oxford University Press in the UK and in certain other countries

Translation, Introduction, Select Bibliography, and Explanatory Notes © John Phillips 2012
Note on Money © David Coward 1992
Chronology © David Coward 2005

The moral rights of the authors have been asserted

First published as an Oxford World's Classics paperback 2012

Impression: 16

British Library Cataloguing in Publication Data

Data available

Library of Congress Cataloging in Publication Data

Data available

ISBN 978–0–19–957284–7

Printed and bound in Great Britain by Clays Ltd, Elcograf S.p.A.

CONTENTS

CONTENTS

INTRODUCTION

INSANE pornographer obsessed with cruel, violent and perverse forms of sex, woman-beater, child rapist, and even murderer—these are just some of the more lurid labels that have been attached to the infamous Marquis de Sade over the last two centuries. Conversely, the French surrealists of the early twentieth century sanctified the 'divine marquis' as arch-transgressor and apostle of freedom. The real Sade, however, is a figure of far greater complexity than allowed by any such simplistic labels, all of which derive from myth rather than fact. He is a figure of uncertainty and contradiction, and at the same time an author of considerable erudition and intellect. His work ranges across a wide variety of genres, from novels, short stories, and plays to political, philosophical, and literary essays. His rhetorical talents and mastery of expression have been widely acknowledged in all of these genres, but it is for his *contes* or novellas, such as the first version of *Justine*, that he has received the most critical praise. It is, however, in the 1791 publication, *Justine, or the Misfortunes of Virtue*, the second, novel-length version of the *Justine* saga, that the author is able to develop and explore at greater leisure the embryonic themes of the original *conte*: the overwhelming force of the sex drive, the corruption of contemporary institutions, especially the aristocracy and the Church, the bankruptcy of certain current philosophical ideas and the astuteness of others, and above all, the absurdity of any notion of divine providence. This doctrine, fundamental to both Christianity and to philosophical optimism, according to which virtue would ultimately be rewarded and vice punished, is dramatically and outrageously reversed in Justine's sorry tale. The effects of such a reversal in the light of the author's declared intention to make the reader prouder of virtue have long been a matter of controversy. We shall return to this question presently. First, given the close relationship between Sade's character and the fictions he created, a brief survey of his life will provide an indispensable context.

The Marquis de Sade, 1740–1814

Donatien-Alphonse-François de Sade was born in 1740, son of

Jean-Baptiste-Joseph-François, Comte de Sade, Lord of Saumane and Mazan, cavalry-officer and diplomat, and of Mlle Maillé de Carman, a lady-in-waiting and poor distant cousin of the Princesse de Condé. The main influences on Sade's young life were his father and his paternal uncle, the Abbé Jacques-François de Sade, who were both active debauchees. At the same time, both were highly cultured men. Sade's father was a close friend of Voltaire and himself wrote verses, while Donatien's uncle in particular had a fine and extensive library which, alongside the classic authors, included all the major works of contemporary Enlightenment philosophy as well as a fair sample of erotic writings. As Donatien spent much of his early childhood at the family chateau of Saumane in Provence in the care of his uncle, he had plenty of time to become well acquainted with this library of free-thinking authors.

The future writer and roué grew up, then, in a world of progressive ideas and libertine tastes. It was also a predominantly masculine world. When he was not in the company of his father and uncle, Donatien's early education was divided between the Jesuit college of Louis-le-Grand in Paris, which he attended alongside other boys of the French aristocracy and haute bourgeoisie between the ages of ten and fourteen, and a young preceptor by the name of Abbé Amblet, who taught him reading, arithmetic, geography, and history. Amblet was a gentle and highly intelligent man, and the only male member of the child's entourage who was not a libertine. From the Jesuits, Sade acquired a taste for rigorous intellectual inquiry, the debating skills of classical rhetoric, and above all, a lifelong passion for the theatre. The Jesuits' enthusiasm at this time for both sodomy and corporal punishment may also have helped shape the young Marquis's nascent sexuality. As for his mother, she appeared to take very little interest in her only child. Her relative absence from his childhood is often seen by critics as the possible source of the mother-hatred that permeates Sade's adult writings.

At the age of fourteen Sade was sent to a prestigious military academy to train to serve in the light cavalry regiment of the King's guard. In 1763, following some years of action in the Seven Years War as a junior officer, the now twenty-two-year-old Marquis left one dissolute life as a soldier for another as a Paris socialite, much to the exasperation of his now destitute father, who determined to find him a wife and a dowry without delay. The Comte quickly came up with the daughter of a senior Paris judge. About the same age as Donatien, Renée-Pélagie de Montreuil came from the recently ennobled bourgeoisie rather than from the traditional aristocracy to which the Sade family proudly belonged, but the Montreuils were well connected and wealthy, and offered a substantial dowry for their eldest daughter. Renée-Pélagie was a plain girl and no great intellect, yet her strength of character and devotion would prove a great support to her husband throughout their long marriage. Her mother, the Présidente de Montreuil, was a formidable woman who would also play a significant role in the Marquis de Sade's destiny.

Following their wedding, on 17 May 1763, the young couple were initially housed by the Montreuils, either in their Paris house or their chateau in Normandy. It was at this time that Sade began to put on plays, allocating parts to his wife and even his mother-in-law, indulging an abiding interest in the theatre.

This domestic harmony was short-lived, however. Only five months after the wedding the Marquis was arrested for the crime of debauchery and imprisoned at Vincennes. Having paid a twenty-year-old Parisian prostitute named Jeanne Testard to spend the night with him, Sade had shocked her religious sensibilities by talk of masturbating into a chalice, and proposing to thrust communion hosts into her vagina. He had then frightened her with whips and other weapons into committing a number of similar sacrilegious acts. On 13 November 1763 the King ordered his release after only three weeks, on condition that he reside at the Montreuils' Norman chateau and stay out of trouble.

In 1764 the Marquis was given permission to move back to Paris. During the next few years Sade fell in and out of love with three women, all actresses that he met while frequenting the theatrical milieu. One might conjecture that this succession of painful amorous experiences eventually had a desensitizing effect on his emotional character. The last of these affairs was with a Mlle Beauvoisin, whom he even passed off as his wife on a visit to La Coste, where the Sade family owned a castle and land.

In January 1767 Sade's father died, at the age of sixty-five. This was a traumatic event for Donatien, who had been very close to the Comte in spite of their many quarrels. Later that year he returned to Paris for the birth of Louis-Marie, the first of Renée-Pélagie's children who would survive into adulthood.

While still in Paris over a year later, on Easter Sunday 1768, Sade picked up a thirty-six-year-old beggar named Rose Keller and, on the pretext of needing a cleaner, took her to a little country house he had rented at Arcueil. Once there, he locked the woman up, ordered her to strip, and whipped her, pouring what felt to her like molten wax into her wounds. Keller later managed to escape from the house and report her experience to the police. Sade was duly arrested and taken to the royal prison at Saumur, where he was held for a fortnight before being transferred to Pierre-Encize, another royal prison near Lyons. After a hearing at which Sade categorically denied any intention of causing Keller serious harm (the medical evidence in fact supported his defence) and claimed that the woman was a prostitute who had accepted money for sexual purposes, he was fined and released after a few months' imprisonment, on condition that he return to Provence and remain there until further notice.

Around this time the huge debts that Sade incurred to pay for his sexual pleasures and also for the theatrical activities at La Coste were beginning to change his mother-in-law's view of him, a process that would culminate eventually in her outright hostility. But the single event that probably did most damage to his relationship with La Présidente was the love-affair with his wife's youngest sister, Anne-Prospère de Launay, who was as beautiful as Renée-Pélagie was plain. Fresh from her convent schooling, and still dressed as a nun, this pretty and, by all accounts, flirtatious twenty-year-old must have represented to Sade all the taboos that his fictional characters would take such pleasure in breaking: virginity, incest, and religion. Another major scandal would soon send them off together into Italy's most romantic city.

On 22 June 1772 Sade and his valet, Latour, set off for Marseilles, ostensibly to secure a loan to pay the Marquis's debts. It was not long, however, before they were looking to spend the money Sade had just borrowed in France's southern city of sin. In humorous self-disguise, the two men swapped names, Sade calling his servant Monsieur le Marquis, while Latour addressed his master as Lafleur (which would later be the name of a valet in *Philosophy in the Boudoir*), and organized a session of debauchery with four young prostitutes, ranging in age from eighteen to twenty-three. The session included acts of flagellation and sodomy. The girls were also asked to swallow pastilles containing cantharides (or 'Spanish fly'), a well-known aphrodisiac, although the intention on this occasion was to cause flatulence, the effects of which Sade found particularly arousing. One of the girls became ill, and complained to the authorities that Sade had tried to poison her. Less than a week later a warrant was issued for the two men's arrest, and on 9 July the police arrived at La Coste to take them into custody, but an actor in Sade's theatre company having warned of the allegations made in Marseilles, Sade and Latour had already fled, accompanied this time by the ravishing Anne-Prospère. In spite of Renée-Pélagie's attempts to bribe the girls into withdrawing their accusations, the two men were found guilty of all charges and condemned to death in absentia (sodomy alone carried the death-sentence at this time), and on 12 September their bodies were symbolically burned in effigy. By now the three fugitives had reached Venice, Sade travelling under the pseudonym of the Comte de Mazan.

This was the first of three Italian trips that Sade undertook between 1772 and 1776 in his attempts to escape French justice. These journeys prompted him to write his first major literary work, *Travels in Italy* (*Voyages d'Italie*), a sort of travelogue with philosophical and historical commentaries, which would not be published until 1795 but which represented an important stage in his formation as a writer and thinker. On the one hand the travel perspective enabled Sade to develop a theme to which he would repeatedly return in his libertine fiction, and which would come to form the basis of his opposition to the absolutism of religious morality: the cultural and historical relativity of human mores. On the other hand, in their increasing improbability, events in the Marquis de Sade's life were beginning to resemble the picaresque adventures of the typical eighteenth-century hero of fiction, and so would also provide ample inspiration, as well as geographical and cultural material, for the novels he would write in the 1790s. During this period Sade managed to elude capture by the French authorities, until he was eventually arrested in Chambéry in December 1772 by order of the King of Sardinia and detained at the sixteenth-century fortress of Miolans. Renée-Pélagie did all she could to obtain his release, but the Montreuils exercised their influence to keep him locked up. At the instigation of Madame de Montreuil, warrants for Sade's arrest were issued and reissued over the next few years. Before the first extended period of Sade's imprisonment, which began in 1777 and was to last until the Revolution, there was one more

scandal which greatly assisted La Présidente in her vigorous campaign
to get her embarrassing son-in-law permanently incarcerated.

During a period of prolonged residence in hiding at La Coste
between 1774 and 1775, the Marquis had hired five girls and a young
male secretary for the winter. It was Anne Sablonnière, a young
woman of twenty-four, otherwise known as 'Nanon', who helped
find the girls and was as a consequence alleged later to have acted as
procuress. There was probably some truth in this, in that the intention had almost certainly been to organize a little harem. In addition
to the six youngsters and Nanon, there was also Renée-Pélagie's
maid, Gothon, a young girl from a Swiss Protestant family. In January
1775 Sade was accused of having abducted the five young girls. This
situation was exacerbated in the spring of that year by Nanon's giving birth to an illegitimate child and claiming that Sade was the
father. This affair was hushed up by the Sade and Montreuil families, who conspired to get Nanon arrested for an alleged theft of
three silver plates and locked away in a house of detention at Arles,
where she would remain for three years. Her baby died of neglect at
La Coste at the age of ten weeks. As for the five girls, four were sent
off to various nunneries to keep them quiet, while one chose to stay
with Renée-Pélagie as scullery-maid. Nevertheless, the whole business had done Sade's reputation considerable damage, and fearing
another police raid on La Coste, he set off again for Italy. It was a year
before he felt safe enough to return to France.

Settling down once more in his chateau in Provence, Sade again
began to recruit young girls. These included a pretty twenty-two-
year-old named Catherine Treillet, whom Sade nicknamed Justine.
Her father, a local weaver, gradually became concerned about the
goings-on at La Coste and decided to take his daughter home by
force. When the daughter refused to go with him, he marched up to
the chateau and fired off a shot at the Marquis. This incident obviously had legal repercussions which contributed to a fateful decision.
In his legal battle with Treillet, Sade determined to seek satisfaction
in the Paris courts, and on 8 February 1777 he and Renée-Pélagie
arrived in the capital, where he learned that his mother had died
three weeks earlier. This was a perfect opportunity for Madame de
Montreuil to get rid of her wayward son-in-law once and for all, and
within a week of his arrival in Paris Sade was arrested and again
imprisoned in the fortress of Vincennes.

The following year the verdict imposed on Sade and his valet for the Marseilles 'poisoning' was in fact annulled by the court at Aix, but Madame de Montreuil was able to have a new *lettre de cachet* issued to keep her son-in-law detained. On the return journey from the Aix appeal to prison at Vincennes, however, the Marquis managed to give his guards the slip when they stopped at a coaching inn at Vincennes, and disappeared into the surrounding countryside, heading for La Coste, which he reached on foot at eight o'clock the next morning. His freedom was short-lived, however, for just six weeks later a detachment of ten armed men stormed the chateau and hauled him back to Vincennes.

This fleeting taste of liberty was the only interruption in a thirteen-year period of detention, initially at Vincennes and then in the Bastille, to which Sade was transferred in February 1784. To fill the long days and evenings he read voraciously, gradually amassing a varied and extensive library which included the classics he had read as a child (for example, Homer, Virgil, Montaigne, La Fontaine, Boccaccio), works of Enlightenment philosophy by Buffon, La Mettrie, d'Holbach, Diderot, Rousseau, and Voltaire, and of course drama and fiction, by Beaumarchais, Marivaux, Voltaire, Defoe, Rousseau, Shakespeare, and many others. In the solitude of his prison-cell Sade began to write in earnest, producing a remarkable number of works in a relatively short time. Indeed, his literary output was so great that in 1788 he was able to compose a comprehensive catalogue of his works, listing no fewer than eight novels and volumes of short stories, sixteen historical novellas, two volumes of essays, an edition of diary notes, and some twenty plays. From this canon of writings only a small number survived the storming of the Bastille in 1789.

All of the plays and two important works of prose—the lengthy epistolary novel *Aline et Valcour*, and the philosophical short story 'Les Infortunes de la vertu' ('The Misfortunes of Virtue'), which would form the basis of the full-length libertine novel *Justine* that Sade would publish after the Revolution—conformed in every sense to accepted literary norms. On the other hand, of the libertine works composed during these prison years, the novel *Les Cent vingt journées de Sodome* (*The One Hundred and Twenty Days of Sodom*), written between 1782 and 1785, and a philosophical essay with strong libertine overtones, *Dialogue entre un prêtre et un moribond* (*Dialogue between a Priest and a Dying Man*; 1782), show a total disregard for the conventions of form as well as of content. The obscene works that he began to produce in prison in the 1780s and completed for publication in the 1790s are of considerably more interest than anything else he wrote.

In the months and weeks immediately preceding the storming of the Bastille on 14 July 1789 angry crowds were in the habit of gathering beneath its walls. Sade quickly saw that the present unrest offered his best chance of freedom in thirteen years, and he shouted to the mob below that the guards were about to cut the prisoners' throats. This provocative act immediately got Sade moved to the lunatic asylum at Charenton, a few miles south of Paris. Ten days later the citizens of Paris invaded the fortress, murdering the governor and plundering or destroying those manuscripts that Sade had not been able to smuggle out of the building. Among the lost works was the unfinished manuscript of *The One Hundred and Twenty Days of Sodom*, which would not resurface until the beginning of the twentieth century. Sade was eventually set free in April 1790 thanks to the abolition by the new National Assembly of *lettres de cachet*, the legal means by which so many had been held indefinitely without trial under the *ancien régime*.

Sade was now a penniless and obese man of nearly fifty. Renée-Pélagie, who had remained utterly devoted to her husband throughout most of his time in prison, had by this time resolved to live alone in a Paris convent and refused to see him. It was not long, though, before the Marquis' old magnetic charm was able to rescue him from dying of starvation in the streets. That summer Sade met the woman who would take his wife's place as lover and loyal companion. Constance Quesnet, a thirty-three-year-old former actress, who was separated from her husband and had a six-year-old son, would remain at his side for the rest of his life. Nicknamed 'Sensible' or 'Sensitive' by Sade because of her highly strung temperament, Constance was a modestly educated but gentle, loving, and intelligent woman. The couple scraped a living on her small allowance, while Citizen Louis Sade, as he was now forced to call himself, tried to get his plays performed at the Comédie française and other leading Paris theatres. These efforts were largely unsuccessful, however, and Sade's increasing poverty, brought about by years of mounting debts and the seizure of his lands under the Revolution, drove him to publish 'well-spiced' novels that he hoped would have a large sale: *Justine, or the Misfortunes of Virtue* in 1791, *Philosophy in the Boudoir* in 1795, *The New Justine* and *Story of Juliette* between 1797 and 1800. Only *Aline and Valcour*, published in 1795, and *Crimes of Love*, a collection of short stories which appeared in 1800, were sufficiently 'respectable' to be published under his own name. Citizen Sade was determined to make money, although in fact, for reasons which have more to do with the prevailing climate of taste in the 1790s than anything else, only the 1791 *Justine* achieved best-seller status.

Although remaining an aristocrat and a monarchist at heart, Sade nevertheless managed to survive the Revolution and the Terror of the Robespierre regime by playing the revolutionary game. This he did admirably, throwing himself energetically into local activities and penning well-received patriotic speeches. Indeed, for a former aristocrat his rise to prominence as a revolutionary was remarkable. He became secretary, then president of his section of the city for a brief period, and was eventually appointed one of the section's twenty judges, positions which he could easily have exploited to avenge himself on the Montreuils, whose death-warrants fate placed before him. A lifelong opponent of the death-penalty, however, Sade saved his in-laws and many others from the guillotine, a decision that eventually led to his arrest on 8 December 1793 on a trumped-up charge. In fact, the real reasons for his arrest were a now unfashionable atheism and 'judicial moderation', an ironic charge in the case of a man whose life and temperament could never have been described as moderate. Moved from one prison to another during the early months of 1794, Sade finally ended up at Picpus near Vincennes, a well-appointed former convent. It was here, from his cell window, that he watched as many of his fellow aristocrats mounted the steps of the guillotine, which had been moved there from the Place de la Révolution (the present-day Place de la Concorde) because of the stench of blood, their corpses being piled into a mass grave dug in the prison gardens. He would later write that the sight of the guillotine did him 'a hundred times more harm' than his imprisonment in the Bastille ever did. Sade himself escaped the guillotine thanks to a bureaucratic mix-up. In July 1794 his name appeared on a list of prisoners to be collected from Paris jails for judgement and execution that day, but as he failed to respond when his name was called he was marked down as absent. Within a short time the political climate had changed again, with Robespierre's own fall from grace and execution, and Sade was freed on 15 October.

For the next five years Sade and Constance got by as best they could. Sade would frequently write desperate letters to his lawyer Gaufridy, begging him to send money, though with little success. By 1799 the former aristocrat was even reduced to working as prompt in a Versailles theatre for forty sous a day.

After more than a decade of freedom, under the strict new censorship laws of the Bonaparte regime, Sade was arrested at his publishers' on 6 March 1801 for the authorship of *Justine*. For the first time in his life he was imprisoned because of his writings. Sade would remain in detention until his death in 1814. Less than two weeks after his arrest the Sade–Montreuil family arranged for the Marquis to be transferred to the Charenton asylum where he had briefly stayed in 1789, in surroundings far more salubrious than any of the Paris prisons. The authorities justified Sade's continued detention and move to an insane asylum by inventing the medical diagnosis of 'libertine dementia', although in no sense could Sade be described as demented. The arrangement was one of pure convenience for the family. With their father out of the way, the Marquis's two sons would have a better chance of finding suitable brides. In fact, Charenton offered Sade a number of distinct advantages. He had an expensively furnished two-room flat, with agreeable views, a library of several hundred volumes, and the freedom to walk in the gardens whenever he liked. Constance was allowed to move into the asylum with him, there were frequent dinner-parties, and Sade enjoyed a stimulating, if at times stormy, relationship with the asylum director, François de Coulmier. The latter was progressive enough to believe in the therapeutic value of drama. Consequently, for the first time in his life Sade was given free rein to indulge his greatest passion. A full-size theatre was built to house an audience of three hundred, and the Marquis given complete control of the rehearsal and performance of plays, which obviously included works written by himself. All of the plays performed at the asylum were wholly conventional in character (unlike the psycho-drama experiments represented in Peter Weiss's 1963 play *Marat-Sade*), and were acted by Sade, Constance, and other inmates with the support of professional actresses brought from the capital. The productions were highly successful and attracted large society audiences.

Sade continued to write at Charenton, producing four novels, of which only three have survived, all conventional historical narratives, a detailed diary, and a significant body of correspondence.

From the autumn of 1812 until his death two years later a sixteen-year-old girl named Madeleine Leclerc, whose mother worked in the asylum, visited Sade on a regular basis to perform paid sexual services, although diary entries suggest that the ageing prisoner doted on the girl and was jealous of her dalliances with young men.

Sade died on 2 December 1814 at the age of seventy-four. His last will and testament had directed that his body be buried without ceremony or headstone on land he had purchased at Malmaison, near Épernon. Acorns were to be sown around the spot, so that 'the traces of my grave will disappear from the surface of the earth as I trust my memory will disappear from the memory of men, except for those few who were kind enough to love me until the last, and fond memories of whom I take with me into my grave'. In complete disregard of these wishes, however, and as a final ironic twist to the colourful life of the eighteenth century's most infamous iconoclast, Sade's younger son, Armand, gave his father a full Christian burial in the Charenton cemetery. The would-be 'martyr for atheism' must have turned in his grave.

The Birth of Justine

There are three versions of Justine's story, which evolved from a hundred-page novella to a two-hundred-page novel and finally to a marathon saga of more than a thousand pages. The original version, 'The Misfortunes of Virtue' ('Les Infortunes de la vertu') was one among the many works penned by Sade during his long years of imprisonment between 1778 and 1790. A novella or short story with satirical aims (critics describe it as a *conte philosophique* or 'philosophical tale'), it was composed in fifteen days in 1787. It was largely conventional in style and lacked any characteristics that might now be termed obscene. Some have found this first draft of Sade's tale of virtue despoiled to contain an intensity and clarity of vision absent from the two subsequent versions, but it was destined never to reach the reading public in the author's lifetime.[1]

---

[1] It was not until 1909 that the manuscript came to light, thanks to the efforts of the poet Guillaume Apollinaire, and it was eventually published in 1930 by Maurice Heine. The novel was not available in unexpurgated form, however, until the 1960s.

The unpublished *conte* was to grow into the novel-length *Justine, or the Misfortunes of Virtue* (*Justine, ou les Malheurs de la vertu*), which appeared in 1791, a year after the author's release from prison. This version, the text translated here, is a predominantly first-person narrative in which Justine herself recounts her adventures to fellow travellers. *The New Justine*, published in 1797, was a greatly extended version of the tale of over a thousand pages, and far more explicit, if not pornographic. This final version, which was accompanied by numerous explicit illustrations, has been described as the most extensive work of print pornography ever undertaken.

Even the 1791 novel was considerably more violent and sexually explicit than the novella, and sold so well that five further editions had to be printed in the space of ten years. While the public's appetite for Sade's first published work was evidently insatiable, critical responses of the time were mixed. A contemporary review praises the author's 'rich and brilliant' imagination, while exhorting young people to 'avoid this dangerous book' and advising even 'more mature' men to read it 'in order to see to what insanities human imagination can lead', but then to 'throw it in the fire'.[2]

Justine was, after all, a 'libertine' novel, and very few such novels were published under the author's real name for fear of imprisonment or worse.[3] Both those found guilty of writing libertine works and their publishers could be sentenced to the guillotine. There were indeed numerous attempts by the authorities during the 1790s to stop sales of the novel, one of many so-called 'philosophical books' sold clandestinely *sous le manteau* or 'under the counter'.

Justine's story consists of a series of increasingly violent episodes of sexual abuse of the young orphan by libertine paedophiles, lascivious monks, murderous pederasts, and a ragbag of colourful characters: thieves, surgeons, counterfeiters, human vampires, and many other sexual predators. Scenes of sexual abuse alternate with long philosophical dialogues, during which the unshakeably devout young heroine attempts to convert all of her abusers to the Christian faith. These dialogues enable the author to lecture the reader on the futility

---

[2] *Journal général de France*, 27 Sept. 1792.

[3] In the seventeenth century the term 'libertine' was used to mean 'free-thinking' on a philosophical level, and was usually applied to atheists. By the beginning of the eighteenth century, however, it was increasingly employed to designate publications of a sexually obscene as well as anti-religious character.

of a belief in God or divine providence, the omnipotence of blind and amoral Nature, and thus to justify all acts of self-gratification at the expense of others.

In this version the account of the sexual cruelty and perversions to which Justine is subjected is given in her own voice, the voice of a sexually inexperienced and pious girl, and so obscenity is largely avoided in the main narrative, at least at a linguistic level.

Justine immediately appears to us as a passive creature, destined for martyrdom. A devout young child of twelve at the beginning of her remarkable odyssey, her religious faith remains implausibly unshaken by the unending catalogue of disasters that befall her throughout her relatively short and miserable existence. Suddenly left orphaned and destitute together with her fifteen-year-old sister, Juliette, she is first described to us in terms of what we would now consider to be a stereotype of feminine beauty (big blue eyes, teeth of ivory, lovely blonde hair). For the modern reader, the same physical features make up another stereotype—the dumb blonde—which is reinforced here by character traits connoting 'girlishness' and vulnerability (ingenuousness, sensitivity, naivety). Like her beauty, these traits can be also read on her physiognomy, at the very surface of her body: modesty, delicacy, shyness, and above all, the 'look of a virgin'. Justine's physical appearance immediately suggests that this is the part she will play: in Sade's terms, she is primed to be a victim of her own virtue (which will prevent her from enjoying the sexual attentions forced upon her, but which, more importantly, will determine the very nature of her attraction for the men and women who abuse her). She will also be the victim of the religious and social prejudices of a society that places a high value on the status of virginity, and in so doing creates a taboo that cries out to be transgressed.

In all of these respects Juliette is an exact opposite: not blonde, but brunette, with eyes not credulously blue but dark and 'prodigiously expressive'; not timid but spirited; not naive but incredulous; not innocent, but worldly wise thanks to the best possible education that a father's untimely ruin will deny her younger sister.

When both parents die and the two girls are left penniless orphans, Juliette's only response is the pleasure of being free. Even if we had not already been told at the beginning of the narrative of the fortune her beauty will help her to amass, we would know from this display of lack of feeling that, far from being a victim, the insensitive and self-serving Juliette will be one of life's winners. Not so the 'sad and miserable Justine'.

In the first two versions, when she finishes her sad tale Justine is recognized by her sister Juliette, whose rich and powerful lover succeeds in rescuing her from the gallows, and she goes to live with them in their chateau. Fate, however, cruelly cuts short Justine's life and her new-found happiness. In a savage metaphor for the sheer perversity of providence, she is finally split asunder by a thunderbolt during a violent thunderstorm. The evolution of this scene and its repercussions in the narrative reflects both the increasingly transgressive sexualization of Justine from one version to the next and, perhaps also, the author's changing attitude to his heroine. In the short story the bolt enters her right breast and comes out through her mouth, whereas in *Justine, or the Misfortunes of Virtue* the bolt exits through her abdomen and in *The New Justine* through her vagina. Furthermore, in the final version, in which there is no happy reunion, Justine's horrific death is not so much an accident as an event engineered by Juliette and her libertine friends, who sadistically drive her outside as the storm reaches its peak.[4]

Justine's Misfortunes

The change of title from one version to another is not without significance. 'Infortunes' connotes the unfortunate fate suffered by virtue through no fault of its own, but the ambiguity of 'Malheurs'— ill-luck, but also misery, the opposite of 'bonheur'—seems to imply that virtue is itself a wretched state, and so anyone embracing it has only herself to blame. In the second version, then, the juxtaposition of the heroine's name with her misery and its cause—*Justine, ou les Malheurs de la vertu*—personalizes the abstract title of the first version, focusing our attention on Justine as the source of her own misfortune.

The Dedication to this edition is addressed to the woman who by

---

[4] The ending of *The New Justine* is substantively different from that of the preceding versions. Having escaped from her death-cell, Justine encounters Juliette, who takes her back to her chateau where she recounts her story. Juliette then in turn relates her own life history, to be found in the companion volumes of *The Story of Juliette*, and Justine's death occurs at the very end of the *Juliette* narrative.

this time had become Sade's devoted companion, the aptly named Constance, and is designed to condition the responses, first of Constance, to whom the author speaks directly, and more generally of all those morally upright citizens that she, in her sensitivity, indirectly represents. Virtue, Sade implies, is best served when shown as the pitiful victim of vice, so that the reader will be unavoidably moved by her plight. Moreover, any attacks upon the work could only come from libertines, whose interest it is to show virtue triumphant; like Molière, his crusading predecessor, its author would then be an innocent victim of injustice and malevolence. Coming from the century's best-known libertine, such sentiments seem motivated less by a genuine love of virtue than by fear of imprisonment for the publication of a libertine novel.

At any rate, Sade was well aware of the novel's potential to shock, as a letter written to his lawyer, Reinaud, clearly reveals: 'A novel of mine is currently being printed, but one too immoral to be sent to a man as pious and as decent as you . . . It is called *Justine, or the Misfortunes of Virtue*. Burn it without reading it if by chance it falls into your hands. I disown it . . .'[5] Read in the light of this letter, the Dedication comes across as a transparently hypocritical attempt to construct a moral lesson. It is hard not to read the novel's 'happy ending' in the same way. Juliette and her lover are sufficiently moved by her sister's sudden death to follow the path of virtue to true happiness. Juliette joins a Carmelite convent and becomes the very embodiment of piety, whilst her lover embarks on a successful and exemplary career in government. On the basis of events that directly contradict the lessons in self-interest of the entire preceding narrative, the reader is invited to draw the wholly implausible conclusion that 'true happiness is found in the bosom of Virtue alone, and that if, for reasons which it is not ours to divine, God allows it to be persecuted on Earth, it is to make up for it in Heaven with the sweetest rewards'.

In stark contrast, the ending of *The New Justine* shows that Sade has abandoned all former pretences at writing a morally uplifting tale. Neither Juliette nor any of her companions undergoes a Pauline conversion to virtue—quite the opposite in fact—and the reader of *Juliette* is left in no doubt as to the rewards of vice.

---

[5] Quoted by Gilbert Lely, Avant-Propos, *La Nouvelle Justine*, 1 (Paris: Union Générale d'Éditions, 1978), 9 (my translation).

Philosophical and Literary Influences

Sade's work is rooted in the literary, political, and above all, philosophical climate of eighteenth-century France, and can best be read as part of an existing tradition, dating back to the mid-seventeenth century, a tradition from which Sade borrows extensively. Many well-known writers before Sade, including the philosophers Diderot and Mirabeau, had composed and published libertine works. Indeed, there was a lively commerce in illicit books in Paris throughout the eighteenth century, particularly in the years leading up to the Revolution. During this period 'philosophical' books, as they were known in the trade, included any work considered subversive by the authorities, from religious satires to political pamphlets attacking the monarchy. Obscenity was often used in such works as a satirical weapon to castigate a repressive and corrupt clergy and a decadent aristocracy. The abuse of rank and an oppressive justice system were also popular targets in this underground literature. Driven partly by similarly satirical intentions, Sade's obscene writings sit within this literary historical context, although his representation of libertinism is more extreme, more graphic, and more horrific than that of any of his predecessors or contemporaries. In our own predominantly secular age it is this depiction of a permissive, perverse, and violent sexuality that carries the most transgressive charge. In contrast, an eighteenth-century society steeped in Catholicism would have found the atheistic basis of Sade's moral philosophy and his blasphemous rejection of all religious belief far less tolerable.

Sade's atheism was heavily influenced by the work of two materialist philosophers of the Enlightenment: La Mettrie's *Man Machine* (1748) and Baron d'Holbach's *System of Nature* (1770). Materialism rejected belief in a soul or afterlife, reducing everything in the universe to the physical organization of matter. According to La Mettrie, scientific observation and experiment are the only means by which human beings can be defined, and this method tells us that Man is quite simply a machine, subject to the laws of motion like any mechanism of eighteenth-century science. The sole purpose of existence in this scheme of things is pleasure—a doctrine espoused with relish by so many of Sade's libertine characters. D'Holbach views the human being as a collection of atoms, so that even the conscience has a material origin, acquired from our education and experience. His system does not, therefore, allow for free will, since all our decisions are determined by our personal interest. For d'Holbach, all morality is a matter of social utility or pragmatism.

Sade described *System of Nature* as the true basis of his philosophy, and indeed lifted whole passages from it practically verbatim to place in the mouths of the libertines as they rail against the various dogmas of religion, especially the illusory concept of virtue. As atheistic materialism's most powerful and most controversial voice, Sade is the dark side of the Enlightenment because he says loud and clear what other Enlightenment philosophers hardly dare to whisper: the death of God and the renaissance of Man from the ashes of a God-centred universe. Sade's originality lies in placing the body at the centre of his atheistic philosophy, in siting philosophy in the boudoir, in making sex the driving force of all human action, more than a century before Freud.

Echoing Voltaire's *Candide*, with which Sade was almost certainly familiar, *Justine* reads as a ferocious satire, attacking the corruption of practically all contemporary institutions, including the judiciary, banking, the bourgeois-dominated world of finances in general, and above all the Catholic Church, its doctrines and its abusive practices.

Sade had good reason to hate all of these institutions. The spendthrift Marquis had frequently been obliged to seek loans at exorbitant rates of interest from greedy bankers. He had suffered years of imprisonment without proper trial at the hands of a corrupt judiciary. As for the Church, Sade's profound hatred of religion had a personal as well as an intellectual origin, given his Spartan education by the Jesuits and, later, his imprisonment for so-called sacrilegious acts. 'When atheism wants martyrs, let it choose them and my blood is ready,' declares the Comte de Bressac, in melodramatic expression of what were essentially the author's own sentiments.

In all these respects Sade's tale is decidedly Voltairean, but where Voltaire never quite found a satisfactory solution to the problem of physical and moral evil, other than to posit the concept of an indifferent God,[6] Sade's libertines dismiss belief in a deity altogether, and

---

[6] The only logical explanation, for Voltaire, to the problem of evil was that God had created the universe, rather like a clockmaker making a clock, had 'wound it up', and then left it to 'run down' on its own. This was the position of the Deist, for whom God existed but was indifferent to Man. On Voltaire's philosophical thought, see the Introduction to Voltaire, *Candide and Other Stories*, trans. and ed. Roger Pearson (Oxford World's Classics)

draw somewhat different conclusions from the observation, familiar to Candide, that the virtuous perish while the wicked survive. Candide and his fellow truth-seekers do eventually find a kind of contentment in the simple virtue of hard work. In contrast, Justine is repeatedly reminded of what the author-narrator had told the reader on the very first page: that 'in a century that is thoroughly corrupt, the safest course is to do as others do'. Jean-Jacques Rousseau's idealistic faith in Man's natural goodness is directly challenged in a dissertation delivered to Justine by Roland the counterfeiter: the only truth is that the strong not only survive but flourish at the expense of the weak. The image of nature presented in the novel is far removed from Rousseau's idealized view of an earthly utopia, inhabited by noble savages and uncorrupted by the evils of civilization. In the original version even Justine herself comes to the conclusion, on encountering the monstrous Roland, that 'Man is naturally wicked'. The note of optimism on which *Candide* ends is completely absent, then, from the far bleaker vision of life and death that closes *Justine*.

The common theme of all three versions of *Justine* is that the heroine's unreasonable attachment to virtue (and in particular to her virginity) attract nothing but misfortune, as she is exploited and abused physically and sexually by almost everyone she encounters, and is even framed for crimes of theft and murder.

This emphasis on Man's wickedness is to be found in two other great works of the period, Samuel Richardson's *Clarissa; or, The History of a Young Lady* (1747–8), in which virtue is also represented as an irresistible object of libertine abuse, and Pierre Choderlos de Laclos's masterly tale of Machiavellian manipulation, *Les Liaisons dangereuses*, published in 1782. Both must have had some influence on Sade. In his *Note on the Novel* (*Idée sur les romans*) of 1800, he lavishes fulsome praise on 'l'immortel Richardson', and although he never referred to *Les Liaisons* by name, we know that he kept a copy of it in his library at the Charenton asylum where he spent the last fifteen years of his life, and it is implausible to think that he had not read it when it was first published. There are, in fact, distinct echoes in the conception of Justine's character of Cécile Volanges, the young, delectable, and sexually innocent girl whom Laclos's libertines, the Vicomte de Valmont and the Marquise de Merteuil, take such pleasure in debauching. Other influences on the writing of Sade's novel can be found among the popular genres of the century:

fairy-tales, the Gothic novel ('roman noir'), and in particular the *conte moral* or 'moral tale'. Among fairy-tale elements of a general nature, which clearly detract from any realistic effect, there are giants (Gernande), and magical healing potions, while Justine's unfortunate experiences in the forest at the hands of Saint-Florent, the Comte de Bressac, and others seems directly inspired by stories of the *Little Red Riding Hood* type, and the great many other fairy-tales known to Sade from his youth in which a credulous young girl, lost in the woods, too willingly places her trust in those she encounters. More specifically, the vampiric Gernande's secret chamber filled with the bloody corpses of earlier spouses is strongly reminiscent of the tale of 'Bluebeard'. Gernande's isolated castle, Roland's mountain fortress, and the labyrinthine monastery of Sainte-Marie-des-Bois, together with their sepulchral trappings of torture-chambers, skulls, and the like, seem to come straight out of the Gothic novel, although the atheistic Sadean version is, of course, completely devoid of the genre's supernatural features.[7]

Narrative and Style

While Sade appears merely to borrow from the fairy-tale and the Gothic novel, it is the *conte moral* that undergoes parodic treatment in *Justine*. The 'recognition scene', a stock situation of the genre, in which characters long separated are tearfully reunited, is amusingly counterfeited in the reunion of the two sisters towards the end of the narrative. The style of the moral tale is parodied through excess—the *ton larmoyant* or 'tearful tone', and the heavy emphasis on *sensibilité* are clearly recognizable here, as in Justine's frequent lachrymose pleadings for mercy. Most controversially of all, the genre's moral aims are outrageously inverted: whereas the moral tale seeks to edify and improve its reader by extolling romantic love and showing how

[7] 'Gothic novels', popular in England especially from around the middle of the eighteenth century, were originally fictions depicting cruel passions and supernatural terrors, usually in a medieval setting, although by the nineteenth century any works with a gloomy, violent, and horrific atmosphere, such as Mary Shelley's *Frankenstein* (1818), came to be described as 'Gothic'. Typical examples contemporaneous with Sade are Horace Walpole's *The Castle of Otranto* (1764), Ann Radcliffe's *The Mysteries of Udolpho* (1794), and M. G. Lewis's *The Monk* (1795), which may itself have been inspired by the *Justine* of 1791. For more on the latter point, see my article, 'Circles of Influence: Lewis, Sade, Artaud', *Comparative Critical Studies* (Spring, 2012).

virtue alone leads to happiness, Sade's narrative demonstrates that
virtue leads repeatedly and inexorably to misery and that human rela-
tions are motivated mainly by lust or self-interest.

   The use of these models drawn from the popular literature of the
time clearly has an impact on the verisimilitude of the narrative.
Whatever her injuries, Justine always makes a perfect and speedy
recovery, often thanks to quasi-magical healing potions, and even the
mark of the thief branded on her shoulder by Rodin is completely
removed by surgeons following her reunion with Juliette. Like the
hero or heroine of some modern comic-book adventure story, she
extricates herself with astounding ease from all of those mortal perils
that beset her. The bloodthirsty Gernande, for example, forgets to
lock the door of her prison, and with one bound, she is free! At the
level of characterization, too, there is little concern with *vraisem-
blance*. In spite of the succession of depraved villains that confront
Justine, her naive credulity followed by her amazement when her
trust is betrayed remain implausibly unshaken. Equally implausible
is the apparently untarnished innocence of a girl who has already
been forced to participate in numerous orgies and should by now be
well used to the naked bodies of both sexes: 'Being little acquainted
with this part of the body,' she earnestly tells her listeners when
the loveliness of a particular female posterior is in question, 'you
will permit me to remain uncommitted on this point' (p. 233).
Characterization is here wholly subservient to plot. At the level of
discourse, finally, there is an equally apparent lack of regard for
plausibility. That the common thieves, Dubois and Ironheart
('Coeur de Fer'), should discourse like philosophers is unlikely, to
say the least, while the necessarily more sophisticated vocabulary
increasingly found in Justine's narrative as the years go by does at
times strain credulity, when we recall that her education was abruptly
terminated at the age of twelve. We should, of course, not be surprised by this lack of attention to verisimilitude. Sade's fiction is a
long distance from the realism that will come to dominate and in
many ways define the novel genre in the nineteenth century.

   Justine's arguments are not only stylistically but also intellectually
sophisticated enough to derive from her creator's own self-questioning.
That Justine is seen to match her opponents in the art of expression
and debate is both essential to the creation of a balanced and therefore
intellectually engaging debate, and necessary to ensure the ultimate

strength and supremacy of the libertine view. Contrastingly, the crude terms in which the libertines describe their sexual lusts are equally an expression of the author's own desires and fantasies, couched in a language that, in the dark confines of his cell in the Bastille, he must have found as titillating as did his libertine characters.

Justine's voice acts as an effective counterpoint to the vulgarity of her captors. As a religious prude she is obliged to avoid such vulgarity, while doing her best to recount her adventures as authentically as possible. This narrative structure imposes creatively productive limitations on a writer who is therefore obliged to come up with acceptable circumlocutions for sexual activities that his character might plausibly employ. Such a strategy produces a story of considerable inventiveness, in which different tones and linguistic registers provide interesting variety at the level of expression. In marked contrast to the verbosity of the libertines (which might be said to be the product of Sade's own tendency to write prose that is excessively convoluted in nature), Justine's voice frequently has a refreshing clarity and simplicity. Moreover, even when she is obliged to employ precious figures of speech to describe those perverse sexual activities she finds especially distasteful and abhorrent, the effect of such self-conscious circumlocution is to amuse rather than to arouse the reader.

This sophistication of style is not present in *The New Justine* and *The Story of Juliette*, in which an exclusively third-person narrator is the dominant voice. In these later works circumlocution and euphemism give way to vulgarism and obscenity, as the abstractions of the libertine dissertation find concrete illustration in descriptions of the sexual acts that precede and follow it. In the many lengthy descriptions of these acts Sade's language eschews the metaphorical, providing direct access to the body, its sexual parts and functions. The result is arguably far less successful, at least from a literary point of view.

Sade and Justine

Like its heroine herself, the *Justine* story emerges from circumstances of misfortune and poverty. Both author and character find themselves in dire straits, but both react differently to their situation. While Sade makes a virtue out of necessity, filling his long years of imprisonment with the writing of plays, novels, and essays, his fictional invention bows to her fate, reacting supinely to the sudden and devastating death of her parents and the ensuing loss of status and wealth.

A minority of critics, however, have argued that Sade actually does identify with Justine as victim, and, given his deep sense of injustice at his treatment by the authorities for actions which he certainly did not consider criminal, this view is perhaps not without substance.

The writing frenzy that produced this first novel-length version suggests an emotional investment in the narrative of the 1791 *Justine* that is absent from *The Story of Juliette*, which was probably written during Sade's prolonged period of freedom in the 1790s. Jean Paulhan has argued that, if the sadistic libertines might be considered personae of the author, he also identifies masochistically with Justine.[8] It is not hard to share this view of a man, writing in the relentless solitude of his prison-cell, tortured by sexual deprivation and by ignorance of the term of his detention, suffering increasingly from eye-trouble—a real problem for the writer Sade had by now become. There is some evidence, too, that the figure of his victim-heroine was drawn from life, which might support the hypothesis of a greater psychological and emotional attachment of the author to Justine than to Juliette. We know that the young female servant at the Sade family chateau of La Coste, whose real name was Catherine Trillet and who went by the nickname of Justine, participated voluntarily in sexual activities with the Marquis, refusing to leave the chateau with her father. She may even have fallen in love with her master, just as the fictional Justine does with the Comte de Bressac. Whatever the truth of their relationship, it does not seem implausible to assume that Sade used the serving-girl as a general model for his literary creation, in the same way that other figures and events from his past appear to have inspired particular scenes in the novel.

Notwithstanding her initial portrayal as the brainless and bashful blonde with an unreasonable and unthinking devotion to virtue, Justine actually behaves in an entirely sensible and sympathetic manner. In spite of himself, Sade creates a figure with whom the reader (and perhaps also the author) is drawn to identify. The centrality of her role as victim is complemented, and indeed enhanced, by the centrality of her

---

[8] See Jean Paulhan, Introduction to *Les Infortunes de la vertu* (Paris: Point du Jour, 1946), pp. ii–xliii, translated as 'The Marquis de Sade and his Accomplice' in *Marquis de Sade, Justine, Philosophy in the Bedroom, and Other Writings* (New York: Grove Weidenfeld, 1990), 3–36.

role as narrator. Because it is Justine and not the author-narrator who has charge of the narrative in the first two versions, she is able to condemn the libertines for their views and is even accorded the right to put her own case at length, for instance, on the question of God's existence. Since she is the principal narrator, both libertines and fellow victims speak through her, which means that we mostly share a point of view that is opposed to and sometimes mocks that of her captors. Moreover, Justine's comradeship with other female victims forms a contrast to the isolation of the libertines, whose alliances are always self-serving, usually temporary, and sometimes Machiavellian in motivation.[9]

Contrary to the impressions given by her initial character-sketch, Justine is intelligent and self-assertive in debates with her libertine captors, who always listen respectfully to her arguments and at times even compliment her on her reasoning. Following a sermon from the thief, Dubois, concerning the justification of crime, for instance, Justine is given a strong counter-argument, challenging the logic of the female libertine on her own ground. Dubois seems unable to respond to Justine's powerful and cogent objections, and has to resort to appealing to her good heart. Justine's opponents are not just monsters, but redoubtable theorists, which makes her arguments all the more impressive in their ability to match their knowledge and rhetoric. According to this view, far from being the naive ingénue, Justine, even in her final incarnation, is actually a smart young lady who simply has a disastrous run of bad luck.

If Sade is saying that misfortune 'naturally' strikes the virtuous, then he is positing a *malevolent* providence—in any event, a force of some kind outside of the human dimension, the existence of which would clearly be in contradiction with his atheistic materialism. It is not Justine's virtue that makes life difficult for her—she finds ways of justifying to herself her acquiescence in the various sexual acts demanded of her—but what Geoffrey Bennington has called the 'double bind' situations that so frequently confront her.[10] In these

---

[9] James Fowler notes the contrast between the isolation of the libertines and the comradeship of their victims: see his *The Libertine's Nemesis: The Prude in Clarissa and the roman libertin* (London: Legenda, 2011), ch. 4. In *Justine, or the Misfortunes of Virtue*, this is particularly noticeable during the Sainte-Marie-des-Bois episode, and to a lesser extent the stay at Rodin's house.

[10] See Geoffrey Bennington, 'Forget to Remember, Remember to Forget: Sade avec Kant', *Paragraph*, 23: 1 (March 2000), ed. John Phillips (Edinburgh: Edinburgh University Press), 75–86.

situations, which involve the choice between two evils, Justine shows herself to be as much a pragmatist as a prude. A good example of the 'double-bind' in the 1791 *Justine* is Bressac's demand that his young captive should poison his aunt. If she refuses, the Comte threatens to find other means of carrying out the murder. On the other hand, if she accepts she may be able to save the woman. This is a moral dilemma that most would find hard to resolve. It transpires that Justine's consenting to do the deed but then attempting to warn Bressac's aunt leads indirectly both to the aunt's poisoning and to her own torture and near death. Here, as frequently elsewhere, it is Justine's very virtue that leads to crime, and yet it would seem that the very notion of the existence of a benevolent providence is put in question by such dilemmas. Fate does exist, but it is evil, not good. Sade's universe is consequently more Manichean than materialist, and the responsibility of individuals like Justine for the plight in which they find themselves is diminished as a result.

The double-bind situations which confront Justine also demonstrate that the trials to which those one might call the 'chief' victims in Sade's world are subjected are not just physical but also—and perhaps more crucially—moral and psychological. Victimhood is not just a passive state in Sade: the victim is frequently joined in debate by her libertine captors, her virtue (and arguments in its defence) tested to breaking-point. The libertines derive as much satisfaction from defeating their victims intellectually as they do from subduing and abusing them physically, while the victims themselves (and Justine offers the best example of this) rise admirably to the challenge with equally forceful and reasoned replies. It is as if Sade were constantly drawn to dialogue with the victim that he himself had become, to interrogate the reasons for his own victimhood through Justine, to put the victim's side of his own nature to the test of logical reasoning and debate. Like her, he would prefer to choose virtue, but like her, he is confronted with the problem that virtuous actions can have evil consequences. From the victim's point of view, it is more dangerous to have a girl kept in ignorance of vice than to educate her in the ways of the world. By the same token, the ostensibly well-intentioned attempts to protect society by imprisoning wrongdoers like the author only serve to turn them into hardened recidivists who will then become an even greater threat to others on their release.

What these dilemmas illustrate is that acts of violence in Sade almost always have a philosophical underpinning and a philosophical context. Such acts are not presented for their own sake, as they would be in some modern forms of violent pornography for example, but as exemplifications of a philosophical point, or as a pretext for philosophical debate. Such episodes also together constitute an important body of evidence for viewing Sade as a moralist. Above all, however, it is the premiss of an authorial identification with his creation emotionally that may most surprise the reader. Justine's most horrendous experiences befall her like the bolt of lightning that finally strikes her dead, without her first being consulted about her readiness to engage in debauchery. She is in a sense, then, a martyr for virtue. The branding Justine receives from Rodin and Rombeau is the mark of the criminal, but it also recalls the stigmata of saints, the outward and visible signs of suffering of the body (like that of Christ during his passion), and as such, the miraculous outward manifestation of inner sanctity. Did Sade, the self-styled martyr, identify unconsciously with his martyred young heroine? Like Justine, Sade suffered much the same reversals of fortune: loss of wealth and property in the Revolution; being branded a criminal (symbolically in his case); what he saw as the abuses of justice in the magistrates courts—Justine's case of arson and murder is heard by a corrupt and lascivious judge—and the threat of the death-penalty; and, not least, the tortures of a captivity whose term was unknown were only too familiar to her creator. When, in the monastery at Sainte-Marie-des-Bois, Omphale tells Justine: 'It is not only the need to requite the passions of these debauchees that is the bane of our lives, it is the loss of our freedom', do we hear the Marquis's own embittered voice?

Reading Justine

Most readers will be shocked by at least some of the sexual activities represented in this novel. In addition to torture and murder, they include paedophilia, sadomasochism, fetishism, and other forms of perversion, much of which is highly problematic from an ethical and moral standpoint. Yet it is these aspects of Sade's work especially that distinguish him from other materialist atheists of his time, and make him unique in the history of literature and philosophy in the modern era. Sade fearlessly explores the darker side of human nature, from which most of us would prefer to avert our gaze: the objectification of human beings, the utter selfishness of lust, the tyranny of an ego unfettered by laws or lacking the humanizing influences of socialization. Sade's exposure of the sexual motive that frequently lies behind human corruption and crime, of the sexual sadism that drives so much violence in human history, is a valuable message that bears repeating today.

There will always be those who are sexually excited by the violent objectification of women. The pleasure of raping virgins owned by so many of Sade's libertines finds its place in the darkest corners of the male sexual imagination. The majority of readers, however, will follow Rétif de la Bretonne's example in finding the more sadistic scenes of Sade's tale morally and physically repugnant.[11] For some, reading Sade as an author of comic fantasy may be one strategy for coping with all but the most extreme sexual violence.[12] Moreover, Sade's writing is probably most subversive and certainly most entertaining when read in this way. Like some dark comic-strip caper set in the Gothic spaces of eighteenth-century French chateaux and monasteries, his libertine fictions marry the obsessiveness of farce (all bottoms and exaggerated body parts) with the gore of horror, both genres situated at some distance from the real.

Ultimately, readers must decide for themselves whether this text suggests sexual fascination with the libertine as fantasy figure of unlimited power, or loathing for the abuse of that power on the part of an embittered victim of the *ancien régime* (the libertines, we remember, are all wealthy and powerful figures in the institutions of pre-revolutionary France). Do the libertines represent the tyrannical powers that imprisoned him, or are they the advocates of a personal freedom he craves? As so often in Sade, there are no easy answers.

The Marquis de Sade's work is vast in scope and has many extraordinary qualities. But he will always be best remembered for his achievements as a pioneering explorer of human sexuality which follow directly from his materialist thinking. Perhaps, though, Sade's most important bequest of all is less specific and more pervasive than any of these: the gift of a healthy scepticism at a time of multiplying fanaticisms, whether of a religious or a political kind. For Michel

---

[11] Rétif de la Bretonne was inspired in 1798 to write *L'Anti-Justine* as an antidote to the cruelty depicted in Sade's works.

[12] The nineteenth-century English poet Algernon Swinburne and his friends roared with laughter as they read *Justine* aloud to each other.

Foucault, Sade straddles the classical and the modern epochs. His work represents in its entirety a thoroughgoing critique of the old monarchical and aristocratic world and of the religious belief that supported it, but also of the dangers of post-revolutionary despotism of any complexion, and this is a critique that went much further than that of any of his contemporaries. In this sense, Sade is one of the first powerful voices of a secular and ultimately more democratic modern world.

Sade's enduring legacy, then, is located less in the detail of his sexually violent scenarios or of his libertines' nihilistic and iconoclastic philosophies than in the central core of his thought, which shifted the emphasis away from a God-centred spirituality to a Man-centred materialism, and which, in so doing, helped to sweep away the pernicious superstitions of the old theocratic order, and contributed to the creation of a modern intellectual climate in which all absolutisms are regarded with suspicion.

If we are to sum him up, we might call Sade an arch-cynic, a questioning voice determined to unpick the threads of all self-righteous orthodoxies, to deflate pomposities and expose inconsistencies and hypocrisies. The reader will be surprised to discover just how often *Justine* strikes a satirical, ironic, or parodic note. Sade is the devil's advocate of philosophical debate, and the more extreme passages in his work are best read as exercises, designed to push the logic of atheistic materialism to its ultimate conclusion.

NOTE ON THE TEXT

Justine, ou les Malheurs de la vertu is the second version of Sade's tale, the only one to be published during the author's lifetime, and consequently the only one whose text can be established with certainty. It was published in 1791, 'En Hollande. Chez les Libraires associés (Paris, Girouard). 2 vol. in-8''.

The novel was published unabridged in *Oeuvres complètes* (Paris: Éd. Cercle du Livre Précieux, 1966–7), vol. 3, and it is this edition that has been used to make this translation.

SELECT BIBLIOGRAPHY

Works by Sade

Les 120 Journées de Sodome (Paris: POL, 1992).

The One Hundred and Twenty Days of Sodom, compiled and translated by Austryn Wainhouse and Richard Seaver (London: Arrow Books, 1990).

La Philosophie dans le boudoir (Paris: UGE 10/18, 1991).

Philosophy in the Bedroom, in *Marquis de Sade, Justine, Philosophy in the Bedroom, and Other Writings*, compiled and translated by Richard Seaver and Austryn Wainhouse (New York: Grove Weidenfeld, 1990).

Les Infortunes de la vertu (Paris: Garnier-Flammarion, 1969).

The Misfortunes of Virtue and Other Early Tales, trans. David Coward (Oxford: Oxford University Press, 1999).

Justine, ou les malheurs de la vertu (Paris: Éditions Gallimard, 1981).

The Crimes of Love, trans. David Coward (Oxford: Oxford University Press, 2005).

La Nouvelle Justine, 2 vols. (Paris: UGE 10/18, 1995).

Histoire de Juliette, ou les Prospérités du vice, in A. Le Brun and J.-J. Pauvert (eds.), *Oeuvres complètes* (Paris: Société Nouvelle des Éditions Pauvert, 1987), vols. 8 and 9.

Juliette, trans. Austryn Wainhouse (London: Arrow Books, 1991; translation first published 1968).

Les Prospérités du vice (Paris: UGE 1969).

Dialogue entre un prêtre et un moribond, in A. Le Brun and J.-J. Pauvert (eds.), *Oeuvres complètes* (Paris: Société Nouvelle des Éditions Pauvert, 1987), vol. 1.

Dialogue between a Priest and a Dying Man, in *The Marquis de Sade, Justine, Philosophy in the Bedroom, and Other Writings*, compiled and translated by Richard Seaver and Austryn Wainhouse (New York: Grove Weidenfeld, 1990).

Correspondance, in *Oeuvres complètes* (Paris: Cercle du livre précieux, 1967), vol. 12.

Lettres à sa femme, ed. Marc Buffat (Paris: Actes Sud, 1997).

Marquis de Sade: Letters from Prison, trans. Richard Seaver (London: Harvill Press, 2000).

Biographies

Bongie, L. L., *Sade: A Biographical Essay* (Chicago and London: University of Chicago Press, 1998).

Lever, Maurice, *Donatien Alphonse François, Marquis de Sade* (Paris: Librairie Artheme Fayard, 1991).
—— *Marquis de Sade: A Biography*, trans. A. Goldhammer (London: HarperCollins, 1993).
du Plessix Gray, Francine, *At Home with the Marquis de Sade* (New York: Penguin Books, 1999).
Schaeffer, Neil, *The Marquis de Sade: A Life* (London: Hamish Hamilton, 1999).
Thomas, Donald, *The Marquis de Sade* (London: Allison & Busby, 1992).

Works about Sade

BOOKS AND EDITED VOLUMES

Allison, D. B., Roberts, M. S., and Weiss, A. S. (eds.), *Sade and the Narrative of Transgression* (Cambridge: Cambridge University Press, 1995).
Barthes, Roland, *Sade, Fourier, Loyola* (Paris: Seuil, 1971).
Carter, Angela, *The Sadeian Woman* (London: Virago Press, 1979).
Darnton, Robert, *The Forbidden Best-sellers of Pre-Revolutionary France* (London: HarperCollins, 1996).
De Jean, Joan, *Literary Fortifications: Rousseau, Laclos, Sade* (Princeton University Press, 1984).
Fowler, James, *The Libertine's Nemesis: The Prude in 'Clarissa' and the 'roman libertin'* (London: Legenda (Modern Humanities Research Association and Maney Publishing), 2011).
Frappier-Mazur, L., *Writing the Orgy: Power and Parody in Sade* (Philadelphia: University of Pennsylvania Press, 1996); first published in French as *Sade et l'écriture de l'orgie* (Paris: Nathan, 1991).
Gallop, Jane, *Intersections: A Reading of Sade with Bataille, Blanchot, and Klossowski* (Lincoln, Nebr., and London: University of Nebraska Press, 1981).
Goulemot, Jean-Marie, *Forbidden Texts: Erotic Literature and its Readers in Eighteenth-Century France* (Philadelphia: University of Pennsylvania Press, 1994); first published in French as *Ces livres qu'on ne lit que d'une main* (Paris: Éditions Alinea, 1991).
Laplanche, J., and Pontalis, J.-B., *The Language of Psycho-Analysis* (London: The Hogarth Press and Institute of Psycho-Analysis, 1985).
Paglia, Camille, *Sexual Personae: Art and Decadence from Nefertiti to Emily Dickinson* (New York: Vintage Books, 1991).
Phillips, John, *Sade: The Libertine Novels* (London and Stirling, Virginia: Pluto Press, 2001).
—— *How To Read Sade* (London: Granta Books, 2005).
—— *The Marquis de Sade: A Very Short Introduction* (Oxford: Oxford University Press, 2005).

Roger, Philippe, *Sade: La Philosophie dans le pressoir* (Paris: Bernard Grasset, 1976).

Warman, Caroline, *Sade: From Materialism to Pornography*, Studies in Voltaire and the Eighteenth Century, 2002:1 (Oxford: Voltaire Foundation, 2002).

ARTICLES

Beauvoir, Simone de, 'Faut-il brûler Sade?', *Les Temps modernes* (Dec. 1951–Jan. 1952); repr. in *Privilèges* (Paris: Gallimard, 1955); English translation: 'Must We Burn Sade?', in *The Marquis de Sade, The 120 Days of Sodom and Other Writings* (London: Arrow Books, 1990), 3–64.

Bennington, Geoffrey, 'Forget to Remember, Remember to Forget: *Sade avec Kant*', in John Phillips (ed.), 'Sade and his Legacy', special edition of *Paragraph*, 23: 1 (Mar. 2000), 75–86.

Goulemot, Jean-Marie, Préface to Sade, *Les Infortunes de la vertu* (Paris: Garnier-Flammarion, 1969), 19–36.

McMorran, Will, 'Intertextuality and Urtextuality: Sade's Justine Palimpsest', *Eighteenth-Century Fiction*, 19: 3 (2007), 127–41.

O'Neal, John, 'Sade's Justine: A Response to the Enlightenment's Poetics of Confusion', in *Eighteenth Century Fiction*, Volume 21, Number 3, Spring 2009, pp. 345–56.

Paulhan, Jean, Introduction to *Les Infortunes de la vertu* (Paris: Point du Jour, 1946), pp. ii–xliii, translated as 'The Marquis de Sade and his Accomplice', in *The Marquis de Sade, Justine, Philosophy in the Bedroom, and Other Writings* (New York: Grove Weidenfeld, 1990), 3–36.

Phillips, John, 'Critique littéraire et intertextualité: le cas de Sade et de Rétif de la Bretonne', in Malcolm Cooke and Marie-Emmanuelle Plagnol-Diéval (eds.), *Critique et Critiques au 18e siècle*, French Studies of the Eighteenth and Nineteenth Centuries, 22 (New York, etc.: Peter Lang, 2006), 269–80.

—— 'La Prose dramatique de Sade: Ce "dangereux supplément"?', special number of *L'Annuaire théâtral*, 41: 'Sade au théâtre: La Scène et l'Obscène' (Spring 2007), 50–62.

—— 'Circles of Influence: Lewis, Sade, Artaud', *Comparative Critical Studies*, 9: 1 (2012), 61–82.

—— 'Obscenity off the Scene: Sade's *La Philosophie dans le boudoir*', *The Eighteenth Century: Theory and Interpretation* (Autumn 2012).

Further Reading in Oxford World's Classics

Diderot, Denis, *The Nun*, trans. Russell Goulbourne.

Laclos, Pierre Choderlos de, *Les Liaisons dangereuses*, trans. Douglas Parmée, intro. David Coward.

Rousseau, Jean-Jacques, *Discourse on the Origin of Inequality*, trans.
    Franklin Philip, ed. Patrick Coleman.
—— *Discourse on Political Economy* and *The Social Contract*, trans.
    Christopher Betts.
Sade, Marquis de, *The Crimes of Love*, trans. David Coward.
—— *The Misfortunes of Virtue and Other Early Tales*, trans. David
    Coward.
Voltaire, *Candide and Other Stories*, trans. Roger Pearson.

A CHRONOLOGY OF THE MARQUIS DE SADE

1740 2 June: birth in Paris of Donatien-Alphonse-François, son of the Comte de Sade (1702–67) and Marie-Éléonore de Maillé de Carman (1712–77), in Paris. He is brought up with his cousin, the Prince de Condé.

1744 Sent to Provence, where he is entrusted to his grandmother Sade, aunts, and an uncle, the licentious Abbé de Sade (1705–77).

1750 Attends the Jesuit Collège Louis-le-Grand in Paris, accompanied by a private tutor, the Abbé Amblet, of whom he grows fond.

1752 Probable date of formal separation of Sade's parents.

1754 24 May: enters an elite military school.

1755 14 December: sub-lieutenant in an infantry regiment. Sees active service in France and Germany in the Seven Years War, which he ends with the rank of captain (1759) and a reputation for lewd conduct.

1763 16 March: demobilized; April: affair with Mademoiselle de Lauris in Avignon; 17 May: marries Renée-Pélagie de Montreuil ('elle n'est pas jolie') in Paris; 29 October: jailed for two weeks at Vincennes for maltreating Jeanne Testard in a Paris brothel. The charge specifies 'extreme debauchery' and 'horrible impiety'; 13 November: released but confined for a period to the country estate of his wife's parents in Normandy.

1764 26 June: delivers a speech to the Dijon *parlement* as the newly appointed lieutenant-general of one of the Burgundy provinces, a post inherited from his father.

1765 Begins, among others, an affair with Mademoiselle Beauvoisin, a dancer. His name recurs in reports of police officers charged with repressing immorality.

1767 The death of the Comte de Sade leaves him with considerable debts. Sade does not take his father's title, and remains 'Marquis'; 27 August: birth of his son, Louis-Marie (d. 1809).

1768 Easter Sunday: encounter with Rose Keller, followed by the scandalous 'Arcueil Affair'. Imprisoned at Lyons, he is freed on 19 November and confined to his chateau at La Coste in Provence.

1769 2 April: returns to Paris; 27 June: birth of his second son, Donatien-Claude-Armand (d. 1847); September–October: travels through the Low Countries.

1770 His unsavoury reputation makes him unwelcome at court and blocks his military career.

1771 17 April: birth of a daughter, Madeleine-Laure (d. 1844); July–September: imprisoned for debt. Returns to La Coste with his wife and her sister, Anne-Prospère (1751–79), whom he promptly seduces.

1772 17 June: start of the 'Marseilles Affair'. Sade, accompanied by his valet and the infatuated Anne-Prospère, flees to Italy; 3 September: Sade and his valet are sentenced to death *in absentia* as poisoners and sodomites, and their effigies are publicly burned at Aix; 8 December: arrested and jailed at Miolans in Piedmont.

1773 30 April: escapes, and by the autumn is back at La Coste.

1774 January: eludes the authorities who, prompted by Madame de Montreuil, look for him at La Coste. Takes refuge in Italy, where he spends the summer; Winter: debauches with servants ('petites filles') at La Coste.

1775 July: facing prosecution for the *petites filles* affair, decamps to Italy.

1776 Summer: returns to La Coste and begins writing his *Voyage d'Italie*.

1777 17 January: after further debauches at La Coste, the irate father of Catherine Treillet fires two shots at Sade; 13 February: having arrived in Paris too late to see his mother before her death on 14 January, he is arrested and imprisoned at Vincennes.

1778 June: at Aix-en-Provence the death sentence passed in 1772 is lifted, but not the *lettre de cachet*, for which he continues to be detained; 16 July: during his return journey to Vincennes Sade escapes; 7 September: recaptured at La Coste. He is sent back to Vincennes, where he remains for the next six years.

1781 April: writes a comedy, *L'Inconstant*, first of a score of plays of which few have survived and only one was performed; 13 July: Renée-Pélagie granted permission to visit her husband. Sade is frequently angry, jealous, and abusive.

1782 12 July: completes the 'Dialogue Between a Priest and a Dying Man'. Begins work on *The 120 Days of Sodom*.

1783 Writes *Jeanne Laisné*, a tragedy. Experiences eye pain brought on by intensive reading.

1784 29 February: the prison of Vincennes is closed and Sade is transferred to the Bastille.

1785 Assembles what he has written of *The 120 Days of Sodom*, which he will never complete. Begins work on *Aline and Valcour*.

1786 Asks Renée-Pélagie to supply details of Spain and Portugal for his 'philosophical novel', *Aline and Valcour*.

1787 13 June: Sade loses control of the management of his affairs; late June–8 July: completes 'The Misfortunes of Virtue', the first version of *Justine*.

1788 First week of March: writes 'Eugénie de Franval'; 1 October: draws up a catalogue of his writings.

1789 Gives Renée-Pélagie *Aline and Valcour* to read; 2 July: from his cell window, Sade, using an improvised loud-hailer, calls for help and says that prisoners are being murdered; 4 July: transferred to the lunatic asylum at Charenton and forced to leave behind his furniture and a number of manuscripts.

1790 2 April: is freed from Charenton following the abolition of the *lettre de cachet* (13 March). The following day Renée-Pélagie refuses to meet him; 9 June: her request for a separation, a preliminary to divorce, is granted. Henceforth, Sade refers to himself as 'Citizen Sade, man of letters'; 25 August: the Comédie Française rejects Sade's comedy *Le Boudoir*, and in the autumn *Le Misanthrope par amour*, also a comedy, and his tragedy *Jeanne Laisné*. Begins a relationship with Marie-Constance Quesnet which will last until his death. Shows moderate sympathy for the new regime and frequents circles favourable to constitutional monarchy.

1791 Sade's financial plight deepens. After the failed flight to Varennes he publishes an *Adresse d'un citoyen de Paris au roi des Français* (*Address by a citizen of Paris to the King of the French*) which is critical of Louis XVI; June: *Justine, or the Misfortunes of Virtue*, published anonymously; 3 September: elected secretary of his District, the Section des Piques; 22 October: *Oxtiern, or the Effects of Libertinage*, performed at the Théâtre Molière.

1792 March: his comedy *Le Suborneur* is withdrawn at rehearsal, being judged 'too aristocratic'; 10 August: effective end of the monarchy; 17–21 September: in Paris political prisoners are massacred. The chateau of La Coste is pillaged by what Sade calls 'brigands' and 'thieves'.

1793 April: to justify the attack on his property, the *département* of the Bouches-du-Rhône adds Sade's name to the list of émigrés; August: saves the lives of his parents-in-law by ensuring that their names are removed from the list of émigrés; 15 November: heads a delegation to the Convention; December: the printer of the completed *Aline and Valcour* is arrested and Sade is imprisoned for 'moderation'.

The emigration of his sons Louis-Marie (September 1791) and Claude-Armand (May 1792) was also held against him.

1794 27 July: Sade condemned to death; 28 July: the fall of Robespierre ends the Terror, and Sade is saved providentially; 15 October: released from detention.

1795 Publication of *Aline and Valcour* 'by Citizen S***', and of *The Philosopher in the Bedroom*, which appears anonymously.

1796 Painful attacks of gout in the spring, followed by an illness which confines him to his bed in June and July; 13 October: sells the chateau of La Coste to Rovère, a supporter of the revolution.

1797 Summer: travels to Provence for first time for twenty years. Continuing efforts to remove his name from the list of émigrés, on which it has appeared by confusion with those of his sons. Publication of *The New Justine, or the Misfortunes of Virtue, followed by the History of Juliette, her Sister, or the Prosperities of Vice*.

1798 Spring: when Gaufridy, his agent in Provence, fails to send him income from his estates, Sade, reduced to penury, is forced to borrow money. Vain attempts to persuade the Théâtre Ribié to accept several plays, which may have included *Fanni, ou les Effets du désespoir*, *Henriette et Saint-Clair*, and *La Tour enchantée*.

1799 February: employed as a prompter in a Versailles theatre; 29 August: a newspaper reports Sade's death; 13 December: a new production of *Oxtiern*, in which Sade plays a minor role.

1800 January: having sold her dresses to buy food, Constance is obliged to seek work to support the family; 8 July: publisher's advertisement for *The Crimes of Love* appears in the *Journal Typographique et Bibliographique*; 18 August: the police seize a new edition of *Justine*. Fearing the worst, Sade again denies authorship; September/October: publication of his *drame, Oxtiern, ou Les Malheurs de la vertu*, and *The Crimes of Love*; 22 October: appearance of Villeterque's review of *The Crimes of Love* in *Le Journal des Arts*. Sade's reply fails to halt references in the press which identify him as the author of *Justine*.

1801 6 March: arrested with his publisher and imprisoned on 3 April at Saint-Pélagie.

1803 14 March: after attempting to seduce male fellow prisoners, is transferred to Bicêtre and thence, on 27 April, to Charenton, to be detained at the family's expense.

1804 8 September: an official inquiry concludes that Sade is 'unreformable'.

1805 Easter Day: helps to serve mass.

1806 30 January: writes his will, which recognizes the part played by Constance Quesnet in saving his life during the Terror of 1794.

1807 5 June: the authorities confiscate *The Days of Florbelle, or Nature Unveiled*, an immense novel begun in 1804. After Sade's death the manuscript was destroyed.

1808 Organizes theatrical performances for the inmates of Charenton; 2 August: a new governor affirms that Sade is not mad and argues that he belongs in a secure prison rather than a hospital.

1809 9 June: death of Louis-Marie, his elder son, in an ambush in Italy.

1810 7 July: death of Renée-Pélagie. In a letter Sade describes his surviving son as astute but litigious, and observes that heaven had given him 'a daughter [Madeleine-Laure] steeped in stupidity and religion', and so unfitted to be a mother that 'it seems more than likely that she will leave this world in the same virginal state as that in which she entered it'.

1811 Start of ultimate liaison, with 16-year-old Madeleine Leclerc, daughter of a Charenton nurse.

1812 September–October: writes *Adelaide of Brunswick, Princess of Saxony*; 6 June: Napoleon definitively rejects Sade's application to be released.

1813 Publishes *The Marquise de Gange* and completes *The Secret History of Isabelle of Bavaria*.

1814 2 December: death of Sade. He is given a religious funeral and is buried, at his own request, in an unmarked grave.

1815 *Justine* and other works are banned.

1834 The word *sadisme* is formally lexicalized in Boiste's *Dictionnaire universel*.

1876 Publication of Krafft-Ebing's *Psychopathia sexualis*, where, together with 'masochism', the word 'sadism' acquired authority as a scientific term.

1904 The publication by Eugen Dühren (Iwan Bloch) of the newly discovered *120 Days of Sodom* marks the beginning of serious intellectual interest in the writings of Sade.

1909 Guillaume Apollinaire publishes a selection of Sade's works, calls him 'the freest spirit', and predicts that he will dominate the twentieth century.

1957 Jean-Jacques Pauvert found guilty of obscenity for publishing scholarly editions of various works by Sade, which, however, become widely available in the permissive 1960s.

1983 HM Customs, using the discretion allowed under the 1876 Act, permits translations of works by Sade, previously banned in the UK, to be imported.

A NOTE ON MONEY

1 liard = 3 deniers
1 sou = 4 liards (later 6)
1 livre = 20 sous
1 écu = 3 livres
1 louis = 8 écus

The smaller coins were widely current at the poorest levels of society, but were very small change to the cultivated classes. An insight into the cost of living is provided by the Reverend William Cole (*A Journal of my Journey to France in 1765* (ed. F. G. Stokes, London, 1931)) who reckoned one louis as the equivalent of an English guinea, the écu at half a crown, and the livre at tenpence or a shilling. It cost him 150 livres to travel by post from Calais to Paris. There, he gave a guinea a week for a hotel room, though could have had full board in the house of a printseller for a guinea and a half. Firewood cost one livre 'a hundred of dry Billets'. For about 5 livres or 4*s*. 6*d*., he and two servants (whom he paid 20 sous a day) ate very well. 'The wine they chiefly drink at Paris is Burgundy: that which I drank commonly, mixed with water, was at 1 *livre* 10 *sóus* per Bottle: a smaller wine for my servant cost 12 *sous* the quart: I gave for incomparable Champaign, sparkling, or as the French call it, *Moussir* [*sic*], also for the non-Moussir Champaign, or what did not sparkle in the glass, for each 3 *livres* a Bottle.' The bill for 'my Dozen of Shirts & 6 Cravatts' came to 214 livres, or £9. 14*s*. 0*d*. and he paid 'Mr Armand for my Coat of Cotton Velvet, & black Velvet flowered waistcoat 176 *livres* 15 *sous*, which is near 8 Guineas.' For a coat and waistcoat for his servant, he paid £3. 10*s*. 0*d*. or about 80 livres.

JUSTINE,
OR THE MISFORTUNES OF VIRTUE

Oh, my friend!

The rewards of crime are like the thunderbolt, whose deceptive fires embellish the skies for an instant before plunging the unfortunate soul they have dazzled into the abyss of death.

To my good friend

YES, Constance, it is to you that I am dedicating this work.* At once
the example and honour of your sex, combining the fairest and most
enlightened intellect with the most sensitive of natures, you alone
can know those sweet tears shed by suffering Virtue. Abhorring the
sophistries of libertinism and irreligion, ceaselessly combating them
by your words and actions, there is no risk that you will be offended
by those employed by the characters of this story. Nor will you be
upset by the cynicism of some passages (which have, in any case, been
toned down as much as possible). Here, furious at being exposed,
this is vice protesting when it is attacked. *Tartuffe* was put on trial
by bigots.* *Justine* will be decried by libertines, and I have little to
fear from them. Once you have understood my motives, they will not
be disavowed by them. My success depends on your opinion alone,
and if you are happy, I may either enjoy universal success or bow to
censure on all sides.

The aims of this fiction (which is not as fictional as some might
think) are doubtless new. The ascendancy of Virtue over Vice, good
rewarded and evil punished, such is the general trend of works of this
nature. Shall we ever tire of reading them!

But everywhere to represent Vice as triumphant and Virtue a victim of its attacks; to show a wretched girl wandering from one misfortune to another; the plaything of wickedness; the butt of every
kind of debauchery; confronted with the most barbaric and most
monstrous tastes; stunned by the most brazen and most specious
sophistries; a prey to the most cunning of seductions and the most
irresistible of subornations; having no other defences against so many
setbacks, so many scourges, so much corruption, but a sensitive
heart, a mind formed by Nature, and a great deal of courage; in short,
to dare to write the boldest of descriptions, the most terrifying of
maxims, all with the most energetic brushstrokes, with the sole aim
of obtaining from all of this one of the most sublime moral lessons
that humanity has ever been taught, was, I am sure you will agree, to
reach this goal by a road seldom trodden before.

Have I succeeded, Constance? Will a tear from your eyes confirm my victory? In short, having read *Justine*, will you say 'Oh, how these portraits of crime make me proud to love Virtue! How sublime she is when she weeps! How beautiful she is in misfortune!'

Oh, Constance! These words need only escape your lips and my labours are rewarded.

PART ONE

THE greatest achievement of philosophy would be the elucidation of the means employed by Providence to achieve the ends which she has in view for Man, and following this, the mapping out of conduct which might assist this unfortunate biped creature to find his way along life's thorny path, so that he may anticipate the strange whims of a destiny that is known by dozens of different names, and yet which he has still not managed to comprehend or define.

If, filled with respect for our social conventions*, and never straying beyond the limits they impose upon us, if, in spite of this, it is the case that we have encountered nothing but thorns, whilst wicked men gathered only roses, those lacking a properly established foundation of virtue to rise above this observation will doubtless conclude that it is better to let oneself be carried along by the current than to fight against it. Will they not say in such circumstances that, however fair it may be, virtue is the worst option available, when it is too weak to combat vice, and that in a century that is thoroughly corrupt, the safest course is to do as others do. With greater knowledge, in other words, and exploiting the insights they have acquired, will they not agree with the angel Jesrad in *Zadig* that there is no evil from which good does not come, and that accordingly, they may indulge in evil, since it is in fact one more way of doing good?* Will they not also conclude that it is indifferent to the great scheme of things whether an individual should prefer good or evil, and that if misfortune persecutes virtue and prosperity rewards crime, all things being equal in the eyes of Nature, it is infinitely better to throw in one's lot with those evil men who prosper than with the virtuous who founder? It is therefore important to forestall these dangerous sophisms and the erroneous philosophy to which they belong, and essential to demonstrate that examples of unhappy virtue, offered to a corrupted soul, which nevertheless retains a few virtuous principles, may bring this soul back to the path of righteousness, as surely as if he had been shown the path of virtue to be glistening with gold and to lead to the greatest rewards. It is doubtless cruel to have to depict a sweet and sensitive woman who is most respectful of virtue as the victim of countless misfortunes, and on the other hand, to show how those who oppress or mortify this same woman prosper. Yet, if one good thing should come from the depiction of these calamities, can one regret having described them? Can one regret the establishment of facts that teach the wise man who reads them the most useful lesson of submission to the will of Providence, and the fatal warning that it is often in order to remind us of our duties that Heaven strikes down before our eyes those who seem to have most perfectly fulfilled their own?

Such are the sentiments that will guide our work, and it is in consideration of these motives that we ask our readers' indulgence for the erroneous ideas which we shall put into the mouths of our characters, and for the, at times, rather shocking events which, out of love for truth, we have felt obliged to place before their eyes.

Madame the Comtesse of Lorsange was one of those priestesses of Venus who owed their fortune to a pretty face and a great deal of misconduct, and whose titles, however pompous they may be, are to be found nowhere but in the archives of Cythera,* shaped by their own impertinence and sustained by the stupid credulity of others. A brunette with a pretty figure, strikingly expressive eyes, and that fashionable incredulousness which, lending even more spice to the passions, makes those women in which it is suspected even more sought after; some malice, no principles, believing nothing to be bad, and yet with not enough depravity in her heart to have extinguished all sensitivity; proud, libertine: such was Madame de Lorsange.

Nevertheless, this woman had received the best of educations. Daughter of a very important banker in Paris, she had been raised with a sister named Justine, three years her junior, in one of the most renowned convents of the capital, where until the ages of twelve and fifteen no teachers, or books, or lessons had been denied to either sister.

At a time so fateful for the virtue of both sisters, they lost all of this in a single day. A ruinous bankruptcy placed their father in such cruel circumstances that he died of grief. His wife followed him to the grave a month later. Two cold and distant relatives deliberated as to what they would do with the young orphans. Their share of an inheritance depleted by debts amounted to a hundred écus each. Since no one cared to take charge of them, the doors of the convent were opened to them, they were given their inheritance, and left free to do whatever they pleased.

Madame de Lorsange, who from that time on called herself Juliette, and whose character and temperament would be no more developed at the age of thirty, the age that she would reach during the course of the story that we are about to relate, appeared sensitive only to the pleasures of freedom without giving a single thought to the cruel circumstances that had broken her chains. As for Justine who, as we have said, was twelve years old, her serious and melancholy nature made her more aware of the full horror of her situation. Endowed with a tenderness and a surprising sensitivity, as opposed to the artfulness and guile of her sister, her innocence and candour would lead her into many traps. This young girl combined all of these qualities with the sweetest physiognomy, wholly different from that with which Nature had adorned Juliette. There was as much modesty, decency, and timidity in the former's features as there was artifice, wile, and coquetry in the latter's. A look of the Virgin, big, blue, soulful eyes filled with animation, a dazzling complexion, a shapely and supple figure, a voice to touch the heart, teeth of ivory, and the most beautiful blonde hair, such was the portrait of this charming younger sister, whose innocent grace and delicate traits cannot be captured by our brushes.

Both girls were given twenty-four hours to quit the convent, leaving it up to them how best to make provision for themselves with their hundred écus. Juliette, who was delighted to be her own mistress, was at first at pains to dry Justine's tears, but seeing that this was to no avail, she began to scold instead of consoling her. She reproached her for her sensitivity, telling her, with a philosophical attitude quite mature for her age, that in this world one should worry only about what affected one personally, that it was possible to find within oneself physical sensations that were delicious enough to extinguish all moral feelings, the shock of which might otherwise be painful; that it was all the more essential to take this approach in that true wisdom consisted infinitely more in doubling the sum of one's pleasures than in multiplying the sum of one's suffering; that, in short, there was nothing one should not do to dull within oneself that perfidious sensitivity that benefited only others, while bringing oneself nothing but grief. However, it is difficult to harden a kind heart which resists the reasonings of an unkind intellect, and takes comfort from the satisfaction it enjoys by standing up to the sophistries of a wit.

Employing other means of persuasion, Juliette then told her sister that the youth and looks enjoyed by both made it impossible for them to die of hunger. She cited the example of the daughter of one of their neighbours, who, having escaped from her father's house, was now kept in the lap of luxury and was doubtless far happier than if she had remained in the bosom of her family. She warned her not to believe that a young girl could only be happy in the state of marriage, and that, imprisoned by the laws of wedlock, she could look forward to few pleasures and a great deal of misery. On the other hand, if they surrendered to the joys of libertinism they would always be able to defend themselves against their lovers' moods, or take consolation in multiplying their number.

Justine was horrified by this speech. She said that she preferred death to ignominy, and in spite of the renewed efforts that her sister made to win her over, she persistently refused to stay with her, now that she saw her determined to behave in a manner that made her tremble.

The two girls therefore separated without promising to see each other again, seeing that their plans were so different. Would Juliette, who, she claimed, was going to become a great lady, be willing to take in a little girl whose virtuous but lowly inclinations might dishonour her? As for Justine, would she want to endanger her morals in the company of a perverted creature who would fall victim to dissoluteness and public debauchery? Both girls therefore bade each other a final farewell, and both left the convent the very next day.

Cosseted in her childhood by her mother's dressmaker, Justine believes that this woman will be sensitive to her plight. She seeks her out, recounts her misfortunes to her, and asks for work... but is barely recognized and brutally dismissed.

'Oh, Heaven!' the poor creature exclaims, 'must even the very first steps that I take in this world be dogged by sorrows? This woman used to love me, why does she reject me now? Alas! It is because I am a poor orphan with no resources, in a world in which people are esteemed only to the extent that they are thought to offer assistance and pleasure in return.'

A tearful Justine goes to see her priest. She describes her condition to him with all the innocence of her young age... she was wearing a little white close-fitting dress, her beautiful hair carelessly tucked beneath a large bonnet. Her bosom could just be discerned, hidden beneath a few ells of gauze, her pretty complexion a little pale owing to the troubles that weighed upon her. Her eyes welled with tears, making them even more expressive.

'As you can see, Monsieur,' she told the holy clergyman, 'I am in a very distressing state for a young girl. I have lost my mother and father. God has taken them from me at the very age when I have most need of their help. They died penniless, Monsieur, we have nothing left. This is all they left me,' she continued, showing him her twelve louis, 'with nowhere to rest my poor head. You'll take pity on me, won't you, Monsieur! You are a minister of the church, and the church has always been the source of all that is good in my heart. In the name of the God that I adore, and whose representative you are, tell me as a second father what I must do, what I must become?'

Ogling Justine, the charitable priest replied that the parish was heavily burdened, that it would be difficult for it to take on new charity cases, but that if Justine were prepared to serve him, that if she were willing to do heavy work, there would always be a crust of bread for her in his kitchen. Saying this, God's spokesman slipped his hand into her cleavage, kissing her in a manner far too worldly for a man of the church. Well aware of his intentions, Justine rebuffed him with these words: 'Monsieur, I ask neither for charity nor for the place of a servant. I have far too recently left a condition above any in which I might feel obliged to aspire to either of these favours, to be reduced to begging for them. I seek the counsel which my youth and misfortune demand, and you offer them to me at too high a price.'

Embarrassed that his intentions had been exposed in this way, the priest threw the little creature out on the spot. Having now been twice rejected on the very first day of her solitary condition, the unfortunate Justine enters a house where she has seen a 'rooms vacant' notice, rents a little furnished room on the fifth floor, paying in advance, and gives vent to tears that her sensitivity and cruelly injured pride render all the more bitter.

If our reader will permit, we shall leave her at this point for a while to return to Juliette, to relate how, from the simple state we saw her in, having no greater resources than her sister, she nevertheless became, over the course of fifteen years, a titled lady with an income of thirty thousand livres, the finest jewellery, two or three houses in both town and country, winning, for the time being at least, the heart, the fortune, and the trust of Monsieur de Corville, councillor of state, a man enjoying the greatest credit and on the verge of becoming a minister. The road to riches was a thorny one, of that there is no doubt. Such ladies make their way by undergoing the harshest and most shameful apprenticeship. In the bed of a prince today, they may perhaps still bear the humiliating marks of the brutality of those libertines into whose hands youth and inexperience had caused them to fall.

On leaving the convent Juliette went to see a woman recommended to her by a young girlfriend in her neighbourhood. Perverted as she wished to be by this very same woman, she approached her, with her little bundle under her arm, her blue coat in disarray, her hair dishevelled, the prettiest face in the world, if it be true that indecency can have charm in the eyes of some. She tells her story to this woman and begs her to protect her as she did her old friend.

'How old are you?' la Duvergier asks her.

'I'll be fifteen in a couple of days, Madame,' Juliette replies.

'And has any mortal ever…?' continued the matron.

'Oh, no, Madame, I swear to you!' replied Juliette.

'But sometimes, in those convents,' said the old woman, 'a confessor, a nun, a companion… I need absolute proof.'

'You are welcome to obtain it, Madame,' replied Juliette, blushing.

After the duenna had equipped herself with a pair of spectacles and scrupulously inspected everything from every angle, she said to the young girl:

'All right, then, you must stay here, pay close heed to my advice, demonstrate acceptance of and submission to my practices, keep yourself clean, be careful with money, honest with me, circumspect with your companions, and crafty with men, and within ten years I shall make you wealthy enough to retire to a second-floor apartment with a chest of drawers, a pier-glass mirror, and a maid, and the skills you will have acquired from me will give you all you need to obtain the rest.'

Having delivered this advice, Duvergier grabs hold of Juliette's little parcel. She asks if she has any money. Juliette is too honest to keep from her that she has a hundred écus, with the result that dear mama confiscates them, assuring her new tenant that she will invest this small sum in the lottery for her, but that young girls should not have money:

'It leads to doing evil,' she tells her, 'and in such a corrupt century as our own, a virtuous girl from a good background should take care to avoid anything that can ensnare her. What I am saying is only for your own good, my dear,' added the duenna, 'and you ought to be grateful to me for what I am doing for you.'

When this sermon is over, the newcomer is introduced to her companions, and she is shown to her room in the house. The very next day her virginity is on sale.

In the space of four months the merchandise is sold to a succession of nearly one hundred people. Some are content with the rose, others, more refined or more depraved (for the question is not yet resolved), want to open up the bud that flowers next to it. Each time Duvergier adjusts and closes them up again, and for four months the wicked woman is still offering her virginity to the public. At the end of this thorny noviciate Juliette is finally granted her patents as a lay sister. From that moment on she is accepted as a bone-fide working girl, entitled from then on to a share of both the hardships and the profits. Another apprenticeship: whilst, save for a few slips, Juliette serves Nature in the first school, she forgets Nature's laws in the second where her morals are completely corrupted. The successes she sees vice achieve totally deprave her soul. She feels that, born to commit crime, she might as well go the whole hog instead of languishing in a secondary role which requires her to commit the same sins and to demean herself just as much, but does not bring her anywhere near the same rewards. A thoroughly debauched old gentleman likes her, and at first books her for a single appointment, but she is skilful enough to persuade him to keep her in great opulence. Eventually she is seen at the theatre and opera, out walking, alongside the leading lights of the order of Cythera. People look at her, talk about her, envy her, and the smart creature plays the game so well that in less than four years she has ruined six men, the poorest of whom had an annual income of one hundred thousand écus. All of which was more than enough to make her reputation. Society people are so blind that the more one of these creatures has demonstrated her dishonesty, the more they long to be added to her list. It would seem that the degree of men's depravity and corruption becomes the measure of those feelings that they dare to show her.

Juliette had just entered her twentieth year when a certain Comte de Lorsange, a gentleman from Anger aged about forty, became so besotted with her that he determined to give her his name. He settled

an annual income on her of twelve thousand livres, bequeathing the
rest of his fortune to her if he should happen to die before her. He
gave her a house, servants, a livery, and the sort of standing in the
world that in the space of only two or three years completely erased
all memory of her origins.

It was now that the wretched Juliette, forgetting all the moral val-
ues of her upbringing and education, perverted by poor counsel and
dangerous books, in pursuit of pleasure alone and determined to
acquire a position in society and avoid a life in chains, dared to contemplate the crime of shortening her husband's life. Having once
conceived this odious plan she dwelt upon it, unfortunately making
up her mind at one of those dangerous moments when the body is
inflamed by moral weakness, moments when nothing stands in the
way of irregular or impetuous desires, so that one denies oneself all
the less, and the intensity of the pleasures experienced is in proportion to the number of laws broken, or rather to their sanctity. If the
dream vanished and one became well-behaved again, the inconvenience would be small. Such is the history of those who make the wrong
judgements. We know full well that they offend no one, but unfortunately some go further. They dare to imagine what the realization of
this idea would mean, since the very prospect of it has just enthralled
and stimulated them so much. The accursed fantasy is made real, and
its existence is a crime.

Fortunately for her, Madame de Lorsange carried out her deed in
such secrecy that she was safe from any retribution, and she saw to it
that all traces of the dreadful crime that put her husband in the tomb
were buried with him.

A comtesse and free once again, Madame de Lorsange resumed
her old habits. Believing that she now had a position in society, however, she conducted herself with a little less indecency. She was no
longer a kept woman but a rich widow who held fine dinner-parties,
to which both court and town were only too glad to be invited. An
upstanding woman, in other words, who could nonetheless be bed-
ded for two hundred louis, and who rented herself out for five hundred a month.

Before she reached the age of twenty-six Madame de Lorsange
made many more brilliant conquests. She ruined three foreign
ambassadors, four tax-farmers,* two bishops, a cardinal, and three
knights of the king's orders. But as it is rare for one to stop at a first

offence, especially when it has been successful, the wretched Juliette soiled her hands with two more crimes similar to the first. One of these was motivated by the theft of a considerable sum entrusted to her by one of her lovers, a sum of which his family had no knowledge and which Madame de Lorsange was able to hide away as a result of this dreadful deed. She committed the second murder in order to get her hands quickly on a legacy of one hundred thousand francs which one of her admirers bequeathed to the care of a third party, who was instructed to pass on this sum to her after his death. Madame de Lorsange added three or four infanticides to these horrors. The fear of spoiling her pretty figure, the desire to hide a double intrigue, all of this made her resolve to stifle in her womb the consequences of her debauchery, and as these crimes, like the others, remained undiscovered, they did not prevent this clever and ambitious woman from daily finding new dupes.

It is true, therefore, that prosperity can reward the very worst conduct, and that in the very midst of corruption and disorder life can be filled with all that men call happiness; that the example of misfortune everywhere pursuing virtue, and which we shall presently offer to our reader, does not torment honest people any the more. The notion that crime flourishes is deceptive, being merely apparent. In addition to the punishment that is doubtless reserved by Providence for those seduced by its successes, do they not nourish in the depths of their soul a worm that ceaselessly gnaws away at them, preventing them from enjoying its false attractions, and in place of delight leaves in their soul only the heart-rending memory of the crimes that have brought them to this pass? As far as the unfortunate person persecuted by fate is concerned, he has his heart for consolation, and the inner joys that virtue gives him soon make up for the injustice of men.

Such, then, was the state of Madame de Lorsange's affairs when Monsieur de Corville, aged fifty and enjoying the credit and consideration that we described above, resolved to sacrifice himself entirely for this woman and to make her forever his. Whether by the attention he lavished upon her, or by various ploys, or because Madame de Lorsange decided that it was in her interests, he succeeded in doing this, and had been living with her to all intents and purposes as his legitimate spouse for four years when the acquisition of a very beautiful property near Montargis required that both spend some time in this province.

One evening, when the weather was so lovely that they decided to prolong their walk from their property as far as Montargis, they were both too tired to undertake the return journey on foot, and so they put up at the inn where the Lyons coach stops, intending to send a rider to fetch a carriage for them. They were resting in this inn, in a cool room on the ground floor leading onto the yard, when the coach of which we have just spoken arrived at this hostelry.

It is quite a popular entertainment to watch people getting off a coach. You can bet on the type of individuals inside, and if you've chosen a whore, an officer, a few priests, and a monk, you are almost sure to win. Madame de Lorsange gets up, Monsieur de Corville follows her, and both enjoy watching the company as they bump their way to the inn. It seemed that everyone had alighted from the carriage when a horseman of the mounted constabulary got out and then helped down one of his travelling companions who had also been seated in the same place, a girl of twenty-six or twenty-seven, dressed in a simple little printed calico, and wrapped from head to foot in a large cloak of black taffeta. She was tied up like a criminal, and was so weak that she would assuredly have fallen over if her guards had not supported her. Madame de Lorsange let out a cry of surprise and horror, whereupon the young girl turned around, revealing the most shapely of figures and the noblest, most pleasing, and attractive of features—in other words, all of those charms most likely to please, rendered a thousand times more piquant by that tender and touching sorrow that innocence adds to beauty's features.

Monsieur de Corville and his mistress could not help being interested in this miserable girl. They approached and asked one of the guards what the unfortunate creature had done.

'She is accused of three crimes,' the trooper replied, 'murder, theft, and arson, but I confess that my comrade and I have never transported a criminal with as much reluctance. She is the sweetest creature, and appears to be the most honest, as well.'

'Oh!' said Monsieur de Corville, 'may it not just be a question of a few minor offences to be tried in the lower courts?... And where did the crimes take place?'

'In an inn a few leagues from Lyons. She was tried in Lyons, and now, according to custom, she is going to Paris for her sentence to be confirmed, and will return to Lyons to be executed.'

Having drawn near to listen to this story, Madame de Lorsange whispered to Monsieur de Corville that she would like to hear the account of this girl's misfortunes from her own mouth, and Monsieur de Corville, who was forming the same wish, communicated it to the two guards, telling them who he was. The guards did not feel able to deny him. They thus decided that they should spend the night in Montargis, and requested suitable lodgings. Monsieur de Corville having accepted responsibility for the prisoner, they untied her, and when she had been given a little food Madame de Lorsange, who could not help taking the keenest interest in her, doubtless wondered to herself: 'This creature who may be innocent is still treated like a criminal, while I am surrounded by prosperity... I, a woman who has soiled her hands with crimes and horrors.' Having seen to it that the poor girl was somewhat refreshed and a little consoled by their attempts to comfort her, Madame de Lorsange charged her to tell them what had happened to place a girl with such a sweet countenance in such dire straits.

'To tell you the story of my life, Madame,' said the beautiful wretch, 'is to offer you the most striking example of the misfortunes of innocence, it is to accuse the hand of Heaven, it is to question the will of the Supreme Being,* it is a kind of revolt against his sacred wishes... I dare not...'

With that, this fascinating young lady began to weep floods of tears. After giving vent to her feelings, she began to recount her story in these words:

You will allow me to conceal my name and my origins, Madame. It may not be illustrious but it is honest, and I could not have anticipated the humiliating circumstances in which you now find me. I lost my parents at a very young age. I hoped, with the little money that they had left me, to be able to secure a suitable position, and turning down all those that were not, I did not notice that I was spending the little I had living in Paris where I was born. The poorer I became, the more I was despised. The more I needed help, the less I hoped to obtain it. But of all the hardships I experienced at the beginning of my unhappy circumstance, of all the horrible propositions that were made to me, I will recount to you only what occurred at the house of Monsieur Dubourg, one of the richest merchants of the capital. The woman I was lodging with had referred me to him as someone whose wealth and credit were most likely to lessen the rigours of my situation. Having waited in this man's antechamber for some time, I was shown in. The forty-eight-year-old Monsieur Dubourg had just left his bed, and was wrapped in an ill-fitting dressing-gown that barely concealed his disarray. His servants were on the point of doing his hair, but he sent them away and asked me what I wanted.

'Alas, Monsieur,' I replied in confusion, 'I am a poor orphan who is not yet fourteen years of age, and who is already familiar with misfortune in all its aspects. I implore your sympathy, have pity on me, I beg you.'

I proceeded to relate all of my ills to him, the difficulty I had had in finding a position, and perhaps even how hard I found it to accept one, not having been born into such a state; my misfortune in the course of my search to have run out of the little money I had... the lack of work, the hopes I entertained that he would provide me with the means of support; in short, all that the eloquence of misfortune dictates, and which is always more acute in a sensitive soul, always a drag on wealth... Having listened to me in a state of considerable distraction, Monsieur Dubourg asked me if I had always been a good girl.

'I would be neither so poor nor so encumbered, Monsieur,' I replied, 'if I had been ready to stop being one.'

'But on what grounds', Monsieur Dubourg retorted, 'do you expect the rich to ease your situation, if you are unwilling to serve them in any way?'

'What kind of services do you speak of, Monsieur?' I replied. 'I am only too willing to render those services that my age and decency allow.'

'The services of a child such as you are of little use in a household,' Dubourg replied. 'Neither your age nor your constitution befits you for the sort of work you are looking for. You would do better to set about pleasing men, and to make an effort to find someone who would consent to take care of you. This virtue that you make such a fuss about is of no use in the world. There's no point in kneeling before its altars, because its vain incense will not feed you. That which flatters men least, that which they consider to be of least importance, that which they despise the most intensely, is the virtue of your sex. In this world, my child, men value only those things that earn money or bring pleasure. What can we profit from the virtue of women? It is their waywardness that serves and entertains us, but their chastity could not be of less interest to us. When people like us give, in other words, it is only ever to receive. Now, how can a little girl like you repay what is done for her except by allowing others to use her body as they wish?'

'Oh, Monsieur!' I replied, my heart heavy with sighs, 'do men no longer have any honesty or benevolence?'

'Very little,' answered Dubourg, 'how can you expect them to when people talk about it all the time? We've got over this madness of obliging others for nothing in return. We've realized that the pleasures of charity were nothing more than the satisfactions of pride, and as nothing disappears so quickly, men started to want pleasures that were more real. We saw that with a child like you, for example, it was infinitely better to take all the pleasures offered by lewdness in return for one's charity than to give assistance for free, a cold and pointless process. The reputation of a liberal, charitable, generous man, even at the moment when he derives the most satisfaction from it, is not worth the least little pleasure of the senses.'

'Oh, Monsieur! With such principles, the unfortunate must surely perish!'

'What does it matter? France has more subjects than it needs. As long as the machine of state runs smoothly, what does it matter how many individuals it sustains?'

'But do you think that children respect their fathers when they are mistreated by them in this way?'

'What does a father care for the love of children that are a nuisance to him?'

'It would be better, then, if we'd been stifled at birth!'

'That is indeed the custom in many countries. It used to be the case in Greece, it still is in China, where unfortunate children are left out to die or are put to death. What's the point of allowing creatures to live who can no longer count on the support of their parents, either because they have been deprived of them or because they have not been accepted by them, and who are nothing but a financial burden on a state that already has more than it can bear? Bastards, orphans, deformed children should be put to death at birth; the first and the second because, having no one who can or is willing to take care of them, they soil society with a scum that can only become fatal to it one day; and the others because they can be of absolutely no use to it. Both of these groups are to society like those fleshy excrescences that suck the sap from healthy branches, weakening and destroying them, or if you prefer, like those parasitical growths that attach themselves to healthy plants, eating away at them and damaging them by feeding on their nutritive seed. What flagrant abuses are those almshouses set up to feed such scum, those richly endowed properties that we are extravagant enough to build for them, as if the human species were so rare, so precious, that we must preserve even its vilest examples! But let us leave aside a politics of which you will understand little, my child. Why complain of your lot, when the remedy lies in your own hands?'

'Oh, Heaven, at what price!'

'At the price of a fantasy, of a thing whose only value is that which your pride gives it. Moreover,' this barbarian continued, rising to open the door, 'that is all I can offer you. Agree to it, or relieve me of your presence. I dislike beggars...'

My tears flowed, I could not hold them back. Would you believe it, Madame, they excited that man instead of moving him. He shut the door and, seizing me by the scruff of the neck, he brutally declared that he was going to force me to do what I would not grant him voluntarily. At that cruel moment, I took courage from my misfortune, eluded his grasp, and rushed to the door, saying as I escaped:

'Odious man! May the Lord, who is just as grievously offended by you as I am, punish you one day as you deserve to be punished for your execrable hardness of heart. You are worthy neither of the wealth that you so vily exploit, nor of the very air you breathe in a world soiled by your barbarity.'

I hastened to tell my landlady how I had been received by the person to whom she had sent me, but imagine my surprise when that wretched woman covered me with reproaches instead of sympathizing with my pain.

'Puny creature,' she said to me angrily, 'do you imagine that men are so stupid as to give charity to a young girl like you without demanding interest for their investment? Monsieur Dubourg was too good treating you as he did. If I'd been in his shoes, I should not have let you leave my house without satisfying me. However, since you do not wish to take advantage of the help I am offering you, make your own arrangements as you please. Tomorrow, it's the money you owe me, or prison.'

'Have pity, Madame...'

'Oh, yes, pity... with pity you die of hunger!'

'But what do you want me to do?'

'You must go back to see Dubourg. You must satisfy him and bring me money. I shall see him and tell him to expect you. I will make up for your stupidity, if I can. I will apologize to him on your behalf, but you must try to behave better.'

Shamefaced and in despair, not knowing where to turn, seeing myself cruelly repulsed on all sides and almost without resources, I told Madame Desroches (as my landlady was called) that I was ready to do anything to satisfy her. She went to see the financier, and upon her return told me that she had found him to be most annoyed, that she had had some difficulty winning him over, and that she had to resort to begging to persuade him to see me again the following morning. However, I should be careful how I behaved, because if I took it into my head to disobey him again he would himself ensure that I was locked up for life.

I arrived at Dubourg's house all of a flutter. Dubourg was alone, and in an even more indecent state than the day before. Brutality, libertinism, all the features of debauchery could be read in his shifty looks.

'You have Madame Desroches to thank', he said to me harshly. 'It is only for her sake that I am willing, out of the goodness of my heart, to give you a second chance. You must be aware how unworthy you are of my benevolence after your conduct yesterday. Undress yourself, and if you offer the least resistance to my desires, two men are waiting in my antechamber to take you to a place you will never get out of alive.'

'Oh, Monsieur,' I said in tears, throwing myself at the feet of this barbarous man, 'give way a little, I beg you! Be generous enough to help me without making me pay so high a price that I would rather offer you my life than submit to it... Yes, I prefer to die a thousand times rather than infringe the principles I learnt in my childhood... Monsieur, Monsieur, do not force me, I beg you! Can you conceive of happiness in the midst of tears and disgust? Do you dare to seek pleasure where all you can find is repugnance? Immediately after committing your crime, the spectacle of my despair will fill you with remorse...'

But the infamies that Dubourg was already indulging in prevented me from continuing. How could I have thought myself capable of moving a man who was already finding my own pain yet one more stimulus for his horrible passions? Can you believe it, Madame? His senses inflamed by the shrill tones of my cries, savouring them with inhumanity, the shameless man was already preparing to carry out his criminal actions! He rose to his feet, and revealing himself to me in a state in which reason rarely triumphs, in which the resistance of the object that drove him crazy merely served to feed his delirium, he brutally seized hold of me and hastily removed those veils that still hid from him what he longed to enjoy. One moment he abused me, the next he flattered me, treating me roughly, then caressing me... oh, dear Lord! What a scene! What an unheard of mixture of cruelty... and lewdness! It seemed as if, in this first of my life's adventures, the Supreme Being wished to fill me once and for all with the horror I should have for the sort of crime that would lead to all of the ills that threatened me. But ought I to complain in that instant? Probably not, since it was to his excesses that I owed my salvation. Had he been less debauched I should have become a dishonoured woman. Dubourg's fires were extinguished in the very effervescence of his actions, Heaven avenged me for the insults to which the monster was intending to subject me, and the loss of his virility before he was able to sacrifice my virtue saved me from falling victim to him.

This made Dubourg all the more impudent. He accused me of being responsible for his weakness, and intended to make up for it with fresh outrages and even more mortifying invectives. There was nothing he said to me, nothing he attempted, nothing that his perfidious imagination, the harshness of his character, and the depravity of his morals did not enable him to carry out. My clumsiness made him impatient. I was far from acting voluntarily, and I still feel remorse... and yet, nothing worked, he was no longer inflamed by my submissiveness. He tried in turn being tender and stern, proper and improper, my slave and my tyrant, but all in vain, for we both ended up exhausted, fortunately without his being able to recover sufficient strength to launch more dangerous assaults against me. He eventually gave up and made me promise to return the following day, and to make sure that I would do so he gave me no more than the amount of money I owed to Madame Desroches. I therefore returned to that woman's house completely humiliated by such an incident and quite resolved, whatever might happen to me, not to expose myself to such things a third time. I warned her of this when paying her, cursing the villain capable of taking such cruel advantage of my misery. However, far from bringing the wrath of God down upon his head, my curses brought him nothing but luck. A week later I learned that this notorious libertine had just obtained a general stewardship from the government that increased his income by more than four hundred thousand livres per annum. I was absorbed by the reflections to which such absurdities of destiny inevitably give rise when a ray of hope appeared for an instant to shine before my eyes.

One day Madame Desroches came to tell me that she had finally found a household where I would be warmly welcomed, as long as I behaved myself well.

'Oh, Heaven, Madame!' I said to her, throwing myself joyfully into her arms, 'that is the very condition that I would lay down myself, and so, as you might imagine, I accept with pleasure!'

The man I was to serve was a well-known Paris moneylender, who had got rich not just by lending at interest but by robbing people with impunity whenever he thought he could get away with it. He lived in the rue Quincampoix, on the second floor of a house, with a fifty-year-old creature he called his wife, who was at least as mean-spirited as he was.

'Thérèse,' this miser said to me (this being the name I had adopted to conceal my own), 'Thérèse, the first rule of my household is probity. If you should ever extort the tenth part of a denier from me I would see you hang, do you understand, my child? The little comfort my wife and I enjoy is the fruit of our hard labours and complete sobriety... Do you eat much, my child?'

'A few ounces of bread a day, Monsieur,' I replied, 'water and a little soup when I am fortunate enough to get any.'

'Soup! My word! Soup! Just listen to this, my dear,' the money-lender said to his wife, 'does not the ever-increasing demand for luxury make you weep! She's looking for a position, she's been dying of hunger for a year, and she expects to eat soup! We make soup barely once a week on Sundays, and we work like slaves! You shall have three ounces of bread a day, my girl, half a bottle of water from the brook, one of my wife's old dresses every eighteen months, and three écus in wages at the end of the year, provided we are happy with your services, if your thrift lives up to our own standards, and if you help the household to prosper by dint of your good order and efficiency. If your work is poor, you can be dismissed in the blink of an eye. You need to clean and polish this six-room apartment three times a week, make our beds, answer the door, powder my wig, do my wife's hair, look after the dog and the parrot, run the kitchen, clean all the kitchen utensils, help my wife when she's making us a bite to eat, and spend four or five hours a day making linen, stockings, bonnets, and other little household items. As you can see, Thérèse, there's not much to do. You'll have plenty of time left over which we will allow you to spend on yourself, as long as you behave yourself, my child, are sober, and above all, economical, that's the main thing.'

You can easily imagine, Madame, that to accept such a position I had to be in the dreadful state I was in. Not only was there considerably more work than my strength could cope with, but could I live on what I was being offered? However, I was at pains not to appear difficult, and was hired on the very same evening.

Although I should be thinking only of appealing to your sympathy, Madame, if my cruel situation might entertain you for a moment or two I might dare to tell you about some of the examples of avarice that I witnessed in that household, but in my second year of service I was overcome by such a terrible catastrophe that I find it hard to dwell on amusing details before recounting my misfortunes to you.

However, Madame, I have to tell you that in Monsieur du Harpin's apartment, the only light was the one he borrowed from the street-lamp that was happily positioned opposite his bedchamber. No one ever used any linen. The clothes I made were stored away and never touched. On the sleeves of Monsieur's jacket, and also on those of Madame's dress, an old pair of cuffs had been sewn onto the material, which I had to wash every Saturday evening. There were no sheets or towels, in order to avoid the need for laundering. Wine was never drunk in the house, pure water being, according to Madame du Harpin, the drink that was both natural and least injurious to man's health. Whenever bread was cut, a basket had to be placed under the knife in order to collect any crumbs, which were then to be added to all the crumbs collected at mealtimes. This dish was fried with a little butter on Sundays, constituting the feast eaten on these days of rest. Clothes and furniture were never to be beaten for fear of wearing them out, but lightly dusted with a feather-duster.* Both Monsieur's and Madame's shoes were shod with iron. They were the same ones they had worn on their wedding-day. An even stranger practice was that which I had to carry out each week. The apartment contained quite a large room whose walls were not papered. I had to scrape a certain amount of plaster from these walls with a knife and then filter this through a fine sieve. The result of this operation became the powder with which I dusted Monsieur's wig and Madame's chignon each morning. Oh, if only these turpitudes were the sole ones that these dreadful people indulged in! There is nothing more natural than the desire to conserve one's wealth and property, but it is not so natural to wish to increase it at the expense of others, and it was not long before I realized that this was how du Harpin acquired his wealth.

On the floor above us lodged an extremely wealthy individual who possessed some very fine jewellery, and with whose belongings, whether because of the neighbourhood or because they had passed through his hands, my master was well acquainted. I often heard him and his wife covet a particular gold casket containing between thirty and forty louis which, he would say, would have remained his had he only gone about matters with greater cunning. In the end, to console himself for giving back the casket, the good Monsieur du Harpin planned to steal it, and I was the one given the task of carrying out the theft.

He lectured me at great length on the neutral consequences of theft, and even of its usefulness in the world, since it restored a kind of equilibrium which the inequalities of wealth completely undermined, and on the rarity of punishment, since it was demonstrable that barely two out of twenty thieves were executed. With an erudition of which I would not have believed Monsieur du Harpin capable, he demonstrated that theft was honoured throughout Greece, that there were still peoples that accepted it, favoured it, and rewarded it as an act of both skill and courage (two virtues essential to any warlike nation). In short, he made much of the credit which would get me out of trouble if I was discovered. Monsieur du Harpin gave me two skeleton keys, one of which would open the neighbour's apartment and the other the writing-desk containing the box in question. He instructed me to bring him this casket immediately, promising that in return for such an important service my wages would be increased for two years by an additional écu.

'Oh, Monsieur!' I cried, trembling at this proposition, 'how can a master dare to corrupt his servant in such a manner? What is to stop me from turning against you the very weapons you are placing in my hands, and how could you object if one day I made you victim of your own principles?'

Du Harpin, in confusion, took refuge in a clumsy subterfuge: he told me that his intention was merely to test me, and that it was lucky for me that I resisted his temptations, that I would have been done for had I succumbed to them. I scoffed at this lie, but I soon realized that it was wrong of me to give such firm responses. Evildoers do not like to meet resistance in those they seek to seduce. There is unfortunately no middle ground once one is unfortunate enough to have become the object of their attentions. From that point on one is obliged to become their accomplice, which is dangerous, or their enemy, which is more dangerous still. If I had had a little more experience of the world I should have left the house that instant, but it was already written in Heaven that every honest impulse that would spring from my heart would meet with misfortune!

Monsieur du Harpin let nearly a month go by—that is, virtually to the end of my second year in his house—without saying a single word or manifesting the slightest resentment at my refusal of his proposal, when one evening, having just retired to my room to enjoy a few hours repose, I suddenly heard my door being forced open and, not without some trepidation, saw Monsieur du Harpin, accompanied by a police superintendent and four soldiers of the watch, standing before my bed.

'Do your duty, Monsieur,' he said to the officer of the law. 'This wretched woman has stolen a diamond from me worth a thousand écus. You will find it in her room or on her person, that's for sure.'

'I? Steal from you, Monsieur?' I said, jumping out of bed in a state of shock. 'Me! Oh, Heaven! You know better than anyone that this is not the case! Who could be more aware than yourself how repugnant such an action would be to me, and that it is not possible for me to have committed it?'

However, making a lot of noise so that I could not be heard, du Harpin continued to give orders for my room to be searched, and the fateful ring was discovered under my mattress. There was no answer to such irrefutable proof, and I was immediately seized, bound, and led away to prison without having a chance to say one word in my defence.

The trial of an unfortunate girl without either influence or protection is soon expedited in a land where virtue is thought incompatible with misery, and where misfortune is sure proof of guilt. In such places, unjust imprisonment on suspicion can persuade a court that the person who must have committed the crime did commit it.* Opinions match the state in which the accused find themselves, and if there is no gold or securities to establish that they are innocent, the impossibility of their innocence is determined once and for all.[1]

In vain did I defend myself or extend the best assistance to the duty lawyer to whom I was briefly allowed access; the accusation came from my master, the diamond had been discovered in my room, and it was clear that I had stolen it. When I attempted to draw attention to Monsieur du Harpin's frightful character to prove that the misfortune that had befallen me was nothing but the fruit of his vengefulness and the result of his desire to be rid of a creature who, knowing his secret, was acquiring power over him, these charges were treated as recriminations, and I was told that Monsieur du Harpin had been known for twenty years as a man of integrity who was incapable of such a dreadful act. I was transferred to the Conciergerie,* where I realized I was about to pay with my life for my refusal to be party to a crime. I was going to die, and only another criminal act could save me. Providence dictated that crime should serve at least once as virtue's shield, saving it from the abyss into which it was about to be plunged by the imbecility of the judges.

In the cell next to me was a woman of about forty, who was as famous for her beauty as for the nature and multiplicity of her misdeeds. Her name was Dubois, and like the unfortunate Thérèse, she was about to be sentenced to death, the only concern of the judges being the manner of her execution. Since she was guilty of all imaginable kinds of crime, they almost felt obliged either to invent some new punishment for her, or to subject her to one from which our sex is normally exempt. I had inspired a kind of interest in this woman, no doubt of a criminal nature, since, as I was to discover later, it was motivated by a strong desire to make a proselyte of me.

One evening, perhaps two days at the very most before the day when both of us were due to hang, Dubois told me not to go to bed and, without attracting attention, to wait with her as close as possible to the prison gates.

[1] Centuries to come will not see such infamy and horrors!*

'Between seven and eight o'clock,' she continued, 'I have arranged for the Conciergerie to catch fire. Many people will doubtless be burnt to death, but this is of no consequence, Thérèse,' this wicked woman had the gall to say to me. 'The fate of others must never count for anything when our well-being is at stake. We shall be saved, that's certain. Four men, my friends and accomplices, will join us, and I guarantee that you will be set free.'

I tell you, Madame, the same divine hand that had just punished my innocence now served my protector's criminal intentions. The place caught fire with horrendous consequences, with twenty-one people burnt alive, but we escaped. That same day we reached the cottage of a poacher in the forest of Bondy, an intimate friend of our gang.

'Now that you're free, Thérèse,' Dubois then said to me, 'you can choose any path through life you please, but I have one piece of advice to give you, and that is to abandon the path of virtue which, as you can see, has never brought you success. A misplaced delicacy led you to the foot of the scaffold, whereas an awful crime saved me from it. Look where good deeds get you in this world. Is it really worth sacrificing yourself for them? You are young and pretty, Thérèse. Give me two years and I guarantee to make your fortune. Don't imagine, however, that I will lead you to its temple by the paths of virtue. When one chooses this path, dear girl, one must be prepared to undertake more than one trade and be party to more than one intrigue. So make up your mind, because we are not safe in this cottage and must leave in a few hours.'

'Oh, Madame', I said to my benefactor, 'I have great obligations to you, and far be it from me to wish to avoid them. You have saved my life, but I find it horrendous that this was done by committing a criminal act. Please believe that, if I had been the one to commit it, I should have preferred to die a thousand deaths than to have suffered the agony of taking part in it. I am aware of all the risks I have run in following those honest instincts which will always remain in my heart, but however thorny the path of virtue may be, I shall always prefer them to the dangerous attractions of crime. There are religious principles in me which, thank Heaven, will never leave me. If Providence makes my life's journey difficult, it is to reward me for it in a better world. I am consoled by such hopes, which may give succour to sorrows, relieve my suffering, fortify me in my distress, and give me the strength to endure all the ills that it will please God to send me. This joy would immediately be extinguished in my soul if I were to soil it with crimes, and in addition to the fear of retribution in this world, I would face the painful prospect of punishment in the next, which would not leave me with a single moment of the peace I desire.'

'Such absurd ideas will soon lead to the workhouse, my girl,' said Dubois, raising her eyebrows. 'Believe me, you should abandon God's justice, his punishments or rewards to come. All that these platitudes are good for is to make us die of hunger. Oh, Thérèse, the hard hearts of the rich justify the bad conduct of the poor. If their purses opened to serve our needs, if humanity reigned in their hearts, then virtues would flourish in ours. But as long as our misfortune and our patient endurance of it, our good faith and our servitude serve only to tighten our chains, our crimes will become their work, and we would be most foolish to refuse to commit them when they can lighten the yoke which our cruel fate imposes on us. We were all born equal in Nature, Thérèse, and if it pleases fate to undermine this first article of the general law, it is up to us to correct such whims and to use our talents to counter the usurpations of those stronger than us. How I love to hear the rich and titled, the magistrates and the priests, how I love to watch them preach virtue to us! It is very hard to keep oneself from stealing when one has three times more than one needs to live! A great strain to never think of murder when one is sur-rounded by sycophants and slaves for whom your will is law! Truly difficult to be temperate and sober when one is at all times surrounded by the most succulent dishes! So difficult for them to be sincere when they have no reason to lie!... But as for us, Thérèse, whom barbarous Providence, which you are mad enough to idolize, has condemned to the humiliation of crawling along like the snake in the grass, we who are looked upon with disdain because we are poor, who are treated like slaves because we are weak, we whose lips are moistened only with gall and whose feet tread upon nothing but thorns, you want us to abstain from crime when its hand alone can open the door to life, can maintain and preserve us in it, and prevent us from losing it! You want us to remain perpetually submissive and degraded, while the class that dominates us enjoys all Fortune's favours and our lot is nothing but hardship, despondency, and pain, only want, tears, the branding of the criminal, and the scaffold! Oh no, Thérèse, no, either this Providence that you revere deserves no more than our contempt, or such is not its will. When you have a better understanding of it, my child, you will be convinced that, if it places us in a situation where evil becomes necessary, and at the same time gives us the chance to commit it, it is because this evil serves the laws of Providence as much as good does, and derives an equal benefit from both. It has created us all equal, but he who disrupts this equality is no more guilty than he who seeks to restore it. Both are acting on inborn impulses, and both should follow these impulses and enjoy them.'

I confess that if I was ever shaken in my beliefs, it was by the seductive arguments of this clever woman, but a stronger voice than hers combated her sophisms in my heart, and acknowledging it, I announced to Dubois that I had made up my mind never to allow myself to be corrupted.

'Very well,' she replied, 'do what you please, I abandon you to your unhappy lot, but if you ever get caught, which is bound to happen, given the fate that inevitably saves the criminal while sacrificing the virtuous, remember at least never to speak of us.'

While we were reasoning thus, Dubois's four companions were drinking with the poacher, and as wine disposes the temperament of the wrongdoer to new crimes and makes him forget old ones, no sooner had our rogues learnt of my resolutions than they decided to make a victim of me, not being able to make me their accomplice. Their principles, morals, the dark lair where we were, the safe situation in which they thought themselves to be, their drunkenness, my age and innocence, all of these things encouraged them. They got up from the table, talked among themselves, and consulted with Dubois, actions whose ominous secrecy made me shudder with horror, and as a result I was finally ordered to prepare without delay to satisfy the desires of each of the four men, either willingly or by force. If I did so willingly they would each give me one écu so that I might go wherever I desired. If violence had to be employed, things would happen just the same, but in order to preserve secrecy they would stab me to death after satisfying themselves and bury me at the foot of a tree.

I need not describe to you, Madame, the effect that this cruel proposition had on me, since you will easily understand it. I threw myself at Dubois's feet and begged her to be my protector once again, but the dishonest creature merely laughed at my tears.

'Oh, fancy!' she said to me, 'what a sad girl you are! I can't believe that you tremble at the prospect of having to serve four tall, handsome boys like these one after the other. Are you aware that there are ten thousand women in Paris who would give half their gold or their jewels to be in your shoes? Listen,' she added, however, after some reflection, 'I have enough influence over those rascals to obtain a reprieve for you on condition that you prove yourself worthy of it.'

'Alas, Madame, what must I do?' I cried in tears. 'Tell me, I am ready.'

'Follow us, join our gang, and commit the same crimes without the slightest repugnance. This is my only price for saving you from another fate.'

I did not think I ought to waver. In accepting this cruel condition I was running new risks, admittedly, but they were less urgent than the present ones. Perhaps I would be able to defend myself against those to come, whereas nothing could protect me from those currently threatening me.

'I will go anywhere with you, Madame,' I said immediately to Dubois, 'I will go anywhere, I promise, just save me from the fury of these men and I shall never ever leave you.'

'Boys,' said Dubois to the four bandits, 'this girl is one of us, I am receiving her into our gang and I beg you not to subject her to any violence. Let's not put her off our profession before she's even started. You can see how her age and looks can be useful to us. We should exploit them to serve our interests, and not sacrifice them to our desires.'

But the energy of passion reaches a certain point in men when nothing can control it. The people I was dealing with were no longer willing to listen. All four men surrounded me, devouring me with their eyes full of fire and threatening me in a manner still more terrible, on the point of seizing me and sacrificing me to their lusts.

'She's got to have it,' said one of them, 'we can no longer give her quarter. Is it not the case that one must prove one's worth to be in a gang of thieves, and won't she be just as useful to us dishonoured as virgin?'

You will understand, Madame, that I am softening the language used, and my descriptions of these scenes will be similarly toned down. Alas! Their obscene nature is such that a more graphic account would make you blush at least as much as it would my innocence.

Alas! Poor timid victim that I was, I trembled with terror, and barely had the strength to breathe. On my knees before the four men, I stretched out my feeble arms in supplication to them and to Dubois in turn.

'One moment,' said one of them, who went by the name of Ironheart and who seemed to be the gang-leader, a man of about thirty-six with the strength of a bull and the figure of a satyr, 'one moment, my friends, it is possible to satisfy everyone. Since this little girl's virtue is so precious to her, and since, as Dubois quite rightly says, this quality may prove necessary to us if we handle it in a different way, let us leave it intact. However, we have to be satisfied; we are no longer in our right minds, Dubois, and in the state we're in now we might cut your own throat if you stood in the way of our pleasure. Thérèse must instantly appear as naked as the day she was born, and she must agree to adopt in turn all the different positions that we require of her, whilst Dubois will calm our ardour, burning incense on the altars to which this creature denies us access.'

'Take off all of my clothes!' I cried. 'Oh, Heaven! What are you asking of me? When I stand naked before you, who will be able to guarantee...?'

But Ironheart, who seemed in no mood to compromise further with regard to my requests, called me names and struck me so brutally that I realized that obedience was my only option. Dubois having been thrust into the same disorderly state as I, he placed himself in her hands, and as soon as I was in the state he wished me to be in, on all fours, which made me look like an animal, Dubois cooled his fires, expertly guiding a sort of monster towards the peristyles of both altars of Nature in turn, such that with each thrust she had to strike these parts hard with her hand, like the battering-ram at the gates of besieged towns in days gone by. The violence of these initial attacks made me recoil. A furious Ironheart threatened me with harsher treatment if I shrank from this one. Dubois was ordered to redouble her efforts, while one of these libertines held me by the shoulders, preventing me from collapsing under the shocks which became so rough that I was battered and bruised, though I could not escape any of them.

'To tell the truth,' stammered Ironheart, 'if I were her I would prefer to open the gates than to see them battered down in this way, but as she does not wish to, we won't fail to make her capitulate... Vigorously, Dubois, vigorously...!' and the explosion of this debauched man's passions, almost as violent as a thunderbolt, died away at the threshold of those orifices which, though molested, remained intact.

The second man made me kneel between his legs, and while Dubois satisfied him like his companion, two activities completely preoccupied him: one moment, in a very nervous fashion, he would strike my cheeks or my breasts with the flat of his hand, and the next, his impure mouth would soil my own. My face and bosom immediately became crimson red... I was in pain, I begged him to stop, and his eyes streamed with my tears, irritating him further, and he redoubled his efforts, whereupon my tongue was bitten and both rosebuds of my bosom were so bruised that I recoiled in pain but I was held fast. I was pushed back onto him, and as greater pressure was applied from all sides, his ecstasy was ensured.

The third made me climb onto two chairs set side by side with a gap between them, and sitting underneath, and excited by Dubois who was positioned between his legs, he pushed me down until his mouth was opposite my temple of Nature. You cannot imagine, Madame, what this obscene mortal had the temerity to request. Whether I wanted to or not, I had to indulge in the lesser functions. Dear Heaven! How depraved must one be to derive a single moment of pleasure from such things. I did what he wanted and inundated him. My total submission induced a delirium in this vile man that nothing else would have brought about without this infamy.

The fourth man attached ropes to all those parts to which it was possible to do so. Holding the bundle in his hand, he sat seven or eight foot away from my body, greatly excited by Dubois's caresses and kisses. With me standing upright, it was by pulling hard in turn on each of these ropes that the savage stimulated his pleasures. I swayed and kept losing my balance, whilst he was in ecstasy whenever I stumbled. Eventually, he pulled on all the ropes at the same time in such an irregular fashion that I fell over beside him. Such was his sole aim, and my forehead, breasts, and cheeks were covered with the proof of a delirium which this mania alone induced.

This is what I suffered, Madame, but my honour at least was respected, if my modesty was not. A little calmer now, these robbers decided to leave, and that very night they arrived at Le Tremblai on their way to the Chantilly woods, where they hoped to pull off a few good strokes.

Nothing could compare with the despair that I felt at having to accompany such people, and I resolved to abandon them as soon as I could without risk. The following night we slept under haystacks on the outskirts of Louvres. I wanted to have Dubois protect me and to spend the night beside her, but I got the impression that she preferred to spend it on business of her own rather than preserving my virtue from the attacks I feared. Three of them surrounded her, and before our eyes the abominable creature gave herself to all three at the same time. The fourth man, the leader of the gang, came up to me.

'Beautiful Thérèse,' he said to me, 'I hope at least that you will not refuse me the pleasure of spending the night with you?' And as he noticed my extreme repugnance: 'Fear not,' he said, 'we'll talk together, and I won't do anything against your will. Oh, Thérèse,' he continued, putting his arms around me, 'is it not sheer folly for you to imagine that you can remain pure in our company? Even if we agreed to let you, how could that be reconciled with all of our interests? My dear child, there's no point in hiding it from you. When we're living in town we intend to dupe men, using your charms to trap them.'

'Well, Monsieur,' I replied, 'since I would certainly prefer death to such horrors, how can I be useful to you, and why won't you let me go?'

'Of course we won't, my angel,' replied Ironheart, 'you must serve our interests or our pleasures. It is your misfortune that imposes this yoke upon you and you must submit to it. But you know this, Thérèse, there is nothing in this world that cannot be accommodated, so listen to what I am saying and determine your own destiny. Agree to live with me, my dear girl, agree to belong to me alone and I shall spare you the sad fate that awaits you.'

'You want me, Monsieur, to become the mistress of a...?'

'Go on, say it, Thérèse, say the word, "of a rogue", that's what you mean, isn't it? You're right, I admit it, but I cannot offer you any other rank. You will understand that our sort cannot marry. Marriage is a sacrament, Thérèse, and as we are filled with the same contempt for all sacraments, we never touch any of them. However, just listen to reason. You cannot avoid losing what you hold dear, and so is it not better to sacrifice it to one man who would then become your protector and support than to prostitute yourself to all?'

'But do I really have no other choice?' I replied.

'You do not, Thérèse, because you are our prisoner, and as La Fontaine* said long ago, force is always the most decisive factor. Indeed,' he went on, 'is it not a ridiculous extravagance to attach so much value, as you do, to the most pointless of things? How can a girl be so simple as to believe that virtue can depend on the degree of width of one part of her body? Oh, what does it matter to men or to God whether this part is intact or sullied? I will go further and say that, since it is Nature's intentions that each individual should fulfil here on earth all the functions for which he or she was designed, and since women exist solely to serve men's pleasure, it is a clear outrage to Nature to resist her intentions for you in this way. You would be a useless, and consequently contemptible, creature in this world. This fanciful good conduct which others have been absurd enough to tell you was a virtue, and which, far from being useful to Nature and society, has clearly outraged both from your childhood on, is nothing more than reprehensible stubbornness of which a person as spirited as you are should not wish to be guilty. Nevertheless, listen to what I am about to tell you, dear girl. I shall prove to you that I want to please you and that I respect your failings. I shall not touch that phantasm, Thérèse, the possession of which pleases you so much. A girl has more than one favour to give, and Venus is worshipped in far more than one temple. I shall be content with the least of these. You know, my dear, near the Cyprian altar there is a dark retreat where love may find a home to seduce us with more energy. This is the altar at which I shall burn my incense. Not the slightest inconvenience there, Thérèse, because if you're afraid of getting pregnant, that could not happen in such a way, so your pretty figure will never be ruined. The maidenhead that is so dear to you will be preserved without a blemish, and whatever use you want to put it to, you will be able to describe it as unsullied. Nothing can betray a girl on that side, however rough and numerous the attacks. Once the bee has pumped out the nectar, the rose's cup closes once more, and one would never have suspected that it had ever opened up. There are girls who have been pleasured for ten years like this, even with several men, and have got married afterwards as untouched virgins. How many fathers, how many brothers, have abused their daughters or sisters in this fashion, without these girls becoming any less worthy of being thereafter sacrificed on the marriage altar!

How many confessors have taken this very same road to satisfaction
without the parents suspecting anything? In short, it is the refuge
of mystery which good conduct combines there with desire. What
more need I say, Thérèse, that temple is both the most secret and the
most voluptuous. There alone can be found what is needed for happiness, and the great ease of the temple next door cannot compare
with the piquant delights of a place that is reached only with effort,
and where one is lodged only with difficulty. It even benefits women,
and those that reason obliges to acquaint themselves with such pleasures never miss the other kind. Give it a try, Thérèse, and we shall
both be happy.'

'Oh, Monsieur,' I replied, 'I have no experience of such things,
but I have heard it said, Monsieur, that this deviation you advocate
offends women in a manner that is even more painful, and offends
Nature even more grievously. The hand of God wreaks vengeance in
this world, as Sodom has shown.'

'What innocence, my dear, what childishness,' continued this libertine, 'who taught you such things? Give me your attention for just
a little while longer, and I shall set your thinking right. The loss of
the seed intended to propagate the human species, dear girl, is the
only crime that can exist. In that case, if this seed in placed in us with
the sole purpose of propagation, then I grant you that it is an offence
to turn it away from its object. But if it can be demonstrated that, in
placing this seed in our loins, Nature's aim is far from being propagation alone, what does it matter, Thérèse, whether it is lost in one
place or another? The man who changes its object in that case does no
more harm than Nature when it makes no use of it. Now, do not
these losses of Nature which we have only to imitate take place in
many cases? The very fact that it is possible for them to happen is a
first proof that they do not offend against Nature. It would be against
all the laws of equity and the most profound wisdom which we recognize in all of Nature's works, to allow anything that offended her.
Secondly, these losses are effected a hundred million times a day by
Nature herself. Nocturnal emissions, the uselessness of seed when
women are already pregnant, are these losses not sanctioned by her
laws, and do they not prove that, perfectly insensitive to whatever
might be the consequences of that fluid to which we are crazy enough
to attach so much value, she allows its loss with the same indifference
with which she brings it about each day? Do they not prove that,

while she tolerates reproduction, it is far from always being her intention; that she wants us to multiply, but that since she gains no more from one of her actions than from another that is contrary to it, the choice that we may make is indifferent to her; that giving us the power to create, not to create, or to destroy, we neither please nor offend her more in selecting from one or other of these options the one that will suit us best; that the one we choose, being the result of her power and influence over us, will surely always please her far more than it will risk offending her? Oh, believe me, Thérèse, Nature is far less concerned about those mysteries which we are foolish enough to worship. Since she allows us to burn our incense at any temple we choose, our sacrifice cannot offend her. The failure to reproduce, the losses of the seed that serves reproduction or its extinction, and even when it has germinated, the destruction of the embryo long after its formation, all of these things, Thérèse, are imaginary crimes which are of no interest to Nature, and which it makes mock of, as it does of all our other institutions that frequently offend instead of serving her.'

Ironheart was getting worked up as he exposed his perfidious ideas, and I soon saw him in that state in which he had scared me so much the day before. In order to make the lesson more effective, he immediately wanted to put theory into practice, and in spite of my resistance, his hands strayed towards the altar which the villain wished to penetrate... I am bound to confess, Madame, that I was blinded by the enticements of this vile man, and by giving some ground, I was pleased to have preserved what seemed to be the most essential of things. I considered neither the inconsistencies of his sophisms nor the risks to myself, since this dishonest man was hugely proportioned and so was not even capable of serving a woman in the least criminal manner. Driven by his inborn wickedness, his sole aim was to cripple me. I was so fascinated to see all of this, I say, that I was on the point of giving way, and by dint of virtue, becoming a sinner. My resolve was weakening and, already master of the throne, this insolent victor was intent on occupying it when the sound of a coach was heard on the highway. Ironheart instantly abandoned pleasure to attend to duty, summoned his gang, and hurried away to commit more crimes. Soon after, screams could be heard, and the triumphant villains returned covered in blood, their arms full of booty.

'We must leave without delay,' said Ironheart, 'we have killed three men, the corpses are lying on the road, and it is not safe for us to stay here any longer.'

The spoils were shared out. Ironheart wanted me to have my share, which amounted to twenty louis, and so I was forced to accept it. I shuddered at having to take such an amount; however, I was given no choice, and so each took his share and we departed.

The next day we were in safe hiding in the forest of Chantilly. Over supper the gang calculated their profits from this last job, concluding that they had not even made two hundred louis.

'It really wasn't worth committing three murders for such a small sum,' said one of them.

'Calm yourselves, my friends,' Dubois replied, 'it wasn't for the money that I encouraged you to show these travellers no mercy, it was for our own safety. These crimes are the fault of the law and not ours. As long as thieves are executed the same as murderers, they will always kill. Since both offences attract the same punishment, why refuse to do murder when it can cover up theft? In any case,' the horrible woman continued, 'what makes you think that two hundred louis are not worth three murders? The value of everything must be calculated only in relation to our interests. The extinction of each of our victims counts for nothing compared with us. It surely wouldn't matter a fig to us whether those individuals were alive or in the tomb. Consequently, if in such a case we can derive the slightest benefit from it, we should without any remorse promote that interest, because where a thing is completely indifferent to us, if we are wise and in charge of events, we should definitely make sure they are profitable for us, regardless of any harm caused to our adversary. This is because there is no reasonable comparison between our concerns and those of others. The former affect us physically, while the latter are of only moral interest to us, and moral feelings are deceptive. Only physical sensations are true. Thus, not only are two hundred louis sufficient justification for the three murders, but even thirty sous would have sufficed, for these thirty sous would have procured a satisfaction for us which, though far smaller, must nevertheless affect us much more keenly than the three murders would have done, the latter having no significance for us. While they are mortally wounded, we do not even suffer a scratch. The weakness of our organs, our feeble-mindedness, the accursed prejudices with which we were raised, the vain terrors of religion or of our laws, all of these things hold back the ignorant from pursuing a career of crime, preventing them from aiming for the biggest prizes. Yet any individual, filled with strength and vigour, endowed with an active and well-organized mind, who puts himself above all others, and rightly so, will be able to weigh their interests against his, scoff at God and men, risk death, and despise laws, in the firm conviction that the only interests he need serve are his own. He will believe that the greatest amount of harm done to others, of which he will have no physical sensation, cannot begin to compare with the least little pleasure bought at the expense of the hugest of crimes. Pleasure fills and is inside him, while he is untouched by the consequences of his crimes which are outside him. Now, I ask, what reasonable man would not prefer what he himself enjoys to what is foreign to him? How could such a man not consent to commit an act, the unpleasant effects of which are external to him, in order to obtain something that to him is most agreeable?'

'Oh, Madame,' I said to Dubois, having asked her permission to respond to these dreadful sophisms, 'do you not realize that you condemn yourself in what you have just said? Such principles could at the very most suit only that person powerful enough to have nothing to fear from others, whereas we, Madame, living in constant fear and humiliation, ostracized by honest people and condemned by all laws, how can we agree to behave in ways that can only serve to sharpen the sword suspended above our heads? Were we not to find ourselves in this sad situation, were we to be in the bosom of society... if we were where we should be, in other words, if not for our misconduct and misfortune, do you imagine that such maxims would suit us more? Can you expect the person who wishes to stand alone in opposition to the interests of others not to perish? Does society not have the right to expel from its bosom those who declare themselves against it? Can those individuals who isolate themselves fight everyone else? Can they truly be happy and tranquil if they do not accept the social contract and do not consent to give away a little of their happiness in order to preserve the rest?* Society only supports itself through the constant exchange of good deeds. These are the ties that hold it together. Those who commit only crimes instead of good deeds, and therefore must be feared, will necessarily be attacked if they are the strongest, or killed by the first person they offend if they are the weakest. In any event, they will be destroyed by the powerful argument that drives men to safeguard their tranquillity and to attack

those who wish to disrupt it. These are the reasons why it is almost
impossible for criminal associations to endure. When the interests of
others are attacked at knife-point, such people must quickly come
together to ward them off. Even among ourselves, Madame,' I dared
to add, 'how can you pretend to maintain harmony when you advise
each individual to pursue his own interests alone? How could you
then object if one of us wanted to stab the others to death in order to
get his companions' share of the spoils for himself? What finer
defence of virtue than the proof of its necessity, even amongst criminals, than the certainty that their unity would not survive for a single
moment without virtue?'

'The fact is, Thérèse, that all your objections are just sophisms,'
said Ironheart, 'and not what Dubois was arguing. It isn't virtue that
keeps criminals together, it's egoism and self-interest, showing your
praise of virtue to be erroneous and based on an illusory hypothesis.
It isn't out of virtue that, considering myself, I suppose, to be the
strongest in the gang, I don't stab my companions to death to get
their share—it's because I would then be all alone and would thereby
deprive myself of the means by which I could secure the fortune that
I expect to obtain with their help. This is the only motive that equally
stays their hand from striking me. Now, as you can see, Thérèse, this
motive is purely selfish, with not the slightest trace of virtue. Whoever
is inclined to stand alone against the interests of society must expect
to perish, you say. Will he not more surely perish if he has nothing
but misery and neglect to live on? What we call the common interest
is only the sum of all individual interests added together, but it is
only by giving way that these individual interests can agree with and
become part of the general interest. Now, what can someone who has
nothing be expected to give? If he does so you will grant that he is all
the more in error, in that he is then giving infinitely more than he
receives, and in such a case the inequality of the bargain must prevent him from concluding it. Trapped in such a situation, is not the
best thing for such a man to do to remove himself from this unfair
society? Should he not accord rights only to a different society of men
who are placed in the same situation as he, and in whose interests it
is to unite their lesser forces in order to combat the greater power
that wished to make the unfortunate individual relinquish what little
he had for nothing in return? But, you will say, will not this bring
about a state of perpetual war? So be it, is this not the natural state of

affairs? Is it not the only one that truly suits us? Men were all born alone, envious, cruel, and despotic, wanting to have everything and give nothing away, constantly fighting each other to pursue their ambitions or defend their rights. The law-maker came along and told them to stop fighting like this. By conceding a little here and there, we can live peacefully together. I do not criticize the basis of this contract, I simply maintain that two different kinds of individual should never have subscribed to it: those who, considering themselves to be the strongest, needed to give nothing away in order to be happy; and those who, being the weakest, found themselves conceding infinitely more than they were promised. However, society is made up only of the weak and the strong. Now, if the social pact was bound to displease both the strong and the weak, it must be far from suiting society as a whole, and the state of war that existed before must be thought infinitely preferable, since it allowed each individual to exercise his strength and industry freely, a freedom of which he was deprived by the unfair social pact which always takes too much away from one group while never granting enough to the other. Thus, the truly wise person is the one who, at the risk of resuming the state of war that reigned before the pact, launches himself with all his might against this pact, violating it as much as he can, in the certain knowledge that whatever profit he makes from these violations will always be greater than what he might lose if he is the weakest, for he was in no better position when he respected the pact. He may become the strongest in violating it, and if the law relegates him to the social class that he wished to leave behind, his last resource is to lose his life, which is an infinitely lesser misfortune than that of living in opprobrium and misery. These, then, are the two options facing us: crime which makes us happy, or the scaffold which stops us from being unhappy. I ask you, my lovely Thérèse, would you hesitate? Can you come up with any reasoning to match this?'

'Oh, Monsieur,' I replied with the vehemence born of a good cause, 'there are thousands, but should this life be the only object of human beings? Is it not the case that every step in our journey, if we are wise, should lead us to that eternal felicity which is virtue's certain reward? Let us just suppose for one moment—although this is rare and goes against the enlightenment of reason, but never mind—that crime may make the rogue who indulges in it here on earth happy; can you imagine that God's justice does not await this dishonest man in another world to avenge his actions in this one? Oh, Monsieur, do not think that this is not so, do not believe that,' I added in tears, 'it is the only consolation of the unfortunate in life, don't take it away from us. If we are abandoned by men, who else but God can avenge us?'

'Who? No one, Thérèse, absolutely no one. In no way is it necessary that misfortune should be avenged. The unfortunate believe in this because they wish it to be so, because the idea of it consoles them, but it is no less false. What is more, it is essential that the unfortunate should suffer. Their humiliation and their pain are numbered among the laws of Nature, and their existence is essential to her overall plan, as is that of the prosperity that crushes them. This is the truth that must stifle remorse in the soul of the tyrant or evildoer, who should not hold back, blindly committing all the harm that occurs to him since it is Nature's voice alone that inspires these thoughts in him. It is the only way in which she makes us agents of her laws. When her secret promptings dispose us to evil, it is because evil is necessary to her, because she wills it, because she demands it, because the sum of crimes is not complete, as required by the laws of equilibrium, which are the only laws that govern her, and so she demands more crimes to ensure a proper balance. He whose thoughts incline to evil should therefore neither hesitate nor be afraid. He must fearlessly commit the crime as soon as he feels the impulse to do so, for he outrages Nature only by resisting it.* But let us leave morality aside for a moment, since you prefer theology. You poor innocent young girl, do you not realize that the religion upon which you base your arguments, being nothing but man's relationship with God, the devotion which the creature believes he owes to his creator, melts into thin air as soon as the existence of this creator is itself proven to be a fantasy? Terrified by the phenomena that they witnessed, the earliest humans had of necessity to believe that a sublime being, unknown to them, was controlling and influencing events. Weakness lies in giving in to or in fearing force. Human intelligence was still too infantile to look for and discover the laws of movement in Nature, the only source of all the mechanisms that overawed men, who found it simpler to assume that Nature was driven by some motor than to see it as its own driving-force. Not thinking that it would be much more difficult to construct and define such a supreme master than to find the cause of the phenomena that astonished them in Nature, they accepted the idea of this sovereign being and founded religions to worship him. From that moment on, each nation created a religion in keeping with its customs, knowledge, and climate, and soon there were as many faiths on earth as peoples, as many Gods as dynasties. Nevertheless, behind all of these idols it was not hard to recognize this absurd phantom, the first fruit of human blindness. He assumed different guises but he was always the same thing. So, tell me, Thérèse, should a wise man renounce the certain and present happiness of this life simply because imbeciles have constructed a pointless chimera and established absurd ways of serving it? Should he, like Aesop's dog,* abandon the bone for the shadows and renounce his real pleasures for the sake of illusions? No, Thérèse, no, there is no God, Nature is sufficient unto itself, and has no need of an author. This supposed author is nothing but the decomposition of its own forces, nothing but what we call in school "begging the question". A God presupposes creation, that is, a moment when there was nothing, or else a moment when all was in chaos. If either of these states was bad, why did your God allow it to exist? If it was good, why did he change it? But if all is good now, your God has nothing more to do. Now, if he is unnecessary, can he be powerful, and if he is not powerful, can he be God? Finally, if Nature drives itself, what is the point of a moving agent? And if the agent acts to move matter, how can it not be matter itself? Can you conceive of the effect of spirit on matter, and matter being moved by a spirit that is unmoved itself? Just think rationally for a moment about all of the ridiculous and contradictory qualities which the fabricators of this wretched fantasy are obliged to attribute to it, and you will see how they destroy one another, how they mutually devour each other; you will realize that this God-phantom, born of either fear or ignorance, is nothing but a revolting platitude which does not deserve either a single moment of our faith or a second of our attention. It is nothing but a pitiable absurdity that insults the intelligence, revolts our senses, a phantom that emerged from the darkness only to sink back into it forever.

'So don't be concerned by the hope or fear of a world to come, Thérèse, an illusion which is nothing but the fruit of these early lies. Above all, stop trying to use it to restrain us. We are merely tiny parts of a vile and brutish matter, and when we die, that is, when we are reunited with other elements of the general mass of things, we shall disappear forever, whatever our behaviour has been. We shall momentarily pass through the crucible of Nature to re-emerge in different forms, without any greater privilege accorded to those who insanely worshipped virtue than to those who indulged in the most shameful excesses, because there is nothing that offends Nature, and all men have come out of her womb just the same. Having behaved during their lives solely according to her impulses, they will all meet the same end and the same fate at the close of their existence.'*

I was about to respond again to these dreadful blasphemies when we heard the noise of a man on horseback close by. 'To arms!' cried Ironheart, who was more concerned to put his theories into action than to consolidate them. We quickly got to business, and a moment later dragged an unfortunate traveller into the clearing where we had made our encampment. Interrogated about why he was travelling so early in the morning on a deserted road, about his age and his profession, the rider replied that his name was Saint-Florent, that he was one of the leading tradesmen of Lyons, that he was thirty-six years old, that he was returning from Flanders which he had needed to visit on personal business, that he had little money on him, but a lot of papers. He added that his valet had left him the day before, and that to avoid the heat of the day he was travelling at night, with the intention of arriving the same day in Paris, where he would take on a fresh servant and would conclude some of his business. Moreover, if he was now on a deserted road he must have taken a wrong turning, having fallen asleep on his horse. That said, he pleaded for his life, offering in return all that he possessed. An examination of his purse proved that this man was the best possible catch. Saint-Florent had nearly half a million payable on demand on the capital,* a few jewels, and around a hundred louis.

'Friend,' said Ironheart to him, shoving a pistol-butt under his nose, 'you must understand that after stealing so much from you, we cannot let you live.'

'Oh, Monsieur!' I cried, throwing myself at the feet of this rogue, 'I beg you not to force me to witness the horrible spectacle of this unfortunate man's death when I have only just joined your gang! Let him live! Don't refuse me the first favour I ask of you!' And having recourse to a singular ruse to legitimate the interest I was appearing to take in this man, I immediately added with some force: 'The name that this gentleman has given leads me to believe that I am closely related to him.' Then, addressing the traveller, I continued:

'Don't be surprised, Monsieur, to come across a relative in such circumstances. I shall explain everything to you. For these reasons,' I continued imploring our leader once again, 'for these reasons, Monsieur, grant me the life of this wretched man and I shall return the favour with the greatest devotion to everything that may serve your interests.'

'You know what the conditions are if I am to grant you the favour you ask, Thérèse,' replied Ironheart, 'you know what I require of you...'

'Well, then, Monsieur, I will do anything,' I cried, throwing myself between this unfortunate and our chief, who was still on the point of cutting his throat... 'Yes, I will do anything, Monsieur, anything at all! Spare him!'

'Let him live,' said Ironheart, 'but he must join our gang. This condition is indispensable, I can do nothing otherwise, or my comrades would not agree.'

The merchant was astonished to hear me claim that we were relatives, but realizing that his life was saved if he agreed to these proposals, he did not waver for a single moment. He was given refreshment, and then, as our people did not wish to leave this place until daylight: 'Thérèse,' Ironheart said to me, 'I call upon you to keep your promise, but as I am exhausted this evening, you may rest beside Dubois and I will call you at sunrise. If you hesitate for one moment, I shall be avenged for your deceit with the life of this scoundrel.'

'Go to sleep, Monsieur, sleep in peace,' I replied. 'Rest assured that I am filled with gratitude towards you and my only wish is to fulfil my part of the bargain.'

Such was certainly my intention, but if ever I believed that pretence was justified, it was on this occasion. Far too trusting, our rogues, having continued drinking, soon fell asleep, leaving me completely free beside Dubois, who was as drunk as the others and soon shut her eyes like them. The moment these rogues fell asleep, I immediately seized the opportunity: 'Monsieur,' I said to the young citizen of Lyons, 'through no fault of my own I was plunged among these thieves by the most awful catastrophe. I execrate both them and that fateful instant that threw me into their path. I most probably do not have the honour to be related to you, having employed this ruse to save you and, if you agree, to escape with you from the clutches of these wretches. The time is right,' I added, 'let us go. I can see your wallet. Let us take that, but leave the cash which is in their pockets. It would be too dangerous to take it back. Let us go, Monsieur, let us go now. You see what I am doing for you. I am placing myself in your hands. Have pity on my plight, and above all, don't be more cruel than these people. Please respect my honour. I entrust it to you. It is my only treasure, so please allow me to keep it. They have not taken it from me.'

I cannot describe the gratitude that Saint-Florent appeared to show me. He could not find the words to express it. However, we had no time for conversation, we had to flee. I carefully removed the wallet and returned it to him. We then hurriedly crossed the copse, leaving the horse for fear that the noise it would make would wake our friends, and as fast as we could reached the path that would lead us out of the forest. We were lucky enough to come out of it by daybreak and without being followed by anybody. By ten o'clock in the morning we reached Luzarches and there, fearing no longer for our safety, we thought only of resting. There are times in life when one feels oneself to be extremely rich though having nothing to live on—this was Saint-Florent's story. He had five-hundred thousand francs in his wallet and not a single écu in his purse. This reflection made him pause before entering the inn...

'Don't worry, Monsieur,' I said to him when I saw his embarrassment, 'the gang of thieves I have quitted have not left me penniless. Here are twenty louis, take them, I beg you, make use of them and give what is left to the poor. Nothing in this world would make me wish to keep gold acquired from murder.'

Saint-Florent feigned a sense of propriety which was quite different from that which I was later to deduce from his behaviour, absolutely refusing to take what I was offering him. He enquired what my plans were, told me that it would be his governing law to see them fulfilled, and that all he desired was to be able to acquit himself towards me:

'It is to you, Thérèse, that I owe my fortune and my life,' he added, kissing my hands, 'and I can do no better than offer both of them to you. Accept them, I beg you, and allow the god of nuptials to strengthen the bonds of friendship.'

I know not why, but whether because of a presentiment or because of a certain coolness, I was so far from believing that what I had done for this young man could attract such sentiments on his part that

I allowed him to read in my expression the refusal which I dared not put into words. He understood, and said nothing more on the subject, confining himself only to what he might do for me.

'Monsieur,' I said to him, 'if what I have done is truly not without merit in your eyes, the only reward I ask of you is to take me with you to Lyons, and there to find a position for me in some honest household where my modesty will no longer be threatened.'

'It's the best thing you can do,' Saint-Florent said to me, 'and no one is better placed than me to grant you this favour. I have dozens of relatives in this town.' And the young merchant then asked me to tell him the reasons why I wished to stay and not to return to Paris, where I had told him I was born. I did so, with as much confidence as artlessness.

'Oh! If that's all it is,' said the young man, 'I can be of service to you before we reach Lyons. You need have no fear, Thérèse, your case is dormant. You won't be pursued—even less so, I assure you, in the refuge where I intend to hide you away. I have a relative near Bondy who lives in a charming place in the surrounding countryside. I'm sure that she will be delighted to have you stay with her. I shall take you there tomorrow.'

Filled with gratitude in my turn, I accepted a proposal that suited me very well. We rested at Luzarches for the rest of the day, and the following day planned to reach Bondy, which is only six leagues away.*

'As the weather's fine,' Saint-Florent said to me, 'I suggest that we make the journey to my relative's castle on foot. When we're there we shall recount our adventure, and our arriving by this means will draw even more attention to our plight.'

Far from suspecting the intentions of this monster or imagining that I was less safe with him than with the dreadful companions I had left behind, I accepted everything he was suggesting without fear or repugnance. We dined and had supper together. He made no objection whatsoever to my taking a separate bedchamber for the night, and once the hottest part of the day was past, and believing him when he said that it would take only four or five hours to reach his relative's house, I left Luzarches with him and we set off on foot towards Bondy.

It was approximately five o'clock in the evening when we entered the forest. Saint-Florent had not gone back on his word for a single moment, still as honest-seeming, still as anxious to prove his feelings towards me. I should not have felt myself to be safer had I been with my own father. The shadows of the night were starting to fill the forest with the kind of religious horror that inspires both fear in timid souls and criminal intent in more ferocious hearts. We were walking along narrow tracks, with myself in front, and when I turned around to ask Saint-Florent whether we should really be taking such remote paths, and whether by chance he had taken the wrong turning and if he thought we would arrive soon, the rogue replied: 'We've arrived, you little whore!', knocking me to the ground with a blow to my head from his walking-stick, rendering me unconscious...

Oh, Madame, I have no idea what this man then said or did, but the state in which I found myself afterwards brought home to me only too clearly the extent to which I had become his victim. It was the middle of the night when I regained my senses. I was at the foot of a tree, well off the beaten track, bruised, bloodied... and dishonoured, Madame. Such was my reward for everything I had just done for this unfortunate man. After doing everything he wished with me, abusing me in every conceivable way, even in that manner that offends most against Nature, the criminal had taken infamy to its most extreme degree by stealing my purse... and with it, all of the money which I had so generously offered him. He had torn my clothes, most of which lay in shreds nearby. I was almost naked, battered and bruised all over my body. Imagine my situation in the darkness, without resources, without honour, without hope, exposed to all dangers. All I wished to do was to leave this world. If a weapon had been available to me I should have had no hesitation in putting an end to a miserable life which had brought me nothing but suffering... 'The monster!' I said to myself, 'what had I done to deserve such cruel treatment from him? I save his life, I return his fortune to him, and he robs me of what I hold most dear! A wild animal would have been less cruel! Oh, mankind, this is how you are when you listen only to your passions! Tigers in the depths of the wildest deserts would be horrified by your crimes.' These initial cries of pain were followed by a few moments of despair. My tear-filled eyes turned automatically towards the Heavens. My heart leapt towards the feet of the Master who resides there... That pure and shining vault... the imposing silence of the night... the terror that froze my senses... that image of Nature at peace contrasting with the upheaval of my distraught mind... all of these things filled me with the darkest horror, which soon made me want to pray. I threw myself at the knees of that God Almighty denied by the impious, hope of the poor and the afflicted.

'Holy and majestic being,' I cried in tears, 'you who at this frightful moment deign to fill my soul with celestial joy, and who have doubtless prevented me from trying to take my life, oh my protector and my guide, I ask for your benevolence, I implore your clemency, look kindly upon my misery and my torments, my humility and my prayers. Almighty God! You know that I am weak and innocent, mistreated and betrayed. I wanted to follow your example by doing good, and it is your will that I be punished for it. Then, let your will be done, my Lord, all its sacred consequences are dear to me, I respect them and shall never complain of them again. But if I am to encounter nothing but thorns here on earth, would it offend you, my sovereign master, if I asked you to use your powers to call me back to you so that I may worship you undisturbed, that I may adore you far from these perverted men who, alas, have brought nothing but evil upon my head, and whose bloody and perfidious hands take pleasure in drowning my sad days in torrents of tears and an abyss of suffering?'

Prayer is the sweetest consolation of the unfortunate, who derive strength from fulfilment of this duty. I got to my feet, my courage renewed, picked up the rags the scoundrel had left me, and hid myself in a copse where I could spend the night with less risk. The safety I now considered I enjoyed, the satisfaction I had just derived from communion with my God, all helped me to get a few hours rest, and the sun was already high in the sky when my eyes opened again. The moment of reawakening is a terrible one for the unfortunate. Refreshed in the gentle arms of Morpheus, the imagination is more quickly and more gloomily filled with terrors which those deceptive hours of rest had erased from the memory.

'Oh, well,' I said to myself as I examined my bruises, 'so it is true that there are human creatures that Nature reduces to the level of wild beasts! What difference is there now between them and me, hiding away in my hole, avoiding men who behave like them? Is it even worth being born to endure such a pitiful fate?' And my tears flowed in abundance as I made these sad reflections. I had only just had these thoughts when I heard noises nearby. Gradually, I could make out the voices of two men, and so I pricked up my ears:

'Come along, my dear friend,' said one of them, 'this place is perfect for us. Here, the cruel and fateful presence of an aunt whom I detest will not prevent me from tasting with you for a moment those pleasures that I find so sweet.'

They approached each other, placing themselves just in front of me so that nothing they said or did could escape my attention, and I saw... Dear Heaven, Madame (said Thérèse, interrupting her story), why is it that fate only ever put me in such awkward situations that it becomes as difficult for virtue to hear their account as for modesty to describe them! That horrible crime which outrages both Nature and social convention, that sin which the hand of God has so often punished, a crime legitimated by Ironheart, suggested by him to the unfortunate Thérèse and consummated with her against her will by the inhuman wretch who has just sacrificed her, that revolting execration was performed before my eyes with all of the impurest inventions and most awful episodes that the most ingenious depravity can imagine. One of these men, the one who indulged in it, was twenty-four years old, well enough attired to make one think that he was of high social rank, the other man, of about the same age, appeared to be one of his servants. The act was scandalous and lengthy. Supporting himself with his hands on the crest of a small hillock opposite the thicket in which I was hidden, the young master laid bare the impious altar of sacrifice to the companion of his debauchery, while the latter, filled with ardour at the sight, caressed his idol, as he got ready to sacrifice it with a blade much bigger and far more frightful than the one with which the leader of the gang of brigands of Bondy had threatened me. Yet, in no way apprehensive, the young master seemed to confront the weapon presented to him with impunity. He teased it, tickled it, covered it with kisses, grabbed hold of it, and penetrated himself with it, in ecstasy as he swallowed it. Inflamed by his criminal caresses, the vile man thrashed around with the blade inside him and seemed to regret that it was not even more daunting. He braved the thrusts, anticipating and responding to them. Two tender and legitimate spouses could not have caressed each other with greater ardour. Their mouths pressed together, their sighs mingled, their tongues intertwined, and I could see that both were drunk with lust, finding the complement of their perfidious atrocities in this orgy of passion. The ceremony was repeated, and the passive partner spared no effort in bringing the incense back to life, employing every means to renew declining strength—kissing, fondling, defilements, debauched actions of the greatest refinement imaginable—and all of these succeeded in rekindling their desires five times in a row, but without either of them changing roles. The young master was always the woman, and although he was able to play the man in his turn, he did not appear to want to do this for one moment. If he visited the altar similar to his own at which the sacrifice was made, it was for the pleasure of the other idol, which never seemed to be threatened by any attack.

Oh, how time seemed to drag! I dared not move for fear of being noticed. Finally, the criminal actors of this indecent scene, their lusts doubtless satisfied, got up to resume their journey along the path that I supposed must take them home, when the master approached the bush where I was hidden. My bonnet betrayed me... he caught sight of it...

'Jasmin,' he said to his valet, 'we've been discovered... A girl has seen our mysteries... Come, let's flush the whore out and find out what she's doing here.'

I saved them the trouble of pulling me out of my hiding-place, immediately dragging myself out and falling at their feet.

'Oh, Messieurs!' I cried, holding my arms out to them, 'please have pity on an unfortunate woman whose lot is more to be deplored than you may think. There are very few reversals of fortune that can equal my own. The situation in which you have found me should not raise any suspicions about me. It is not so much my fault as the result of my misfortune. Rather than adding to the ills that have befallen me, I beg you to lessen them by providing me with the means to escape the bad luck that dogs me.'

The Comte de Bressac (for such was the young man's name), into whose hands I had fallen, was not favoured with an abundance of sympathy in his heart, but rather possessed a considerable degree of wickedness and libertinism in his head. It is unfortunately all too common to see how libertinism can extinguish pity in man. Its usual effect is to harden the heart, either because most of its crimes require an apathy of the soul, or because the violent effects that this passion has on the entire nervous system reduces the strength of its functioning. However this may be, a libertine is rarely a sensitive man. Moreover, this natural harshness in the type of individuals whose character I am describing was joined in Monsieur Bressac by such an inveterate disgust for our sex, and such a strong hatred for

everything that characterizes it, that it was very difficult for me to
find in his heart those feelings that I wished to arouse in him.

'My little dove,' the Comte said to me harshly, 'if you are looking
for people to make fools of, you'd better look elsewhere. Neither my
friend nor I ever worship at the impure temple of your sex. If it's
charity you're asking for, go and look for people who like doing good
works. We never do anything of the sort... but speak, wretch, did
you see what passed between this gentleman and myself?'

'I saw you both chatting on the grass,' I replied, 'nothing else,
Monsieur, I assure you.'

'I want to believe you,' said the young Comte, 'for your own good.
If I thought that you could have seen anything else, you would never
leave this forest... Jasmin, it's still early. We have the time to hear
this girl's adventures, and afterwards we'll see what must be done
with her.'

These young men sat down and ordered me to sit beside them.
Then I skilfully recounted all of the misfortunes that had assailed me
since I came into the world.

'Come, Jasmin,' said Monsieur de Bressac, getting to his feet as
soon as I had finished, 'let us be fair for once. Just Themis* has condemned this creature. Let us not allow the goddess's intentions to be
cruelly frustrated. Let us carry out the death sentence that this young
criminal has incurred. Far from being a crime, this little murder will
merely constitute reparation of the moral order. Since we are unfortunate enough to disturb it sometimes, let us have the courage to
restore it, at least when the occasion presents itself...'

And having lifted me from where I sat, the cruel men were already
dragging me into the woods, laughing at my tears and my cries.

'Let's bind her by all four of her limbs to four trees to form a rect-
angle,' said Bressac, stripping me naked. Then, using their scarves,
handkerchiefs, and garters, they made ropes with which I was instantly
bound, as they had planned, that is to say, in the most cruel and most
painful manner that is possible to imagine. One cannot express how
much I suffered. It seemed to me that my limbs were being torn off,
and that my stomach, facing downward and dragged by its own weight
to the ground, must be ripped open at any moment. Sweat ran down
my brow, I existed only in the violence of pain. If it had ceased to com-
press my nerves, I should have been seized by mortal anguish. The
villains enjoyed watching me in this position, applauding their efforts.

'That's enough now,' said Bressac finally, 'I think she's been frightened enough for the time being. Thérèse,' he continued, releasing my bonds and ordering me to get dressed, 'follow us and hold your tongue. If you do what I say, you won't have cause to regret it. My aunt requires another companion. Trusting that what you have told me is true, I am going to introduce you to her. I shall vouch to her for your conduct, but if you abuse my favours, if you betray my trust or do not submit to my will... see these four trees, Thérèse, and the area they enclose, a place that was to be your grave, and remember that this gloomy spot is only one league from the castle to which I am taking you, and that the slightest act of disobedience will see you brought back here straightaway.'

I immediately forgot my misfortunes, threw myself at the Comte's feet, and in tears I gave him my word that I would do what he asked. However, he was as insensitive to my joy as to my pain: 'On your feet,' said Bressac, 'your behaviour will speak for you, it alone will determine your fate.' We walked on, Jasmin and his master talking softly together, with me following humbly without saying a word. In less than an hour we reached the castle of Madame la Marquise de Bressac, whose magnificence and large number of servants made me realize that whatever position I was to be given in this household, it would surely be of greater benefit to me than that of chief housekeeper at Monsieur du Harpin's. I was made to wait in a servants' hall, where Jasmin obligingly offered me everything he could to make me feel at home. The young Comte went to see his aunt and tell her about me. Half an hour later he came to fetch me himself to introduce me to the Marquise.

Madame de Bressac was a woman aged forty-six, still very beautiful, who seemed to me to be honest and sensitive, although there was a little severity in her principles and manner of speaking. She had been widowed two years earlier by the young Comte's uncle, who had given her nothing when he married her but his fine name. All the wealth and property that Monsieur de Bressac might hope to acquire would be inherited from his aunt, what he had got from his father affording him scarcely enough to provide for his pleasures. To this Madame de Bressac added a considerable pension, but it was not enough. There was nothing so expensive as the Comte's pleasures. These may not have cost as much as others, but they were far more frequent. The household required fifty thousand écus income, and

Monsieur de Bressac was all alone. It had never been possible to persuade him to take up an occupation. Anything that got in the way of
his libertine activities was so unbearable to him that he could not
assume the responsibility. The Marquise lived on the property for
three months a year, spending the rest of the time in Paris, and these
three months, which she required her nephew to spend with her,
were like torture for a man who abhorred his aunt; he felt that he was
wasting all the time he spent away from a town which for him was the
centre of his pleasures.

   The young Comte ordered me to recount to the Marquise all of
the things I had told him, and as soon as I had finished Madame de
Bressac said to me: 'Your candour and your naivety leave me in no
doubt that you are telling the truth. The only other information I
shall try to discover about you is whether you are really the daughter
of the man you claim to be. If you are, I knew your father, and this
will be one more reason for me to take an interest in you. As for the
business at du Harpin's, I can sort that out in a couple of visits to the
Chancellor, who has been my friend for many years. He is the most
honest man in the world, and all we need do is prove your innocence
to him and all accusations made against you will be erased forever.
But remember, Thérèse, that I am promising to do this only on condition that you conduct yourself impeccably. So you see that the
gratitude I expect from you will always benefit you.'

   I threw myself at the Marquise's feet, assuring her that she would
not be displeased with me. She gently pulled me up and immediately
gave me the position in her service of second chambermaid. Three
days later the enquiries Madame de Bressac had made in Paris were
answered, and they were just as I hoped they would be. The Marquise
praised me for not deceiving her, and all thoughts of misfortune
finally vanished from my mind, to be henceforth replaced by nothing
but expectations of the sweetest consolations I might be permitted to
entertain. However, it was not decreed in Heaven that poor Thérèse
should ever be happy, and if fortuitously she was able to enjoy a few
moments of tranquillity, it was only to make those horrific times that
were to follow all the more bitter.

   We had scarcely arrived in Paris when Madame de Bressac set
about working in my favour. The presiding judge agreed to see me
and listened to the account of my misfortunes with interest. Du
Harpin's calumnies were recognized as such, but any attempts to

punish them would be vain. Du Harpin had with impunity circulated counterfeit banknotes, and in the process ruined several families while making nearly two million for himself, and he had fled to England. As far as the fire at the Palace prisons was concerned, they were convinced that if I had profited from the event, at least I had had no hand in it, and I was assured that the case against me had been dropped without the magistrates who were handling it having to take any other measures. I was given no more information about this and accepted what I was told. You will soon see whether or not I was right to do so.

It is easy to understand how such actions formed an attachment between Madame de Bressac and myself. Indeed, she showed me all manner of kindnesses... how could such acts not have bound me forever to such a precious protectress? Yet it was far from the young Comte's intentions for me to form such an intimate attachment to his aunt... But now is the time to paint this monster's portrait for you...

Monsieur de Bressac combined the most seductive countenance with the charms of youth. If his figure or his features had a few faults, it was because they put me too much in mind of that softness, that nonchalance, that belongs only to women. It seemed that, in lending him the attributes of this sex, Nature had also endowed him with the same tastes. And yet, what an evil spirit lay concealed beneath these feminine charms! All the vices that characterized the souls of criminals could be found there: wickedness, debauchery, contempt for all duties, and principally for those with which Nature appears to delight us, found in him their strongest expression. Greatest among all his faults, however, was that of hatred for his aunt. The Marquise did everything possible to bring her nephew back to the path of virtue. Perhaps she went about this with too much rigour, and the result was that, even more inflamed by the effects of this severity, the Comte indulged his tastes with all the greater impetuosity and the poor Marquise's only reward for her efforts was to be hated all the more.

'Don't imagine', the Comte often said to me, 'that everything my aunt does for you comes from her alone, Thérèse. You should know that if I did not keep after her all the time, she would scarcely remember that she promised to help you. She claims to be doing everything herself, whereas it is all my own work. Yes, Thérèse, oh yes, it is to me alone that you should be grateful, and you should be aware that the gratitude I expect of you is all the more disinterested in that, however pretty you may be, I have no desire to enjoy your favours. No, Thérèse, the services I expect of you are of quite a different kind, and when you are quite convinced of all I have done for you, I hope that I shall find in your heart what I have a right to expect.'

These words seemed so obscure to me that I had no idea how to respond, and yet I did so just in case, and maybe too readily. Should I be honest with you? Alas, yes, because to hide my faults from you would be to betray your trust and ill repay the interest that my misfortunes have inspired in you. You should know, then, Madame, that the only voluntary fault with which I must reproach myself... a fault, did I say?... a folly, an extravagance... there was never anything like it... but at least it is not a crime, only an error for which I alone was punished, and which the just hand of God did not appear to need in order to plunge me into the abyss which was soon to open up beneath my feet. However unworthily the Comte de Bressac had behaved towards me the first day we had met, it had nevertheless been impossible for me to set eyes on him without feeling myself drawn towards him by a movement of tenderness that nothing could quell. In spite of all my reflections on his cruelty, his distant attitude to women, the depravity of his tastes, and the moral gulf that separated us, nothing in the world could extinguish such a gripping passion, and if the Comte had asked me to lay down my life, I would have sacrificed it for him a thousand times. He was a long way from suspecting my feelings... the ungrateful man was far from understanding the reason for the tears I shed daily. However, it was impossible for him not to suspect my desire to anticipate everything that might please him. He could not have been unaware of my attentions. Blind as they doubtless were, they went so far as to encourage his faults, as much as decency would allow, and to keep them hidden from his aunt. This behaviour had in some way won his trust, and because everything associated with him was so precious to me and I was so blind to his coldness towards me, I was sometimes weak enough to believe that he was not indifferent towards me. Yet how the excess of his licentiousness quickly disabused me. This was so great that even his health suffered as a result. I occasionally took the liberty of pointing out to him the disadvantages of his conduct. He would listen to me without repugnance, and after I had finished would say to me that there was no cure for the type of vice that he loved.

'Ah, Thérèse,' he cried one day enthusiastically, 'if only you knew the charms of this fancy, if you could understand how sweet is the illusion of being a woman! It's an unbelievable mental aberration! You abhor this sex and yet wish to imitate it. Oh, how sweet it is when you succeed, Thérèse, how delicious it is to be the whore of anyone who wants you, and taking delirium and prostitution to its greatest degree, to be in succession on the same day the mistress of a picklock, a marquis, a valet, a monk, to be in turn cherished, caressed, envied, threatened, beaten, at one moment victorious in their arms, and the next, victim at their feet, moving them with caresses, reviving their ardour with excesses... Oh, no, no, Thérèse, you cannot understand what such pleasures are like for a temperament such as mine... but quite apart from morality, if only you could imagine what the physical sensations of this divine preference are like! It's impossible to bear it, it's such an intense feeling, and the pleasures awakened are so piquant that you lose your mind, you go crazy. A thousand kisses, each more tender than the previous one, do not adequately match the intoxication into which we are plunged by our lover. Cradled in his arms, our mouths glued together, we would like our whole existence to be united with his, we would like to become one with him. If we dare to complain, it is of being neglected. We would like him to be stronger than Hercules so that he might enter us and fill us up. We want that precious seed that he shoots like a flame into the depths of our bowels to make our own squirt into his hands because of its heat and force... Do not imagine, Thérèse, that we are made like other men. We are quite differently constructed. When God created us, he arranged for that sensitive membrane that covers the temple of Venus in you women to adorn the altars at which our Celadons worship.* We are just as much women there as you are at the sanctuary of reproduction. There is not a single one of your pleasures that is unknown to us, not one that we cannot enjoy, but we also have our own, and it is this delicious combination that makes us the men on earth most sensitive to pleasure, the best able to feel it. It is this enchanting combination which makes any correction of our inclinations impossible, and which would turn us into enthusiasts and fanatics if one were stupid enough to punish us... in the end, this conjunction ensures that we will continue to adore the charming deity that has us under its spell until we die!'

Thus spoke the Comte in praise of his bad habits. Whenever I tried to speak to him of the Being to whom he owed everything and of the concerns that such disorders caused to his respectable aunt, all I got from him was resentment and bad temper, and above all, impatience at seeing riches in such hands and for so long, wealth which, he would say, ought to belong to him. All I could see was the most deeply rooted hatred for this honest woman and the most demonstrable revolt against all the instincts of Nature. Could it, then, be true that when one has managed to transgress the sacred instincts of this law so absolutely in one's tastes, the necessary consequence of this initial crime should then be a frightful tendency to commit all others?

Sometimes I had recourse to the resources of religion. Almost always consoled by these, I tried to fill the soul of this pervert with its solace, in the near certainty that I could restrain him with the bonds of religion if I managed to get him to share its attractions, but the Comte would not allow me to use such weapons for long. Declared enemy of our most holy mysteries, opinionated critic of the purity of our dogmas, savage opponent of the existence of a Supreme Being, Monsieur de Bressac, instead of allowing me to convert him, sought rather to corrupt me.

'All religions proceed from a false premiss, Thérèse,' he would say to me, 'all assume the worship of a creator to be necessary, but this creator has never existed. In this regard, remember the sensible precepts of that Ironheart who, according to you, Thérèse, had forced you to think, just as I am doing. There is nothing more correct than that man's principles, and the low esteem in which you are stupid enough to hold him does not take away his right to argue. If all of Nature's products are effects resulting from the laws that govern it, if perpetual actions and reactions presuppose the movement necessary to its essence, what of that sovereign master that fools gratuitously ascribe to it? This is what your wise teacher told you, dear girl. According to this, what are religions if not the break with which the tyranny of the strongest holds the weakest in check? With this aim in mind, the strongest dares to tell him whom he wishes to dominate that a God forged the cruel chains that bind him, and stupefied by his misery, the latter blindly believes everything he is told. Can the religions born of such deceit deserve any respect? Is there a single one, Thérèse, that does not bear the imprint of imposture and stupidity? In all of them, what do I see? Mysteries that make reason tremble, dogmas that outrage Nature, and grotesque ceremonies that inspire nothing but derision and disgust. But of all of these, if there is one that especially deserves our hatred and contempt, Thérèse, is it not that barbaric law of Christianity into which we were both born? Is there any more odious?... any that makes the heart and spirit heave as much?

'How can intelligent men still give any credence to the obscure sayings and so-called miracles of the vile founder of this frightening creed? Has there ever existed a trickster more deserving of public indignation! How could a leprous Jew, who was born of a whore and a soldier* in the most wretched corner of the universe, have dared to pass himself off as the instrument of him who, people say, created the world? You must admit, Thérèse, that to have such exalted pretensions you need some nobility at the very least. What can this ridiculous ambassador lay claim to? What did he do to prove his mission? Did the earth change its complexion? Did those scourges with which it was afflicted disappear? Did the sun shine upon it night and day? Did all vices cease to soil its surface? Were we henceforth to see only happiness reign? Not at all! It was by magic tricks, capers, and word-plays that God's envoy introduced himself to the world. It was in the respectable company of workmen, artisans, and ladies of pleasure that Heaven's minister arrived to display his greatness. It was by getting drunk with some and sleeping with others that God's friend, God himself, came to subject the hardened sinner to his laws. It was by inventing tricks based on whatever might satisfy either his desires or his greed that the rogue wished to demonstrate his mission. In spite of all this, he is a great success, a few related groups join the rascal, and a sect is formed. This rabble's dogmas manage to seduce a handful of Jews. Slaves of the Roman empire, they must have joyfully embraced a religion which released them from their chains only to prepare them for the yoke of religion. Their motives are suspected, their intractability becomes clear, the rebels are arrested, and their leader perishes, but he dies in a manner that is probably far too lenient for his type of crime, and as a result of an unforgivable lack of reflection, the vulgar fellow's disciples are allowed to disperse instead of being put to death with him. People are gripped by fanaticism, women wail, madmen argue, imbeciles believe, and the most contemptible of men, the clumsiest of rascals, the greatest imposter who had ever lived is God, the son of God equal to his father. Suddenly all his delusions are sanctified, all his sayings become dogmas, and his stupid ideas mysteries. The bosom of his fabulous father opens to receive him, and this Creator, who was alone hitherto, has now become a trinity to humour a son worthy of his greatness. But does this holy God stop there? Certainly not. His celestial powers will lend themselves to much greater favours. At the whim of a priest, that is, of a knave full of lies and crimes, this great God who created all we see will condescend to come down to earth millions of times a morning and enter a piece of pastry, which has to be digested by the faithful and will soon be transformed in the depths of their bowels into the vilest excrement, and all for the satisfaction of his beloved son, the odious man who invented this monstrous impiety at an inn supper. As he himself said, let it be so. He said: this bread that you see will be my flesh and you will eat it as such. Now, I am God, so God will be eaten by you, therefore, because I have said so, the Creator of Heaven and Earth will be changed into the vilest matter than can be expelled by the human body, and man will eat God because this God is good and all-powerful. However, this nonsense spreads. This growth is attributed to its reality, its greatness, its sublimeness, to the power of him who introduced it, and the nonsense spreads for the simplest of reasons, whilst the prestige so falsely acquired has only ever won over rogues on the one hand and imbeciles on the other. This outrageous religion finally establishes itself on the throne, and it is a weak, cruel, ignorant, and fanatical emperor* who wraps it in the diadem of royalty and in this way soils the whole world with it. Oh, Thérèse, what weight can these considerations carry with a critical and philosophical mind? Can the wise see anything in this dreadful collection of fables but the fruit of the imposture of some men and the false credulity of a greater number? If God had wanted us to have any kind of religion, and if he were truly all-powerful, or rather, if there really were a God, would he have communicated his commands to us by such absurd means? Would it be through the medium of a despicable bandit that he would have shown us how to serve him? If this God that you speak of is supreme, if he is all-powerful, if he is just, if he is good, will it be by tricks and conundrums that he would wish to teach me how to know and serve him? Sovereign engine of the universe and of the heart of man, can he not instruct us by means of the stars or convince us by engraving himself in man's heart? Let him one day imprint the law that would please him and that he would like to give us at the sun's centre and in tongues of fire. From one end of the universe to the other, all mankind would see it and read it, and would in consequence be guilty if they did not then follow it. But to declare his wishes only in some unknown corner of Asia, to choose the most double-dealing and the most superstitious of peoples as followers, and the vilest, most ridiculous, and most roguish working man as representative, to muddle up the message so much that it is impossible to comprehend, to teach it only to a tiny number of individuals while leaving everyone else in the dark, and to punish them for remaining there... Oh, no, Thérèse, no, no, such atrocities cannot be our guide. I would rather die a thousand times than believe in them. When atheism wants martyrs, let it choose them and my blood is ready.* We should detest these horrors, Thérèse. The best documented outrages should serve to strengthen the contempt that they rightly deserve... I had scarcely opened my eyes when I detested these simple delusions. From that moment, I made it my rule to trample them underfoot, and took an oath never to return to them. Do as I do if you wish to be happy, detest, renounce, curse as I do both the odious object of this frightful cult and the cult itself, created for fantasy and, like fantasy, made to be vilified by all those who claim to be wise.'

'Oh, Monsieur,' I replied in tears, 'you would deprive a wretched girl of her fondest hope if you cast a slur in her heart on that religion which consoles her. Firmly attached to what it teaches, absolutely convinced that all of the attacks it suffers are nothing but the effects of libertinism and passion, would I sacrifice the idea I hold most dear, that which is closest to my heart, to sophisms and blasphemies that fill me with horror?'

I added a thousand other arguments to these, but the Comte just laughed at them, and his specious principles, expressed with a more virile eloquence and supported by authors which I am glad to say I have never read, attacked those I had read every day but without shaking my faith in them. Madame de Bressac, who was filled with virtue and piety, was not unaware that her nephew justified his waywardness with reference to the latest paradoxes. She frequently complained about them to me, and as she was gracious enough to ascribe a little more common sense to me than to her other female servants, she liked to confide her concerns in me.

Yet her nephew's bad behaviour towards her now knew no bounds, the Comte having reached the point of hiding nothing from her any longer. Not only had he surrounded his aunt with all of the dangerous scoundrels who served his pleasures, but he had even been bold enough to declare to her in my presence that if she was still minded to oppose his tastes, he would convince her of the charms they offered by indulging them before her very eyes.

I groaned with horror at such behaviour. I tried to find personal reasons to stifle in my heart the unhappy flame of passion that burned there, but is love an illness that one can recover from? All of my attempts to quell it merely served to make its flame burn more brightly, and the perfidious Comte never appeared more lovable to me than when I had taken account of everything that should have made me detest him.

I had now been in this house for four years, still tormented by the same worries, still consoled by the same sweet thoughts, when this abominable man, finally believing he could trust me, dared to reveal to me his infamous designs. At that time we were in the country, and I was alone with the Comtesse, her principal maid-servant having got permission to remain in Paris for the summer to assist her husband with some business or other. One evening, shortly after I had retired, I was taking the air on the balcony of my bedchamber, not being able to sleep because of the extreme heat, when the Comte suddenly knocked on my door, begging me to allow him to talk with me. Alas! Every moment granted me by this cruel author of my woes seemed too precious to me to refuse a single one. He entered, carefully closing the door behind him, and sat on a chair beside me:

'Listen to me, Thérèse,' he said to me with a little hesitation, 'I have something to tell you of the greatest consequence. Swear to me that you will never reveal anything I am going to say.'

'Oh, Monsieur,' I replied, 'how can you think me capable of abusing your trust?'

'You do not know the risks you would be taking, should you happen to prove to me that I was wrong to trust you!'

'To lose your trust would be the very worst of my fears, and I need no greater threat.'

'Well, then, Thérèse, I have condemned my aunt to death... and your hand will be my instrument.'

'My hand!' I cried, recoiling in horror. 'Oh, Monsieur! How could you conceive such plans?... Oh, no, take my life if you must but do not ever imagine that you can persuade me to commit the horrific act you are proposing.'

'Listen, Thérèse,' the Comte said to me, calmly leading me back to his subject, 'I suspected you would react with repugnance, but as you are an intelligent girl, I flatter myself that I can overcome it... that I can prove to you that this crime, which seems so enormous to you, is in fact just a simple affair. Your untrained mind must confront two heinous crimes, Thérèse: the destruction of a creature who is like us, and the greater evil that this destruction represents when this creature is close to us. As far as the crime of destruction of one's fellow is concerned, rest assured, my dear girl, that this is purely illusory. The power of destruction is not in the gift of Man. He may, at the most, change the form of things but he does not have the power to annihilate. Now, all forms are equal in the eyes of Nature. Nothing is lost in the immense crucible in which Nature's changes are carried out. All the pieces of matter which end up there are continually reborn in other guises, and whatever our feelings towards them may be, Nature is not outraged by any, not a single one could offend against it. Whatever we destroy replenishes its powers, renews its energy, but no act of destruction weakens it, none works contrary to it... Oh, what does it matter to Nature's eternal creation that the mass of flesh which today makes up a biped creature should tomorrow be reproduced as a thousand different insects? Dare we say that the construction of this two-footed animal is more valuable to it than that of a tiny earthworm, and that Nature must take a greater interest in it? If, therefore, the degree of attachment, or rather of indifference, is the same, what can it matter to her that the sword of one man can change another man into flies or blades of grass? When I have been convinced of the exalted status of our species, when it has been demonstrated to me that we are so important to Nature that these transmutations necessarily offend against its laws, then I shall be able to believe that murder is a crime, but when the profoundest investigations have proved to me that everything that lives on this globe, including the most imperfect of Nature's works, is of equal value in its eyes, I shall never admit that the transformation of one of these beings into a thousand others can in any way be injurious to its plans.* I say this: all men, all animals, all plants that grow, feed, and are destroyed, reproducing themselves by the same means, never truly die but merely undergo variation and modification. All, I say, appearing today in one form and a few years later in another, may change a thousand times in a single day at the whim of the creature that wishes to transform them without a single law of Nature being broken at any time. I tell you that this happens without such changes doing anything but good since, in decomposing individuals whose reconstitution once again becomes necessary to Nature, they merely return to Nature by an action incorrectly described as criminal. She is consequently deprived of this creative energy by those who, through stupid indifference, dare not undertake any transformations. Oh, Thérèse, it is only man's pride that made murder a crime. Imagining himself to be the most sublime being on the planet and the most essential to it, this vain creature proceeded from this false principle to ensure that any action that would destroy his fellows must necessarily be a foul one, but his vanity, his folly, in no way changes the laws of Nature. There is no person that does not at bottom experience the most vehement desire to be rid of those who bother him or whose death may bring him some profit, and do you imagine, Thérèse, that there is such a great difference between this desire and its consequence? Now, if these impressions come to us from Nature, how can we assume that they offend it? Would she inspire in us actions that would do it harm? Ah, rest assured, my dear girl, there is nothing that we feel that does not serve her. All the promptings she sends us are the instruments of her laws. Human passions are nothing but the means which she employs to achieve her aims. When she needs more individuals, she inspires love in us and thus creates them. When destruction becomes necessary to her, she fills our hearts with vengeance, avarice, lewdness, and ambition, and so we have murders, but she has always worked in her own interests, and without suspecting it, we have become the credulous agents of her whims.

'Oh, no, Thérèse, no, Nature does not place in our hands the means to disrupt her economy. Can it make any sense to say that the weakest can really offend against the strongest? What are we relative to her? Can she, when creating us, have placed in us anything capable of harming her? Can this stupid supposition be reconciled with the certain and sublime ways in which we see her achieve her goals? Oh, if murder were not one of man's actions that best fulfilled her intentions, would she allow it to take place? Therefore, how can it harm her to imitate her? Can she be offended to see man do to his neighbour what she herself does to him every day? Since it is demonstrable that she can reproduce only by destroying, if we destroy incessantly, are we not acting in conformity with her wishes? In this sense, therefore, the man who devotes himself to it with the greatest enthusiasm will incontestably be the one who serves her best, since he will be the one who cooperates most with intentions constantly manifested by her. The first principle and the finest quality of Nature is the movement that constantly drives her, but this movement is nothing but a perpetual succession of crimes. It is by crimes alone that this is preserved. The being that is most like Nature and that is consequently the most perfect of beings will therefore necessarily be the one whose most active movement becomes the cause of many crimes whilst, I repeat, the inactive or indolent being, that is to say, the virtuous being must certainly be the least perfect in her eyes, since it has only apathetic or peaceful tendencies which would constantly keep everything in chaos if it were to be dominant. A balance must be preserved, and this can be done only by dint of crimes. Thus, crimes serve Nature. If they serve her, if she requires them, if she wants them, can they offend her, and who can be offended by them if she is not? But the creature I am destroying is my aunt… Oh! Thérèse, how frivolous these ties are in the eyes of a philosopher! Permit me not even to talk about them, such is their futility. Can these despicable chains, the fruit of our laws and political institutions, have any significance in the eyes of Nature? Leave aside your prejudices, then, Thérèse, serve me, and your fortune is made.'

'Oh, Monsieur!' I replied to the Comte de Bressac, full of fear, 'this indifference which you assume to be present in Nature is yet again nothing but the product of your intellectual sophistry. Deign rather to listen to your heart, and you will hear it condemn these false arguments inspired by libertinism. Return to your heart as judge and you will find it to be the sanctuary where the Nature that you outrage wishes to be listened to and respected. If that is where Nature expresses the profoundest horror of the crime which you are contemplating, will you grant me that it is to be condemned? I know that you are presently blinded by your passions, but once these are extinguished you will be eaten away by remorse. The greater your sensitivity, the more you will be tormented by its pricks… Oh, Monsieur! Preserve and respect the life of this gentle and precious friend. Do not sacrifice her or you will die of despair! Every day… every instant, you would see before your eyes that dear aunt that your blind fury would have plunged into the tomb. You would hear her plaintive voice once again pronounce those sweet words that were the joy of your childhood. She would appear in all your waking moments and would torment you in your dreams. With her bloody fingers, she would reopen those wounds that you would have torn into her flesh. From that time on you would not enjoy a single happy moment on this earth, all of your pleasures would be sullied, all of your thoughts would be troubled. A celestial hand, whose power you do not know, would avenge the life you would have destroyed by poisoning your own, and you would die from the mortal regret of daring to carry out your crimes before you could enjoy their rewards.'

I was in tears as I said these words on my knees at the Comte's feet. I begged him by all that he found most sacred to forget an infamous aberration that I swore to him I would keep secret all my life… but I did not know the man I was dealing with, I did not know the extent to which passions engendered crime in this perverse soul. The Comte rose icily to his feet.

'I see clearly that I was mistaken, Thérèse,' he said to me, 'I am perhaps as dismayed for your sake as for mine. No matter, I shall find other means and you will have lost a great deal without your mistress having gained anything.'

This threat changed all of my thinking. By not agreeing to carry out the crime proposed to me, I risked much on my own account and my mistress would certainly die. By agreeing to be his accomplice, I would protect myself from the Comte's wrath and I could definitely save his aunt. This reflection, which was the work of an instant in me, made up my mind to accept everything, but as such a sudden change of heart might have appeared suspect, I made my acquiescence seem harder to win over, forcing the Comte to keep repeating his sophisms to me. Gradually, I began to look as if I had no answers to them and Bressac believed he had defeated me. I made it seem as if my weakness were ascribable to the power of his rhetoric, and finally gave in. The Comte threw himself into my arms. How this gesture would have filled me with joy, if it had had another cause… What am I saying? Such times were long gone. His horrible behaviour, his barbaric schemes, had stifled all the feelings that my weak heart had dared to entertain, and now he was nothing but a monster in my eyes…

'You are the first woman I have embraced,' the Comte said to me, 'and truly I do so with all my heart… You are delicious, my child!

A ray of wisdom has penetrated your mind! Is it possible that such a charming intellect should have remained in the dark for so long?'

We then agreed on what we would do. In a couple of days' time, more or less, depending on how easy I would find it, I was to empty a small packet of poison given to me by Bressac into the cup of chocolate that Madame was accustomed to take in the morning. The Comte would ensure that I was immune from any prosecution. He would issue me with a contract for two thousand écus annual income on the very day of the execution. He made me these promises without explaining in what ways I would benefit from them, and we separated.

Meanwhile, something so very singular occurred, something so revealing of the atrocious thought processes of the monster I was dealing with, that I must interrupt for a moment the account that you are doubtless awaiting of the outcome of the adventure in which I had become involved.

Two days after our criminal pact, the Comte learnt that an uncle whose legacy he did not expect to receive had just left him an annual income of eighty thousand livres... Oh Heaven!, I said to myself when I heard this news, is this how divine justice punishes those who plot crimes! Then, soon recovering from this blasphemous reaction to divine Providence, I knelt down and begged God's forgiveness, flattering myself that this unexpected event would at least change the Comte's plans... How wrong I was!

'Oh, my dear Thérèse,' he said to me, having come up to my room the very same evening, 'see how I am being showered with good fortune! As I have often told you, the idea of a crime or its execution is the surest means of attracting luck. Only wicked men do so.'

'What's that, Monsieur?' I replied. 'So this fortune which you were not expecting has not persuaded you to wait patiently for the death that you wish to hasten?'

'Wait?' the Comte abruptly replied. 'I won't wait a single moment, Thérèse. Let me tell you that I am twenty-eight years old, and that it is hard to wait at my age. No, please realize that this in no way changes our plans, and assure me that the whole business will be completed before we are due to return to Paris... tomorrow or the day after tomorrow at the very latest. I am already anxious to pay you the first quarter of your annuity, to place into your hands the document that secures it for you.'

I did my best to disguise the fear that this excess of eagerness inspired in me, and I resumed my earlier resolve, quite persuaded that if I did not commit the horrible crime to which I had agreed, the Comte would soon notice that I was toying with him, and that if I warned Madame de Bressac, whatever measures the revelation of this plan made her adopt, the young Comte would still see that he had been betrayed and would immediately take more certain steps that would bring about the aunt's death just the same while exposing me to all of the nephew's revenge. The path of justice was the only option left, but nothing in the world could have made me resolve to take it. I determined, therefore, to warn the Marquise. Of all possible alternatives, this one seemed the best one to me and I chose it.

'Madame,' I said to her the day following my last meeting with the Comte, 'I have something of the greatest importance to disclose to you, but no matter how closely it concerns you, I am determined not to say anything unless you first give me your word of honour not to bear any grudge against Monsieur your nephew for what he has the audacity to be planning... You will, of course, act, Madame, taking all necessary steps, but you will not say a word. Please promise me this, or else I shall keep silent.'

Madame de Bressac, who believed that it was just a matter of her nephew's usual outrages, took the oath that I had demanded of her and I revealed all. The unfortunate woman burst into tears on learning of this infamy.

'The monster!' she cried. 'Have I ever done anything that was not in his interests? If I wished to warn against his vices, or cure him of them, what other motive but his happiness could make me be so harsh? And is it not thanks to me that he has inherited this legacy? Oh, Thérèse, Thérèse, give me solid proof that this plan is true... put me in a position whereby I cannot have the slightest doubt. I need anything that can help extinguish in me all those feelings that my deluded heart still dares harbour for that monster...'

So then I showed her the packet of poison. It would have been hard to produce better proof. The Marquise wanted to try it out, so we gave a small dose to a dog, which we shut away and which died two hours later in horrible convulsions. Madame de Bressac could have no more doubts, and she determined to act. She instructed me to give her the rest of the poison, and immediately wrote a letter to the Duc de Sonzeval, a relative of hers, bidding him to pay a secret visit to the minister in order to report the crime plotted by her nephew and of which she was about to become the victim, to obtain a 'lettre de cachet',* and to come with all possible speed to her home to deliver her from the villain who was conspiring so cruelly against her life.

However, this abominable crime was destined to take place. By a divine will that defies comprehension, virtue was bound to yield to the machinations of the wicked. The animal on which we had conducted our experiment revealed all to the Comte, who heard it howling. Knowing that this dog was dear to his aunt, he asked what had happened to it. Those he spoke to, not knowing anything, gave no clear response. From that moment he began to harbour suspicions. He did not say a word, but I could see that he was troubled. I told the Marquise about his mood, she became more concerned, though all she could think of doing was to send the letter with all possible haste and to do all she could to keep its purpose secret. She told her nephew that she was sending someone by coach to Paris to ask the Duc de Sonzeval to take charge immediately of the legacy which he had just inherited from his uncle, because if no one appeared she feared there might be lawsuits. She added that she was bidding the Duc to come and give her all the necessary information so that she might decide to accompany her nephew if the business required it. The Comte, who was too good at reading expressions not to see confusion on his aunt's face and not to observe some embarrassment on my own, divined everything and put himself even more on his guard. On the pretext of taking a walk, he left the castle grounds and waited for the messenger at a spot where he was bound to pass by. Being more loyal to him than to his aunt, this man was perfectly willing to hand him his dispatches, and, convinced of what he doubtless called my treachery, Bressac gave the messenger a hundred louis with the order never to reappear at his aunt's. He then returned to the castle with rage in his heart. He contained himself, nevertheless. He came to find me, cajoled me as was his wont, asked me if the deed would take place the following day, pointing out to me that it was essential that it occurred before the Duc's arrival, then calmly went to bed without giving anything away. I was completely fooled by him and so had no cause for alarm at that moment. If this terrible crime was carried out as the Comte later informed me, he must have committed it himself, though I have no idea how. I conjectured many things, but it would serve no purpose to relate these to you. Let us come rather to the cruel manner in which I was punished for not having wanted to assume responsibility for it. The day after the messenger's arrest Madame took her chocolate as usual and rose to wash and dress. She seemed agitated and seated herself at table. I had scarcely left the room when the Comte approached me.

'Thérèse,' he said to me with the greatest sang-froid, 'I have found a safer means than the one I had proposed to you to carry out our plans, but I need to explain the details to you and dare not come into your bedchamber so often. Be at the corner of the grounds at five o'clock precisely. I shall meet you there and we shall take a walk in the woods, where I shall explain everything to you.'

I confess to you, Madame, that whether because Providence allowed it or through excess of trust or sheer blindness, nothing prepared me for the shocking misfortune that awaited me. I felt so certain that the Marquise's secret and her plans were safe that I never imagined that the Comte could have discovered them, and yet I was nervous.

According to one of our tragic authors, 'perjury is a virtue when there is a threat of crime',* but perjury is always odious to the delicate and sensitive soul who feels obliged to have recourse to it. I felt unhappy with my role.

In spite of this, I presented myself at the meeting-place and the Comte did not keep me waiting long. He approached me in a gay and carefree manner, and we went into the forest without there being any indication of anything but the laughter and jesting which he was used to share with me. When I wished to turn the conversation to the subject that had prompted him to ask for our meeting, he kept telling me to wait, that he feared we might be observed and that we were not yet in a safe place. Imperceptibly, we reached the four trees to which I had been so cruelly attached. I started upon seeing this spot, and the full horror of my fate then presented itself to me. Imagine how my fears grew when I saw how this dreadful place had been prepared. Ropes hung from one of the trees. Three monstrous hounds were tied to the other three, and appeared just to be waiting for me to satisfy the hunger evident from their wide-open and salivating jaws. They were under the control of one of the Comte's favourites.

Then the perfidious creature turned to me, addressing me henceforth only in the coarsest of terms: 'F—ing bitch,' he said to me, 'do

you recognize this bush from which I dragged you like a wild animal
to give you back the life which you deserved to lose?... Do you recognize these trees from which I threatened to hang you again if you
ever gave me occasion to repent my kindness to you? Why did you
accept the mission I asked you to undertake against my aunt if you
intended to betray me, and in what way did you imagine you would
be serving virtue by risking the freedom of the one to whom you
owed your happiness? Of these two crimes, why did you choose the
most abominable one?'

'Alas! Did I not choose the least abominable one?'

'You should have refused,' continued the Comte furiously, seizing
me by the arm and shaking me violently, 'yes, you should have definitely refused and not agreed to betray me.'

Then Monsieur de Bressac told me everything he had done to
intercept Madame's messages, and how the suspicion had taken root
in him, prompting him to divert them.

'What has your falseness led you to do, unworthy creature?' he
continued. 'You have risked your life without saving my aunt's. The
deed is done and I shall reap its rewards on returning to the castle,
but you must die and you must learn before you expire that the
path of virtue is not always the safest one, and that there are circumstances in this world when complicity with a crime is preferable to
treachery.'

And without giving me time to reply, without showing the slightest pity for the cruel state I was in, he dragged me towards the tree
prepared for me and where his crony was waiting.

'Here she is,' he told him, 'the woman who intended to poison my
aunt and who has perhaps already committed this frightful crime, in
spite of my attempts to prevent it. I should probably have done better
to place her in the hands of Justice, but she would then have lost her
life and I want to let her live so that she may suffer longer.'

The two villains then grabbed hold of me and in an instant had me
stripped bare. 'What a lovely bottom!' said the Comte in tones of the
cruellest irony, and brutally touching it, 'what superb flesh!... an
excellent lunch for my hounds!'

Once I no longer had a stitch on me, I was attached to the tree by
a rope tied around my back, leaving my arms free to defend myself as
best I could, and thanks to the slack left on the rope I was able to
move forward or back about six feet. Once I was in this position, the

Comte, who was very worked up, came close to look at my expression, and then encircled me. From the harsh manner in which he touched me, it seemed to me that his murderous hands intended to compete in rage with his dogs' razor-like teeth.

'Come,' he said to his assistant, 'release these animals, it is time.'

They are unchained, the Comte excites them, all three of them hurl themselves at my poor body. It is as if they are sharing it so that none of its parts is exempt from their furious assaults. I try to throw them off in vain, they just tear me apart with greater fury, and during this horrible scene Bressac, the unworthy Bressac, as if my torments had ignited his perfidious lusts... the infamous Bressac indulged himself in criminal caresses with his crony.

'That's enough,' he said after a few moments, 'tie the dogs up and let us leave this wretch to her sad fate.'

'Well, Thérèse,' he said to me in a low voice as he released my bonds, 'as you can see, virtue often costs you dear. Don't you think that a pension of two thousand écus would have been preferable to the bites that now cover you?'

But in the awful condition I was in, I could hardly hear him. I threw myself at the foot of the tree and nearly lost consciousness.

'I've been good enough to save your life,' said the villain, inflamed by my suffering, 'take care at least how you use this favour...'

He then ordered me to get up, gather my clothes, and leave that place as fast as I could. As blood was flowing from all over my body, I picked some grass to freshen myself and clean myself so that my clothes, the only ones I had left, would not be stained, while Bressac walked up and down, far more preoccupied with his own thoughts than with me.

The swelling of my flesh, the blood that still streamed out of me, the dreadful pain I endured, all of this made the business of getting dressed almost impossible, and yet the dishonest man who had just put me in this cruel state... he for whom I would previously have laid down my life... never deigned to show me the least sign of sympathy. As soon as I was ready, he said: 'Go where you wish, you must have some money left and I won't take it from you, but watch that you don't reappear in any of my town or country houses. There are two powerful reasons for this prohibition. It's best that you know first and foremost that the business you thought was concluded is not finished. You were told that it was, but you were misled. The charge against you has not been dropped. You were left in this situation so that we could see how you would behave. Secondly, you will be regarded in public as the Marquise's murderer. If she is still breathing, I shall ensure that she carries this thought with her to the grave, the entire household will know it. So there will be two charges against you instead of one, and in place of a vile usurer as adversary, a rich and powerful man will be determined to drive you into Hell if you abuse the life that his pity grants you.'

'Oh, Monsieur,' I replied, 'however severely you have treated me, you may have nothing to fear from my behaviour. I thought I ought to take steps against you to save your aunt's life, but I shall not do so just for the sake of the unfortunate Thérèse. Farewell, Monsieur, may your crimes make you as happy as your cruelty causes me to suffer, and whatever fate Heaven has in store for me, as long as it preserves my lamentable life I shall devote it entirely to praying for you.'

The Comte looked up. He could not help scrutinizing me at these words, and as he saw me about to collapse and streaming with tears, the cruel man walked away, no doubt afraid of showing emotion, and I never saw him again.

Left abandoned to my pain, I slumped at the foot of the tree and there gave it full voice, so that the forest echoed with my laments. I pressed my miserable body against the earth and showered the grass with my tears.

'Oh, my Lord,' I cried, 'you willed it so. It was your eternal decree that the innocent should become the prey of the guilty. Do what you will with me, Lord, I am still a long way from the torments you suffered for us. May those that I am enduring in adoration of you make me one day worthy of the rewards you promise to the weak, when they offer up their tribulations to you and glorify you in the midst of their pains!'

Night was falling and it was becoming impossible for me to go any further. I could scarcely stand up. I glanced at the bush in which I had slept four years earlier, in circumstances that were almost as miserable. I dragged myself over to it as best I could, and lying in the same place, tormented by my still-bleeding wounds, overwhelmed by my troubled thoughts and my broken heart, I spent the cruellest night it is possible to imagine.

The vigour of my age and of my temperament having given me a little strength at daybreak, and too afraid to stay close to that cruel castle, I hurried to distance myself from it. I left the forest and, resolved to reach the first habitation that I came across, entered the small market-town of Saint-Marcel, which was about five leagues from Paris, and asked for the house of the surgeon, which was pointed out to me. I begged him to dress my wounds, telling him that, having fled from my mother's house in Paris because of an affair of the heart, I had been ambushed by robbers at night in the forest, who, in revenge for my resistance to their lusts, had set their dogs on me.

Rodin, as this surgeon was called, examined me very carefully but found nothing dangerous in my wounds. He would, he said, have guaranteed to restore me in less than a fortnight to the health I enjoyed before my adventure if I had arrived at his house immediately afterwards, but the night and my worried state had poisoned my wounds and it would take a month for me to get better. Rodin put me up in his house, took care of me as best he could, and a month later my body bore no more traces of Monsieur de Bressac's cruelty.

As soon as my physical condition permitted me to take the air, my first concern was to try to find in the town a young girl adroit and intelligent enough to go to the Marquise's castle to find out everything that had happened since my departure. It was not really curiosity that drove me to do this, curiosity alone being obviously dangerous and certainly quite out of place, but I had left the money I had earned at the Marquise's in my room. I had scarcely six louis on me and had then more than forty at the castle. I could not imagine that the Comte would be so cruel as to refuse me what so rightly belonged to me. Persuaded that once he had recovered from his initial anger he would not wish to be so unjust towards me, I wrote as touching a letter as I could. I carefully concealed from him the place where I was living and begged him to send my old clothes on to me with the little money that belonged to me in my room. A twenty-five-year-old peasant woman, quick-witted and humorous, undertook to deliver my letter and promised that she would discreetly obtain enough information to satisfy me on her return with regard to all the matters which I explained needed clarification. I enjoined her above all to hide the name of the place where I was, not to speak of me in any way at all, and to say that she had been given the letter by a man who had brought it more than fifteen leagues from there.

Jeannette left, and twenty-four hours later she brought me back the response. I still have it, here it is, Madame, but before reading it, please listen to what happened at the Comte's after I had left.

The Marquise de Bressac, having fallen dangerously ill the very same day that I left the castle, had died two days later in excruciating pains and convulsions. Her relatives came quickly, and her nephew, who appeared to be completely devastated, claimed that his aunt had been poisoned by a chambermaid who had fled the same day. They had started to search for her, intending to put the wretched woman to death if she were found. Moreover, as a result of his inheritance the Comte was now considerably wealthier than he had thought. The Marquise's strongbox, wallet, and jewels, none of which were known to exist, gave her nephew, in addition to an annual income, more than six-hundred thousand francs in effects and cash. People said that this young man could scarcely hide his joy behind his mask of affected grief, and having deplored the fate of the unfortunate Marquise and sworn to avenge her if they laid hands on the guilty party, the relatives summoned to attend the autopsy demanded by the Comte had left the young man in full and quiet possession of his wickedness. Monsieur de Bressac had himself spoken to Jeannette, asking her various questions to which the young woman had replied with such frankness and firmness that he had resolved to give her his response without pressing her further.

'Here is that fateful letter,' said Thérèse, handing it to Madame de Lorsange, 'yes, here it is, Madame, it is sometimes close to my heart, and I shall keep it until I die, read it, if you can, without trembling.'

Having taken the note from the hands of our beautiful adventuress, Madame de Lorsange read the following:

'A wicked girl capable of poisoning my aunt has the cheek to dare write to me after this loathsome crime. The best thing she can do is to keep herself well hidden. She can be sure that she will be in trouble if she is discovered. What does she dare ask for? Does she speak of money? Anything she may have left behind makes up for the thefts she committed, either during her time in the house or when she carried out her last crime. She should avoid sending another letter like this one, because I tell her that we would have the messenger taken into custody until the criminal's hiding-place became known to the justice system.'

'Please continue, my dear child,' said Madame de Lorsange, handing the note back to Thérèse. 'All of these events are quite horrific. To be swimming in gold and refuse to give an unfortunate girl what she legitimately earned when she had no intention to commit any crime is a gratuitous infamy that is without parallel.'

Alas, Madame! (Thérèse continued, resuming the thread of her story), I wept for two days over this unfortunate letter. I was hurt more by the horrible allegations it contained than by its refusal of my request. So I am guilty, I cried, now I am denounced to the law a second time for having obeyed its laws too scrupulously! So be it, I am not repentant. Whatever may happen to me, at least I shall know no remorse as long as my soul is pure and the only thing I have done wrong is to have listened too much to those sentiments of equity and virtue which will never abandon me.

Yet it was impossible for me to believe that I was being sought by justice, as the Comte claimed. This was so implausible, since it would be dangerous for him to have me brought in front of a court, and I imagined that at bottom he must be far more nervous about seeing me than I had reason to tremble at his threats. These reflections made me determine to remain where I was, and even to find a position, if that were possible, until I had increased my funds enough to be able to leave; but before I tell you what I decided to do, it is necessary to give you some idea of this man and his surroundings.

Rodin was a man of forty years, with brown hair and a heavy brow, a keen eye and a strong, healthy demeanour, and yet at the same time a libertine air. With a background well above his rank, possessing an income of between ten and twelve thousand livres, Rodin practised the art of surgery purely out of interest. He had a very fine house in Saint-Marcel which he shared only with two serving-girls and his daughter, having lost his wife some years earlier. His daughter, a young woman by the name of Rosalie who had just reached her fourteenth year, combined all of those charms capable of creating a sensation: a fresh, round face with extraordinarily animated expression, sweet and piquant features, the prettiest mouth possible, big brown eyes full of soul and feeling, chestnut hair falling down to her waist, a lovely complexion of remarkable delicacy, a bosom that was already the most beautiful to be found, and at the same time a witty, vivacious personality, and one of the dearest souls that ever Nature had created. As regards the companions with whom I was to serve in this household, these were two peasant girls, one of whom was a governess and the other a cook. The one exercising the former function was probably around twenty-five years old, the other was between eighteen and twenty, and both were extremely pretty. The choice of these young women made me suspicious about Rodin's keenness to keep me in his house.

Why does he need a third woman, I said to myself, and why does he want pretty ones? I thought, there is definitely something in all this that does not conform to those accepted morals from which I do not wish to stray. I must be on my guard.

I consequently asked Monsieur Rodin to allow me to spend another week recovering at his place, with the assurance that by the end of that time he would have my response to what he was offering me. I took advantage of this interval to form a closer bond with Rosalie, determined to accept a position in her father's house only if there was nothing in it that might make me take offence. With this in mind, I kept a careful watch over everything, and the very next day noticed that this man had an arrangement that from that moment made me extremely suspicious about his conduct.

Monsieur Rodin ran a boarding-school in his house for children of both sexes. He had been granted permission to do this when his wife was still alive, and no one had thought it best to revoke it when he lost her. Monsieur Rodin's pupils were few in number but carefully chosen. In all, he had only fourteen girls and fourteen boys. He never took any below the age of twelve and they were always sent away at sixteen. There was none so pretty as the pupils admitted by Rodin. If one was presented to him with physical defects or no figure, he was astute enough to reject them on umpteen pretexts that were always based on sophisms which no one could answer. Thus, either he never had a full number of boarders, or else those he did have were always charming. These children did not eat at his place but came to the house twice a day, from seven to eleven in the morning and from four till eight in the evening. If I had not seen all of this little troop before, it was because I had arrived at this man's during the holidays when the schoolchildren were not around, reappearing only as I began to recover.

Rodin ran the school himself, his governess taking charge of the girls' class until he took this over as soon as he had finished teaching the boys. He taught these young pupils to write, as well as arithmetic, a little history, drawing, and music, and in all of these lessons he was the only master.

I first expressed my astonishment to Rosalie that her father could exercise the function of surgeon and at the same time that of a schoolmaster. I said to her that it seemed odd to me that, being able to live confortably without pursuing either of these professions, he should take the trouble to attend to them himself. Rosalie, with whom I got along very well, began to laugh at my observation. The way in which she reacted to what I was saying only served to make me more curious, and I entreated her to open up to me completely.

'Listen,' this charming girl said to me with all the candour of her age and all the naivety of her amiable character, 'listen, Thérèse, I shall tell you everything, because I can see that you are an honest girl... incapable of betraying the secret that I am about to confide in you. Assuredly, dear friend, my father can do without all this, so if he pursues either of the professions that you have seen him exercise, he has two motives for doing so which I shall now explain to you. He practises surgery for the love of it, for the mere pleasure of making new discoveries in his art. He has made so many of them, he has published such well-received studies based on his experiments, that he is generally accepted as being the most brilliant man in France today. He worked in Paris for twenty years, and he retired to the countryside for his enjoyment. The official surgeon in Saint-Marcel is a man named Rombeau, whom he has taken under his wing and whom he involves in his experiments. Do you want to know what makes him run a boarding-school now, Thérèse?... Libertinism, my child, nothing but libertinism, a passion carried to the extreme in him. My father finds in his pupils of both sexes objects whose dependence on him makes them submissive to his leanings, and he takes advantage of this... But just a moment... follow me, Rosalie said to me, today is actually Friday, one of the three days in the week when he corrects those who have made errors, and it is in this type of correction that my father takes a personal pleasure. Follow me, I tell you, and you'll see how he goes about it. We can watch from a closet in my bedchamber which is next door to the room where he conducts his investigations. I'll take you there, but no noise, and above all, take care never to speak a word regarding what I have told you or what you are about to see.'

It was too important to me to find out about the morals of this new person who was offering me a refuge to neglect anything that might reveal them to me. I followed Rosalie, who sat me next to the dividing-wall, which was sufficiently badly assembled that the gaps in its planks gave enough light to see all that took place in the adjoining room.

We had scarcely assumed our post when Rodin entered, bringing with him a fourteen-year-old girl, fair of complexion and as pretty as a picture. The poor creature, her eyes full of tears, unfortunately all too aware of what awaited her, moaned as she followed her harsh teacher, and threw herself at his feet, begging for mercy, but it was the very severity of the inflexible Rodin that kindled the first sparks of his pleasure, already evident in the ferocity of the looks he gave her...

'Oh, no, no,' he cried, 'no, no, this has happened with you too many times, Julie. I regret all my kindnesses to you because they have just led you to commit new faults, but could the gravity of this one allow me to use clemency, even assuming that I wanted to?... a note passed to a boy as you came into class?'

'Monsieur, I protest that I did not!'

'Oh! I saw you, I saw you.'

'Don't believe a word of it,' Rosalie said to me, 'these are faults he invents to give him the excuses he needs. This little creature is an angel, it's because she resists that he treats her so harshly.'

Meanwhile Rodin, who has become quite worked up, seizes the girl's hands and ties them above her head to the ring of a pillar situated in the middle of the punishment room. Julie has no more defences... except, that is, for her lovely face languidly turned towards her torturer, her beautiful hair falling around her shoulders, and the tears that are streaming down the prettiest, sweetest, most captivating of features. Rodin becomes excited contemplating this tableau, and covers Julie's imploring eyes with a blindfold so that she can't see anything any more. Rodin, now more at ease, removes the veils of her modesty, lifting the shirt tucked under her corset to the middle of her back... What white skin, what loveliness! ... rose petals scattered on lilies by the hands of the Graces themselves. Who could be so unfeeling as to subject such fresh, such piquant charms to torture? What monster could take pleasure from pain and tears? Rodin contemplates this scene... his wild eyes devour and his hands dare to profane the flowers that his cruelty is about to wither. They are just in front of us, so that no gesture escapes our attention. One moment the libertine begins to reveal all of these sweet features that enchant him, and the next he hides them again. He offers them to us in every conceivable form, but it is the sweet ones that he is most fond of. Although the true temple of love is within his reach, Rodin stays faithful to his idol and does not even glance in that direction, and even fears its appearance. If her position exposes it, he covers it. The slightest deviation would disturb his devotion, he wants nothing to distract him from it. Finally, his fury knows no bounds, he expresses it first with invective, then he bombards the poor, unfortunate little thing with threats and improper suggestions, and she trembles beneath the blows which she sees are about to tear her apart. Rodin, no longer in control of himself, grabs hold of a handful of birch-rods from a basin of vinegar where they have acquired more flexibility and bite. 'Come,' he says, approaching his victim, 'prepare yourself to suffer,' and vigorously striking these bundles directly onto all those parts of her body presented to him, the cruel man first delivers twenty-five blows which soon transform the tender rosiness of her fresh young skin into bright vermilion.

Julie was screaming... her screams pierced my very soul, while tears ran from beneath her blindfold, dropping like pearls onto her lovely cheeks, making Rodin even more furious... He runs his hands over the bruises on her body, touching and squeezing them, as if about to launch fresh assaults. These do indeed quickly follow his first attacks. Beginning once more, Rodin's blows are all preceded by some invective, threat, or reproach... blood is drawn and Rodin is in ecstasy, delighting in the contemplation of the visible proofs of his ferocity. He can contain himself no longer, on fire in the most indecent manner. He has no qualms about displaying this indecency. Julie cannot bear to look... in an instant he is poised to enter her hole, and would like to enter victorious but dares not. Recommencing new tyrannies, Rodin whips her repeatedly with all his might, and these lashes finally succeed in opening up that refuge of grace and sensual delight. He is beside himself, so drunk with lust that he is no longer in possession of his senses, shouting, swearing, blaspheming; nothing is safe from his barbarous blows. Everything he sees is treated with the same severity, nevertheless the villain stops, realizing the impossibility of taking things further without risking losing the strength that he will need for fresh assaults.

'Get dressed,' he says to Julie, untying her and adjusting his dress, 'and if anything of the kind happens with you again, remember that you won't get away with it so easily.'

Once Julie has returned to her class, Rodin goes into the boys and comes back straightaway with a young schoolboy of fifteen, as fair as a summer's day. Rodin scolds him, but probably because he feels more comfortable with him, cajoles and embraces him as he tells him off:

'You deserve to be punished,' he says to him, 'and so you shall be...'

With these words, he exceeds all bounds of decency with this child. Nothing escapes his attention, nothing is left out, the veils are lifted, things begin to stir. Rodin threatens him, caresses him, kisses him, curses him, while his impious fingers seek to awaken sensations of voluptuousness in this young boy and demand the same in return.

'Well, lovely though it is,' the satyr says to him, as he contemplates his success in this regard, 'you are now in a state that I forbade you to enter... I'll wager that with only two strokes more, it would shoot all over me...'

Confident of the excitement he is causing, the libertine steps forward to accept the boy's homage, and his mouth is the temple that will receive this sweet incense. His hands cause the jets to spurt, he guides them into his mouth and drinks them greedily, while he himself is on the point of exploding, but he is determined to reach his goal.

'Oh, I shall punish you for this blunder!' he says, rising to his feet. He takes the young man's hands and, gripping them, has unrestricted access to the altar at which he desires to sacrifice his fury. He pulls it open, covers it with kisses, and pushes his tongue deep inside. Rodin, drunk with love and ferocity, fills the air with expressions of both.

'Oh, you little rogue!' he cries, 'I'm going to pay you back for the effect you're having on me!'

Rodin picks up the birch-rods and whips him. Doubtless because he is more excited than with the young vestal virgin, his blows become much harder and much more numerous. The child weeps and Rodin is in ecstasy, but he is tempted by new pleasures. He unties the child and quickly proceeds to make new sacrifices. A little girl of thirteen follows the boy, and she is succeeded by another schoolboy, followed by a young girl. Rodin whips nine children, five boys and four girls.

The last one is a young boy of fourteen with delicious features. Rodin attempts to enjoy him, but the schoolboy resists. Mad with lust, he whips him, and losing control the villain spurts the frothy jets of his passion all over the molested parts of his young pupil, drenching him from top to toe. Furious that he did not have sufficient strength to contain himself at least until the end, our disciplinarian unties the child with annoyance and sends him back to class, assuring him that he'll make up for it. This is what I heard. These are the events I witnessed.

'Oh, Heaven!' I said to Rosalie when these dreadful scenes were over, 'how can one indulge in such excesses? How can one take pleasure in the infliction of pain?'

'Oh, you don't know it all,' replied Rosalie, 'listen,' she said to me as we returned to her bedchamber, 'what you have seen has proved to you that when my father finds little resistance in these young pupils, he takes his horrific actions much further, abusing girls in the same way as he does boys' (as Rosalie explained to me, these crimes were just like those which I had feared I would myself suffer at the hands of the leader of the gang of thieves following my escape from the Conciergerie, crimes that the merchant from Lyons actually did inflict upon me). 'By this means,' continued this young person, 'the girls are not dishonoured, there are no pregnancies to fear, and nothing to stop them from finding husbands. There isn't a single year when he does not corrupt nearly all the boys like this, and at least half of the other children. Of the fourteen girls that you have seen, eight are already sullied in this way, and he has enjoyed nine boys. The two women who serve him are subjected to the same horrors... Oh, Thérèse,' added Rosalie, throwing her arms around me, 'oh, dear girl, me too, he seduced me when I was an innocent young thing. By the time I was eleven years old I had already become his victim... Alas, this took place before I could defend myself from him...'

'But Mademoiselle,' I interrupted her apprehensively, 'what about religion? This recourse at least remained open to you... Could you not consult a confessor and tell him everything?'

'Oh, don't you realize that as he perverts us he stifles in us all the seeds of religion, and that he forbids us to practise all of its rites, and in any case, how could I? He has scarcely educated me. The little he has told me about these things was from fear that my ignorance might betray his impiety. But I have never been to confession, I have never made my first communion. He knows so well how to ridicule all of these things, to remove all trace of them from us, that those he has suborned are cut off from their duties for good, or else, if they are forced to carry them out because of their family, they do so in a luke-warm fashion or with such complete indifference that he has nothing to fear from any indiscretion on their part. But let yourself be convinced, Thérèse, by your own eyes,' she continued, quickly pushing me into the closet from which we had just emerged, 'come, this chamber in which he punishes his pupils is the same one where he enjoys us. The class is over now, the time has come when, excited by the preliminaries, he will come and make up for the constraints that his prudence sometimes imposes on him. Stand where you were before, dear girl, and your eyes will discover everything.'

Despite my reluctance to watch these new horrors, it was never-theless better for me to go back into this closet than to be overheard talking to Rosalie during classes. Rodin would undoubtedly have become suspicious. I therefore took up position. I had scarcely done so when Rodin came into his daughter's room and led her into the chamber where he had just been. The two serving-girls of the house-hold soon joined them, and then, having no more constraints, the lewd Rodin indulged himself freely and without any modesty in all the abnormal acts of his debauchery. The two peasant girls, com-pletely naked, are severely whipped. While he directs blows against one of these, the other whips him in turn, and meanwhile he applies the filthiest, the most frenetic, the most disgusting caresses to the same altar in Rosalie who, raised up on an armchair, sticks it up in the air for him. It is finally the turn of this unfortunate girl. Rodin ties her to the post as he did his schoolgirls, and whilst his serving-maids took it in turn to scourge him, and sometimes both together, he whipped his daughter, striking her from the middle of her back right down to the bottom of her thighs, ecstatic with pleasure. He is agi-tated in the extreme, screaming and blaspheming, as he delivers his blows. He immediately presses his lips to every spot where his rods leave their mark—the inside of the victim's altar and her mouth… everywhere except the front is sucked hard by his mouth. Soon, without even changing position but just making it more accessible, Rodin penetrates the tight refuge of pleasure. Meanwhile, the same throne is offered by his governess for him to embrace, and the other girl whips him as hard as she can. Rodin is in ecstasy, ripping and cleaving flesh, a thousand kisses each hotter than the previous one expressing his desire for what is being presented to his lewdness. The bomb explodes and, drunk with passion, the libertine dares to taste the sweetest pleasures that incest and infamy have to offer.

Rodin went off to eat. After such exploits, he needed to restore his strength. That evening there were classes and punishment, and so I could have observed more scenes if I had wished, but I had seen enough to convince myself and to decide how to respond to this villain's offers. The time for me to give him my answer was approaching. Two days after these events he came to my room himself to ask me what I had decided. I was in bed at the time. On the pretext of checking whether there remained any traces of my wounds, so that I could not object, he insisted on examining me naked, and as he had been doing this twice a day for a month without my noticing anything in him so far that might offend against my modesty, I did not feel able to resist. But Rodin had other plans on this occasion. When he had the object of his devotion within his grasp, he put one of his legs around my back, gripping me so hard that I was, so to speak, defenceless.

'Thérèse,' he then said to me, his wandering hands leaving me in no doubt as to his intentions, 'you are now completely recovered, my dear, so now you can show me the gratitude with which I know your heart is full. This is easily done, all I want is this,' the rogue continued, holding me still with all the strength he could summon... 'Yes, this is the only reward I want, this is all I ask from women... but this is one of the loveliest I have ever seen in my entire life!' he continued. 'How round it is! How firm!... What exquisite skin!... Oh, I just have to enjoy it!'

So saying, Rodin, who was probably already prepared to carry out his mission, was obliged to let go of me for a moment in order to make it possible, and I took advantage of the time this gave me to free myself from his grip: 'Monsieur,' I said to him, 'please believe, I beg of you, that nothing in this whole world could persuade me to submit to the horrors that you seem to desire. I owe you a debt of gratitude, I agree, but I will not acquit it at the cost of a crime. I am doubtless poor and miserable, nevertheless, here is the little money I possess,' I continued, offering him my poor purse, 'take what you consider appropriate and permit me to leave this house, I beg you, just as soon as I am able.'

Confounded by a degree of resistance which he did not expect from a girl devoid of resources and whom, according to that injustice usual among men, he supposed to be dishonest for the simple reason that she was in a state of misery, Rodin looked at me closely.

'Thérèse,' he went on after a moment, 'you're in no position to play the virgin with me. It seems to me that I had the right to a few kindnesses on your part. Never mind, keep your money, but do not leave me. It suits me very well to have a good girl in the house. I'm surrounded by girls who are far from being so... Since you appear to be so virtuous, I hope that you will therefore be like that in every respect. This is in my interests, my daughter likes you, she has just begged me again to persuade you not to leave us. So I invite you to stay with us.'

'Monsieur,' I replied, 'I would not be happy here. The two women who serve you aspire to all the feelings you are able to have for them. They would be jealous of me, and sooner or later I would be forced to leave you.'

'You need have no fear of that,' replied Rodin, 'you mustn't be afraid of any of the consequences of jealousy from those women. I know how to keep them in their place and to protect yours, and you alone will enjoy my confidence at no risk to yourself. But it is right for you to know that to continue to be worthy of it, the chief quality I demand of you, Thérèse, is absolute discretion. Many things happen here, many of which will offend against your virtuous principles, but you must see all and hear all, my child, and never say a word... Oh, stay with me, Thérèse, stay here, my child, I shall be delighted to keep you. In the midst of so many vices to which I am drawn by a fiery temperament, an unbridled spirit, and a very spoilt nature, I will at least have the consolation of having a virtuous person near at hand. I will be able to take refuge in her bosom as at the feet of a God when I am sated with my debauchery...'

'Oh Heaven!' I thought at that moment, 'so virtue is necessary, it is indeed indispensable to man, since even the vicious criminal is himself obliged to seek reassurance in it and to take shelter in its arms.' I then recalled how Rosalie had urged me not to leave her, and believing that I recognized some good principles in Rodin, I firmly accepted a position with him.

'Thérèse,' Rodin said to me a few days later, 'I'm going to put you with my daughter. That way, you won't have anything to do with my two other women, and I shall give you three hundred livres in wages.'

Such a position was a real stroke of luck for one in my circumstances. Burning with the desire to bring Rosalie back into the ways of righteousness, and maybe even her father himself, if I managed to gain some influence over him, I had no regrets about what I had just done... having had me dressed appropriately, Rodin lost no time in taking me to his daughter, announcing to her that he was giving me to her. Rosalie greeted me with unparalleled cries of joy, and I was quickly settled in.

A week had not passed when I began to work hard to convert the two of them, but Rodin's obstinacy thwarted all of my efforts. 'Do not think', he would reply to my wise counsels, 'that the homage I have paid to virtue in you is proof, either that I esteem virtue or that I would wish to prefer it to vice. You would be quite wrong to imagine this, Thérèse. Anyone who, based on what I have done for you, deduced from my actions either the importance or the necessity of virtue would be sorely mistaken, and I should be very upset if you believed that such were my thoughts. The hovel that offers me shelter during the hunt when the fierce rays of the sun are shining directly onto me is certainly not an edifice of any utility, its necessity being purely circumstantial. I am exposed to some danger, I find something that protects me from it and make use of it, but is this something any less useless, can it be any less despicable? In a totally depraved society, virtue would be pointless. Since ours is not of that nature, we must certainly either play the game or make use of it in order to have less to fear from those who follow its path. If no one did so, it would become useless. Therefore, I am not wrong when I maintain that whether virtue is necessary is just a matter of opinion or circumstance. Virtue is not a world of priceless worth, it is just a way of behaving that varies according to climate and consequently has nothing real about it, and that alone reveals its futility. Only those things that are constant are truly good. That which perpetually changes could not aspire to the character of goodness, which is why the immutable was ranked among the perfections of the Eternal, but virtue is totally devoid of this character. There are no two races on the surface of the globe that are virtuous in the same way, therefore there is nothing real, nothing intrinsically good about virtue, and it in no way deserves our adoration. You must use it as a prop, and diplomatically adopt the style of the country where you live so that those who practise it out of taste, or who are obliged to respect it because of their situation, leave you in peace, and in order that the virtue that is respected where you are protects you through the weight of convention against attacks from those who profess vice. But once again, all of this is a matter of circumstance, none of it attributing any real merit to virtue. Moreover, certain virtues are impossible for some men to follow. Now, how can you persuade me that a virtue which combats or is contrary to the passions can be found in Nature? And if it is not in Nature, how can it be good? The men in question will assuredly prefer the vices that are opposed to these virtues, since they offer them the only way of living that is best suited to their physique or their organs. According to this hypothesis, therefore, there will be vices that are very useful. Now, how can virtue be useful if you demonstrate to me that its opposite can be so? The response to that is that virtue is useful to others, and in that sense it is good, for if it is accepted that one should do only what is good for others, they will do only good to me in my turn. Such reasoning is nothing but sophistry. For the little good I receive from others based on the fact that they practise virtue and that I am obliged to practise it in turn, I make a million sacrifices that in no way compensate me. Receiving less than I give, I am therefore making a bad bargain, experiencing much more harm from the privations I endure in order to be virtuous than I receive good from those who do it.* Since this arrangement is not equal, I should therefore not submit to it. If I am virtuous, it is certain that the amount of good I do to others will not make up for the trouble I endure in forcing myself to behave virtuously, and would it therefore not be better for me to renounce the idea of creating a happiness for them that must necessarily cost me as much suffering? There just remain the wrongs I as a wicked man can do to others and the wrongs they will do to me in turn if everyone is like me. Given a complete circularity of vice, I am definitely running risks, I admit. However, the trouble caused me by the risks I take is compensated for by the pleasure of causing risks to others. Thus is balance maintained, and everyone is more or less equally happy, which is not, and could never be, the case in a society where some are good and others bad because this mixture gives rise to perpetual traps that do not exist in the other scenario. In a mixed society there are diverse interests, and such diversity is the source of an infinite number of misfortunes, while in the other arrangement all interests are equal, each individual member being endowed with the same tastes, the same leanings, all heading towards the same goal, and everyone is happy. But, idiots will tell you, evil does not make you happy. No it does not, when people agree to worship good. But if you see no value in what you call good, if you debase it, you will then revere only what you were stupid enough to call evil, and all men will have the pleasure of committing it, not because it will be permitted (that would sometimes be a reason for its attraction to lessen), but they will no longer be punished for it by laws which, by virtue of the fear they inspire, diminish the pleasure that Nature has given crime. Let's imagine a society where it is accepted that incest (to take this offence as an example among many), that incest, I say, is a crime. Those who indulge in it will be unhappy because the general opinion, laws, religion, everything will conspire to spoil their pleasure. Those who want to commit this wrong and who dare not do so will be equally miserable because of these restraints. Thus, the law that proscribes incest will have done nothing but make people unhappy. Where, in a neighbouring society, incest is not a crime, those who do not wish to engage in it will not be miserable, and those who do will be happy. Thus, the society that has permitted this act will serve men better than that which has made the same act into a crime. The same is true of all those other acts stupidly considered criminal. If you regard them as such, you make lots of people unhappy. If you allow them, no one complains, since he who likes such acts quietly indulges in them, and he who doesn't care about them either manifests a kind of indifference towards them that is in no way painful, or compensates for the harm he might have been done by a host of other injuries which he in turn inflicts on those against whom he had a grievance. Thus, everybody in a crime-ridden society is either very happy or is in a state of unconcern that is not harmful. Consequently, there is nothing good, nothing respectable, nothing that can make people happy in what we call virtue. Those who practise it, therefore, have no reason to be proud just because the particular type of constitution of our societies obliges us to pay it homage. It is purely a matter of circumstance or convention, but in point of fact this cult is illusory, and to worship virtue for even a single moment does not make it any more attractive.'

Such was the infernal logic of Rodin's miserable passions, but

Rosalie, far sweeter, far less corrupted, Rosalie who detested the horrors to which she was forced to submit, was more amenable to my opinions. I earnestly desired to have her make her first communion, yet to do so would have necessitated confiding in a priest, and Rodin did not want such men in his house, detesting them as much as the cult they professed. He would not have tolerated one near his daughter for anything in the world, and it was just as impossible to take this young person to a confessor. Rodin never let Rosalie go out unaccompanied. We therefore had to wait for some opportunity to present itself, and while we waited I gave the young girl instruction. By giving her a taste for virtue, I also inspired in her a taste for religion, revealing to her the holy doctrines and sublime mysteries, and linking both of these so closely in her young heart that I made them indispensable to her happiness.

'Oh, Mademoiselle,' I said to her one day as she shed tears of compunction, 'can man be so blind as to believe that he is not destined for a better life? Is it not enough that he has been endowed with the power and the ability to know his God for him to be convinced that this favour has been granted to him so that he may fulfil the duties it imposes on him? Now, what can be the basis of the worship of the Eternal Being if not that virtue which He himself exemplifies? Could the Creator of so many marvels have any other laws but good? And can our hearts please Him if good is not their very substance? It seems to me that with sensitive souls, the only signs of love we need send this Supreme Being are those inspired by gratitude. Has He not favoured us in giving us the ability to enjoy the beauties of this universe, and do we not owe Him some gratitude for such a boon? But a stronger reason yet establishes and confirms the universal chain of our duties: why should we refuse to fulfil those required by His laws since these are the same ones as those which consolidate our happiness among men? Is it not sweet to feel that we render ourselves worthy of the Supreme Being just by exercising those virtues that must ensure our contentment on earth, and that the means which make us worthy of living among our fellow creatures are the same ones as those that give us the certainty of being reborn before God's throne! Oh, Rosalie, how blind are those who would wish to take this hope away from us! Deceived and seduced by their miserable passions, they prefer denial of the eternal verities to a renunciation that would make them worthy of them. They prefer to say: *We are deceived,* rather than to admit that they are themselves deceived. The idea of the losses that they face would disturb their unworthy pleasures. It seems less frightful to them to annihilate all prospect of paradise than to deprive themselves of that which must gain a place there for them. But when these tyrannical passions grow weak in them, when the veil is rent, when nothing in their corrupt souls can any longer equal that majestic voice of the God that they denied in their delirium, oh, Rosalie, how terrible must be their change of heart, and how dearly the remorse that goes with it must make them pay for that moment of error that blinded them! This is the condition in which man must be judged so that his own conduct be regulated. We should not believe what he says when he is intoxicated or when he is carried away by the fever of passion. Only when he can reason calmly, in possession of all his faculties, may he seek truth and find it. Only then do we seek that holy Being of our own volition, the God that we hitherto denied. We implore his help and he consoles us. We pray to him and he listens. Ah, why, then, would I deny him, why would I ignore the God who is so necessary to my happiness? Why would I prefer to say, like the soul who has strayed, *There is no God*, when the heart of the reasonable man at every moment offers me proofs of the existence of this divine Being? Is it therefore better to dream with those who are mad than to reason with the wise? Everything is deducible from this first principle: once God exists, this God deserves to be worshipped, and the basis of this faith is incontestably Virtue.'

From these first truths I was easily able to deduce the rest, and Rosalie the deist had soon become a Christian. But I repeat, how was I to turn theory into practice? Forced to obey her father, the most Rosalie could do was to respond to him with disgust, and with a man like Rodin could this not become dangerous? He was intractable, impervious to all of my beliefs, but if I could not manage to convince him, at least he could not shake my faith.

However, such a schooling and the very real and permanent dangers that it represented made me tremble for Rosalie, to the point that I did not feel at all guilty in encouraging her to flee this perverted house. It seemed to me that wrenching her from the bosom of her incestuous father was a lesser evil than leaving her there exposed to all the risks she might run. I had already gently broached this subject, and I was possibly not that far from succeeding, when suddenly Rosalie disappeared from the house without its being possible for me to know where she was. When I enquired of Rodin's women or of Rodin himself as to her whereabouts, I was assured that she had gone to spend the summer at a relative's house ten leagues away. When I asked around the neighbourhood, people first expressed astonishment at such a question coming from someone in the household, and then they would give me the same answer as Rodin and his servants: they had seen her and kissed her goodbye the previous day, the very same day of her departure, and I received everywhere the same response. When I asked Rodin why I had not been told that she had left, and why I had not followed my mistress, he assured me that the only reason had been to avoid a painful scene for both of us, and that I would no doubt soon see my beloved Rosalie again. I had to accept these excuses, but I found it more difficult to be convinced by them. Was it plausible that Rosalie, Rosalie who loved me so much, could have agreed to leave me without saying a word! And from what I knew of Rodin's character, there was much left unsaid regarding the wretched girl's fate. I therefore resolved to do all I could to find out what had become of her, and every means seemed acceptable to me to achieve this.

The very next day, finding myself alone in the house, I carefully search every corner. Thinking I can hear moans coming from a very dark cellar, I draw nearer. A pile of wood appears to block a narrow, concealed door. I move closer, pushing all obstacles aside... fresh noises can be heard... I believe I recognize the voice... I listen hard... there is no doubt in my mind.

'Thérèse,' I hear her cry at last. 'Oh, Thérèse, is that you?'

'Yes, dear, sweet friend,' I cried, recognizing Rosalie's voice... 'Yes, it is Thérèse, sent by Heaven to help you...'

I ask her so many questions that she scarcely has the time to answer. I finally discover that, a few hours before her disappearance, Rombeau, Rodin's friend and colleague, had examined her naked, and that she had received the order from her father to submit to the same horrors with Rombeau as those Rodin demanded of her daily, that she had resisted, but that a furious Rodin had seized her and himself subjected her to his colleague's outrageous assaults; that then, leaving her still naked, the two friends had whispered together for a very long time, returning to inspect her again from time to time, and to enjoy her in the same criminal manner, or to mistreat her in a hundred different ways; that after four or five hours of this scenario

Rodin had told her categorically that he was going to send her to the country to stay with one of his female relatives, but that she must leave right away and not say anything to Thérèse, for reasons which he would himself explain to her the following day at his relative's house, where he would be joining her without delay. He had given Rosalie to understand that she was to marry, and that this was why his friend Rombeau had examined her to ascertain whether she was able to bear children. Rosalie had actually left, accompanied by an old woman. She had crossed the village, bidding several acquaintances farewell as she went, but just as soon as night had fallen her chaperone had taken her back to her father's house, where she had arrived at midnight. Rodin, who was waiting for her, had seized her, stifling her cries with his hand, and without saying a word had thrown her into this cellar, where she had in fact been quite well fed and cared for since.

'I fear the worst,' added this poor girl, 'my father's behaviour towards me since that time, the things he says to me, all the events that preceded Rombeau's examination, everything, Thérèse, everything proves that these monsters are going to use me for some of their experiments, and that your poor Rosalie is done for.'

After the tears that flowed in abundance from my eyes, I asked this poor girl if she knew where the key to the cellar was kept. She did not know, yet she did not think that they were in the habit of taking it away with them. I searched for it in every corner but in vain, and the time came when they were due back without my having been able to give this dear child any other help but words of consolation, hope, and tears. She made me swear to return the following day. I promised to do so, and even assured her that if, by then, I had made no satisfactory discoveries concerning her, I would leave the house immediately, I would make an official complaint to the courts, and whatever the cost, would rescue her from the dreadful fate that threatened her.

So I go back upstairs. Rombeau was having supper that evening with Rodin. Resolved to do anything to throw light on my mistress's fate, I hide next door to the apartment where the two friends are, and their conversation leaves me in no doubt at all about the horrible plan they were both hatching.

'Never', said Rodin, 'will human anatomy be in such a perfect condition for the examination of the organs as in a child of fourteen or fifteen years who has died a cruel death. This is the only way we can obtain a complete analysis of such an interesting subject.'

'The same applies to the membrane that is proof of virginity,' replied Rombeau. 'A young girl is essential for this examination. What do we observe at the age of puberty? Nothing. Menstruation tears the hymen and any examination becomes imprecise. Your daughter is exactly what we need. Even though she is fifteen, she does not yet have her periods. The way in which we have enjoyed her has not damaged this membrane, and we can examine her without any qualms. I am delighted that you have finally made up your mind.'

'I certainly have,' replied Rodin. 'I find it odious that such futile considerations should impede scientific progress. Have great men ever allowed themselves to be held back by such miserable chains? And when Michelangelo wanted to paint a Christ in the nude, did he let his conscience prevent him from crucifying a young man and copying him in his agony? But when we wish to make progress in our field, how necessary these same methods must be! How can it be at all wrong to permit oneself to use them? If the sacrifice of a single person saves a million lives, can one hesitate when the cost is so small? Is the murder that we are going to commit any different in nature from that carried out by our laws, and is not the object of these laws that people find so wise the sacrifice of one subject in order to save a thousand?'

'It is the only way to learn,' said Rombeau, 'and in the hospitals where I worked throughout my youth I witnessed a thousand such experiments. Because of the ties that bind you to this creature, I confess that I was afraid you would hesitate.'

'What! Because she is my daughter? A feeble excuse!' cried Rodin. 'What importance do you imagine this relationship has in my heart? I consider the fruit of a little sperm in the same way (apart from its weight) as I do that which I enjoy losing for pleasure. I have never attached more importance to either one. We have the right to take back what we have given. The right to dispose of one's children has never been contested in any nation on this earth. The Persians, the Medes, the Armenians, the Greeks* practised it fully. The legal system devised by Lycurgus, the model of all lawmakers, not only gave fathers every right over their children, but even condemned to death those whose parents did not wish to feed them, or those who were deformed. A great number of savages kill their children as soon as they are born. Almost all of the women of Asia, Africa, and America abort them without incurring any blame. Cook encountered this custom on all of the islands of the South Seas.* Romulus permitted infanticide. The law of the Twelve Tables also tolerated this, and until Constantine the Romans exposed or killed their children with impunity. Aristotle advocates this so-called crime. The sect of the Stoics considered it as laudable, and it is still very much the custom in China. Every day in the streets and canals of Peking can be found more than ten thousand individuals sacrificed or abandoned by their parents, and whatever a child's age, in this wise empire, a father need only put it in the hands of a judge to get rid of it. According to the laws of the Parthians, one could kill one's son, daughter, or brother, even in adolescence. Caesar found this custom widespread among the Gauls. Several passages of the Pentateuch prove that it was permissible for God's people to kill their children, and indeed, God himself demanded it of Abraham. According to a famous modern thinker, for a long time it was believed that the prosperity of empires depended on the slavery of children, a view based on the soundest principles of reason. After all, if monarchs can think that they are authorized to sacrifice twenty or thirty thousand of their subjects in a single day in their own interests, why should a father not be master of the lives of his children when he considers it appropriate? What absurdity! What inconsistency and what weakness in those who are bound by such chains! The authority of a father over his children, the only real one, the only one which is the basis of all others, is dictated to us by the voice of Nature herself, and a careful study of its workings offers us examples all the time. Tsar Peter had no doubt whatever about this right. He exercised it himself and addressed a public declaration to all divisions of his empire, stating that, according to laws both human and divine, a father had a total and absolute right to sentence his children to death without appeal and without consulting anyone else's opinion. It's only in our barbaric country of France that this right has been removed, because of a pity that is both absurd and misplaced. No,' continued Rodin with passion, 'no, no, my friend, I shall never understand that a father who was willing to give life should not be free to give death. It is the ridiculous price we attach to this life that makes us talk nonsense all the time about the circumstances that drive a man to rid himself of his fellow creatures. Believing that existence is the greatest thing we own, we stupidly imagine that we are committing a crime if we remove those who enjoy it, yet the cessation of this existence, or at least of what follows it, is no more evil than life is good, or rather, if nothing dies, if nothing is destroyed, if nothing is ever lost in Nature, if all of the decomposed parts of any body are just waiting to be dissolved to reappear immediately in new forms, the act of murder is without importance and so how can one consider it wrong? Even if it were just a personal whim, I should regard the act as a perfectly simple matter, even more so when it becomes necessary to an art that is so useful to mankind... When it can offer such great insights, it is no longer an evil, my friend, no longer a heinous offence, it is the best, the wisest, the most useful of all actions, and to deny oneself the opportunity would be the real crime.'

'Ah!' said Rombeau, full of enthusiasm for such frightening maxims, 'I approve of what you are saying, my dear fellow, your wisdom enchants me, but I am astonished by your indifference. I thought you were in love.'

'I, in love with a girl?... Oh, Rombeau, I thought you knew me better. I make use of such creatures when I have nothing better. The extreme penchant I have for pleasures of the kind you see me indulge in makes all those temples where that kind of incense can be offered very precious to me, and to multiply them, I sometimes combine a young girl with a pretty boy. But once any of these unfortunate females has fed my illusions for too long, I am overcome with disgust, and I have only ever known one way of satisfying it deliciously... Do you understand, Rombeau? Chilperic*, the greatest sensualist among the kings of France, thought the same. He would say openly that one could make use of a woman for want of anything better, but on the express condition that she should be exterminated as soon as one had enjoyed her.[1] That little bitch has been serving my pleasures for five years now, and it's time she paid for putting an end to my intoxication with her life.'

The meal was nearly over, and judging from the behaviour of these two wild men, from their conversation, their actions, their plans, and their state of mind, which bordered on delirium, I realized that there was not a moment to lose and that the unfortunate Rosalie's death was to take place that same evening. I ran to the cellar, determined to rescue her or die in the attempt.

---

[1] See a small volume entitled *The Jesuits in Fine Fettle*.*

'Oh, my dear friend,' I cried out to her, 'there is not a moment to lose... the monsters... it's going to happen this evening... they are on their way...'

And saying this, I made the most violent attempts to break down the door. One of my blows makes something drop to the floor, I grope for it, it's the key, I pick it up and make haste to open the door... I embrace Rosalie, I urge her to flee, encouraging her to follow my lead, and she runs after me... Dear Heaven! It was once again written that virtue should succumb and that the tenderest feelings of commiseration would be most harshly punished. Alerted by the governess, Rodin and Rombeau suddenly appear, the former seizing his daughter just as she is stepping over the threshold of the door, beyond which she has only a few more steps to make in order to be free.

'Where are you going, you wretched girl?' cried Rodin stopping her in her tracks, while Rombeau seized hold of me... 'Ah!' he continued looking at me. 'This mischievous young woman was helping you to escape! So this is what your great virtuous principles have brought you, Thérèse... to abduct a young girl from her father!'

'Certainly,' I replied firmly, 'and I must do this when that father is barbaric enough to conspire against his own daughter's life.'

'Ah! Ah! Spying and seduction!' Rodin continued. 'All of the most dangerous vices in a servant. Come up, come up, we must examine this business.'

Dragged upstairs by these two rogues, we reach the apartments and the doors close behind us. Rodin's unfortunate daughter is tied to the columns of a bed, and these crazy men turn all their rage against me. I am assailed by the harshest invectives, and the most frightening judgements are pronounced against me. My fate is to be dissected alive so that they may examine the beatings of my heart and make the kind of observations about this part of the body that would be impossible to carry out on a corpse. Meanwhile, they undress me, and I become the object of the most indecent assaults.

'Above all,' says Rombeau, 'I am of the opinion that we should attack the fortress that your good conduct has preserved... How superb it is! Just look at the silken rosiness of those two half moons that defend the entrance! No virgin was ever fresher!'

'Virgin! Well, she is almost,' says Rodin... 'She was violated just once against her will, and not the least little thing since. Let me look for a moment...'

And the cruel man mingles gestures of adoration with those rough and ferocious caresses that degrade the idol instead of honouring it. If there had been birch-rods to hand, I would have been cruelly treated. They talked of caning me, but as there were none to be found they contented themselves with what they could do with their hands. They beat me red raw... the more I defended myself, the faster they held me. However, when I realized that they were contemplating more grievous acts, I threw myself at the feet of my tormentors, offering them my life, and begging them not to dishonour me.

'But since you are not a virgin any longer,' said Rombeau, 'what does it matter? No guilt will attach to you, you have already been raped, and so when we rape you again there will not be the slightest stain on your conscience. All will have been taken from you by force...'

And consoling me in this manner, the outrageous man was already laying me on a sofa.

'No,' said Rodin, restraining his companion's enthusiasm to which I was about to fall victim, 'no, let us not waste our energies on this creature. Remember that we cannot put off any longer the operations planned for Rosalie and that we need all our strength to carry these out. We must find other ways of punishing this wretched girl.'

So saying, Rodin placed an iron in the fire. 'Yes,' he continued, 'we can punish her a thousand times more than if we took her life. Let us brand her and so stigmatize her. In addition to all the scars she already has on her body, this debasement will get her hanged or ensure she dies of hunger. At least, she will suffer until then and our revenge will be longer-lasting and so more delicious.'

Rombeau seizes hold of me and, taking the red hot iron with which thieves are branded, the abominable Rodin applies it to my shoulder.

'Let her dare appear in public now, the whore,' the monster continued, 'let her just dare, and by revealing this ignominious letter I shall have sufficient legitimate reasons for having her dismissed with such swiftness and secrecy.'

They put a dressing on me, clothe me, fortify me with a few drops of liqueur, and taking advantage of the dark hours, the two friends lead me to the edge of the forest and cruelly abandon me there, having again brought home to me the dangers I would run if I dared to lodge a complaint in the state of degradation I was now in.

No other girl would have taken this threat seriously. Once it had

been possible for me to prove that the treatment that I had just under-
gone was not the work of any court of justice, what had I to fear? But
my weakness, my natural timidity, the nightmares of my misfortunes
in Paris and in the Bressac castle all filled me with bewilderment and
terror. I thought only of fleeing, far more affected by the pain I felt at
leaving an innocent victim in the hands of those two criminals who
were probably on the point of sacrificing her, than I was by my own
troubles. More upset and preoccupied than in physical pain, I
instantly set off on foot, but having no sense of direction and not asking the way, all I did was to encircle Paris, and on the fourth day of
my journey I had only got as far as Lieusaint. Knowing that this road
could take me in the direction of the southern provinces, I then
resolved to follow it and, if possible, to reach those distant lands,
imagining that the peace and quiet so cruelly denied me in my homeland perhaps awaited me on the other side of France. Fateful error!
How many torments I still had to suffer!

Whatever trials I had had to undergo thus far, at least my innocence was still intact. I had simply fallen victim to a number of monstrous assaults, or with few exceptions, at any rate, and could still
count myself one of the class of honest women. In fact, I had only
been really defiled by a rape that occurred five years earlier and the
effects of which had now healed... a rape that was consummated in an
instant during which my numb senses had not even allowed me to
feel what was happening. Moreover, what did I have to reproach
myself with? Nothing, oh, not a single thing, my heart was pure. But
I was too arrogant and my presumptuousness was asking to be punished. The outrages that awaited me would be such that it would soon
no longer be possible for me to cherish the same consoling thoughts
in the depths of my soul, however unwillingly I took part in them.

This time, I had my entire fortune on me, that is, about a hundred
écus, the sum total of everything I had saved at the Bressacs' and
what I had earned at Rodin's. In the depths of my misfortune, I still
felt pleased that these resources had not been taken from me. I flattered myself that, given the frugality, temperance, and thrift to which
I was accustomed, this money would suffice at least until I was able to
find a position. The outrage that I had just suffered was not visible. I
imagined that I would be able to keep it hidden and that this stigma
would not prevent me from earning a living. I was twenty-two years
of age, enjoying good health and an appearance thanks to which it

was my misfortune to win admirers everywhere. I also had some virtues which, while they had always brought me bad luck, still consoled me, as I have just told you, and made me hope that Heaven would eventually grant them, if not rewards, at least some cessation of the ills which they had attracted to me. Full of hope and courage, I continued on my journey as far as Sens, where I rested for a few days. After a week I was completely recovered. Perhaps I would have found some position in this town but, driven by the need to distance myself as much as possible, I set off again with the intention to seek fortune in the Dauphiné.* I had heard a great deal of this area and imagined I would find happiness there. We shall see how successful I was.

Whatever the circumstances of my life, the sentiments of religion had never left me. Despising the vain sophisms of the strong-minded, believing them all to come from libertinism much more than from any firm conviction, I preferred to follow my conscience and my heart, finding in both all necessary responses to them. Often forced by my misfortunes to neglect my religious duties, I made up for this whenever I found an opportunity to do so.

I had just left Auxerre on 7 August—I shall never forget that time. I had covered about two leagues, and as I was starting to suffer from the heat, I climbed up to the top of a small hillock covered with a clump of trees, not far from the road, intending to refresh myself and to take a nap for a couple of hours at less cost than in an inn and in greater safety than on the highway. I settled myself at the foot of an oak tree, and after a frugal breakfast I sank into sweet repose. Having enjoyed a long and tranquil sleep, I opened my eyes to gaze upon the agreeable landscape that stretched before me into the distance. To my right lay a forest, from the middle of which, about three or four leagues distant, a small bell-tower rose modestly into the air... a place of pleasing solitude, I said to myself, that was calling to me... you must be the refuge of gentle and virtuous recluses who give their lives completely to God and their duties, or of holy hermits exclusively devoted to religion... Far removed from that pernicious society where innocence is constantly haunted by crime, which damages and destroys it... oh! all of the virtues must reside there, I'm sure, and when the crimes of men exile them from this earth, it is there in that solitary retreat that they shall find refuge, in the bosom of those fortunate beings who cherish and cultivate them each and every day.

I was lost in these thoughts when a girl of about my age tending sheep on this plateau suddenly caught my attention. I asked her about this dwelling and she told me that I was looking at a Benedictine convent, occupied by four hermits unequalled in religion, continence, and sobriety. 'Once a year, people make a pilgrimage there to a miraculous virgin from whom the pious obtain everything they ask for.' Immediately impelled by a strange desire to go and beg for help at the feet of this Holy Mother of God, I asked the girl if she would come and pray with me. She replied that this was impossible as her mother was waiting for her, but that it was easy to reach the place. She showed me the way, assuring me that the Father Superior of the convent was the most respectable and the most sainted of men, and that he would receive me perfectly well and would offer me all the help that I might require. 'His name is Dom Severino,' the girl continued, 'he is Italian and a close relative of the Pope, who showers him with blessings. He is kind, honest, willing, aged fifty-five years, more than two-thirds of which he has spent in France... you will be pleased with him, Mademoiselle,' continued the shepherdess, 'go and enlighten yourself in that calm and holy place, and you will come out a better person.'

This account spurred me on all the more, and it became impossible for me to resist the violent desire that I felt to go and visit this holy church and there to make reparation for the sins I was guilty of by performing a few acts of piety. Even though I myself was in need of charity, I gave the girl an écu and set off on the road to Sainte-Marie-des-Bois, such being the name of the convent towards which I now directed my steps.

PART TWO

ONCE I had descended onto the plain I could no longer see the bell-tower. The forest was my only guide, and I began to think that the distance I had to cover, and which I was yet to discover, was far greater than I had estimated it to be. Yet I was not discouraged, and arriving at the edge of the forest and seeing that I had enough daylight left, I resolved to press on, imagining that I might still reach the monastery before nightfall. However, I could see no sign of humanity... not a single house, and I chanced to follow the only path, which itself appeared to be rarely used. I had already gone at least five leagues without seeing anything when, the sun having completely ceased illuminating the universe, I seemed to hear the sound of a bell... I listen, I walk in the direction of the noise, I increase my step, the footpath becomes a little wider, and finally I catch sight of hedges and soon after, the monastery. Its rural isolation was the most complete, there being no neighbouring habitation, the closest being six leagues away, and the monastery was surrounded by thick copses on every side. It was situated in a hollow, and it had taken a long descent to reach it. This was the reason why I had lost sight of the bell-tower once I had reached the plain. Adjacent to the walls of the monastery was a gardener's hut, and it was here that enquiries were to be made before entering. I ask this porter if I may be permitted to speak with the Father Superior. He enquires what I want of him. I give him to understand that I am drawn to this holy retreat by my religious vocation, and that all of the hardships I have endured to reach it would be more than justified if I might be allowed for a single moment to throw myself at the feet of the miraculous Virgin and of those saints of the church in whose house her divine image is preserved. The gardener rings the bell and enters the monastery, but as it is late and the good fathers are having supper, it is some time before he returns. Eventually, he reappears with one of the monks.

'Mademoiselle,' he says to me, 'this is Dom Clement, the bursar of the monastery. He has come to see whether what you're after is worth disturbing Father Superior for.'

Clement, whose name could not have been less suited to his appearance, was a man of forty-eight years, hugely corpulent and gigantic in size, with a fierce and sombre look, expressing himself only with harsh words spat out by a raucous organ—the true figure of a satyr. He had the appearance of a tyrant and he made me tremble... Then, without its being possible for me to prevent it happening, the memory of my earlier misfortunes presented itself to my troubled memory in hues of blood...

'What is it you want?' this monk said to me in the most rebarbative manner; 'is this the time to come to a church?... You have all the look of an adventuress.'

'Holy man,' I said prostrating myself, 'I thought that the house of God was open at all hours. I have come a long way to visit you, filled with fervour and devotion. I ask for my confession to be heard, if possible, and when the inner depths of my conscience are revealed to you, you will know whether or not I am worthy to prostrate myself at the foot of the holy image.'

'But this is not the time for confessions,' said the monk, adopting a softer tone, 'and where will you spend the night? We do not run a hostel... you should have come in the morning.'

I then told him the reasons that had prevented me from doing so, and without a word of reply, Clement went off to inform the Father Superior. A few minutes later the church door opened and Dom Severino himself came out to the gardener's hut to invite me into the church with him.

Dom Severino, of whom I had better give you an idea straight-away, was a man of fifty-five years as I had been told, but he was good-looking, with a complexion that was still young in appearance, with a strong build and the limbs of Hercules, and all this without any rough edges. Overall, a kind of elegance and softness of features predominated, indicating that in his youth he must have possessed all those attributes that make a man handsome. He had the most beautiful eyes in the world, noble features, and the most honest, the most gracious, the most courteous tone of voice. An agreeable sort of accent which, though none of his words was corrupted, nevertheless betrayed his regional origins, and I confess that all the outward grace of this cleric to some degree calmed those fears that the previous one had instilled in me.

'My dear girl,' he said to me courteously, 'although the hour is inconvenient, and we are not in the habit of receiving visitors so late, I will hear your confession nevertheless, and after that we will think about how we can make the most suitable arrangements for you to spend the night until the time comes tomorrow when you can worship the holy image that has drawn you here.'

We enter the church, the doors close, and a lamp is lit next to the confessional. Severino tells me to go inside. He sits and bids me confide in him in total confidence.

After humbling myself, I am completely reassured by a man who seems so gentle, and I hide nothing from him. I confess all of my sins to him, I recount to him all of my woes, I even tell him about the shameful mark that the barbaric Rodin branded me with. Severino listens to all this with the greatest attention, and with an air of pity and interest. He even has me repeat some of the details, and yet some of his words and gestures betray him. Alas! I did not realize this until later. When I was able to think more calmly about this incident, it was impossible for me not to remember that the monk had on several occasions touched himself in ways that proved that the questions he asked of me were largely dictated by passion, and that not only did these questions linger over obscene details but even affected to place importance on the following five points: 1. Whether it was true that I was an orphan and born in Paris. 2. Whether I definitely had neither parents, nor friends, nor protectors, nor anyone finally to whom I could write. 3. Whether I had confided my intention to come there in no one but the shepherdess who had told me about the monastery, and whether I had arranged to meet her again on the way back. 4. Whether I had definitely not seen anyone since my rape, and whether I was sure that the man who had abused me had also done so on the side condemned by Nature as well as on the side that Nature allows. 5. Whether I thought I had not been followed and whether anyone had seen me enter the monastery.

Having satisfied himself on these questions with the most modest, the most sincere, and the most innocent of expressions: 'So then,' the monk said to me, getting to his feet and taking me by the hand, 'come, my child, tomorrow I shall give you the sweet satisfaction of taking communion at the foot of the icon that you have come to visit, but first let us attend to your basic needs,' and he led me to the back of the church...

'Where are you taking me?' I said to him with an anxiety which I felt unable to suppress... 'Why are we going inside?'

'Where else, charming pilgrim?' the monk replied, letting me into the sacristy. 'Are you afraid of spending the night with four holy hermits?!... Oh, you'll see that we shall find ways of entertaining you, my dear little angel, and if we are unable to give you great pleasure, at least you shall serve ours to the greatest degree.'

These words make me shiver. A cold sweat runs through me and I reel. It is night, no light guides our steps, and my terrified imagination places the spectre of death before my eyes, waving his scythe above my head. My knees give way... At this, the monk's expression suddenly changes, and he pulls me to my feet with a curse: 'Whore,' he says to me, 'walk! Don't think of moaning or resisting, because such things would be futile.'

These cruel words give me back my strength, I sense that I am lost if I weaken, and I get to my feet...

'Oh, Heaven!' I say to this villain, 'must I once again be the victim of my pious sentiments? Must the desire to get close to what is most respectable in religion be again punished as a crime!...'

We keep on walking, penetrating the darkest corridors where there is nothing to tell me where we are or what our destination will be. I was in front of Dom Severino, and could feel him breathing heavily and uttering incoherent words. One would have thought he was drunk. From time to time he would stop me, putting his left arm around my body while his right hand slid under my skirts from behind, impudently running it over that rude part that we share with men and which is the sole object of devotion for those who prefer this sex in their shameful pleasures. This libertine even dared on several occasions to run his mouth over this spot and into its most secret place. Then, we would start walking again. We come to a staircase, and at the bottom of thirty or forty steps a door opens, I am blinded by flashes of light, and we enter a charming and magnificently lit room. There, I see three monks and four girls seated around a table, being served by four other women who are completely naked. This scene makes me tremble. Severino gives me a push and I am in the room with him.

'Gentlemen,' he says as we enter, 'allow me to present a true phenomenon to you. Here is a Lucrecia who, though she bears on her shoulder the mark of a loose woman, has in her conscience all the candour, all the naivety of the Virgin... A single rape attack, my friends, and that was six years ago, so she's almost a Vestal Virgin... truly I give her to you as such... moreover, she has the most beautiful...

Oh, Clement, how you're going to enjoy this lovely flesh... what elasticity, my friend! What creaminess!'

'Oh, f——!' says Clement, half drunk, getting up and coming towards me, 'delighted to make her acquaintance! I must verify these facts!'

I will keep you in suspense with regard to my situation for as little time as possible, Madame (said Thérèse), but I am obliged to interrupt the thread of my story for a moment in order to describe the new people I find myself with. You know Dom Severino and have an idea of his tastes. Alas! His depravity in this area was such that he had never tasted other pleasures, and yet this was inconsequential for the operations of Nature, since his bizarre fantasy was to choose only narrow paths, and this monster was equipped with faculties that were so enormous that even the broadest of roads would have seemed too narrow to him.

As for Clement, his portrait has already been drawn. To his outward appearance, which I have already described, add ferocity, a tendency to tease, the most dangerous deceitfulness, an intemperate nature in every respect, a biting sarcasm, a corrupt soul, the cruel tastes of Rodin with regard to his pupils, no feelings, no delicacy, no religion, such a jaded temperament that for the last five years he had been incapable of enjoying any other pleasure than that for which barbarism had given him a taste, and you will have the most complete image of this vile man.

Antonin, the third actor of these detestable orgies, was forty years of age, small, thin, extremely vigorous, as redoubtably equipped as Severino and almost as wicked as Clement, and a devotee of the latter's pleasures, though indulging himself in them less fiercely; for while Clement's sole intention in practising this bizarre mania was to provoke and tyrannize over a woman, without which he could not obtain his pleasure, Antonin pursued them with delight, in all the purity of Nature, employing the element of flagellation solely to give the girl he was honouring with his favours more fire and more energy. In short, the former had a taste for brutality, while for the latter it was merely a refinement.

Jerome, the oldest of these four recluses, was also the most debauched one of them all. All the tastes and passions, all the most monstrous perversions came together in the soul of this monk. He combined the whims of the others with that of liking to receive upon himself that which his confederates gave to the girls, and if he was the agent (which was frequently the case) it was always on condition that he be treated the same way in his turn. Moreover, all the temples of Venus were the same to him, but as his strengths were beginning to decline, he nevertheless had for some years preferred the one which, requiring no effort from the agent, left the job of awakening sensations and producing ecstasy to the other person. The mouth was his favourite temple, and while he indulged himself in this pleasure of choice, he would employ a second woman to arouse him with the aid of birch-rods. Moreover, this man's character was just as sly, just as wicked, as those of the others, and whatever form vice might assume in him, he was sure immediately to find followers and temples in this infernal house. You will understand this more readily, Madame, when I explain its make-up to you. Prodigious funds had been acquired to provide the Order with this obscene retreat, which had existed for more than a hundred years and was always inhabited by the four richest and most advanced clerics of the Order, by those who were most high-born and whose libertinism was strong enough to warrant their being buried in this dark lair, the existence of which would never be revealed, as you will see from those things I have yet to explain. But let us return to the descriptions of its inhabitants.

The eight girls who were at supper that evening were so far apart in age that it would be impossible for me to sketch them for you collectively—an oddity that I found astonishing—and so I must necessarily confine myself to a few details. Let us begin with the youngest and proceed in that order.

The youngest of the girls was barely ten years old: the unkempt countenance of a child, with pretty features, the look of someone humiliated by her fate, nervous and trembling.

The second girl was fifteen years old: same nervous expression, an air of modesty forced upon her, but an enchanting face, and overall a very attractive girl.

The third was twenty years of age: an artist's dream model, blonde, with the most beautiful hair, fine, regular, gentle features; appeared more broken in.

The fourth was thirty: she was one of the most beautiful women it was possible to find; candour, honesty, and decency in her attitude, and all the virtues of a gentle soul.

The fifth was a young woman of thirty-six, three months pregnant: a brunette, full of life with lovely eyes, but one who, it seemed to me, had lost any remorse, any decency, any reserve she might have had.

The sixth was the same age: as tall as a tower and built in proportion to her height, with beautiful features, a true colossus whose shape was spoilt by plumpness; she was naked when I saw her, and I could easily make out that there was not a single part of her big body that did not bear the imprint of the brutality of those villains whose pleasures her unlucky star made her serve.

The seventh and eighth were two very beautiful women of about forty.

Let us now continue the story of my arrival in this foul place.

As I have already told you, I had scarcely entered when each of the monks came up to me. Clement was the boldest, and his vile mouth was soon glued to mine. I turned away in horror, but I was made to understand that any resistance would be nothing but affectation that would prove useless, and that the best thing for me to do was to follow the other girls' example.

'I'm sure you will understand,' Dom Severino said to me, 'that it would be futile to attempt any resistance in the inaccessible retreat in which you find yourself. You have, you say, experienced many woes, but the greatest one of all for a virtuous girl is still missing from the list of your misfortunes. Was it not high time that this proud virtue hit the rocks, and can one still be almost a virgin at the age of twenty-two? You can see here other girls who, like you, wished to resist when they first arrived and who, as you will prudently do, submitted in the end when they saw that their defensive attitude could only lead to their being badly treated. It is only right to point out to you, Thérèse,' continued the Father Superior, showing me scourges, birch-rods, ferulas, riding-switches, ropes, and numerous other kinds of instruments of torture... 'Yes, it is right for you to know that this is what we use with rebellious girls. Have a look and decide whether you wish to be convinced. In any case, what do you expect to find? Fairness? It has no place here. Humanity? Our only pleasure is to violate its laws. Religion? It counts for nothing with us. Our contempt for it increases the more we know of it. Parents? Friends? Judges? There is none of these in this place, my dear girl. All you will find here is egoism, cruelty, debauchery, and the most sustained impiety. Total submission is therefore your only option. Have a good look at the impenetrable refuge you're in. No living being ever comes here. The monastery could be invaded, searched, and set fire to, but this hiding-place would still not be discovered. It is an isolated construction, buried underground, surrounded on all sides by six unbelievably thick walls, and here you are, my girl, with four libertines who certainly have no wish to spare you and who will be excited all the more by your pleas, your tears, your utterances, your cries, and your prostrations. So who can you turn to for help? To that God that you have come to beg for help with so much zeal, and who rewards you for your fervour by luring you more effectively into the trap? The mythical God that we ourselves outrage daily here by insulting his vain laws? You can see, then, Thérèse, that there is no power of whatever kind you may suppose, that can manage to wrench you from our grasp. Not in the order of what is possible, nor in that of miracles is there any kind of means that may succeed in preserving any longer that virtue that you are so proud of, that may, in other words, prevent your becoming in every sense and in every way the victim of the libidinous excesses in which all four of us intend to indulge ourselves with you... So take your clothes off, whore, give your body to our lusts, let it be soiled by them this instant, or the most cruel treatment will prove to you those risks that a wretch like you runs in disobeying us.'

This speech... this terrible command, left me without options, I realized, but would I not have been at fault had I not said what my situation still permitted and my heart prompted me to say? I therefore threw myself at Dom Severino's feet, and employed all the eloquence of a soul in despair to beg him not to take advantage of my condition. I shed the bitterest tears in his lap, and dared to try out on this man everything I imagined to be the most persuasive, everything I believed to be the most pathetic... What use was any of this, dear Lord! Did I not know that tears are just one more attraction in the eyes of the libertine? How could I doubt that all of my attempts to move the hearts of these barbarians would merely serve to inflame them...?

'Take this bitch,' said Severino in fury, 'grab hold of her, Clement, strip her naked this minute. She must learn that compassion never stifles Nature among people like us.'

Clement was foaming at the mouth, my resistance having worked him up, and he grabbed me with a wiry arm. Punctuating his utterances and actions with terrible blasphemies, he ripped my clothes off in seconds.

'What a beautiful creature!' said the Father Superior, running his fingers over my back, 'may God strike me dead if I ever saw one better made! My friends,' this monk went on, 'let us put some order into our business. You know our welcome procedures, and she must go through all of them without exception. During this time, the other eight women must position themselves around us in order to anticipate our desires or to arouse them.'

Immediately a circle formed, I was placed in the middle, and there, for more than two hours, I was examined, considered, and touched by these four monks, receiving from each of them in turn either praise or criticism.

You will permit me, Madame (said our beautiful prisoner with a blush), to keep from you some of the obscene details of this odious ceremony. Let your imagination paint for you everything that debauchery may inspire wicked men to do in such circumstances. Let it see them move in turn from my fellow prisoners to me, let it compare, scrutinize, confront, and discourse, and it will truly still have only the faintest idea of what transpired. The initial orgies were doubtless rather mild compared with all of the horrors that I would soon undergo.

'Come,' said Severino whose prodigiously increased desires could no longer contain themselves, and who gave the impression in this terrible state of a tiger ready to devour its victim, 'let each one of us introduce her to his favourite enjoyment.'

Placing me on a couch in the attitude suited to his execrable plans, and getting two of his monks to hold me still, the evil man attempts to satisfy himself with me in that perverse and criminal manner that is only able to make us resemble the sex that we have not by denigrating that which we have. However, either the lewd man is too generously proportioned or Nature revolts in me at the very suggestion of such pleasures. He cannot overcome the obstacles. Scarcely has he presented himself than he is immediately repulsed… He withdraws, he pushes, he tears, but all of his efforts are in vain. This monster's fury directs itself to the altar that he wishes in vain to penetrate. He strikes it, pinches it, bites it. Fresh trials are born from the depths of his brutality. My pummelled flesh becomes more receptive, the pathway opens up, and the ram penetrates. I utter terrible cries. Soon the entire object is engulfed, and instantly spurting a venom that drains all his strength, the serpent finally yields with tears of rage at the movements I am making to free myself. I had never suffered so much in my whole life.

Clement comes forward. He is armed with birch-rods, his perfidious intentions transparent in the looks he gives me. 'Let me!' he says to Severino. 'Let me avenge you, Father. I shall punish this stupid creature for resisting your pleasures.'

He needs no one to hold me. Placing one arm around me, he pushes me onto one of his knees, thus lifting my stomach and making the place that will serve his whims more accessible. At first he makes a few tentative strokes, apparently intending only to try things out, but soon on fire with lust, the cruel man strikes as hard as he can. Nothing is exempt from his ferocity. From the middle of my back to the top of my legs, I feel the villain's attentions everywhere. Daring to fill these cruel moments with love, he glues his mouth to mine and breathes in those sighs that pain wrenches from me... My tears flow, he devours them, in turn kissing, threatening, and continuing to strike me. As he performs these actions, one of the women excites him. On her knees in front of him, she works at it in diverse ways with both hands. The more she succeeds, the greater the violence of the blows I receive. I am about to be torn apart, but there is no sign that my suffering is at an end. All may be exhausted, but in vain. The end that I await will be the work of his delirium alone. Suddenly, he is gripped by some fresh cruelty. My bosom is at this brute's mercy, it arouses him, the cannibal takes hold of it with his teeth and bites it. This excess precipitates the attack and the incense escapes. His ejaculations are accompanied by dreadful screams and terrible blasphemies, and the exhausted monk abandons me to Jerome.

'I shall not be any more dangerous to your virtue than Clement,' this libertine says to me, caressing the bleeding altar at which this monk has just made his sacrifice, 'but I want to kiss those cracks. To be worthy enough to open them up as well, I must pay them a little homage. I want more than that,' the old satyr continued, introducing one of his fingers where Severino had been, 'I want the hen to lay, and I want to eat its egg... is there one?... yes, indeed there is!... Oh, my child, how soft it is!...'*

His mouth takes the place of his fingers... I am told what I must do and perform the act with disgust. In the situation I am in, alas, how can I refuse! The shameless man is happy... he swallows, then getting me to kneel before him, he presses himself against me in this posture, and his ignominious passion is sated in a place that makes any complaint impossible. While he does all this, the fat woman whips him, and another, positioned level with his mouth, fulfils the same duty to which I have just been submitted.

'It is not enough,' says the villain, 'into each of my hands she must... One can't have too much of that sort of thing...'

The two prettiest girls approach. They obey. Such are the excesses to which Jerome is brought by the desire for satiety.

In any case, foul acts have made him happy, and half an hour later, with a repugnance that it is easy for you to divine, my mouth receives the disgusting homage of this vile man.

Antonin appears: 'Let's have a look at this virtue that is so pure,' he says. 'Damaged by a single assault, that can scarcely have left any trace.' His weapons have taken aim, and he would willingly profit from Clement's actions. As I have told you, active beatings please him as well as it does this monk, but as he is in a hurry, the state I have been left in by his confederate suffices for him. He examines this state of affairs, enjoys it, and leaving me in the posture so favoured by them all, for a moment he paws the two half moons that defend the entrance. He furiously shakes the temple porticos and has soon reached the sanctuary. Though just as violent as Severino's, the assault is made in a pathway less narrow and is not so hard to bear. The vigorous athlete seizes hold of my hips, and giving impetus to the movements that I cannot make, he furiously throws me up and down on top of him. It seems from the redoubled efforts of this Hercules that, not content with being master of the place, he intends to reduce it to powder. Such terrible attacks, which are so new to me, make me succumb, but without any concern for my pains, the cruel conqueror thinks only of increasing his pleasures. All the others stand around him, exciting him and abetting his lusts. Opposite him, raised up on my back, the fifteen-year-old girl, her legs wide open, offers his mouth the altar on which he is sacrificing with me, and at leisure he sucks up that precious sap of Nature, the emission of which is barely accorded by her to this young child. Kneeling before my victor's thighs, one of the old women excites them with her foul tongue, arousing his desires and driving them to the point of ecstasy, while the debauched man excites a woman with each of his hands, the better to inflame himself. There is not one of his senses that is not tickled, not one that does not contribute to the culmination of his delirium. He is close to it, but my unremitting horror of all of these infamies prevents me from sharing it... He reaches this alone, his thrusts, his cries, all announce it, and in spite of myself, I am inundated with the proofs of a fire which I was only the last to light. I finally collapse on the throne where I have just been sacrificed, my pain and my tears, my despair and my remorse now being my only signs of life.

However, Dom Severino orders the women to feed me, but I am a long way from accepting these attentions, and my mind is assailed by a fit of intense sorrow. I who made my virtue the foundation of all my happiness and all my glory, I who consoled myself for all the ills of fortune with my good behaviour, I could not bear the horrible idea of seeing myself so cruelly sullied by those from whom I might have expected the greatest succour and consolation. My tears flow in abundance, my cries echo through the rafters. I roll on the floor, beating my breast, tearing out my hair, calling out to my torturers and begging them to end my suffering... Would you believe it, Madame, this awful spectacle arouses them even more.

'Ah!' says Severino. 'No sight has ever excited me more than this! Look at the effect she's having on me, my friends. It's incredible what female suffering does to me!'

'Let's take her again,' says Clement, 'and to teach her for screaming like that, the wretched girl should be treated more cruelly in this second assault.'

This plan has scarcely been conceived than it is executed. Severino comes forward but despite what has just been said, his desires have need of a greater degree of arousal and it is only after he has employed Clement's cruel methods that he manages to find the strength necessary for the accomplishment of his new crime. Good God, what an excess of ferociousness! Could it be that these monsters intended to go so far as to choose a peak of my moral agony as violent as the one I was now experiencing to subject me to physical torments of such barbarity!

'It would be unfair for me not first and foremost to employ with this novice what serves us so well as a scenario,' says Clement as he begins to act, 'and I promise you that I will treat her no better than you have.'

'One moment,' says Antonin to the Father Superior whom he saw was about to grab hold of me again, 'while your zeal expresses itself in the posterior regions of this lovely girl, it seems to me that I can worship the God on the other side. We can place her between us.'

I am positioned such that I can again offer my mouth to Jerome. This is demanded of me, Clement puts himself in my hands, and I am forced to excite him. All of the priestesses surround this dreadful group, each one serving the actors within it, knowing how she should excite them further. Meanwhile, I must suffer it all, I alone bearing the full weight of it. Severino gives the signal, the other three closely follow, and for the second time, there I am shamefully soiled by the proofs of the disgusting lust of these shameless villains.

'That's enough for the first day,' says the Father Superior. 'Now she must be shown that her companions are treated no better than her.'

I am placed on a raised armchair, and there I am obliged to contemplate the new horrors that are to end the orgies.

The monks are in a line and all the sisters parade before them, receiving a stroke of the whip from each. They are then forced to excite their torturers with their mouths while the latter torment and insult them.

The youngest, the one who is ten years old, places herself on the couch and each cleric comes to subject her to a punishment of his choice. Next to her is the fifteen-year-old girl whom the monk that has just inflicted the punishment must enjoy in his own way. She's the butt of their jokes. The eldest of the girls must follow the monk whose turn it is, to serve him either in this operation or in the final act. Severino uses his hand alone to molest the girl who offers herself to him and wastes no time in penetrating the sanctuary that delights him and that is presented to him by the girl who has been placed nearby. Armed with a handful of nettles, the old woman does to him what he has just done himself. It is from these painful titillations that the intoxication of this libertine is born... If you ask him, will he admit to being cruel? He has done nothing that he does not himself endure.

Clement gently pinches the little girl's flesh. The pleasures on offer nearby are no longer available to him, but he receives the same treatment he has meted out and he leaves at the feet of his idol the incense that he no longer has the strength to throw into the sanctuary.

Antonin amuses himself by pummelling hard those fleshy parts of his victim's body. Inflamed by the leaps she is making, he falls upon that part of her body offered to his pleasures of preference. He is in turn pummelled and beaten, and he is intoxicated by these torments.

Old Jerome just uses his teeth, but every bite leaves a mark from which blood immediately spurts. After a dozen or so, their favourite victim offers him her mouth. There he quenches his fury while he is himself bitten as hard as he has done.

The monks drink and replenish their energies.* The thirty-six-year-old woman, three months pregnant as I have told you, is positioned by them on an eight-foot high pedestal. There being space for only one leg, she is obliged to keep the other one in the air. All around her are mattresses covered with brambles, holly, and thorns to a thickness of three feet, and she is given a flexible pole to support her. It is easy to see how, on the one hand, it is in her interest not to fall, and on the other, how impossible it is for her to keep her balance. It is these two alternatives that the monks find entertaining. All four ranged around her, each of them has one or two women to excite him in various ways during this spectacle. Pregnant though she is, the unfortunate woman maintains her position for nearly a quarter of an hour, but eventually her strength fails her, she falls onto the thorns, and our villains, drunk with lust, approach to deliver the abominable homage of their ferocity onto her body for the last time. They then retire.

Father Superior put me in the hands of one of his girls, aged thirty, of whom I have spoken to you. Her name was Omphale. She was charged with instructing me and settling me in to my new home, but I neither saw nor heard anything that first evening. Exhausted and in despair, my only thought was to find a little repose. In the bedchamber that was allocated to me I noticed other women who were not present at supper. I left the inspection of these new girls until the following day and focused only on resting a while. Omphale left me alone, going off to bed herself. I was scarcely in bed when the full horror of my fate presented itself to me most vividly. I could not get over either the insults I had suffered or those I had been made to witness. Alas! If sometimes my imagination had wandered into these pleasures, I had believed them to be as chaste as the God who inspired them, and given as consolation to humans by Nature. I assumed them to be born of love and delicacy. I was a long way from believing that man could only find pleasure by following the example of wild animals and making his neighbour tremble... Then thinking again about my lot as determined by fate... 'O just Heaven?' I said to myself, 'it is now absolutely clear to me that no act of virtue can flow from my heart without being immediately followed by suffering! And dear Lord, what harm was I doing, wanting to perform my religious devotions in this monastery? Did I offend against Heaven in wishing to pray to it? O incomprehensible decrees of Providence, deign to reveal yourself to me,' I continued, 'if you do not want me to rebel against you!' Bitter tears followed these reflections and I was still drowning in them when day broke. Omphale came up to my bed.

'Dear companion,' she said to me, 'I have come to exhort you to take courage. I wept just like you in the early days, but now I have become used to the situation and you will become accustomed to it as I have done. It is terrible at the beginning. It is not only the need to requite the passions of these debauchees that is the bane of our lives, it is the loss of our freedom and the way in which we were brought to this awful house.'

Unfortunates find consolation in the sight of others like them. However painful my suffering, I put it aside for a moment to ask my companion to tell me about the evils I should expect to encounter.

'One moment,' my teacher said to me, 'get up, let us first walk round our refuge and observe your new companions. We shall talk later.'

Following Omphale's advice, I saw that I was in a very large dormitory, containing eight fairly clean little beds. Next to each bed was a closet, but all the windows that lit either these closets or the bedchamber were raised five foot from the floor and barred inside and out. In the middle of the main chamber was a large table fixed to the floor for eating and working. The chamber had three other doors reinforced with iron. No iron bars on our side, and enormous bolts on the other.

'So this is our prison?' I said to Omphale.

'Alas, yes, my dear,' she replied. 'This is our only abode. The other eight girls have a similar room nearby, and we never communicate except when it pleases the monks to bring us together.'

I entered the closet that was to be mine. It was about eight foot square. Daylight came into it as with the other room through a very high window with iron bars. The only furniture consisted of a bidet, a washstand, and a night-commode. When I returned I was surrounded by my companions, who were eager to see me. There were seven of them, and I was number eight. Omphale, who lived in the other room, was in this one only to give me instructions. If I wished, she would stay there, and one of the other girls would replace her in her chamber. I requested this arrangement and it was agreed. But before I get to Omphale's story, it seems essential to me to paint the portrait of those seven new companions given to me by fate. I shall proceed in order of age as I have done for the others.

The youngest was twelve years old, with very animated and vivacious features, the most beautiful hair, and the prettiest of mouths.

The second was sixteen. She was one of the loveliest blondes that you could ever see, with truly delicious features and all the graces, all the gentleness of her years, combined with an attractive air, borne of her sadness, that made her a thousand times lovelier still.

The third was twenty-three: very pretty, but in my opinion the charms with which Nature had endowed her were spoilt by an excess of effrontery and impudence.

The fourth was twenty-six and was fashioned like Venus, though her curves were a little too pronounced; a dazzling white skin; a gentle, open, and humorous physiognomy, beautiful eyes, a mouth that was too large but which framed admirable teeth, and the loveliest blonde hair.

The fifth was thirty-two: she was four months pregnant, with a rather sad, oval face, huge eyes filled with animation, a very pale complexion, a delicate constitution, a gentle voice, and lacking in freshness; naturally libertine; I was told that she exhausted herself.

The sixth was thirty-three; a tall, strapping woman with the fairest countenance in the world and beautiful curves.

The seventh was thirty-eight; a true model of shape and beauty; she was the senior of my dormitory. Omphale warned me of her mean spirit and, in particular, of her taste for women.

'The real way to please her is to give in to her,' my companion told me, 'to resist her is to bring down on one's head all of the ills that can afflict us in this house. Think carefully about this.'

Omphale asked Ursule—this was the senior's name—for permission to instruct me. Ursule consented to this on condition that I would kiss her. I approached her. Her foul tongue met mine, while her fingers set to work to create feelings that she was a long way from obtaining from me. Yet, in spite of myself, I had to submit to everything, and when she thought she had triumphed she sent me back to my closet, where Omphale spoke to me in the following terms.

'All of the women you saw yesterday, my dear Thérèse, and those you have just seen, are divided into four groups of four girls each. The first is called the group of children, and contains girls from the tenderest age to sixteen years. They are identifiable from their white dress.

'The second group, whose colour is green, is called the group of the young, and contains girls from sixteen to twenty-one.

'The third is known as the group of the age of reason, and is dressed in blue. It contains women from twenty-one to thirty, and is the one in which we both find ourselves.

'The fourth group, dressed in bronze, is reserved for the more mature women and is composed of all those over thirty.

'The suppers of the reverend fathers either include these girls chosen indifferently from all groups, or else they appear by group. All depends on the whims of the monks, but outside the suppers they are mixed up in the two dormitories, as you can judge from those who inhabit our own.

'The instruction I have to give you', Omphale told me, 'must be contained in four principal categories. In the first, we shall consider everything that concerns the house. In the second, we shall place all that touches the girls' conduct, their punishment, their food, etc., etc., etc. The third category will instruct you regarding the organiza- tion of the monks' pleasures and the manner in which the girls serve them. The fourth will outline for you the history of discharges and changes.

'I shall not describe the approaches to this dreadful house, Thérèse, you know them as well as I do. I shall speak only about the interior. This has been shown to me so that I may paint a picture of it to new- comers and so that this instruction may remove from them any wish to escape. Yesterday Severino explained some of this to you and he did not deceive you, my dear. The church and the building attached to it make up what may strictly speaking be called the monastery, but you don't know the location of the lodgings we inhabit and how they are reached. At the end of the sacristy behind the altar is a door hid- den in the wood panelling and opened by a spring. This door leads into a corridor that is as dark as it is long, and the many turnings of which fear no doubt prevented you from noticing when you were brought in. First, this corridor descends because it has to pass under a ditch thirty feet deep, then it climbs up again on the other side of the ditch until it is a mere six feet beneath the ground, and in this way it arrives in the underground spaces of our building at about one quarter of a league's distance from the other one. Six thick surrounding fences make it impossible to see this building, even by climbing to the top of the church bell-tower. The reason for this is simple. The building is very low, at no more than twenty-five feet in height, while the fences, some of which consist of walls, others of quickset hedges growing very close to each other, are each more than fifty feet high. From whichever side you look at this section, therefore, it can only be taken for a copse in the forest, but never for a place of habitation. As I have just said, it is thus through a trapdoor leading into the underground spaces that can be found the exit to the dark corridor that I have just described and which it is impossible for you to recall, given the state you must have been in when you went through it. This building here, my dear, is composed of underground caverns, a suite of rooms on another floor, a mezzanine, and a first floor. Above is a very thick roof, on top of which is a lead basin filled with earth in which evergreen bushes are planted and which, combined with the hedges that surround us, give the whole thing the appearance of a still more real-looking piece of land. The underground caverns form a large room in the centre and eight closets around it, two of which serve as dungeons for girls who have merited this punishment, and the other six as cellars. Above is located the supper room, kitchens, pantries, and two closets where the monks spend time when they wish to indulge in solitary pleasures with us away from the eyes of their fellow brothers. The mezzanines are composed of eight dormitories, four of which have a closet. These are the cells where the monks sleep and where they take us when their lubriciousness requires us to share their beds. The other four dormitories are those of the servant brothers, one of whom is our jailer, the second the monks' valet, the third their surgeon, who has everything required for emergencies in his cell, and the fourth is the cook. These four brothers are deaf and dumb. As you can see, there would be little point in expecting any help or consolation from them. Anyway, they never stop to speak to us and we are strictly forbidden from talking to them. The upper floor of these mezzanines houses the two seraglios.

They are both perfectly identical. It's as you can see, a large bed-chamber containing eight closets. So, as you can imagine, my dear girl, even supposing one could smash the bars of our casement-windows and get down through the window, we would be a long way from being able to escape, since we would still have to cross five quickset hedges, a thick, high wall, and a wide ditch. Even if we did manage to overcome these obstacles, where would we find ourselves? In the courtyard of the monastery, which is itself thoroughly secured and which, it would be immediately obvious, could not offer any guaranteed way out. One means of escape, less perilous maybe, would, I confess, be to find in our underground caverns the mouth of the passage that leads there, but how could we reach these caverns which, like us, are perpetually enclosed? Even if we could reach them, we still could not find this opening. It leads into some hidden corner unknown to us and itself barricaded with metal grilles for which they alone have the key. However, even if all of these obstacles could be overcome and we reached the passageway, the road would be no safer for us. It is full of traps known only to them, and into which those who tried to follow it without them would inevitably fall. You must therefore renounce all hope of escaping, Thérèse, because it is impossible. Let me tell you that if it were feasible I would have fled this detestable place long ago, but it cannot be done. Those who are here leave only when they die, hence the haughty, cruel, and tyrannical behaviour of these villains towards us. Nothing fires their imagination like the impunity guaranteed them by this inaccessible retreat. Certain never to have any other witnesses of their excesses but the very victims that requite their lusts, quite sure that their crimes will never be revealed, they carry them to the most odious extremes. Free of all legal restraints, having infringed those of religion, uninhibited by remorse, there is no atrocity that they do not allow themselves, and in this criminal apathy their abominable passions are all the more voluptuously titillated by the knowledge that nothing, they say, inflames them as much as solitude and silence, as much as weakness on the one hand and impunity on the other. The monks sleep regularly every night in this building, they come here at five o'clock in the evening, and return to the monastery the following morning at around nine o'clock, except for one of them whose turn it is to spend the day here and who is known as the duty officer. We shall examine his work presently. As for the four brothers, they never budge. In every dormitory we have a bell which rings in the jailer's cell. Only the senior has the right to ring, but when she does so, when she or we are in need of help, this immediately arrives. When they return each day the fathers bring all necessary provisions themselves and entrust them to the cook, who uses them as ordered. There is a fountain in the underground caverns, and all kinds of wine in abundance in the cellars. Let us move on to the second category, pertaining to the girls' dress, their food, punishment, etc.

'Our number is always the same. Things are arranged in such a way that there are always sixteen of us, or eight in each dormitory, and as you can see, always wearing the uniform of our group. No day goes by without our being given the clothes of the group which we are entering. Every day we wear the underclothes in that colour belonging to our group. In the evening we are in dressing-gowns of this same colour, our hair done as best we can. The senior of the dormitory has total power over us and it is a crime to disobey her. She is entrusted with the job of inspecting us before we present ourselves at the orgies, and if things are not in the desired state, she is punished the same as we are. The faults we can commit are of several types. Each one carries its own particular penalty, the list of which is posted in both bedchambers. The duty officer, the person who, as I shall explain to you presently, comes to give us our orders, selects the girls for supper, inspects our living-quarters, and hears the senior's complaints, this monk, I say, is the one who each evening doles out the punishment that each girl has merited. Here is the list of these punishments according to the crimes that have incurred them:

'Not getting up in the morning at the prescribed hour, thirty lashes of the whip (for it is almost always in this manner that we are punished, it being relatively simple for an episode of these libertines' pleasures to become their correction of choice); presenting, either by misunderstanding or by any cause whatever, a part of the body in the act of pleasure instead of the one desired, fifty lashes; having the wrong clothes or hairstyle, twenty lashes; failing to give advance warning of a period, sixty lashes; on the day when the surgeon has confirmed your pregnancy, a hundred lashes; negligence, inability, or refusal in all matters of lust, two hundred lashes. And how many times does their infernal wickedness find fault with us here when we have not committed the slightest error? How many times does one of them suddenly demand what he knows full well we have just accorded to another, and which cannot therefore be repeated straightaway? Yet we still have to suffer the punishment. Our complaints and pleadings are never listened to. We must obey or be punished. Errors of conduct in the chamber or disobedience to the senior, sixty lashes. A tearful, sorrowful, or remorseful appearance, and even the slightest suggestion of a return to religious belief, two hundred lashes. If a monk chooses you to taste the final stages of pleasure with you and he cannot enjoy these, whether it's his fault, which is very common, or whether it's yours, three hundred lashes on the spot. The slightest air of revulsion at the monks' propositions, of whatever nature these might be, two hundred lashes. A plan to escape, a rebellion, nine days imprisonment, completely naked, and three hundred lashes of the whip every day. Conspiracies, unruly gatherings, mutinous whisperings involving one or more, as soon as these are discovered, three hundred lashes. Plans to commit suicide, refusal to eat properly, two hundred lashes. Any show of disrespect to the monks, one hundred and eighty lashes. These are our only rules, otherwise we can do whatever we like. We can sleep together, argue, fight between ourselves, indulge in the greatest excesses of drunkenness and gluttony, swear and blaspheme. None of these things are of any consequence, and not a single word is said to us about these faults. We are scolded only for those which I have just told you about, but the overseers can spare us much of this trouble if they so wish. Unfortunately, this protection is bought only with favours that are often more disagreeable than the punishments they earn. They have the same tastes in both dormitories, and it is only by granting them favours that one can manage to gag them. If one refuses to give them what they ask, they multiply the sum of one's faults beyond all reason, and far from scolding them for their injustice, the monks we serve constantly encourage them to do this, doubling the penalties. They are themselves subject to all the same rules, and moreover, are very severely punished if they are suspected of being indulgent. It is not that these libertines need all of this to deal severely with us, but they are delighted to have excuses. Our natural looks lend charm to their lust which feeds upon it. We are each given a small provision of linen when we arrive here. Everything is given to us by the half-dozen, and renewed annually, but we have to surrender what we bring. We are not allowed to keep the slightest little thing. Any complaints from the four brothers I spoke to you about and from the overseer are heard, and we are punished merely on their say-so. However, at least they expect nothing from us, and there is less to fear from them than from the overseers, who are very demanding and extremely dangerous when their behaviour is driven by capriciousness or revenge. Our food is very good and always in great abundance. If they did not derive pleasure from this, perhaps this aspect would not be so favourable, but as their filthy debauches benefit from it, they spare no expense to gorge us with food. Those who like to whip us keep us nice and plump, and those who, as Jerome was telling you yesterday, like to watch the hen lay, thanks to an abundance of food, are sure of a greater quantity of eggs. Consequently, we are served four times a day. We are given breakfast between nine and ten o'clock, and we always have poultry with rice, fresh or stewed fruit, tea, coffee, or chocolate. Dinner is served at one o'clock. Each table of eight is served the same food: an excellent soup, four entrées, a roast dish and four side-dishes, and dessert in all seasons. At half-past five, tea is served, and we have fruit or patisseries. Supper is of course excellent if it is taken with the monks. If we do not share this, as there are only four of us per bedchamber, we are served three roast dishes and four side-dishes at the same time. We each have a daily ration of one bottle of white wine, one of red, and half a bottle of liqueur. Those who do not drink so much are free to give their share to others. There are some very greedy girls among us who drink an astonishing amount, get drunk, and are not reprimanded for any of this. The same applies to those for whom these four meals are still not enough. They only have to ring and they are immediately brought what they ask for. The overseers force us to eat at meals, and if a girl persisted in not wanting to do so, for whatever reason, the third time she would be severely punished. The monks' supper is composed of three roast dishes, six entrées followed by a cold dish and eight side-dishes, fruit, three different sorts of wine, coffee, and liqueurs. Sometimes all eight of us are at table with them. Sometimes they force four of us to serve them, and these girls eat later. It also happens from time to time that they have only four girls at supper, and then an entire group is together, but when there are eight of us, there are always two girls from each group. Needless to say, no one from the outside ever visits us. No stranger under any pretext whatever is admitted into this building. If we fall ill we are looked after by the brother surgeon alone, and if we die it is without any religious succour. We are tossed into one of the gaps between the hedges, and that's that, but incredibly cruel though it may sound, if the illness becomes too grave or if contagion is feared, they do not wait until we are dead to bury us. We are taken and placed where I have told you while still alive. During the eighteen years since I've been here I have seen more than ten instances of this unparalleled ferocity. Their answer to that is that it is better to lose one than to risk the loss of sixteen, and moreover, that the life of a girl is such a small loss, and one which is so easily replaced, that it can be the cause of few regrets. Let us move on to the organization of the monks' pleasures and to all that pertains to this subject.

'We rise here at exactly nine o'clock in the morning in all seasons. We retire to bed at a late hour more or less, owing to the monks' supper. As soon as we are up, the duty officer arrives to make his inspection. He sits in a big armchair and there, each of us is obliged to go and stand before him, her skirts raised on the side he likes. He touches, he kisses, he examines, and when all have fulfilled this duty, he selects those who must attend at supper. He prescribes for them the state in which they must present themselves, he hears complaints from the overseer, and punishments are imposed. They rarely leave without requiring some lewd scene of debauchery in which all eight of us take part. The superior directs these libidinous acts, which demand the most complete submission on our part. It is often the case that before breakfast one of the reverend fathers summons one of us to his bed. The brother jailer brings a card bearing the name of the girl required, and even if the duty officer is occupied with her, he does not have the right to retain her, she leaves and comes back when she is dismissed. Once this first ceremony is finished, we have breakfast. From then on until the evening we have nothing to do, but at seven o'clock in the summer and six in the winter they come to fetch those who have been chosen. Brother jailer leads them away himself, and after supper those who are not kept for the night return to the seraglio. Often no one stays, it being the new girls who are sent for to spend the night. They are also told several hours in advance what they should wear and where they are to go. Sometimes there is only the duty girl who sleeps over.'

'The duty girl,' I interrupted, 'what is this new position?'

'It's this,' replied my storyteller. 'On the first of every month each monk adopts a girl who must be his servant and butt of his shameless desires. Only the overseers are excused because of their dormitory duties. They can neither change them in the course of the month, nor choose them two months in succession. There is nothing so cruel, so harsh, as the duties this service involves, and I don't know how you will take to it. As soon as the clock strikes five in the afternoon the duty girl goes down to the monk she serves, staying with him until that time the following day when he re-enters the monastery. She meets up with him again as soon as he comes back. She spends the few intervening hours eating and resting, for she has to stay awake during those nights she spends with her master. Let me repeat that this unfortunate girl is there to serve as butt to all of the whims that may pass through this libertine's head: blows, whippings, beatings, indecent proposals, orgasms, she has to endure it all. She must be up all night in her boss's bedchamber, always ready to lend herself to the passions that may excite this tyrant. But the most cruel, the most ignominious instance of this servitude is the awful obligation she is under to make her mouth or her breasts available to either one of this monster's needs. He never uses any other vessel, she must receive it all, and the slightest repugnance is immediately punished with the most barbaric torments. In all the scenes of lust it is these girls who assist in their pleasures, who take care of them, and who mop up any dirt. If a monk is soiled when he has just enjoyed a woman, it is up to the next girl to clean it with her mouth. Should he wish to be excited, it is this unfortunate's duty, she must accompany him to any spot, dress him, undress him, in short, be ready to serve him at any moment. She is always in the wrong, and always beaten. At supper, her place is either behind her master's chair or at his feet like a dog, under the table or kneeling between his thighs, exciting him with her mouth. Sometimes she serves as his seat or his candlestick. At other times all four girls will be positioned around the table in the most lewd, and yet at the same time the most awkward, attitudes. If they lose their balance, they risk either falling onto thorns placed nearby, or breaking a limb, or even getting killed, which is not unheard of, and meanwhile the villains rejoice and debauch them-selves, over-indulging themselves as they please with food, wine, lust, and cruelty.'

'Oh, Heaven!' I said to my companion, trembling with horror, 'how can one take things to such extremes? What a hellish place!'

'Listen, Thérèse, listen, my child, you are still a long way from knowing everything,' said Omphale. 'The state of pregnancy, which is revered outside in the world, is certain to attract the censure of these monsters, and does not excuse a girl from punishment or from duties. On the contrary, it is a cause of suffering, humiliation, and anxiety. How many times have their blows brought about abortions in those whose fruit they decide not to pick, and if they do pick it, it is in order to enjoy it. What I am telling you here should be enough to persuade you to avoid falling into that condition as long as possible.'

'But how can one?'

'Without a doubt, there are certain sponges...,* but if Antonin catches sight of them, you won't escape his wrath. The surest way is to stifle the voice of Nature by calming their fantasies, and with such villains this is not difficult. Moreover,' continued my teacher, 'there are contiguous and related matters here which you would not suspect, and which it is right to explain to you, but as these belong to the fourth category, that is, that of our recruits, discharges, and changes, I shall move on to this category and include this small detail in it. You are not unaware, Thérèse, that the four monks who make up this monastery are at the head of the Order, all four being from distinguished families, and all four rich in their own right. Independently of the considerable funds provided by the Benedictine Order for the upkeep of this voluptuous retreat, to which all hope to come in their turn, those who are here contribute a considerable part of their wealth to these funds. These two sources of income together amount to more than a hundred thousand écus a year, which are spent only on fresh recruits and household expenses. They have a dozen women on whom they can absolutely rely, and whose sole duty is to bring them each month a girl between the ages of twelve at the least and thirty at the most. The subject must be free from any fault and endowed with the greatest possible number of qualities, but above all she must be high-born. These abductions, all well paid for and always carried out a long way from here, never entail any drawbacks. I have never heard of any pursuits. The extreme care they take keeps them hidden from the world. They place no value whatsoever on virginity, so that a girl who has already been seduced or a married woman is equally pleasing to them. On the other hand, there must be an abduction and it must be recorded. These circumstances excite them. They want to be certain that their crimes cost tears, which is why they would send away any girl who came to them voluntarily. If you had not defended yourself so ferociously, they would not have recognized a true profundity of virtue in you, and consequently, the certainty that they were committing a crime, and they would have sent you away within twenty-four hours. Thus, all those here are of the noblest origins, Thérèse. You are looking, dear friend, at the only daughter of the Comte of ——, snatched in Paris at the age of twelve, and ensured of a dowry of one hundred thousand écus one day. I was taken from the arms of my governess, who was conducting me on her own by coach from one of my father's country estates to the Abbey of Panthemont where I was brought up. My governess disappeared—she had probably been bribed—and I was brought here post-haste. The same is true of all of the others. The twenty-year-old girl belongs to one of the most distinguished families of Poitou. The sixteen-year-old is the daughter of the Baron of ——, one of the greatest lords of Lorraine. Counts, dukes, and marquises are the fathers of the twenty-three-year-old, the twelve-year-old, and the thirty-two-year-old, so there is not a single girl here who cannot lay claim to the noblest of titles, and not one that is not treated with the greatest ignominy. However, not content with such horrors, these dishonest men also wished to dishonour their very closest relatives. The young lady of twenty-six, without a doubt one of the most beautiful among us, is the daughter of Clement, and the thirty-six-year-old is Jerome's niece.

'As soon as a new girl has arrived in this cesspit of impurity, once she has been taken from the world forever, another girl is immediately taken away, and this, dear girl, this is the complement of our suffering. The cruellest of our woes is not to know what happens to us in these terrible and worrying discharges. It is absolutely impossible to say what becomes of us on leaving this place. We have as much proof as our solitude enables us to acquire that the girls substituted for by the monks never reappear. They themselves inform us of this. They do not hide from us that this retreat is our tomb, but do they murder us? Dear Heaven! Could murder, the most execrable of crimes, be for them what it was for the infamous Maréchal de Retz,* a kind of jouissance the cruelty of which, titillating their perfidious imagination, might plunge their senses into a greater intoxication?[1] Accustomed to find pleasure in pain alone, to find pleasure only in torments and torture, could it be possible that they are deluded

---

[1] See *The History of Brittany* by Dom Lobineau.*

enough to believe that, by redoubling, by increasing the initial cause of their delirium, they are bound to make it more perfect? As lacking in principles as they are in faith, morals, or virtues, and profiting from the misfortunes into which their initial crimes plunged us, could these rascals seek satisfaction in a second crime that took our life? I know not... if they are quizzed about it, they mumble, at times responding in the negative, at times in the affirmative. What is certain is that, in spite of the promises they have made to us to complain to the authorities about these people and to work to free us, not one of these girls has ever kept her word... Once again, I say, do the monks placate us, or do they make it impossible for us to bring charges? When we ask those who arrive to give us news of those who have left us, they never know anything. So what happens to these unfortunates? That's what torments us. That's the dreadful uncertainty that fills our days with misery. I've been in this house for eighteen years and I've already seen more than two hundred girls leave... Where are they? They all swore to serve us, so why has not a single one kept her word?

'Moreover, nothing explains why we're kept here... age, changes in our looks, nothing makes any difference... their only rule is capriciousness. They'll send away today the girl they caressed the most yesterday, and the one they're most tired of they'll keep for ten years. That's the story of the overseer of this dormitory. She's been in the house for twelve years, and she's still fêted; I've seen them send away fifteen-year-old children whose beauty would have made the Graces jealous, just so they could keep her. The girl who left a week ago was not even sixteen. She was as lovely as Venus herself, and they had enjoyed her for less than a year, but she fell pregnant, which as I have told you, Thérèse, is a serious failing in this house. Last month they got rid of a seventeen-year-old, a year ago a twenty-year-old, eight months pregnant, and recently a girl the instant she felt the first pains of labour. Don't imagine that conduct makes any difference, because I've seen girls who were attentive to their every desire and who left after six months, while they have kept other girls who are sullen and temperamental for many years. So there is no point in recommending a particular kind of behaviour to our new arrivals. The whims of these monsters infringe all taboos, and are the only laws governing their actions.

'When a girl is to be sent away, she is informed of this in the

morning, never earlier than that. The duty officer appears at nine
o'clock as usual, and he says, I suppose: "Omphale, the Monastery is
discharging you, I shall come to fetch you this evening." Then he
continues with his duties, but you do not show yourself to him at
inspection. Then he goes out. The girl dismissed embraces her companions, she promises again and again to serve their interests, to
lodge a complaint, to let everyone know what is going on, the time
comes, the monk appears, the girl leaves, and nothing more is ever
heard of her. Meanwhile, the supper takes place as usual. The only
things we have noticed on such days is that the monks rarely reach
the final phases of their pleasures. It is as if they are holding themselves back, and yet they drink much more, sometimes even to the
point of intoxication. They send us away much earlier in the evening,
without keeping a single girl to sleep with, those girls on duty retiring
to the seraglio.'

'Very well,' I said to my companion, 'if no one has kept her promise, it is because you have been dealing only with weak creatures, who
are easily intimidated, or with children who have not dared to do
anything for you. I am not afraid of being killed, at least, I don't
believe that is what is happening. Reasonable men cannot possibly
take their criminal actions so far... I realize that... After what I have
seen, perhaps I should not excuse these men as I do, but it is not possible, my dear, for them to commit horrors the very notion of which
is inconceivable. Oh, my dear friend,' I continued with affection,
'will you make that same promise with me which I swear I shall not
break?... will you?'

'Yes.'

'Well, then, I swear to you on all that I hold most sacred, on the
God who gives me breath and whom alone I adore... I promise that I
shall destroy these infamies, or that I shall die in the attempt. Will
you make the same promise to me?'

'You need not doubt it,' replied Omphale, 'but you must realize
that these promises are pointless. Girls who were angrier than you,
more determined, better connected, and who were, in short, the most
loyal friends, have failed to keep the same oaths. Permit me, my dear
Thérèse, given my cruel experience, to regard our own vows as vain
and not to place any more faith in them.'

'What of the monks?' I said to my friend, 'are there also changes
among them? Do new ones frequently arrive?'

'No,' she replied, 'Antonin has been here for ten years, Clement for eighteen years, Jerome for thirty, and Severino for twenty-five. The Father Superior was born in Italy and is a close relative of the Pope's, with whom he is on good terms. It's only since he has been here that the alleged miracles of the Virgin have assured the monastery's reputation and have prevented its scandalmongering enemies from observing what goes on here too closely. However, the house was already established just as you see it now when he arrived here. It has operated in the same way for more than a hundred years, and during this time all of the Father Superiors who have come have maintained an order so advantageous to their pleasures. Severino, the greatest libertine of his century, got himself posted here with the sole intention of leading a life conducive to his tastes. His intention is to preserve the secret privileges of this abbey for as long as he can. We belong to the diocese of Auxerre, but whether the Bishop is aware of them or not, we never see him appear here, he never ever sets foot in the monastery. Generally speaking, very few people come here, except around the time of the festival of Our Lady in August. From what the monks tell us, fewer than ten people a year come to this house. Nevertheless, whenever a group of strangers do present themselves the Father Superior is probably careful to receive them well. They are impressed by an outward appearance of piety and austerity, and they go away happy, praising the monastery, and these criminals enjoy an impunity deriving from the good faith of the people and the credulity of the devout.'

Omphale had scarcely ended her instruction when the clocks chimed nine o'clock. The overseer called to us to come quickly, and indeed the duty officer appeared. This was Antonin. We lined up, as was the custom. He cast a lazy eye over the group, counted us, and then sat down. We then went one by one to raise our skirts in front of him, as far as the navel on one side, and the middle of the back on the other. Antonin received this homage with the indifference of satiety, and without the slightest emotion. Then, looking at me, he asked me how I was coping with the experience. Seeing that all I could do in response was to shed tears… 'She'll get used to it,' he said with a laugh, 'there is not a house in France where girls are better educated than here.' He took the list of the guilty from the hands of the overseer, then, still addressing me, he made me tremble. Every gesture, every movement that seemed certain to submit me to the will of these libertines was for me like a death sentence. Antonin orders me to sit at the edge of a bed, and once I am in this position, he tells the over-seer to come uncover my breasts and lift up my skirts to just beneath them. He himself then places my legs as far apart as possible, and sits directly opposite me. One of my companions comes and positions herself on top of me in the same attitude, so that it is the altar of reproduction that offers itself to Antonin instead of my face, and if he comes, he will have these attractions level with his mouth. A third girl kneeling before him excites him with her hand, while a fourth girl, totally naked, points out with her fingers those parts of my body that he should strike. Imperceptibly, this girl excites me as well, and with both his hands, Antonin repeats what she is doing to me to the two other girls on either side of him. You cannot imagine the bad language and obscene suggestions that this debauchee uses to excite himself. Eventually, he is in the state he wishes to be in and is led to me, while all the others work to arouse him as he is about to come, fully exposing his posterior parts. Omphale grabs hold of them, doing all she can to excite them, rubbing, kissing, and defiling them, and burning with lust, Antonin hurls himself upon me... 'I want her to get pregnant this time,' he says furiously... These moral turpitudes precipitate the physical crisis. Antonin, whose habit was to utter ter-rible cries in these final moments of his intoxication, lets out a dread-ful shriek. All the girls surround him, doing what they can to inten-sify his ecstasy, and the libertine reaches this amidst the most bizarre episodes of lust and depravity.

These kinds of groupings were often performed, it being the rule that whenever a monk came in whatever manner this might happen, all of the girls should then surround him in order to arouse his senses from every direction, so that, if I may be allowed to express myself thus, pleasure might penetrate him more effectively through every single pore.

Antonin went out and had breakfast served to him. My compan-ions forced me to eat, which I did to please them. We had barely finished eating when the Father Superior came in. Seeing us still at table, he excused us from performing the same ceremonies for him as those we had just performed for Antonin. 'We must think of dressing her,' he said looking at me. So saying, he opened a wardrobe and threw onto my bed several pieces of clothing of the colour stipulated for my class. 'Try on all of these,' he said to me, 'and give me your own clothes.'

I did what he told me, but suspecting this would happen, I had prudently taken out my money during the night and hidden it in my hair. As each garment was removed, Severino's eagle eyes fixed themselves on that part uncovered and his hands immediately wandered over it. When I was half-naked the monk seized hold of me, placing me in the position most suited to his pleasures, that is to say, the exact reverse of that attitude which Antonin had just required of me. I should like to have asked him for mercy, but seeing that his eyes were already full of fury I thought it best to show obedience. I positioned myself as required, the others surrounded him, his attention fixed on the obscene altar that delighted him. His hands squeezed it, his mouth glued itself to it, his eyes devoured it... he was at the pinnacle of pleasure.

If it is acceptable to you, Madame (said the beautiful Thérèse), I am going to confine myself to an abbreviated account of the first month I spent in this monastery, that is, of the main episodes of this period. The rest would be too repetitive. The monotony of my stay there would convey itself to my story, and so it seems best to move immediately thereafter to the event that finally got me out of this foul cesspit.

I was not expected at supper on this first day, but merely called upon to spend the night with Dom Clement. Following the custom, I presented myself at his cell a few moments before he was due to return. The brother jailer took me there and locked me inside. He arrived as intoxicated by wine as by lust, followed by the twenty-six-year-old who at that time was his duty girl. Having been told what I must do, I knelt down as soon as I heard him coming. He came up to me, looked at me carefully as I humiliated myself before him, then ordered me to get up and to kiss him on the mouth. He savoured this kiss for several minutes, getting as much out of it as it was possible to do. While this was going on, Armande, as the girl who served him was called, undressed me bit by bit. She began by uncovering my bottom, and when she had done so she quickly turned me round in order to expose to her uncle that organ so dear to his tastes. Clement examined it, touched it, then sitting in an armchair, he ordered me to come and let him kiss it. Armande, in between his knees, excited him with her mouth, while Clement thrust his own into the sanctuary of the temple that I presented to him, his tongue straying into the path located in its centre. His hands explored the same altars in Armande, but as he found the clothing that the girl still wore to be in the way, he ordered her to remove it, which she quickly did, repositioning herself close to her uncle so that, arousing him with her hand, she was also more easily accessible to Clement's grasp. The unholy monk, similarly preoccupied with me, then ordered me to fill his mouth as freely as possible with those winds that my bowels might produce. This fancy seemed revolting to me, but I was still far from knowing all the irregularities of debauchery. I obeyed and soon suffered from the effects of this intemperance. His arousal being even stronger, the monk became more ardent, and suddenly bit into the globes of flesh I was presenting to him in six different places. I let out a cry and leap forward, he gets up and comes towards me with anger in his eyes, asking me if I know what I am risking by disturbing him... I apologize profusely, he seizes me by my corset which still covers my bosom and tears it off together with my shirt in less time than I am taking to tell you about it... He brutally grabs hold of my breasts, calling them names and squeezing them hard. Armande undresses him, and so all three of us are now naked. For a moment he is preoccupied with Armande, furiously smacking her with his hand. He kisses her on her mouth, biting her tongue and lips, and she cries out. At times the pain brings tears from the girl's eyes in spite of herself. He gets her to climb onto a chair and demands the same act from her that he required of me. Armande complies while I excite him with one hand and whip him gently with the other, and during this lust he also bites Armande, but she contains herself and does not dare move. However, the monster's teeth have imprinted themselves on the skin of this lovely girl, and the marks are visible in several places. Then, turning suddenly, he says to me: 'Thérèse, you are going to suffer cruelly.' (He need not have said this, his eyes betraying his intentions all too clearly.) 'You shall be beaten all over,' he tells me, and so saying, he has again seized hold of my breasts, which he is handling roughly, rubbing the ends with the tips of his fingers, and causing me very sharp pains. I dared not say anything for fear of antagonizing him further, but my brow was covered in perspiration, and in spite of myself my eyes filled with tears. He turns me around and makes me kneel on the edge of a chair with my hands holding the back. I am not to move even for an instant under pain of the gravest consequences. Once I am finally in position and well within his reach, he orders Armande to bring him birch-rods, and she hands him a long, thin bundle. Clement grabs them and, advising me not to move, he begins with twenty or so blows on my shoulders and the top of my back. He then leaves me for a moment, and comes back to take Armande and place her six feet away from me, also on her knees on the edge of a chair. He declares to us that he is going to whip both of us together, and that the first of the two of us to let go of the chair, to utter a cry, or to shed a tear will immediately be subjected by him to any punishment that he deems fitting. He applies the same number of blows to Armande as he has just given me, in exactly the same places. He seizes hold of me again, kisses every spot that he has just molested, and, raising the switches, he says to me: 'Hold very still, whore, you're going to be treated like the lowest creature you are.' With these words, he delivers fifty strokes concentrated exclusively from the middle of the shoulders to the lower back. He then turns to my companion and treats her in the same manner. We did not utter a word. All that could be heard were a few low, restrained groans, and we had enough strength to hold back our tears. However strongly aroused the monk's passions were, however, no sign of them was yet apparent. From time to time he became very excited, but without anything popping up. Approaching me closely, he spends a few moments inspecting the two still-intact globes of flesh which are about to endure the same onslaught in their turn. He squeezes them and cannot resist pushing them apart, tickling them, and kissing them again repeatedly. 'Come on,' he says, 'be brave...' Blows instantly rain down on these mounds, bruising my flesh down to my thighs. Extremely animated by the way I'm jumping up and down, and by the grinding of my teeth and the contortions that the pain wrenches from me, observing them with delight, he expresses the sensations that grip him on my mouth, embracing it with ardour... 'I like this girl,' he cries, 'there's not one I've whipped that has given me so much pleasure,' and turns to his niece, treating her with the same barbarity. There remained the lower part of the body from the top of the thighs down to the ankles, both of which he struck with the same ardour. 'Come,' he says again, turning me round, 'let's change hands and have a go here.' He gave me around twenty strokes from the middle of my stomach to the bottom of my thighs, then, making me spread them, he struck me hard inside the lair that my position exposed to him. 'There's the bird I want to pluck,' he said. A few lashes having penetrated quite deeply, owing to the care he was taking, I could not stifle my cries. 'Aha!' said the villain, 'I've found your sensitive spot. We shall very soon visit it more thoroughly.' Meanwhile, his niece is placed in the same posture and treated in the same manner. He finds in her too the most delicate spots of a woman's body, but whether out of habit or courage or fear of incurring harsher treatment, she has the strength to contain herself, and only a few shudders and involuntary twitches are noticeable. However, some changes occurred in the physical state of this libertine, and although things still had very little consistency, the constant action of rubbing seemed to be producing results.

'Kneel down,' the monk said to me, 'I am going to whip you on your bosom.'

'On my bosom, Father?'

'Yes, on these two lubricious lumps that excite me only when I do this.' So saying, he squeezed and squashed them violently.

'Oh, Father! This part of my body is so delicate that you're going to kill me.'

'That doesn't matter as long as I am satisfied,' he said, and he applied five or six more blows which I was fortunately able to fend off with my hands. Seeing this, he ties them behind my back, and because he has cruelly ordered me to keep silent, all I have now to beg for mercy are my facial expressions and my tears. I therefore attempt to move him... but in vain. He aims a dozen savage blows at my breasts, which I can no longer defend. Terrible lashes dig into my flesh, marking it instantly with my blood. The pain caused me to shed tears that fell upon the traces of this monster's rage, rendering them, according to him, a thousand times more attractive... He kissed them, he devoured them, returning again and again to my mouth and my eyes swimming in tears which he sucked lubriciously. Armande is positioned, her hands are bound, and she offers up her beautifully rounded bosom, as white as alabaster. Clement makes as if to kiss it but actually bites it... He finally strikes it, and her lovely skin, so white and so plump, soon offers her torturer little more than a vision of bruises and bloody weals. 'One moment,' says the raging monk, 'I want to thrash the most beautiful of bottoms and the softest of bosoms at the same time.' With me still kneeling, he positions Armande on top of me, and has her spread open her legs so that my mouth is level with her genitals and my breasts are between her thighs underneath her bottom. In this way, the monk has everything he wants

within reach: he has Armande's buttocks and my titties in full view.
He strikes both enthusiastically, but in order to spare me blows that
are becoming much more dangerous for me than for her, my companion is good enough to lower herself and, in so doing, to keep me
safe, herself receiving lashes in the process that would have certainly
hurt me badly. Clement becomes aware of her ruse and makes us
change position. 'She won't gain anything by this,' he says angrily.
'Even if I am prepared to spare that part of her body today, I shall be
able to molest another part that is at least as delicate.' As I rose to my
feet, I saw that so many infamies had not been committed in vain,
because the debauched monk was now in the most splendid state, in
which he raged all the more. Deciding to change weapons, he opens
a cupboard containing several straps, and takes one out that is iron-
tipped and which makes me tremble. 'Look, Thérèse,' he says to me,
showing it to me, 'see how delicious it is to whip with this... You will
feel it... You will feel it, you wicked little thing. But for the time
being, I just want to use this one...' It consisted of twelve small knotted ropes bound together. At the end of each rope was a knot stronger
than the others and as large as a plum-stone. 'Come on, gee up!... gee
up!' he said to his niece. The latter, who knew what he was talking
about, immediately went down on all fours, her back raised as far as
possible, and told me to do likewise, which I did. Clement sits astride
my back, his head facing my behind, while Armande's faces him.
Now that both of us are well within his reach, the rogue darts furious
looks at the charms we are offering him. However, as this posture
causes us to open as wide as possible that delicate part that distin-
guishes our sex from men, the barbarian aims all his blows at it, penetrating into the interior with far greater ease than the tips of the
rods, his rage leaving deep marks there. He strikes first the one, then
the other. As skilful a horseman as he is bold as a flagellator, he
changes mount several times. We are exhausted, and the sensations
of pain are so violent that it becomes almost impossible to bear them.
'Get up,' he then says to us, picking up the birch-rods again, 'yes, get
up and be afraid.' His eyes are gleaming and he is foaming at the
mouth. Now, our entire body is under threat and we try to avoid his
blows... we run into every corner of the chamber like lunatics... he
follows us, striking out indifferently at one or the other of us. The
villain covers us in blood, finally cornering both of us by the bed,
where he redoubles his blows. The unfortunate Armande receives

one on her breasts that makes her reel. This final horror precipitates the climax, and while my back suffers its cruel effects, my bottom is showered with the proofs of a delirium, the results of which are so dangerous.

'Let us go to bed,' Clement finally says to me, 'maybe that's enough for you, Thérèse, but it's certainly not enough for me. One never tires of this mania, though it is merely a pale reflection of what one would really like to do. Ah! dear girl, you know not how far our depravity can take us, to what depths our intoxication can make us sink. You don't understand the violent commotion that results from the electric fluid produced by the pain of the object that serves our passions. How aroused we are by its suffering! The desire to increase it... that is where these fantasies may come to grief, I know, but is such a danger to be feared by those who laugh at everything?'

Although Clement was still in a lively mood, nevertheless, seeing that his senses had become much calmer, and wishing to respond to what he had just said, I dared to reproach him with the depravity of his tastes, and it seems to me that the way in which this libertine justified these deserves to be included in the confessions you have asked me to make.

'The most ridiculous thing in the world, my dear Thérèse,' Clement said to me, 'is doubtless to want to argue about people's tastes, to challenge them, to blame men for them, or to punish them if they are not in conformity, either with the laws of the country in which one lives, or with social conventions. Indeed! Men will never understand that there are no tastes, however bizarre, however criminal they may be supposed to be, that do not derive from the kind of make-up we have been given by Nature! That said, I ask you by what right one man dare demand that another man should reform his tastes or model them on the social order! By what right even should laws that are made for man's happiness alone dare to deal severely with him who cannot change his ways or could do so only at the expense of that very happiness that the laws are designed to preserve on his behalf? In any case, even if an individual wished to change his tastes, can he do so? Is it in our nature to remake ourselves! Can we become different from what we are? Would you demand it of a deformed man, and is this lack of conformity in our tastes different on a moral level from the imperfection of the deformed man on a physical level? Let's examine the question in detail, if you wish. I can see that you have a mind, Thérèse, capable of understanding it. I also see that you have already been struck by two irregularities among us. You are amazed by the feeling of piquancy experienced by some of our fellow brothers for things vulgarly known as fetid or foul, and you are similarly astonished that our sensual faculties may be stimulated by actions which, according to you, are simply manifestations of ferocity. Let us analyse both of these tastes, and let us attempt, if possible, to convince you that there is nothing simpler in the world than the pleasures that result from them.

'It is strange, you claim, that dirty, dissolute things are able to produce in our senses an effect essential to their delirium, but before expressing surprise at this, my dear Thérèse, you should understand that objects only have that value in our eyes which our imagination creates for them. Given this constant truth, it is therefore quite possible that not only the most bizarre, but even the vilest and most frightful things may affect us very appreciably. The imagination of Man is a faculty of the mind in which objects are conjured up and modified, and thoughts are formed via the organ of the senses, all deriving from his first glimpse of these objects. However, this imagination, which itself results from the type of mental organization with which Man is endowed, perceives the objects only in a particular manner, and then creates thoughts only according to the effects produced by the impact of objects perceived. A comparison will make what I am describing easier for you to grasp, Thérèse. I am sure you have seen mirrors of differing shapes, some of which reduce objects in size while others enlarge them; the latter make them look awful while the former lend them charm. You can now imagine that if each one of these mirrors combined the creative with the objective faculty, they would each give a completely different image of the same man who looked at himself in it. Would this image not derive from the way in which the mirror had perceived the object? If, in addition to the two faculties which we have just ascribed to this mirror, it also possessed that of feeling, would it not have for this man which it saw in a particular way the kind of feeling of which it was now capable for the sort of being that it reflected? The mirror that saw him as handsome would love him, while the mirror that saw him as frightful would detest him, and yet it would still be the same man.

'Such is the human imagination, Thérèse. The same object is represented by it in as many different ways as it has different attitudes, and according to the image of the object received by this imagination, whatever it may be, it will decide to love or hate it. If the imagination is struck by the perceived object in an agreeable way, it will like and prefer it, even though this object may intrinsically have nothing really attractive about it. And even though this object may have a particular value in the eyes of another, if it strikes an individual's imagination in a disagreeable manner, the latter will keep his distance from it because none of our feelings is formed or manifested except as a result of the impact of different objects on our imagination. It should be no surprise, then, that what is very pleasing to some can be displeasing to others, and conversely, that the most extraordinary thing can still find followers... The deformed man can also find mirrors that make him handsome.

'Now, if we concede that the pleasures of the senses are always dependent on the imagination, always governed by the imagination, we cannot be surprised by the number of variations that the imagination can create for these pleasures, by the infinite multiplicity of tastes and different passions to which the different deviations of this imagination will give rise. Although lewd, these tastes should not startle us more than those of a simple nature. There is no reason to find a preference at table any less extraordinary than a preference in bed, and in either case, it is no more surprising to worship a thing that the majority of men find detestable than it is to love another thing that is generally acknowledged to be good. To like what others like demonstrates conformity in the organs, but nothing in favour of the beloved object. Three-quarters of the world can find the smell of a rose delicious without this being a reason either to condemn that quarter who may find it smells bad, or to show that this smell is truly agreeable.

'Therefore, if there exist beings in the world whose tastes shock all accepted standards, not only should we not be astonished by them, not only should we not preach to them or punish them, but we should serve their interests, make them happy, abolish all restraints upon them, and if we wish to be just, provide them with every means to satisfy themselves without risk, because it was no more their choice to have strange tastes than it was yours to be witty or stupid, to have a fine figure or to be a hunchback. It is in the mother's womb that our leanings to one thing or another are formed. The first objects we encounter and the first words we hear determine the scope and nature of our tastes.* It is then that our tastes are fixed, and nothing in the world can henceforth destroy them. No matter how a child is brought up, nothing changes them, and the person who is destined to be a criminal will just as surely become so, however well he is educated, as the person whose organs dispose him to virtue will follow the path of righteousness, even if his teacher has failed him. Both have acted in accordance with their make-up, with the impressions that they have received from Nature, and one is no more deserving of punishment than the other is deserving of reward.

'What is quite odd is that as long as we are speaking only of trifling things, we are not surprised by differences in taste, but once it is a matter of lust, there is such a commotion, with women constantly defending their rights, women whose weakness and lack of status mean they have nothing to lose, trembling each time something is taken from them—if unfortunately one includes actions that shock their beliefs, these are crimes deserving the scaffold! And yet, what injustice! Is the pleasure of the senses supposed to make a man any better than the other pleasures of life? In short, must the temple of reproduction attract us any more strongly, awaken our desires any more surely, than that part of the body that is most contrary to it, or most distant from it, or than those more repulsive or disgusting things which emanate from such a body? It should not be any more surprising, it seems to me, to find that a man has singular tastes in the pleasures of libertinism than to find that he has such an approach to other aspects of life! Once again, in both cases, his singularity is the product of his organs. Is it his fault if what interests you has no meaning for him, or if he is excited only by what you find repugnant? What man would not instantly change his tastes, his attachments, his leanings, across the board, and would not prefer to be like everyone else rather than to be unusual, if he could choose to do so? Those who wish to deal severely with such a man are motivated by the most stupid, the most barbaric intolerance. Whatever his deviations might be, society should find him no more guilty than the person who, as I have just said, came into the world half-blind or lame, and it is just as unjust to punish or to mock the one as it would be to afflict or to ridicule the other. The man endowed with singular tastes is ill, or if you like, he is a woman suffering from hysterical vapours. Has it ever occurred to us to punish or to torment either of these? Let us be equally fair towards the man whose whims surprise us. Just like the

man who is ill or the woman who suffers from the vapours, he is more
to be pitied than blamed. This is the excuse for the behaviour of such
people from a moral point of view. It could doubtless apply just as
easily on a physical level, and when our knowledge of anatomy is
perfected, we will be able to use it to demonstrate easily the relationship between the constitution of man and the tastes that have formed
him. Pedants, executioners, turnkeys, legislators, tonsured rabble,
where will all of you be when we reach that point? What of your laws,
your morality, your religion, your scaffolds, your Heaven, your gods,
your Hell, when it is proven that particular types of fluid or of fibre
or a given degree of acidity in the blood or in the brain are enough to
turn men into the object of either your rewards or your punishments!

  'But let us continue. You are astonished by cruel tastes! What is
the aim of the pleasure-seeking man? Is it not to arouse his senses in
every way possible, and thereby to get the most pleasure from the
final crisis?... a precious moment which determines whether this
crisis is good or bad, depending on how much energy is invested in
it? Now, is it not an untenable sophism to dare to claim that to get the
best out of it, it must be shared by the woman? Is it not clearly visible
that the woman cannot share anything with us without taking from
us, and that everything she steals from us must necessarily be at our
expense? So I ask you, in what way is it necessary for a woman to
orgasm when we do? Is there any other reason for this than having
one's pride flattered? And does one not, on the contrary, feel this
pride in a far more exciting manner by ruthlessly preventing this
woman from reaching orgasm so that you alone do so, in order that
nothing should prevent her from focusing on your own orgasm?
Does not tyranny give a much stronger boost to pride than benefi-
cence? In short, is not the man who dominates much more obviously
the master than the man who shares? But how can it enter the head of
any reasonable man that there was any room for delicacy in sexual
pleasure? It is absurd to maintain that it is a necessary part of it. Not
only does it contribute nothing at all to the pleasure of the senses, it
positively hinders it. Love and pleasure are two quite different things,
as demonstrated by the fact that one can love every day without having pleasure, and have pleasure even more frequently without loving.
Any degree of tenderness that one uses in one's own pleasures to
increase the woman's will necessarily reduce that of the man, and so

long as he aims to give pleasure, he will assuredly not experience any himself, or else his pleasure will be purely intellectual, in other words, imaginary and totally inferior to that of the senses. No, no, Thérèse, I cannot say this too often, it is not at all the case that pleasure must be shared in order to be intense, and to make this sort of pleasure as intense as it is capable of being, it is, on the contrary, absolutely essential for the man to pleasure himself at the expense of the woman, and, regardless of any sensation she may experience, for him to take from her anything that may increase the extent of his own pleasure, without having the slightest regard for the effects on the woman, for these effects would distract him. He either wants the woman to share his pleasure, in which case he experiences none himself, or else he is afraid that she might suffer pain, and then he is distracted. If egoism is the first law of Nature, it is most certainly in the pleasures of lust more than anywhere else that our celestial mother wants it to be our only motive. To neglect or disturb the woman's pleasure is of little significance if the man's is thereby increased, because if in so doing he gains something, he is in no way affected by the loss experienced by the object that serves him, and it must be a matter of indifference to him whether this object is happy or unhappy, provided that he himself is delighted. There is really no kind of relationship between him and this object. It would therefore be crazy for him to concern himself with the sensations of this object at the expense of his own, totally ridiculous to refuse to increase his own in order to have an effect on sensations that are foreign to him. That said, if the individual in question is unfortunately made in such a way that he can get excited only by producing painful sensations in the object that serves him, you will admit that he must do so without remorse, since his aim is to obtain pleasure, regardless of any effect on this object... We shall return to this question, but let us take things in their proper order.

'Solitary pleasures, then, do have some charms, and can do so more than any others. If this were not so, how could so many old or deformed men enjoy themselves? They are quite sure that no one loves them, quite certain that it is impossible for others to share what they feel—do they experience pleasure any the less? Do they want to experience only the illusion of it? They are completely selfish in their pleasures, and it is obvious that their sole concern is how to enjoy them, that they are prepared to sacrifice anything to obtain them, while the object that serves them is never expected to possess any properties but those of passivity. It is thus in no way necessary to give pleasure in order to receive it, the happy or unhappy situation of the victim of our debauchery being absolutely indifferent to the satisfaction of our senses, and so the state of their heart or mind is not relevant in the slightest. This object may indifferently enjoy or suffer from what you do to them, they may love or hate you. All such considerations count for nothing once our senses are in play. Women, I confess, may establish contrary maxims, but women who are nothing more than pleasure machines, nothing but pleasure's breastplates, come a cropper whenever this kind of pleasure has to be properly defined. Is there a single reasonable man who wishes to share his pleasure with prostitutes? And yet, are there not millions of men who derive great enjoyment from these creatures? All such individuals are convinced of the ideas I am putting forward and put them into practice without the slightest doubt, ridiculing those who legitimate their actions according to good principles. The latter do so because the world is full of living statues who come and go, who act and eat and digest without ever being aware of anything.

'Given that solitary pleasures are demonstrated to be just as delicious as others and actually far more so, it therefore becomes quite obvious that these pleasures, enjoyed independently of the object that serves us, are not only a long way from anything that might please it but are even contrary to its own enjoyment. I will go further and say that my pleasures can derive from the imposition of pain, from humiliation or from torture, without this being in any way extraordinary, and without the consequence being anything other than a much more certain increase in pleasure for the despot who torments and humiliates it. Let us attempt to demonstrate this.

'The pleasurable feeling is nothing more than a sort of vibration in our body produced by the impact on our senses brought about by the imagination aroused by the memory of a lubricious object, or by the presence of this object, or better still by irritation felt by this object of the kind that excites us the most. Thus, our moment of pleasure, that inexpressible sensation that makes us crazy, that transports us to the highest level of happiness that man can reach, will only ever be triggered by two causes: either by the real or imaginary perception in the object that serves us of the kind of beauty that arouses us most, or by watching this object experience the strongest possible sensation.

Now, there is no more vivid sensation than pain. Its impressions are sure, they do not deceive like those of the pleasure that women constantly feign and which they practically never feel. Moreover, how much self-esteem must one need, how much youth, strength, and health, to be certain of producing in a woman that dubious and unsatisfactory impression of pleasure? The impression of pain, on the contrary, does not require the least little thing. The more faults a man has, the older he is, the less lovable he is, the better he will succeed. As far as the objective is concerned, this is more likely to be achieved, since we have established that our senses are never more closely affected, I mean to say, that they are never more aroused than when we have produced the greatest possible impression in the object that serves us, by whatever means. The man, then, who can create the most tumultuous effect in a woman, who can best shatter this woman's whole body, will have truly succeeded in obtaining for himself the greatest possible amount of pleasure, because the shock he feels, deriving from the impact others experience and being necessarily caused by that impact, will necessarily be more vigorous if the impact on others has been painful than if it has only been sweet and tender. It follows that the egotistical sensualist, who is convinced that his pleasures will be vivid as long as they are complete, will therefore inflict the strongest possible dose of pain on the object that serves him whenever he has the power to do so, in the certain knowledge that the thrill he gets out of it will only be in proportion to the degree of impact he has produced.'

'These doctrines are horrendous, Father,' I said to Clement, 'they can only lead to a taste for cruelty and horror.'

'So what?' the barbarian replied. 'I repeat, are we masters of our tastes? Should we not give in to the influence of those we have received from Nature, as the proud crown of the oak tree bows to the storm that shakes it? If Nature were offended by these tastes it would not inspire them in us. It is impossible for us to receive any urge from her that is designed to outrage her, and in this absolute certainty we may indulge in all our passions, whatever form they make take and however violent they may be, quite sure that any disadvantages occasioned by their impact are merely part of Nature's plan, of which we are the involuntary instruments. And what are the consequences of these passions to us? When one wants to enjoy oneself by performing some act or other, the consequences are irrelevant.'

'I am not talking about the consequences,' I suddenly interjected, 'it is a question of the thing itself. Obviously, if you are the stronger one and if your atrocious principles of cruelty drive you to seek pleasure in pain alone, with a view to increasing your sensations, you will imperceptibly succeed in inflicting pain on the object that serves you to a degree of violence capable of taking her life.'

'So be it. That is to say, because of tastes given to me by Nature, I will have served the designs of Nature which creates only by destroying and never inspires in me the idea of destruction unless it needs to create. In other words, I will have taken an oblong piece of matter and formed three or four thousand round or square pieces out of it. Oh, Thérèse, how can such actions be crimes? How can one give this name to actions that serve Nature? Does man have the power to commit crimes? When, preferring his happiness to that of others, he overturns or destroys all that he finds in his way, has he done anything but serve Nature, whose primary and surest promptings command him to make himself happy, whatever the cost to others? The doctrine of loving one's neighbour is a fantasy that we owe to Christianity and not to Nature. The follower of the Nazarene, tormented and unhappy, and consequently the state of weakness that was supposed to invite tolerance and humanity, necessarily had to establish this fantastic relation between one human being and another. He was supposed to preserve his own life by helping his neighbour to flourish. But the philosopher does not accept such fanciful relationships. Having regard for himself alone in the world, he looks after his own interests in all things. If he humours or is kind to others for a single moment, he does so only in proportion to the profit he believes he can derive from such actions. Should he no longer have need of them, or once he has the upper hand, he then abjures forever all of those wonderful doctrines of humanity and benevolence to which he subscribed for tactical reasons alone. He is no longer afraid to make everything serve him, to possess all that surrounds him, and, whatever the cost of his pleasures to others, he indulges them without thinking and without remorse.'

'But the man you describe is a monster.'

'The man I describe is Nature's own.'

'He is a wild beast.'

'Well, is not the tiger or leopard of which this man is the image, if you like, created like him by Nature and created to fulfil the intentions of Nature? The wolf that devours the lamb accomplishes the will of our common mother, like the wrongdoer who destroys the object of his vengence or of his lubricity.'*

'Oh, you can say what you like, Father, but I shall never accept such destructive lusts.'

'Because you are afraid of becoming their object, and that is egoism. Let us swap roles, and you'll see what I mean. Ask the lamb, and he will not accept either that the wolf may devour him. Ask the wolf what use the lamb serves, and he will answer, to feed me. Wolves eating lambs, lambs devoured by wolves, the strong killing the weak, the weak falling victim to the strong, such is Nature, such are her designs, such is her plan. A perpetual action and reaction, a host of vices and virtues, in short, a perfect balance resulting from the equality of good and evil on earth, a balance that is essential to the preservation of the stars, to life, and without which everything would instantly be destroyed. Oh, Thérèse, this Nature would be most astonished if it were able to talk to us for a moment and we told it that these crimes that serve it, that these heinous crimes which it requires and which it inspires in us, are punished by laws which we are assured reflect its own. "Imbecile," it would reply, "sleep, drink, eat, and commit such crimes without fear whenever you like. All of these so-called infamies please me, and I want them to happen because I inspire them in you. It is not up to you to decide what offends and what delights me. Understand that there is nothing in you that does not belong to me, nothing that I have not put there for reasons which it is not appropriate for you to know; that the most abominable and the most virtuous of these acts are both just ways of serving me. Do not restrain yourself, therefore, flout your laws, your social conventions and your gods, listen only to my voice, and believe that if there is a crime in my eyes, it is to oppose those things I inspire you to do, either by your resistance or by your sophisms."'

'Oh, dear Heaven!' I cried, 'you make me tremble. If there were no crimes against Nature, where does that insuperable repugnance come from that we feel for certain transgressions?'

'Such repugnance is not dictated by Nature,' the rogue quickly replied, 'it comes only from a lack of habit. Is this not the case with certain foods? Although they are excellent, do they not repulse us simply because we are not accustomed to them? Yet, would we dare say in consequence that these dishes are not good? If we make an effort to overcome our revulsion, we will soon agree that they are tasty. We find medicines revolting, even though they are good for us. Let us accustom ourselves to evil in the same way, and we will soon find it to have nothing but charms for us. This momentary repulsion is a trick, a coquetry of Nature, far more than a warning that it is outraged by such a thing. In this way, it prepares us to experience the pleasures of triumph, and increases those of the very act itself. Better, Thérèse, than that: the more horrific the act seems to us, the more contrary it appears to be to our habits and customs, the more taboos it infringes, the more it shocks all our social conventions, the more it offends against what we believe to be the laws of Nature—on the contrary, the more it is useful to Nature itself. It is only ever by dint of crimes that it reasserts those rights that virtue constantly takes away from it. If a crime strays only a little from the path of virtue, it will establish the balance indispensable to Nature more slowly, but the more serious the crime is the more it redresses the balance, and the more it counterbalances the sway of virtue which would other-wise destroy everything. Let he who is contemplating a crime or has just committed one, then, put aside his fears, for the greater the scale of his crime, the better it will have served Nature.'

These horrific doctrines soon turned my thoughts to Omphale's feelings about the way in which the girls left this dreadful house. It was at that moment, therefore, that I conceived the plans that you shall see me subsequently carry out. Nevertheless, in order to get everything clear, I could not help putting a few more questions to Father Clement.

'At least,' I said to him, 'you don't keep the unfortunate victims of your passions forever. I suppose you send them away when you're tired of them?'

'Most certainly, Thérèse,' the monk answered me. 'You have entered this house only to leave it again when all four of us have agreed to retire you. This will definitely happen to you.'

'But are you not afraid', I went on, 'that younger and less discreet girls may go and report what happened in your house?'

'That's impossible.'

'Impossible?'

'Absolutely.'

'Could you explain to me why?'

'No, that's our secret, but I can assure you that, regardless of your discretion or lack of it, it will be perfectly impossible for you ever to say a single word about what goes on here when you leave. So you see, Thérèse, I cannot recommend that you be discreet. Attitudes of restraint will in no way limit the expression of my desires...'

And with these words, the monk fell asleep. From that moment on, it was no longer possible for me not to see that those unfortunates who were dismissed were subjected to the most violent treatment, and that the awesome security that was boasted of was the fruit of their deaths alone. My resolve was strengthened all the more by this realization: we shall soon see with what consequences.

As soon as Clement was asleep, Armande approached me.

'He'll soon wake up like a madman,' she said to me. 'Nature only puts his senses to sleep so that, after a short rest, they are endowed with far greater energy. One more scene and then we'll be left alone until tomorrow.'

'But what about you?' I said to my friend. 'Do you not sleep for a little while?'

'How can I?' replied Armande. 'If I did not stand by his bed, keeping watch over him, and my negligence was noticed, he would be capable of sticking a knife in me.'

'Oh, Heaven!' I said, 'what? Even when he is asleep this villain wants those around him to suffer!'

'Yes,' my companion replied, 'it is the very barbarity of this idea that makes him awaken with such fury, as you will see. In this, he is like those perverted authors whose corruption is so active and so dangerous that their sole aim in publishing their dreadful doctrines is to extend the sum of their crimes beyond the grave. They can do no more themselves, but their accursed writings will cause more crimes to be committed, and this sweet notion which they take with them to the grave consoles them for the fact that death forces them to give up doing evil.'

'The monsters!' I cried...

Armande, who was a very gentle creature, kissed me, shedding a few tears, then resumed pacing around the roué's bed. Two hours later the monk did indeed wake up in a state of prodigious agitation, and seized hold of me with such force that I thought he was going to suffocate me. His breathing was quick and laboured, his eyes gleamed, and he uttered a string of unconnected words that were nothing but blasphemies or libertine expressions. He called to

Armande, demanding whips, and resumed flogging the two of us, but far more vigorously than he had done before falling asleep. He seemed to want to end the session with me. I screamed at the top of my voice. To put an end to my suffering, Armande excited him violently so that he lost control, and finally, overcome by the most violent sensations, the monster lost his ardour and his desires in the eruption of burning floods of seed.

All was quiet for the rest of the night. On rising, the monk did no more than touch and examine both of us, and as he went off to say mass, we returned to the seraglio. The overseer could not help lusting after me in the state of arousal she claimed I must be in. How could I defend myself, exhausted as I was? She did what she wanted, enough to convince me that even a woman, schooled in such a way, and quickly losing all the delicacy and restraint of her sex, was bound to commit obscene and cruel acts following the example of her tyrannical masters.

Two nights later I slept with Jerome. I shall not describe his horrific behaviour to you, it was even more terrifying. My God, what a school! After a week, I had finally done all the rounds. Then Omphale asked me whether or not it was true that, of them all, Clement was the one I had the most to complain about.

'Alas!' I replied, 'in the midst of so many horrors and so much filth, it really is hard to say which of these villains is the most odious. I am sick and tired of all of them, and would like to get out of here now, whatever fate awaits me.'

'Your wish may soon be granted,' replied my companion; 'the feast is almost upon us, and this event rarely takes place without bringing them more victims. They either seduce young girls in the confessional, or they whisk some away if they can. So many new recruits, which always means discharges...'

This famous festival arrived... you would not believe the monstrous impieties of the monks during this event, Madame! They decided that a miracle, visible to all, would greatly increase their glorious reputation. Consequently, they took Florette, the youngest of the girls, and dressed her up just like the Virgin Mary. They then attached her to the wall behind the recess with ropes that could not be seen, and ordered her suddenly to lift up her arms solemnly to Heaven when the host was raised. As this little creature was threatened with the cruellest punishments if she said a single word about this, or if she did not play her part as required, she gave a superb performance, and the trick fulfilled all their expectations. The people announced that it was a miracle, left valuable offerings to the Virgin, and went away more convinced than ever of the efficacy of our Heavenly mother's grace. Heaping sacrilege upon sacrilege, our libertines had Florette appear at the evening orgies in the same clothes that had brought her so much adoration, and each of them indulged his odious passions by subjecting her in this costume to whatever took his fancy. Their sacrileges did not stop there, once this first crime had aroused them. Having stripped the child naked, they lay her face down on a large table, lit candles, and placing the image of our Saviour in the middle of her back, they had the temerity to consummate the most sacred of our rites on her behind. I fainted at this horrible sight, I just could not stand it. Seeing me in this condition, Severino said that, in order to accustom me to it, I must also serve as an altar in my turn. I was seized and laid in the same place as Florette. The sacrifice was carried out, and the host... that sacred symbol of our august religion... Severino took hold of it and shoved it into the obscene location of his sodomite pleasures... he crushed it, cursing all the while, ignominiously assaulting it with the frantic thrusts of his monstrous dart, and blaspheming, squirted the foul floods of his lusts onto the very body of his Saviour...

I was dragged motionless from his hands. They had to carry me to my room, where I wept for a whole week over the horrible crime which I had helped to commit in spite of myself. This memory still wounds my soul, I cannot think of it without shuddering... Religion for me is linked to emotion. Anything that offends against it or outrages it makes my heart bleed.

The appointed time of the month for discharges was close when Severino came into our dormitory one morning at about nine o'clock. He appeared very worked up, and there was a sort of manic look in his eyes. He examined us, and arranged us both in turn in his favourite position, paying particular attention to Omphale. He stood still for several minutes gazing at her in this posture, growing secretly excited, kissing what was before him, making it look as if he was ready to consummate the act but without actually doing so. Then bidding her get up, he looked at her with rage and malevolence, and kicked her hard in the crotch, sending her flying twenty feet across the room.

'The community is discharging you, whore,' he told her, 'we are tired of you. Be ready to leave at nightfall. I shall come to fetch you myself.' With that, he went out. As soon as he had gone, Omphale got up and threw herself in tears into my arms.

'Well!' she said to me, 'after the infamy and cruelty of the preliminaries, can you still be in any doubt as to what follows? Oh dear Lord, what will become of me!'

'Calm yourself,' I said to the poor girl, 'I'm prepared to do anything now. I am just waiting for the right opportunity. Perhaps it will present itself sooner than you think. I shall expose these horrors. If it is true that their treatment of us is as cruel as we have reason to believe, try to delay things a little, and I shall snatch you from them.'

Omphale swore to do me the same service if she were released, and we both wept. The day passed uneventfully. At about five o'clock Severino came back up himself.

'Come,' he said abruptly to Omphale, 'are you ready?'

'Yes, Father,' she replied, sobbing, 'may I just kiss my companions goodbye?'

'There is no point,' said the monk, 'there's no time for a tearful scene, come along, they're waiting for us.' She then asked if she should take her old clothes with her. 'No,' said the Father Superior, 'does not everything belong to the house? You have no more need of those things.' Then, correcting himself like someone who has said too much, he added:

'Those clothes will no longer be of use to you. You'll have others made to fit you that will suit you better, just take what you are wearing now.'

I asked the monk if he would at least allow me to accompany Omphale as far as the main door of the house, but he responded with a look that made me recoil in horror... Omphale went out, her expression filled with anxiety and tears. As soon as she was outside, I threw myself on my bed in despair.

Accustomed to these events, or fooling themselves as to their consequences, my companions took less part in them than I did, and the Father Superior returned an hour later. He had come to take the girls required for supper, of whom I was one. There can't have been more than four women, the twelve-year-old girl, the sixteen-year-old, the twenty-three-year-old and myself. Everything happened

more or less as on previous days. The only differences I noticed
were that the duty girls were not there, that the monks frequently
whispered into each other's ears, that they drank a lot, that they concentrated on violently arousing their desires without ever allowing
themselves to consummate them, and that they sent us away much
earlier without keeping any of us to sleep with... What conclusions
were to be drawn from these observations? I made them because you
notice everything in such circumstances, but what could I deduce
from them? Oh, my perplexity was such that not a single idea came
into my head without its being immediately contradicted by another.
Recalling Clement's remarks, I should probably have feared the
worst, and yet hope... that deceptive hope that consoles us, that
blinds us, and that therefore does us almost as much good as not,
hope, I say, would reassure me... So many horrors were foreign to
me that it was impossible for me to bear them! I went to bed in this
terrible state—persuaded one moment that Omphale would not fail
to keep her oath, convinced the next that the cruel treatment to which
she would be subjected would render her impotent to help us. This
was my eventual opinion when three days had passed without my
hearing anything of her.

On the fourth day I was again among a large number of carefully
selected girls required at supper. On that day the eight most beautiful
women were present, among whom I was honoured to be included.
The duty girls were also there. As soon as we entered, we saw our
new companion.

'Young ladies, this is the girl that the community has chosen to
replace Omphale,' Severino told us. So saying, he tore the mantlets
and veils from the girl's face and shoulders, and we saw a young person of fifteen years, of the most pleasing and most delicate appearance. She gracefully raised her lovely eyes to look at each of us. They
were still wet with tears but were full of interest. She had a slight and
supple waist, a dazzlingly fair complexion, the most beautiful hair in
the world, and something so seductive overall that it was impossible
to look upon her without feeling attracted to her in spite of oneself.
Her name was Octavie, and we soon discovered that she was a young
lady of the highest rank, born in Paris and en route from her monastery to marry the Comte de ——. She had been abducted from her
carriage with two governesses and three footmen. She did not know
what had become of her retinue. She had been taken on her own at

nightfall, blindfolded, and brought to the spot where we now saw her, in complete ignorance of what had happened to her.

No one had yet said a single word to her. Ecstatic for the time being at the sight of so many charms, our four libertines only had the strength to admire them. The omnipotence of beauty commands respect. Even the most corrupt of villains is obliged to pay homage to it in spite of his wicked heart, an obligation he never resists without regret, but monsters such as those we were dealing with do not languish under such constraints for long.

'Come, my lovely child,' said the Father Superior, pulling her impudently towards the armchair upon which he was seated, 'come, let's see whether the rest of your charms are equal to those which Nature has placed so profusely on your physiognomy.' And as this beautiful girl became distraught, as she blushed and tried to free herself, Severino seized hold of her roughly, saying: 'Listen here, little Agnès, and understand that we require you to strip naked immediately.' And with these words, the libertine slipped one hand under her skirts, while keeping a tight hold of her with the other. Clement came forward, lifted Octavie's clothes halfway up her back, and in so doing exposed the sweetest and most appetizing attractions that it is possible to see. Severino, who was touching her but had not noticed these, bent down to look, and so all four had to agree that they had never seen anything so beautiful. Meanwhile, poor modest Octavie, who was quite unused to such outrages, shed tears and tried to defend herself.

'Let us undress her, let us undress her,' said Antonin, 'I've never seen anything like this.' He helped Severino, and in a flash the young girl's charms were laid bare before our eyes. Assuredly, there was never a skin more fair or a body so well put together... Lord, what a crime!... Must so much beauty, so much freshness, so much innocence, so much delicacy become the prey of these barbarians! In shame, Octavie does not know where to turn to hide her charms. Everywhere are eyes devouring her and brutal hands defiling her. The circle forms around her, and as with me, she is passed all the way round it. The brutal Antoine did not have the strength to resist. A cruel attack precipitates the sacrifice and incense lies steaming at the foot of his god. Jerome compares her to our young companion of sixteen, doubtless the prettiest girl in the seraglio. He places the two altars of his religion side by side.

'Oh, what lovely white skin! what grace!' he says, fondling Octavie, 'yet, what gentleness and freshness this one also possesses. Truly,' the monk continues, burning with desire, 'I can't decide.' Then, glueing his mouth to the charms that confront him, he cries: 'Octavie, the apple is yours, and yours alone, give me the precious fruit of the tree that my heart adores... Oh, yes, yes, let me have either of them, and I guarantee the prize of beauty for ever more to whoever serves me first.'

Severino sees that it is time to think of more serious things. Absolutely incapable of waiting, he seizes hold of the unfortunate girl, positions her to suit his desires, but not managing to arrange things quite as he wishes, he calls Clement over to help him. Octavie weeps, but they pay her no attention. The indecent monk looks at her with fire in his eyes. In complete control, he seems to consider all avenues in order to launch his attack more successfully. He employs no ruses or other approaches... would he gather roses with so much charm by removing the thorns? However enormous the disproportion between the conquest and the assailant, the latter is no less willing to engage in combat. A piercing cry announces victory, but nothing moves the enemy. The more the captive begs for mercy, the more vigorously she is assailed. The wretched girl fights in vain, but is soon sacrificed.

'Victory was never harder won,' said Severino as he withdrew, 'I thought that for the first time in my life I would fail just as I was about to enter port... Oh, how tight it was, how hot! It's the Ganymede of the gods!'

'I must bring her back to the organ you have just soiled,' said Antonin, grabbing hold of her there, and not allowing her to get up, he added: 'there is more than one breach in the walls.'

And proudly approaching her, he has entered the sanctuary in a flash. Fresh cries can be heard.

'May God be praised,' said the dishonest gentleman, 'I would have doubted that I was successful were it not for the victim's groans, but my triumph is assured by her blood and tears.'

'In truth,' said Clement, coming forward with birch-rods in his hand, 'I shall not alter that sweet posture either, it is too favourable to my desires.'

Jerome's duty girl and the thirty-year-old were holding Octavie. Clement looked closely at her, touching her all over, while the terrified girl begged him to stop, and yet could not move him.

'Oh, my friends,' said the monk in triumph, 'how can one resist whipping a pupil when she displays such a lovely arse to us?'

The air soon echoed with the swishing of canes and the dull crack of their blows on her beautiful flesh mingled with Octavie's cries, which the monk answered with blasphemies. What a scene was performed in the midst of us all before these libertines who responded with a thousand obscenities! They applauded and encouraged him, as Octavie's skin changed colour, shades of deepest scarlet appearing on her lily-white complexion. But what might perhaps please love for a moment if the sacrifice were conducted with moderation, greater rigour turns into a terrible crime against its laws. Nothing can stop the perfidious monk. The more the young pupil complains, the greater the Father Superior's severity. From the middle of her back to the bottom of her thighs, all is treated in the same manner, and the perfidious man finally requites his lust upon the bleeding marks of his pleasures.

'I shall be less savage than that,' said Jerome, taking hold of the girl and glueing himself to her coral lips, 'this is the temple where I shall sacrifice...! Into this enchanting mouth.'

I can say no more... It was a foul reptile soiling a rose. My comparison tells you all.

The rest of the evening progressed in similar fashion, except that, as the beauty and touchingly young age of this girl inflamed these villains even more, they redoubled all of their infamies, and if this wretch was finally sent back to her chamber, lending her at least the few hours rest she needed, it was much less because of their commiseration than their satiety.

I should have really liked to be able to console her on that first night, but as I was obliged to spend it with Severino, I would have been the one, on the contrary, who would have been in great need of help. I had had the misfortune, not to please—the word would not be appropriate—but to excite more strongly than any other girl the infamous desires of this sodomite. He now wanted me almost every night. Worn out by this new girl, he was in need of support. Doubtless afraid of not now being able to cause me enough pain with the terrible weapon with which he was endowed, on this occasion he had the idea of perforating me with one of those objects used by nuns which decency forbids me to name and which was enormous in size, but I had to go along with it all. He inserted this weapon into his favourite temple. A number of thrusts sufficed to push it deep inside. I cried out, but the monk just laughed. After a few more thrusts he suddenly pulled this instrument out violently and himself penetrated the gaping hole that he had just opened up... What a whim! Is this not exactly the opposite of all those things that men should desire? Yet, who can define the soul of a libertine?* We have known for a long time that this is one of Nature's mysteries, and she has still not explained it to us.

In the morning, finding himself somewhat refreshed, he wanted to try out a different form of torture, and showed me an even bigger instrument. This one was hollow and equipped with a piston that squirted an incredibly powerful stream of water through an aperture which produced a jet of more than three inches in circumference. This enormous instrument itself had a circumference of nine inches and was twelve inches long. Severino had it filled with very hot water, intending to stick it inside me from the front. Terrified by such a prospect, I threw myself at his feet to beg for mercy, but he was in one of those accursed moods in which pity has no voice, stifled by the far more eloquent passions which replace it with a cruelty that is often extremely dangerous. The monk threatened me with all his anger if I did not play along, and I was forced to obey. The perfidious machine penetrated me by two-thirds, and the tearing it caused me, combined with the instrument's extreme heat, almost made me lose the use of my senses. All the while, the Father Superior kept cursing those parts he was molesting, and had another girl excite him. After a quarter of an hour of these lacerating thrusts, he released the piston which squirted boiling water deep inside my womb... I fainted, and Severino was in ecstasy... His rapture was at least as great as my pain.

'That's nothing,' the scoundrel said when I had recovered my senses, 'we sometimes treat these charms far more harshly here... Christ! We have a salad of thorns, well seasoned with pepper and vinegar, which we shove inside with the point of a knife, that's what they need to revive them. I shall sentence you to this the first time you commit a fault!' said the villain, still fingering his sole object of devotion. However, after the debauches of the previous night just a few acts of sacrifice had exhausted him and I was dismissed.

On returning to my room, I discovered my new companion in tears and did what I could to calm her, but it is not easy to come to terms with such a dreadful change of circumstances. Moreover, this young girl was extremely devout, virtuous, and sensitive, and consequently her situation seemed all the more terrible to her. Omphale had been right to tell me that the length of time girls had been in the monastery had absolutely no influence on the choice of dismissals, and that, simply dictated by the monks' whims or by their fear of searches made after the girls' abduction, they could be dismissed after a week just as easily as after twenty years. Octavie had not been with us for four months when Jerome came to tell her she was leaving. Although it was he who had enjoyed her the most during her stay in the monastery, and who might have cherished her and so wanted to prolong his enjoyment of her, the poor child left, making us the same promises as Omphale had done. She did not keep them any more than Omphale did.

From that moment on I directed all my thoughts to the plan I had formulated after Omphale's departure, resolved to do anything to escape this den of iniquity, and my determination to succeed knew no fear. What might I expect in carrying out my plan? Death! And what was I certain to encounter if I stayed? Death. And if I succeeded, I would be saved. There was therefore no reason to hesitate, but before I could act, those fateful examples of how vice is rewarded were destined once again to be enacted before my eyes. It was written in the great book of Destiny, in that obscure book known to no mortal man, it was written there, I say, that all those who had tormented and humiliated me, who had kept me in chains, would forever be rewarded for their crimes in front of my eyes, as if Providence had undertaken to show me the futility of virtue... Baneful lessons from which I still did not learn, and were I again to escape from the sword suspended above my head, will not prevent me from continuing to be the slave of the deity that rules my heart.

One morning, without our expecting it, Antonin appeared in our bedchamber and announced to us that the Reverend Father Severino, relative and protégé of the Pope, had just been appointed head of the Benedictine Order by His Holiness. The very next day this cleric did indeed leave, without seeing us. We were told that we were expecting another who was far superior in debauchery to all those who remained—further reasons for hastening my plans.

The day following Severino's departure the monks decided to dismiss another of my companions. I chose for my escape the very same day that the fate of this wretch was announced, so that the monks would be preoccupied and pay me less attention.

We were at the beginning of spring, when the length of the nights still favoured my plans a little. I had been making preparations for two months without their suspecting anything. With an old pair of scissors I had found I was gradually sawing the bars of my closet. I could already get my head through them easily, and I had made a rope from my bed-linen that was more than adequate to cover the twenty or twenty-five feet that Omphale had told me was the height of the building. When my old clothes had been taken from me I had been careful, as I told you, to take out my few savings, amounting to nearly six louis, and I still had these carefully hidden. As I set off, I put this money back into my hair. Almost everyone from our dormitory was at supper that evening, and being left alone with one of my companions who retired to bed as soon as the others had gone downstairs, I went into my closet. Once safely inside, I uncovered the hole that I was careful to block up every day, tied my rope to one of the bars that was not damaged, and then by this means slid down it, soon reaching the ground. It was not this part that I found difficult. The six enclosures ringed by walls or by hedges that my companion had told me about were quite a different matter.

Once there, I realized that each space or circular alley between each hedgerow and the next was not more than eight feet wide, and it was this proximity that at first sight gave the impression that everything in this area was just an overgrown clump of trees. It was a very dark night. As I followed this first circular alleyway round to see if I could find an opening in the hedgerow, I passed below the supper-room, and seeing that they had all left, my anxiety greatly increased. However, I continued searching and in this way arrived level with the window of the great underground hall which was located underneath the room reserved for day-to-day orgies. I could see that this room was well lit and I was bold enough to approach it, looking down into the room from where I was standing. My unfortunate companion was stretched out on a rack. She had little hair left and was doubtless destined to undergo some dreadful torture which would finally set her free of all her woes... I trembled, but was soon amazed by what I saw then. Either Omphale did not know everything or she had not told me all, for I saw four naked girls in this cellar who appeared very beautiful and extremely young to me, and who certainly did not belong to our group. So there were other victims of the lust of these monsters in this dreadful refuge... other unfortunate girls unknown to the rest of us... I hastened to flee, and continued to follow the path round until I was right on the other side opposite the cellar. Having failed so far to find an opening in the hedge, I resolved to make one. Without anyone noticing, I had equipped myself with a long knife. I set about working with it. Despite the gloves I was wearing my hands were soon covered in cuts, but nothing stopped me. The hedge was more than two feet thick, but I managed to open it up sufficiently to reach the second enclosure. There, I was astonished to feel the earth to be soft, giving way beneath my feet, and I sank into it up to my ankles. The further I advanced through these dense copses, the darker they became. Curious to know the reason for this change in terrain, I felt with my hands... Oh, Heaven! I was holding a skull! Dear God! I thought in horror, this is doubtless the cemetery where these torturers throw the bodies of their victims, just as I had been told. They scarcely take the trouble to cover them with earth! This skull was perhaps that of my dear Omphale, or of the unfortunate Octavie, so beautiful, so sweet, so good, and who appeared on earth like the rose of whose loveliness she was the very image! Alas! That would have been my fate, too! Why not simply submit to it? What would I gain from leaving, only to find new setbacks? Have I not committed enough crimes here? Have I not here become the cause of enough crimes? Oh, let me fulfil my destiny! Oh, earth, open up and swallow me! When one is as forsaken, as poor, as abandoned as I, why should one make such efforts to lead such a pointless existence any longer in the company of such monsters!... No, no, I must avenge virtue in chains... She expects me to have the courage to do so... I should not allow myself to be cowed... I must go forward. It is essential that the world be rid of villains as dangerous as these. Must I fear causing the loss of a handful of men's lives in order to save those of millions of individuals, sacrificed to their savagery or their philosophy?

And so I cut through the hedge at the place where I was. This one was thicker than the other. The further forward I went, the harder it became. I do manage to make a hole, but the soil closes up on the other side... there is no longer any sign of those same horrors I had just encountered. In this way, I arrive at the edge of the ditch without finding the high wall that Omphale had told me about. It probably did not exist, it being likely that the monks only told us about it to scare us more. Less shut in on the other side of this sixfold enclosure, I was better able to make out the objects around me. The church and the main building that backed on to it were immediately visible to me. The ditch bordered both. I was careful not to attempt to cross it from here. I followed the edge round, and finding myself eventually opposite one of the forest paths, I resolved to cross it there and to set off along that road when I had climbed up the other side. This ditch was very deep but, fortunately for me, it was dry. As it was brick-lined there was no way of sliding down, and so I jumped. A little stunned by my fall, it took me a few moments to get back on my feet... I carried on and reached the other side without encountering any obstacles, but how was I to climb up! Searching carefully for a suitable spot, I eventually found one where a few bricks had come loose, giving me the chance to use them as rungs and to stick my foot into the earth to support myself. I had soon almost reached the top, when everything gave way under my weight and I fell back into the ditch beneath all the debris I had dislodged. I thought I was dead. This fall, which was an involuntary one, had been harder than the other. What's more, I was completely covered by all the material that had fallen on top of me. Some of this had struck me on the head and my skull was cracked. Oh, dear Lord! I said to myself in despair, let us not go any further, let us stay here. This is a warning from Heaven, which does not want me to go on. My ideas are probably wrong. Perhaps evil is of some use on earth, and when the hand of God wills it so, perhaps it is wrong to oppose it! But quickly revolted by such an idea, which was the all-too-sorry fruit of the corruption that had surrounded me, I removed all the debris I was covered with, and finding it easier to climb up to the hole I had just made because of the fresh holes that had appeared, I tried again with renewed courage and got to the top in a flash. All of this had taken me further away from the path I had caught sight of before, but, having carefully sought it out, I managed to get onto it and began to flee with all speed. I found myself outside the forest before the end of the day, and was soon on the hillock from which, to my misfortune, I had spotted that dreadful monastery six months earlier. Perspiring heavily, I rested for a moment. My first thought was to fall to my knees and beg God's forgiveness once again for the sins I had been forced to commit in that odious receptacle of impurity and crime. Tears of regret soon

flowed from my eyes. Alas! I said to myself, I was far less of a criminal when I left that same path last year, prompted by a principle
of devotion so fatally deceived! Oh, dear God, what a state I am
now in! These gloomy reflections were dispelled a little by the pleasure of finding myself free again, and I continued on my way to Dijon,
imagining that only in that city would my grievances be legitimately
received...

Here Madame de Lorsange wished to persuade Thérèse to draw
breath, at least for a few moments. She certainly needed to do so.
The passion she invested in her story, the wounds that these gloomy
accounts reopened in her heart, all finally forced her to pause for a
little while. M. de Corville had refreshments brought in, and after a
short rest, our heroine resumed the tale of her deplorable adventures
as follows:

On my second day my initial fears about being pursued had completely vanished. It was extremely hot and, taking my usual precautions, I had left the path to find some shelter where I might have a
light meal that would fortify me before evening. A little copse in the
wood to the right of the path, in the middle of which flowed a clear,
bright stream, seemed to me the perfect spot to refresh myself. My
thirst quenched by this pure, fresh water and nourished by a little
bread, I rested with my back against a tree and allowed the pure, still
air to circulate through my veins, restoring my strength and calming
my senses. There, my thoughts turned to that destiny, one practically without example, which, in spite of the thorns surrounding me
on my journey of virtue and whatever might happen to me, always
brought me back to my religious faith, to acts of love and submission
to the Supreme Being who inspires it and of whom it is the very
image. A sort of enthusiasm had just gripped me. Mercifully, I told
myself, the good Lord that I adore has not abandoned me, since I
have even now found the means to repair my strength. Is it not to
Him that I owe this good fortune? And are there not individuals on
this earth to whom it is refused? So, I am not entirely wretched, since
there are still those more to be pitied than I... Ah, am I not far less to
be pitied than those unfortunates that I am leaving behind in that den
of vice, from which God in His goodness has saved me by some sort
of miracle?... And, full of gratitude, I had sunk to my knees, turning

to the sun as the finest work of the Godhead, as that which is the greatest manifestation of His greatness, and finding in the sublime beauty of this star a fresh impulse to pray and offer thanks, when suddenly I felt myself to be seized by two men who, having covered my head to stop me seeing what was happening and crying out, bound me like a criminal and dragged me off without uttering a word.

We had been walking like this for two hours without its being possible for me to see which road we were on when, hearing me breathing with difficulty, one of my guides suggested to his companion that they remove the veil covering my head. He agreed to this, and I could breathe. I also noticed that we were in the middle of a forest, on a road that was fairly wide though little used. A myriad gloomy thoughts then entered my head, and I feared that I was being taken back to their odious monastery.

'Oh, Monsieur!' I said to one of my abductors, 'I beg you to tell me where you are taking me! May I not ask what you intend to do with me?'

'Calm yourself, my child,' this man said to me, 'the precautions we are obliged to take should not cause you any anxiety, because we are taking you to a very kind master. There are excellent reasons why he feels it necessary to employ such mysterious methods to select chambermaids for his wife, but you will be fine there.'

'Alas, sirs!' I replied, 'if all you wish is to make me happy, there is no reason to restrain me. I am a poor orphan who is greatly to be pitied, I have no doubt. All I ask for is a position somewhere, and if this is what you are giving me, why would you be afraid that I might run away?'

'She's right,' said one of the men, 'let's make her more comfortable and just keep her hands bound.'

They did this, and we continued on our way. Seeing that I came quietly, they even answered my questions, and I eventually learnt from them that the master to whom they were taking me was called the Comte de Gernande, that he was born in Paris and possessed considerable wealth in that part of the country, amounting in all to more than five hundred thousand livres income which, according to one of my guides, was his alone to enjoy.

'Alone?'

'Yes, he is a solitary man, a philosopher. He never sees anyone. On the other hand, he is one of the greatest gluttons in Europe. There isn't a single man in all the world who is capable of eating as much as him. I needn't tell you any more, you'll see for yourself.'

'But why these precautions, Monsieur?'

'I'll explain. Our master has the misfortune of having a wife who has lost her mind. She must be kept under surveillance. She does not leave her room and no one wishes to serve her. There would have been no point proposing it to you because, if you'd known about this, you would never have accepted. We are obliged to abduct girls by force to exercise this sad duty.'

'What! Do you mean that I will be a prisoner serving this lady?'

'Actually yes, that's why we are holding you like this. You'll be comfortable there... you need not worry, perfectly comfortable. Apart from these constraints, you will want for nothing.'

'Oh, dear Heaven! What a situation!'

'Come, come, my child, be brave, you'll be able to leave one day and your fortune will be made.'

My guide had scarcely finished speaking when we caught sight of the castle. It was a superb and vast building isolated in the middle of the forest, but the number of people in this grand edifice was considerably smaller than it appeared capable of housing. The only parts of the castle where I saw some activity and comings and goings were the kitchens, which were situated in cellars beneath the centre of the main building. All the rest was as solitary as the location of the castle. No one took any notice of us when we entered. One of my guides went down to the kitchens while the other presented me to the Comte. He was at the end of a vast and superb apartment, wrapped in a dressing-gown of Indian satin and lying on an ottoman with two young men next to him. They were so indecently, or rather so ridiculously attired, and coiffeured with such style and elegance that I at first took them for girls. When I had examined them more closely, I eventually realized that they were both boys, one of whom was fifteen years old or thereabout, the other sixteen. They appeared extremely good-looking, but were both in such a state of passivity and prostration that I first thought they were ill.

'Here's a girl, Monseigneur,' said my guide, 'she seemed to us to be just what you require. She is sweet-natured, honest, and all she asks for is a position in service. We hope that you will be pleased with her.'

'Very good,' said the Comte, barely glancing at me, 'you will lock the doors before retiring, Saint-Louis, and you will allow no one to enter unless I ring for them.'

Then the Comte got up and came over to examine me. While he is looking me up and down, I can describe him to you. The singularity of his portrait merits your attention for a moment. Monsieur de Gernande was at that time a man fifty years of age, nearly six foot tall and monstrously fat. His countenance was more terrifying than anything I've seen: the length of his nose, his thick, dark eyebrows, his wicked black eyes, his wide mouth and bad teeth, his dark, bald forehead, the sound of his raucous and frightening voice, his enormous hands and arms, all contributed to make him a gigantic individual whose appearance inspired much less confidence than fear. We shall soon see whether the morality and actions of this centaur matched his terrifying appearance. Following the most cavalier and cursory of examinations, the Comte asked me how old I was.

'Twenty-three years, Monsieur,' I replied.

He followed up this initial question with a few more about my history. I told him everything about myself, and did not even leave out the branding I had received from Rodin. When I had described my miserable condition to him, proving to him that misfortune had ever dogged my steps, the hateful man said to me harshly: 'So much the better, you'll fit in more easily here. It is but a very small misfortune that bad luck pursues that abject race of people that Nature condemns to crawl alongside us on the same earth. They are more active and less insolent in consequence, and better fulfil their duties towards us.'

'But sir, I have told you of my origins, which are not lowly.'

'Yes, yes, I know all that, people always pretend to be all sorts of things when they are nothing or in misery. The illusions of pride must necessarily offer consolation for the ills of fortune. It's then up to us to believe what we want to about these tales of the high-born brought low by the blows of fate. Anyway, I don't care about any of this. I find that you have the look and more or less the dress of a servant, and so I shall take you on as such, if it pleases you. However,' this hard man continued, 'whether or not you will find happiness is entirely in your hands. If you are patient and discreet, I shall send you away in a few years with sufficient means to live on without needing to find another situation in service.'

Then he took hold of one arm and then the other, and folding my sleeves up to the elbow, carefully examined them, asking me how many times I had been bled.

'Twice, Monsieur,' I told him, rather surprised by this question, and I explained when and in what circumstances in my life this had taken place. He pressed his fingers on the veins to make them stand out, in order to proceed with this operation, and when they had reached the desired point, he applied his mouth to them and sucked. From then on I had no doubt that libertinism was part of this hateful man's way of life, and the torments of anxiety were again awakened in my heart.

'I have to know what you look like,' continued the Comte, staring at me in a manner that made me tremble. 'The duties you must perform require that you possess no physical disabilities, so let's see what you have.'

I objected, but all the muscles of the Comte's terrifying physique seemed disposed to anger, and he sternly declared that he would not advise me to play the prude with him, since he had the means certain to make women see reason.

'What you have told me', he said to me, 'does not suggest that you are especially virtuous, and so any resistance on your part would be as out of place as it would be ridiculous.'

With these words, he gestured to his young boys, who immediately came up to me and set about undressing me. With individuals as weak and as enervated as those around me, it would most assuredly not have been difficult to defend myself, but what would have been the point? The anthropophagus who set them onto me could have pulverized me with a single blow of his fist, had he so wished, and so I realized that I was obliged to give in. I was undressed in a flash, and scarcely had this been done when I noticed that once again I was making these two Ganymedes laugh.

'My friend,' the younger boy said to the other, 'a girl is a lovely thing... but what a shame there's nothing down there.'

'Oh!' said the other boy, 'there's nothing more vile than that hole. I wouldn't touch a woman, even for a fortune.'

And while my front passage was so sarcastically ridiculed by them, the Comte, intimate devotee of the behind (regrettably, alas, like all libertines!), was examining mine with the greatest attention; handling it roughly, kneading it forcefully, and pinching my flesh between his fingers, he pummelled it until it was black and blue. He then made me walk a few steps forward and backwards towards him so that he would not lose sight of his chosen part. When I had got back to him, he made me bend over, stand upright, clench my buttocks, then spread them. He often knelt before this part of my body, which alone interested him. He directed kisses to several different spots, several even to the most secret of orifices, but all these kisses were the epitome of suction, not one of them that did not have this action as goal. He seemed to suckle each of the spots to which he applied his lips. It was during this examination that he asked me to recount every detail of what had been done to me at the monastery of Sainte-Marie-des Bois, and not noticing that I was redoubling his lusts in telling these tales, I naively told him everything with complete candour. He called one of his young men over, and placing him next to me, undid the knot of a long piece of red ribbon that held up a pair of white gauze pants, revealing all those charms hidden by this garment. After a few gentle caresses directed to the same altar upon which the Comte had made his sacrifice with me, he completely changed the focus of his attention and began to suck the part of this child that characterized his sex. He continued touching me. Whether out of habit on the young man's part, or skill on the part of this satyr, within a very few minutes Nature vanquished filled the mouth of the latter with the liquid that spurted from the member of the former. This is how this libertine exhausted these unfortunate children that he kept in his house and the number of whom we shall soon see. He weakened them in this manner, and this was the cause of the languid state in which I had found them. We shall now see how he managed to put the women into the same state, and the real reason why he kept his own wife in seclusion.

The homage that the Comte had paid to me had lasted a long time, but without the slightest infidelity to the temple that he had chosen: neither his hands, nor his looks, nor his desires had deviated from it for an instant. Having also sucked the other young man and received and devoured his seed in the same way: 'Come,' he said to me, bidding me follow him into an adjoining closet without even letting me recover my clothes, 'come, I am going to show you what is going on here.'

I could not conceal my dreadful anxiety, but there was no way of turning my fate around, I had to drain the chalice that was presented to me to the dregs.

Two other young men of sixteen, just as handsome, just as weak as the first two that we have left in the drawing-room, were working at a tapestry in this closet. They rose when we entered.

'Narcissus,' said the Comte to one of them, 'this is the Comtesse's new chambermaid, and I have to put her to the test. Give me my lancets.'

Narcissus opened a cupboard and immediately took out everything needed for blood-letting. I will leave it to you to imagine what happened to me. My torturer saw my confusion, but just laughed.

'Get her ready, Zephire,' said Monsieur de Gernande to the other young man, and approaching me, this child said to me with a smile:

'Don't be afraid, Mademoiselle, it can only do you the greatest good. Position yourself like this.'

I had to kneel on the edge of a stool, placed in the centre of the chamber, with my arms held by two black ribbons attached to the ceiling. I had hardly adopted this posture when the Comte approached me, lancet in hand. He was scarcely breathing, his eyes sparkled, and he wore a frightening expression. He bound my arms, and in less than the blink of an eye he had pierced both of them. He let out a cry, accompanied by a few blasphemies, as soon as he saw blood, and went to sit six feet away opposite me. The light garment that covered him was soon unwrapped, Zephire kneeling between his legs to suck him, while Narcissus, both feet resting on his master's chair, offered him to suck the same object that Gernande himself had the other boy pump. Gernande grabbed hold of Zephire's thighs, squeezing them and pressing himself against them, and yet stopped doing so to cast fiery looks at me. Meanwhile, my blood was gushing out of me, falling into two white basins placed under my arms. I soon felt myself weaken.

'Monsieur,' I cried, 'have pity on me, I am fainting.'

And I tottered, though I could not fall since I was held up by the ribbons. However, with my arms waving around, and my head wobbling on my shoulders, my face was drenched with blood. The Comte was drunk with lust... but I did not see the end of this procedure, fainting before it reached its climax. Perhaps he was not able to achieve this until he saw me in this condition, perhaps his supreme ecstasy depended on this image of death? Whatever the truth of this, when I recovered my senses I found myself in an excellent bed, with two old women nearby. As soon as they saw that my eyes were open they offered me broth, and every three hours excellent soups for forty-eight hours. When this time was up Monsieur de Gernande sent word for me to get up and come to speak to him in the same drawing-room where he had received me when I arrived. I was taken there, still a little weak and yet in quite good health.

When I arrived, the Comte bade me sit and said to me: 'Thérèse, I shall not subject you to such trials very often, you are useful to me for other purposes. However, it is essential that I explain my tastes to you and the way in which you will come to an end in this house if you betray me, if you have the misfortune to allow yourself to be suborned by the woman with whom I am going to place you. This woman is my wife, Thérèse, a status that is doubtless the most deadly she could have, since it obliges her to lend herself to the strange passion of which you have just been victim. Do not imagine that I treat her in this way out of vengeance, or contempt, or any feeling of hatred; it is simply a matter of passion. Nothing equals the pleasure I feel spilling blood... I am in ecstasy when it flows. I have never enjoyed this woman any other way. It's three years ago since I married her, and every four days precisely since then she undergoes the same treatment that you experienced. Her extreme youth (she is not yet twenty years old), the special care that we take of her, all this sustains her, and as we restore in her what we force her to lose, she has been in very good health since that time. Given such a condition, you will understand that I cannot allow her to go out or to be seen by anyone. I therefore give out that she is mad, and her mother, the only relative she has left, and who lives in her castle six leagues from here, is so convinced of this that she does not even dare come to see her. The Comtesse begs for mercy often enough, and there is nothing she will not do to move me, but she will never succeed. My lusts have dictated her sentence, which cannot be changed, and she will continue in this way for as long as she is able. She will want for nothing during her life, and as I enjoy exhausting her, I shall keep her going for as long as possible, and when she is no longer able to stand it, all well and good. She is my fourth and I shall soon have a fifth. Nothing concerns me less than the fate of a woman. There are so many in the world, and it is good to make changes.

'Be that as it may, Thérèse, your job is to take care of her. She regularly loses two bowls of blood every four days, but does not faint any more. She has gained strength from the habit, her exhaustion lasts for twenty-four hours, and she is well for the remaining three days. However, as you will readily understand, this life displeases her and there is nothing she would not do to escape it, nothing she would not undertake to communicate her true condition to her mother. She has already seduced two of her maids, whose scheming was discovered in time to stop them succeeding. She herself is responsible for the loss of those two unfortunates, and she repents it now. Acknowledging the unchanging nature of her fate, she makes the best of it and promises not to make any further attempts to seduce the people I place around her. But this secret, Thérèse, what happens to those who betray me, all this obliges me to surround her only with people abducted as you have been, in order to avoid in this way any prosecutions. Having taken you from no one, and so not having to answer for you to anyone, I am in a better position to punish you if you deserve it, in a manner which, although it may rob you of your life, cannot attract any sort of investigations or other unwelcome attention. From this time on, therefore, you no longer belong to the outside world, since you can disappear from it whenever I wish. So you see that such is your fate, my child: happy if you behave yourself well, dead if you seek to betray me. In any other case, I would ask for a response, but I have no need of one in view of the situation you are in. I have you in my power and you must obey me, Thérèse... let's go and see my wife.'

Finding no arguments to voice against such a true account, I followed my master. We crossed a long gallery, as dark and as secluded as the rest of the castle. A door opened and we entered an antechamber, where I recognized the two old women who had looked after me while I was poorly. They rose and led us into a magnificent apartment, where we found the wretched Comtesse doing frame embroidery on a chaise longue. She got up when she caught sight of her husband.

'Sit down,' the Comte said to her, 'you have my permission to remain seated while you hear what I have to say. I have at last found you a chambermaid, Madame, and here she is,' he continued, 'I hope you will recall the fate which you brought upon the others, and that you will not try to plunge this one into the same misfortune.'

'There would be no point,' I then said, full of desire to serve this unfortunate and wishing to disguise my intentions; 'yes, Madame, if I may be allowed to stress this to you, it would be pointless, because

I shall immediately report every word you say to me to Monsieur your husband, and I shall certainly not risk my life to serve you.'

'I shall not undertake anything that might place you in such a position, Mademoiselle,' said this poor woman who did not yet understand my reasons for speaking thus, 'rest assured, all I ask of you is to take care of me.'

'I shall be attentive to all your needs, Madame,' I replied, 'but that is all.'

And, delighted with me, the Comte shook my hand, whispering in my ear: 'Good, Thérèse, your fortune is made if you behave as you say you will.' The Comte then showed me my room adjoining the Comtesse's, and pointed out to me that there was no hope of escape from this apartment, which was everywhere secured by solid doors and windows that were framed with double grilles.

'There is a terrace, of course,' Monsieur de Gernande continued, leading me into a small garden located on the same level as the apartment, 'but given its elevation, I feel sure you won't be wanting to gauge the height of the walls. The Comtesse may come here to take the air whenever she pleases, and you will keep her company... farewell.'

I returned to my mistress's side, and as we began by silently studying each other, I was able to capture her well enough during these first few moments to provide a portrait of her.

Aged nineteen-and-a-half years, Madame de Gernande had the loveliest and the most majestic figure it was possible to see, not one of her gestures or movements that was not graceful, not one of her looks that was not full of feeling. Although she was blonde, her dark eyes were so beautiful that nothing could compare with their expressiveness, but a sort of languor, the result of her misfortunes, softened their lustre, making them a thousand times more attractive. She had the whitest skin and the loveliest hair, a tiny mouth, too small perhaps, and yet I would have been surprised if anyone considered this a fault. It was a pretty rose not fully opened, but her teeth were so white... her lips so red... it seemed as if Cupid had painted them with colours borrowed from the goddess of flowers. Her nose was narrow and aquiline, pinched at the top and crowned with two ebony eyebrows, her chin was extremely pretty, and in short, she had the loveliest oval-shaped face in which reigned overall a sort of charm, naivety, and candour that would have led one to take her enchanting countenance for that of an angel rather than the physiognomy of a mortal. Her arms, her bosom, her buttocks, were so round and white that she might have served as an artist's model. The temple of Venus was covered with a thin, dark moss, below which were a pair of well-rounded thighs, and what I found astonishing was that, in spite of her misfortunes, her plumpness remained unaffected. Her chubby, round buttocks were as plump and fleshy and firm as if she had a fuller figure and had always lived in the happiest of surroundings. And yet, everywhere on her body could be seen the terrible traces of her husband's libertinism, but, I repeat, without spoiling anything... the overall image was that of a beautiful lily where the bee has left a few marks. Madame de Gernande combined so many gifts with a sweet nature, a gentle and romantic turn of mind, and the most sensitive heart! She was talented and well-educated... and possessed a natural gift for seduction that only her vile husband could possibly have resisted. The sound of her voice was so charming and so devout. Such was the Comte de Gernande's unfortunate wife, such was the angelic creature against whom he had plotted. It seemed that the more inspiring she was, the more she inflamed his ferocity, and that the abundance of gifts she had received from Nature only served as further promptings to this villain's cruelties.

'What day were you bled, Madame?' I said to her, in order to make it clear to her that I knew everything.

'Three days ago,' she told me, 'and it's tomorrow...' Then, with a sigh, she added: 'Yes, tomorrow... Mademoiselle, tomorrow... you will be witness to this fine spectacle.'

'And is Madame not growing weaker?'

'Oh, dear Heaven! I am not yet twenty years old, and I'm sure that one is no weaker at the age of seventy. But I am comforted by the thought that it will soon end. I cannot possibly live long like this. I shall go to join my Father, I shall go to seek in the arms of the Supreme Being a repose that men have so cruelly denied me in this world.'

These words broke my heart. I disguised my feelings, though, wishing to retain my composure, but I secretly promised myself from then on that I would rather lay down my life a thousand times, if it came to it, than fail to rescue this unfortunate victim of a monster's debauchery from her sorry fate.

It was time for the Comtesse's dinner. The two old women came to tell me to take her into her room, and I passed the information on to her. Being used to this, she immediately went out, and assisted by the two valets who had seized me, the two old women served a sumptuous meal at a table where my place was set opposite my mistress. The valets then retired and the two women informed me that they would not budge from the antechamber, so as to be close enough to receive the orders of Madame relating to anything she might desire. I told the Comtesse this, she took her place, and invited me to do likewise with a friendly and affable air that completely won me over. There were at least twenty dishes on the table.

'As far as such things are concerned, you can see that I am well taken care of, Mademoiselle,' she said to me.

'Yes, Madame,' I replied, 'and I know that it is Monsieur le Comte's wish that you should want for nothing.'

'Oh, yes, but as such attentiveness is motivated solely by cruelty, it has little effect on me.'

Given her state of exhaustion and strong natural impulse to repair herself constantly, Madame de Gernande ate a great deal. She expressed a wish for young partridges and a Rouen duckling, which were immediately brought to her. After the meal she went to take the air on the terrace, holding my hand. It would have been impossible for her to go ten paces without my help. It was then that she showed me all those parts of her body that I have just described to you. She showed me her arms, which were covered in scars.

'Oh, it's not just there,' she said to me, 'there isn't a single spot on my miserable body where he does not enjoy seeing blood flow.'

And she showed me her feet, her neck, beneath her breasts, and several other fleshy parts that were equally covered in scars. On that first day I restricted my comments to a few mild expressions of sympathy, and we retired.

The next day was the Comtesse's fateful day. Monsieur de Gernande, who did not proceed with this operation until after dinner, which he always had before his wife's, sent word to me to come and eat with him. It was then, Madame, that I saw this ogre behave in such a terrifying manner that I could not believe my eyes. Four valets, among whom were the two who had brought me to the castle, served this astonishing meal. It deserves to be described in detail, and I shall do so without any exaggeration. I am sure that they did not serve any more just for me, and so what I saw was customary each day.

They served two soups, one a consommé flavoured with saffron, the other a ham bisque. The middle dish was sirloin of English beef, eight hors d'oeuvres, five of which looked to be lighter but were not, a head of wild boar in the midst of eight roast dishes which were accompanied by two services of side-dishes, and sixteen fruit desserts. There were ice-creams, six sorts of wine, four kinds of liqueur, and coffee. Monsieur de Gernande helped himself to all the dishes, some of which were completely devoured by him. He drank twelve bottles of wine, four Burgundies to begin with, four bottles of Champagne with the roast course, then a bottle each of Tokay, Mulseau, Hermitage, and Madeira with dessert. He ended the meal with two bottles of Caribbean liqueur and ten cups of coffee.*

As fresh after all that as if he had just woken up, Monsieur Gernande said to me: 'Let's go and bleed your mistress. You will tell me, please, whether I treat her as well as I do you.'

Two young boys whom I had not seen before, the same age as the other ones, were waiting for us at the door of the Comtesse's apartment. It was there that the Comte informed me that he had twelve such, that he had replaced each year. These ones appeared still prettier to me than any of those I had seen previously. They were less nervous than the others. We entered... All of the ceremonies that I am going to describe to you now, Madame, were those required by the Comte. They were observed regularly each day, the only thing that varied being the location of the bleedings.

Simply attired in a dress of flowing muslin, the Comtesse dropped to her knees as soon as the Comte entered.

'Are you ready?' her husband asked her.

'For anything, Monsieur,' she humbly replied. 'You know full well that I am your victim, and that your wish is my command.'

Monsieur de Gernande then told me to undress his wife and to bring her to him. However repugnant I found all these horrors, as you know, Madame, I had no option but to submit completely to his will. Look upon me, I beg you, as nothing but a slave in all that I have recounted to you and all that I have yet to tell you. I complied only when I could not do otherwise, but I did not act willingly in any of these scenarios.

I therefore lifted my mistress's dress and led her naked to the side of her husband, who was already seated in a large armchair. Well acquainted with this ceremony, she got up onto this chair and of her

own accord offered him that favourite part of her body to kiss which
he had enjoyed so much in me, and which seemed to arouse him
equally in all persons, whatever their sex.

'Spread them, Madame!' the Comte said roughly to her...

And for a long time he enjoyed what he liked to see, getting her to
adopt different positions in turn, half-opening and then squeezing it
shut again. With the tips of his fingers or his tongue he tickled the
narrow orifice, and soon, carried away by the ferocity of his passions,
he would nip her flesh, squeezing and scratching it. And as each small
wound opened up, he would immediately glue his mouth to it.
During these cruel preliminaries I would hold down his unfortunate
victim, and the two young boys, completely naked, would do duty for
him. Taking turns to kneel between his legs, they used their mouths
to excite him. It was then that I saw, not without astonished surprise,
that this giant, this sort of monster whose very appearance terrified
people, was scarcely a man. The thinnest, the tiniest excrescence of
flesh, or to employ a more precise comparison, what one would see in
a three-year-old infant was the most you could make out in an individual who was so huge and so corpulent everywhere else, and yet his
sensations were none the less acute, and every shiver of pleasure was
in him an attack of spasms. After this initial session he lay on the
couch and got his wife to straddle him so that her behind still covered
his face, while she rendered him the same service of sucking with her
mouth that he had just received from the young Ganymedes, who
were now both simultaneously excited by him with his hands.
Meanwhile, my own worked upon his behind. I tickled and defiled it
in every possible way. Having adopted this approach for more than a
quarter of an hour without any effect, I had to change tack. By order
of her husband, I laid the Comtesse on her back on a chaise longue,
with her thighs as wide open as possible. The sight of what she
opened up like this threw the Comte into a kind of rage... he thinks
for a moment, he darts thunderous looks, he blasphemes, then he
throws himself like a madman upon his wife, pierces her with his
lancet in five or six places on her body, but all of these wounds were
slight, producing a few drops of blood at the most. These initial cruelties finally ceased, to give way to others. The Comte sits again, letting
his wife breathe for a moment, to focus his attention on the two
favourites. He made them suck each other, or else he positioned them
in such a way that while he was sucking one, the other sucked him,

and so that the one he was sucking performed the same service with his mouth to the one by whom he was sucked. The Comte received much but gave nothing. His satiety and his impotence were such that the very greatest efforts could not even drag him from his torpor. He appeared to experience very violent titillation, but nothing happened. Occasionally, he commanded me to suck his little friends myself, and straightaway to deliver the incense that I collected into his mouth. He finally set each one in turn on the wretched Comtesse. These young men went up to her, insulted her, and were insolent enough to beat her and slap her face, and the more they molested her, the more they were praised, the more they were encouraged by the Comte.

Gernande then turned his attentions to me. I was in front of him with my bottom level with his face, and he paid homage to his God but did not molest me. I do not know why he did not torment his Ganymedes either, while assaulting the Comtesse alone. Perhaps the honour of belonging to him had become a right to be mistreated by him. Perhaps he was really excited by cruelty only because of the element of force in these outrages. Anything is possible in the minds of such individuals, and you can bet that whatever appears most criminal will be what inflames them the most. He finally places his young men and me beside his wife, mixing us together, man, woman, man, woman, and all four of us presenting our behinds to him. He first stands opposite, inspecting us from a little distance, then he comes closer, touching, comparing, caressing us. The young men and I were not made to suffer from this, but whenever he came to his wife, he would plague and torment her one way or another. The scene changed once again. He had the Comtesse laid on her stomach on a sofa, and taking each of the young men in turn, he introduced them himself into the narrow canal offered to them by Madame de Gernande's position. He allows them to become excited there but it is in his mouth only that the sacrifice must be consummated. He sucks each of them equally as they withdraw. While one performs, he has himself sucked by the other, and his tongue strays to the throne of pleasure presented to him by the boy performing. This activity is lengthy and the Comte tires of it, so he gets up and wants me to take the Comtesse's place. I immediately beg him not to require this of me, but in vain. He places his wife on her back along the length of the sofa, makes me lie on top of her, with my bottom turned towards him, and commands his favourites to probe me by the forbidden route. He brings each to me, introducing them into me with his own hands. I am then obliged to excite the Comtesse with my fingers and kiss her on the mouth. As for him, his offering is the same. As each of his favourites cannot act without displaying one of the sweetest objects of his devotion to him, he takes full advantage of this, and as with the Comtesse, after a few thrusts, the boy who is drilling me must go and squirt into his mouth the incense brought forth for me. When the young men have finished, he presses himself against my bottom, as if he wishes to replace them.

'There's no point in this,' he cries, 'that's not what I need... to business... to business... however woeful my state may appear... I cannot wait any longer... come, Comtesse, your arms!'

He then seizes her ferociously, positions her as he had me, with her arms attached to the ceiling by two black ribbons. I am charged with the job of securing the strips of cloth. He inspects the bindings, and finding them inadequate, he tightens them, so that, he says, the blood will come out with greater force. He feels the veins and pierces both of them almost at the same time. The blood spurts out a long way, and he is in ecstasy. Again positioning himself opposite while these two fountains flow, he has me kneel between his legs so that I may suck him. He gets both of his favourites to do the same in their turn, all the time keeping his eyes fixed on those jets of blood that inflame him. As for myself, certain that the instant that the crisis he hopes will take place will signal the end of the Comtesse's trials, I do all I can to hasten it, and as you can see, Madame, I have become whore through good-will and libertine through virtue. The dénouement that we awaited so desperately finally arrived. I had no idea how violent and dangerous it would be, since I had fainted the last time it had occurred... Oh, Madame, what frenzy! Gernande was delirious for almost ten minutes, thrashing around like a man in the throes of an epileptic fit and uttering cries that must have been audible a league away. His cursing was excessive, and striking out at all around him, he was terrifying to behold. The two favourites were knocked down, and he was about to hurl himself upon his wife but I managed to contain him. He let me finish sucking him, the need he had of me making him respect me. I eventually was able to calm him down by releasing from him that burning liquor, the heat, thickness, and above all abundance of which put him into such a frenetic state that I thought he was about to expire. Seven or eight spoons would scarcely have sufficed to contain the amount, and its consistency was thicker than the thickest porridge. This happened without an erection, and with the very appearance of exhaustion. Such contrarieties are better explained by those familiar with the art. The Comte ate excessively, and expended energy in this fashion only when he bled his wife, that is, every four days. Was this the cause of this phenomenon? I know not, and not daring to offer reasons for what I do not understand, I shall do no more than describe what I saw.

In any event, I ran to the Comtesse, staunched the flow of her blood, untied her, and lay her on a sofa in a state of extreme weakness, but the Comte suddenly left the room with his favourites without showing the slightest concern, and without deigning even to glance at the wretched victim of his rage, leaving me to restore everything to order as I wished. Such is the fatal indifference that, more than anything else, characterizes the mind of a true libertine. If he were carried away only by the ardour of his passion, remorse would be painted in his features when he saw the deadly consequences of his delirium. But if his soul is totally corrupt, he will not fear such consequences, observing them without pain or regret, perhaps even exhibiting still some trace of those vile lusts that produced them.

I helped Madame de Gernande to retire. From what she told me, this time she had lost much more than usual, but she was treated with so much care and so many restoratives that two days later there was no trace left of her ordeal. That same evening, as soon as I had completed my duties with the Comtesse, Gernande summoned me to go and speak with him. He was having supper, and I was obliged to serve him at this meal, which was conducted by him with even more intemperance than dinner. Four of his favourites accompanied him at table. Regularly every evening the libertine drank himself to intoxication, but twenty bottles of the most excellent wines were scarcely sufficient to achieve this, and I frequently saw him get through thirty. Supported by his favourites, the libertine then went to bed each evening with a couple of them, but he put no personal effort into any of this, which was nothing more than a rehearsal for the main performance.

However, I had found the secret of winning this man's highest esteem. He openly confessed that few women had pleased him as much. This helped me to gain his confidence, which I exploited solely to serve my mistress.

One morning, when Gernande had summoned me to his study to inform me of some new plans for libertine activities, and having listened carefully to him and applauded him warmly, when I saw that he was in quite a calm mood I tried to touch his heart with regard to the plight of his unfortunate wife.

'Is it possible, Monsieur,' I said to him, 'that a woman can be treated in such a manner, even regardless of all her ties to you? Please deign to consider the touching graces of her sex.'

'Oh, Thérèse,' replied the Comte, 'how can someone with intelligence try to calm me down with arguments that positively work me up all the more! Listen, my child,' he went on, bidding me sit next to him, 'whatever invectives you hear me proffer against your sex, no emotion, please. I shall bend to reasoned argument if it is well made.

'I ask you, Thérèse, what is your justification for claiming that a husband should be obliged to make his wife happy? And by what right does this wife dare demand it from her husband? The necessity of such a mutual obligation can rightfully only exist between two beings who possess an equal capability to harm each other, and consequently between two beings of equal strength. Such an association can only exist where a pact is immediately formed between these two beings to use their strength only in such a fashion that can cause no harm to either of them, but this ridiculous covenant could assuredly not exist between a strong individual and a weak individual. By what right could the latter demand that the former should spare him, and how could the strong ever be so stupid as to agree to do so? I can agree not to use my superior force with a person who is able to inspire fear by virtue of his own, but on what grounds would I reduce the impact of my strength against a person subjected to me by Nature? Do you reply, out of pity? This feeling is compatible only with that being who is like me, and as he is selfish, it would take effect only on the tacit condition that the individual who inspires pity in me will feel the same way with respect to me. But if I consistently prove myself to be superior in strength to him, so that his sympathy becomes useless to me, I am never obliged to agree to any sacrifice in order to obtain it. Would I not be a fool to pity the chicken killed for my dinner? This creature, which is too far beneath me and has no relationship whatever with me, could never inspire any feeling in me. Now, the relationship of a wife with her husband is no different in effect from that of the chicken with me. Both are domestic animals which we are obliged to make use of, that we must exploit in accordance with the uses with which Nature endows them, and without there being any difference of any kind between them. But I ask you, if Nature's intention was that your sex was created for the happiness of ours, and vice versa, would this blind Nature have been so inept in the construction of both of these sexes? Would it have given them both such grave faults that a mutual estrangement and antipathy were inevitably bound to result? There is no need to look for any further examples, just tell me, I beg you, Thérèse, given the character you know I have, what woman could I make happy, and conversely, what man can enjoy pleasuring a woman unless he is endowed with the gigantic proportions necessary to satisfy her? Will it, in your opinion, be his moral qualities that will make up for his physical inadequacies? And what reasonable person, knowing women well, will not cry with Euripides:* "He among the gods who gave birth to woman can boast of having produced the worst among all creatures and the most tiresome for man." If, then, it is proved that the two sexes are not at all compatible with each other, and that there is not a single complaint made by one that is not immediately applicable to the other, it is consequently false that Nature has created them for their reciprocal happiness. It may have granted them the desire to get close to each other in order to achieve the goal of propagation, but not to link up with a view to finding mutual happiness. Therefore, being in no position to expect to receive the pity of the stronger, and no longer being able to argue that the latter can find his happiness with her, the weaker of the two has no other alternative but submission. As, in spite of the difficulty of achieving this mutual happiness, it is up to the individuals of both sexes to strive to do this, the weaker must by her submission attract to herself the only bit of happiness that it is possible for her to enjoy, and the stronger must work at achieving his own by whatever means of oppression that it pleases him to employ, since it is proven that the strong are happy only when exercising their faculties of strength, that is, through the greatest possible oppression. Thus, this happiness that the two sexes may find in each other can be found by one through blind obedience and by the other through the greatest possible domination. If it were not Nature's intention that one of the sexes should tyrannize the other, would she not have created them of equal strength? In making one inferior to the other in all respects, has she not adequately indicated that her will was for the stronger to make use of those rights that she has given him? The more the stronger extends his authority, the more he in doing so makes the woman that fate has bound to him unhappy, and the better he fulfils Nature's intentions. This process is not to be judged according to the complaints of the weaker being. In this case, the judgements could only be faulty, since in making them, you would be espousing the thoughts of the weak alone. The action must be judged according to the power of the strong and the degree to which he has extended his power, and when the effects of this strength have been felt by a woman, one must then examine what a woman is, and how this despicable sex has been seen from antiquity to our own times by three-quarters of the peoples of the earth.

'Now, what do I see when I proceed to an objective study of this question? A puny creature, who is always inferior to man, infinitely less handsome than he, less ingenious, less wise, constituted in a disgusting fashion, entirely opposite to what may please a man, to what may delight him... an unhealthy creature for three-quarters of her life, incapable of satisfying her husband during those times when Nature subjects her to childbearing, sour, cantankerous, and haughty in temperament, tyrannical if she is accorded rights, base and grovelling if she is in subjection, yet always false, always mean, always dangerous; a creature so perverse, finally, that it was seriously debated at several sessions of the Council of Mâcon* as to whether this bizarre individual, as different from man as the ape in the forest, could lay claim to the title of human being, and whether this could reasonably be granted to it. Yet could this be an error of that time, and is woman more favourably regarded by earlier generations? Was this odious sex, which we now dare to idolize, honoured by the Persians, the Medes, the Babylonians, the Greeks, the Romans? Alas, I see her at all times oppressed, everywhere rigorously kept apart from serious affairs, everywhere despised, demeaned, shut away. In short, women are everywhere treated like beasts that one makes use of when required, and that one then immediately shuts away again in the harem. If I pause for an instant in Rome, I hear Cato the Wise* cry out to me from the world's ancient capital: "If men were without women they would still converse with the Gods." I hear a Roman Censor begin his harangue with these words: "Gentlemen, if it were possible for us to live without women, we would then know true happiness." I hear the poets sing in the theatres of Greece: "Oh, Jupiter! Why were you obliged to create women? Could you not have given birth to humans by better and wiser methods, in short, by means that would have spared us the scourge of women?" I see these same people, the Greeks, hold this sex in such contempt that laws were required to force a Spartan to procreate, and that one of the sentences of these wise republics was to force a wrongdoer to dress as a woman, that is, to clothe himself as the vilest and most contemptible creature they knew.

'But there is no need to look for examples in centuries so far removed from us. How is this wretched sex seen even today all over the world? How is it now? I see women shut away throughout the whole of Asia, serving there as slaves to the barbaric whims of despots who molest and torment them, who make play of their suffering. In America I see races human by nature, Eskimos, practise every possible kind of benevolence amongst men, and treat women with every conceivable harshness. I see them humiliated, prostituted to strangers in one part of the world, and serving as currency in another. In Africa, where they are doubtless far more downtrodden, I see them doing the work of beasts of burden, ploughing the soil, sowing the land, and serving their husbands on their knees. Shall I follow Captain Cook in his new discoveries? Will the charming isle of Tahiti, where pregnancy is a crime that sometimes leads to the mother's being put to death, offer me happier women? On other islands discovered by this same mariner I see them beaten and tormented by their own children, while the husbands themselves join their family in treating them more harshly still.

'Oh, Thérèse, do not let any of this amaze you, and do not be any more astonished by the widespread rights that husbands have had over their wives since time immemorial. The closer people are to Nature, the more they follow its laws. A woman can have no other relationship with her husband than that of a slave with her master. She certainly has no right to pretend to any higher status. One must not confuse with rights those absurd abuses which, while degrading our own sex, elevated yours for an instant. One must look for the cause of these abuses, say what they are, and thereafter, follow once again the wise counsels of reason. Now, here is the origin of that fleeting respect that your sex won in times past, Thérèse, and which still today, and without their realizing it, takes advantage of the good-will of those who continue to show this respect.

'Among the ancient Gauls, that is, in the only part of the world where women were not entirely treated like slaves, they would pre-dict the future and bring people good luck. The people imagined that they succeeded in this practice only because of the close commerce they doubtless had with the gods. Hence they were, in a way, associ-ated with the priesthood, and enjoyed a measure of the consideration shown to the priests. Chivalry was established in France according to these prejudices, and finding them favourable to its spirit, it adopted them, but as with all else, the causes were forgotten and the effects endured. Chivalry disappeared, but the antiquated notions it had nourished increased. This ancient respect accorded to an imaginary status did not die away even when the basis of this status disappeared. Witches were no longer respected but whores were venerated, and what was worse, men continued to slit each other's throats for them. The minds of philosophers should no longer be influenced by such platitudes, and putting women back in their proper place, as willed by Nature and acknowledged by the wisest peoples, they should see women only as individuals created for their pleasure and subjected to their whims, as creatures whose weakness and spitefulness should deserve nothing but their contempt.

'However, not only have all the peoples of the earth enjoyed the most extensive rights over their women, Thérèse, there have even been those who condemned them to death as soon as they came into the world, keeping alive only a small number necessary to the repro-duction of the species. Those Arabs known by the name of Koreihs used to bury their daughters as soon as they reached the age of seven on a mountainside near Mecca, because, they said, such a vile sex seemed to them unworthy of staying alive. In the harem of the King of Achem, if there was even the suspicion of infidelity, for the slight-est disobedience in the service of the Prince's pleasures, or as soon as they inspired disgust, they immediately received the most awful punishment. On the banks of the Ganges they are obliged to sacrifice themselves upon the remains of their husbands, being of no more use in the world once their masters are no longer able to enjoy them. Elsewhere they are hunted like wild animals, and it is an honour to kill many. In Egypt they are sacrificed to the gods, in Formosa they are trampled underfoot if they become pregnant. Under Germanic laws, he who killed a female stranger was fined only ten écus, or nothing at all if she was his own or a courtesan. In short, everywhere, I repeat, everywhere I see women being humiliated, molested, everywhere sacrificed to the superstition of priests, to the barbarity of husbands, or to the caprices of libertines. And because I have the misfortune to live in a nation that is still primitive enough to lack the courage to abolish the most absurd of prejudices, I am supposed to deprive myself of those rights that Nature grants me over their sex! I should renounce all of those pleasures arising from these rights!... No, no, Thérèse, that is not fair. I shall conceal my behaviour, since I must, but in this retreat where I hide away I shall compensate myself in secret for those absurd restrictions that legislation imposes on me, and here I shall treat my wife according to the rights granted by all the laws of the Universe, of Nature, and of my own heart.'*

'Oh, Monsieur,' I said to him, 'it is impossible to convert you!'

'That is why I would not advise you to undertake it, Thérèse,' Gernande replied, 'the tree is too old to bend. At my age, one can take a few more steps on the road of evil, but not a single one on the road to good. My principles and my tastes have made me happy since my childhood, they have always been the sole basis of my behaviour and my actions. Perhaps I shall go further, I feel that it is possible, but not to turn around, no. I hold the prejudices of men in too much horror, I hate their civilization, their virtues, and their gods too profoundly ever to sacrifice my leanings to them.'

From that moment, I clearly saw that I had no other alternative but to use trickery and to join forces with the Comtesse if I was to deliver either her or myself from this house.

After spending a year in her household, I had opened up my heart to her all too readily for her not to be convinced of my desire to serve her, and for her not to realize what had first made me act differently. I revealed myself to her even more, she yielded to me, and we made our plans together. We were to apprise her mother of the situation, opening her eyes to the Comte's infamies. Madame de Gernande was in no doubt that this unfortunate lady would instantly come to free her daughter from her chains, but how were we to manage this, we were so securely held, constantly kept under surveillance? Being accustomed to scaling ramparts, I scrutinized the one below the terrace. It was scarcely thirty foot high. I could not see any surrounding wall, and believed that, once we were at the bottom of this wall, we would be on the forest paths, but the Comtesse had arrived in this apartment at night and, never having left it, was unable to confirm my impressions. I agreed to try climbing down. Madame de Gernande sent her mother a letter that was the most likely to move her and determine her to come to the aid of such an unhappy daughter. I stuffed the letter in my cleavage, I embraced my dear, charming mistress, and then, with the aid of our sheets, as soon as night fell, I slid down to the foot of the fortress. Oh, Heaven, what did I see, realizing that I was a long way from being outside the enclosure! I was still in the grounds, in grounds surrounded by walls the sight of which had been hidden from me by the great number of trees and the thickness of their foliage. These walls were more than forty feet high, covered on top with glass, and prodigiously thick... What was to become of me? Dawn was about to break. What would they think, on seeing me in a place from which I was clearly planning flight? Would I be able to escape the Comte's fury? There was no reason to suppose that this ogre would not drink my blood to punish me for such a crime! It was impossible to go back, as the Comtesse had pulled up the sheets. To knock at the gates would be certain to betray me, and so I was very close to losing my head completely and hysterically surrendering to the effects of my despair. If I had discerned some degree of compassion in the Comte's heart such hope might perhaps have led me astray for a moment, but a tyrant, a barbarian, a man who detested women and who, he said himself, had for a long time been searching for an opportunity to sacrifice one by draining her of her blood drop by drop in order to see how many hours she might stay alive in this way... there was no doubt that I would become the subject of this experiment. Not knowing, therefore, what was to become of me, finding dangers everywhere, I threw myself at the foot of a tree, resolved to await my fate and resigning myself in silence to the will of Eternal God... Finally, day broke. Dear Heaven! The first object that presented itself to me... was the Comte himself. It had been dreadfully hot during the night, and he had come outside to take the air. He thinks he is mistaken, he believes he is seeing a ghost, he shrinks back, courage rarely being the virtue of villains. I rise trembling to my feet and prostrate myself before him.

'What are you doing here, Thérèse?' he said to me.

'Oh, Monsieur, punish me,' I replied, 'I have done wrong and have no defence.'

In my terror I had unfortunately forgotten to tear up the Comtesse's letter. Suspecting I have it, he asks me for it, and I am about to deny it, but seeing the fateful letter sticking out of the handkerchief in my bosom, Gernande seizes hold of it, reads it furiously, and orders me to follow him.

We return to the castle by a secret staircase leading down beneath the vaults. The profoundest silence still reigned there. After a few twists and turns, the Comte opens a dungeon and throws me into it.

'Impudent girl,' he then says to me, 'I had warned you that the crime you have just committed was punishable here by death. Prepare yourself, therefore, to suffer the punishment which you have brought upon yourself. After dinner tomorrow I shall come to dispatch you.'

Once again I throw myself at his feet, but grabbing hold of my hair, he drags me all around the floor of my cell, repeating this several times, finally hurling me hard enough against the walls to crush me to death.

'You deserve to have all four veins opened this instant,' he said as he closed the cell door, 'and if I am delaying your sentence, rest assured that it is only to make it all the more horrible.'

He is outside and I am shaking in the most violent manner. I cannot describe to you the night I spent. The torments of my imagination combined with the physical pains that this monster's initial cruelty had just caused me made it one of the most dreadful nights of my life. You cannot conceive the anguish of a wretch who awaits her punishment at any time, from whom all hope has been taken away, and who does not know whether each moment she is still breathing will be the last moment of her life. Unsure what sentence awaits her, she pictures it to herself in a thousand different ways, each more horrible than the other, and she thinks the slightest noise she hears is that of her executioners approaching. Her blood curdles, her heart stops, and the sword that will end her days is less cruel than these fatal moments when death threatens her.

It is likely that the Comte began by exacting revenge on his wife. The event that saved me will convince you of this, as it did me. I had been in the awful state I have just described to you for a day-and-a-half without anyone coming to help me, when my door opened and the Comte appeared. He was alone and his eyes gleamed with fury.

'You must have a good idea of the kind of death that you are about to suffer,' he said to me. 'Your perverse blood must flow in abundance. You will be bled three times a day. I want to see how long you can live like that. This is an experiment I have been longing to conduct, you know, and I thank you for providing me with the means.'

And with revenge his sole concern, the monster makes me stretch out an arm, pierces it, and after two bowls of blood, binds the wound. He had scarcely finished when shouts could be heard.

'Monsieur... Monsieur,' cried one of the old women who served us, as she ran up to speak to him... 'come quickly, Madame is dying, and she wishes to speak to you before she breathes her last.'

And the old woman flew back to her mistress's side.

However accustomed one might be to crime, it is rare that the news of its commission does not frighten the person who has just committed it. Such terror avenges virtue. This is the moment when it reclaims its rights. Gernande goes out in distraught mood, forgetting to lock the doors, and despite being weakened by being bled and starved for more than forty hours, I take my chance and flee from my cell. All the doors are open, so I cross the courtyards and reach the forest without being seen. 'Just walk,' I tell myself, 'walk with courage. Even if the strong despise the weak, there is an all-powerful God who protects and will never abandon them.' My head filled with these thoughts, I walk on with renewed spirit, and before night has fallen I find myself in a cottage four leagues distant from the castle. Still having a little money left, I am able to take care of myself as best I can, and had recovered in a few hours. I set out again at daybreak. Renouncing all thoughts of lodging complaints, whether new or old, and having enquired after directions, I headed towards Lyons, where I arrived a week later, a little weak and ill, but fortunately I was not followed. There, my only thought was to recover my health before reaching Grenoble, where I still expected to find happiness.

One day, when I chanced to glance at a foreign gazette, imagine my surprise when I saw crime rewarded in it in the shape of one of the main authors of my woes crowned with success. According to this newspaper, Rodin, the surgeon of Saint-Marcel, that unspeakable villain who had punished me so cruelly for having tried to prevent him from murdering his daughter, had just been appointed Principal Surgeon of the Empress of Russia, at a considerable salary. 'Good luck to him, the rogue,' I told myself, 'so be it, if Providence wills it so, while you, wretched creature, must suffer, suffer without complaint, since it is said that trials and tribulations must be virtue's miserable lot. No matter, I shall never take against it.'

I had not yet seen an end to these striking examples of the triumph of vice, examples so discouraging for virtue, and the prosperity of the person I was about to encounter would doubtless vex and astonish me more than any other, since this prosperity was that of one of those men who had inflicted the bloodiest outrages on me. I was preparing myself to leave when one evening I received a note, delivered to me by a footman dressed in grey who was completely unknown to me. On handing it to me, he told me that his master had charged him to obtain a reply from me without fail. This note read as follows: 'A man who has done you some wrong, and who thinks he recognized you in Bellecour Square, is anxious to see you in order to make reparation for his conduct. Come to meet him quickly. He has things to tell you which may acquit his debt to you.'

This note was not signed, and the footman offered no further information. When I declared to him that I was resolved not to reply as long as I did not know who his master was, he said: 'It is from Monsieur de Saint-Florent, Mademoiselle. He had the honour to make your acquaintance some time ago in the Paris region, and he maintains that you did him a favour which he is anxious to repay. Now that he is in charge of this town's business affairs, he enjoys both a great reputation and wealth that mean he is in a position to show you his gratitude. He is waiting for you.'

I quickly reflected on all this: 'If this man were not well intentioned towards me,' I said to myself, 'is it likely that he would write to me, that he would communicate with me in such a manner? He has remorse for his past infamies, he is shocked to recall that he took away from me what was most dear to me, that by a number of horrific deeds he reduced me to the cruellest state a woman can find herself in... yes, yes, there is no doubt that he is remorseful and I would be guilty in the eyes of the Supreme Being if I did not consent to alleviate his remorse. Moreover, am I in a position to reject the support on offer? Should I not rather waste no time in accepting all he is offering to relieve my suffering? This man wishes to see me in his mansion, and his wealth must surround him with people in whose presence he has too much self-respect to dare fail me again, and in the state I'm in, dear God!, can I inspire anything but pity?' I therefore assured Saint-Florent's servant that at the stroke of eleven o'clock the following day I should be pleased to call upon his master, that I congratulated him on the ways in which fortune had favoured him, and that I was a long way from being similarly blessed.

I returned to my room, but my mind was so preoccupied with what this man wished to say to me that I did not get a wink of sleep. I finally arrive at the address I had been given. It was a superb mansion, with a host of servants, and the humiliating looks these rich scoundrels gave me, scorning my misfortune, had quite an effect on me, and I was on the point of withdrawing when the same servant who had spoken to me the previous day approaches me and, reassuring me, leads me to a sumptuous drawing-room, where I easily recognize my torturer, despite his being forty-five years old now and its being almost nine years since I last saw him. He does not get up, but he commands his servant to leave us alone and gestures to me to come and perch on a chair beside the huge armchair where he is seated.

'I wanted to see you again, my child,' he said with a humiliating tone of superiority, 'not that I believe I have done you great wrongs, not that troublesome memories force me to make reparation when I think myself to be above such things, but I remember that during the little time we knew each other you showed spirit, and this is needed for what I have to propose to you. If you accept my proposal, the services I shall require from you and the fortune I possess will give you the resources you need, and which you would hope to acquire in vain otherwise.'

I was about to respond by reproaching him for the frivolousness of this approach when Saint-Florent silenced me.

'What's past is past,' he told me, 'that was passion and nothing more, and my principles lead me to believe that the fire of our passions should not be dampened in any way. When the passions speak, they must be obeyed, that is my law. When I was ambushed by the gang of thieves that you were with, did you hear me complain of my fate? One must console oneself and work hard if one is the weakest, and enjoy all of one's rights if one is the strongest, that's my philosophy. You were young and pretty, Thérèse, we were in the depths of a forest, there is no pleasure in the whole world that arouses my senses like the rape of a virgin girl. That is what you were and I raped you. Perhaps I would have done worse things to you if what I was attempting had not been successful, and if you had resisted my advances, but I robbed you and left you without resources on a dangerous road in the middle of the night. I had two motives for this second crime. I needed money, not having any. As for the other reason that drove me to commit this act, there is no point in explaining it to you, Thérèse, because you would not understand it. Only those who know man's heart and have studied its innermost recesses, who have visited the most impenetrable corners of that dark labyrinth, could explain this succession of misdeeds to you.'

'What, Monsieur! the money I had given you... the favour I had just done you... repay all I had done for you with such black treachery?... and you say that that is understandable, that it can be excused?'

'Oh, yes, Thérèse, the proof is that, having just robbed and assaulted you... (for I beat you, Thérèse), I had not gone twenty yards when, thinking of the state I left you in, I instantly recovered enough strength from these thoughts for fresh outrages which I would perhaps not have subjected you to otherwise. You had lost only one of your maidenheads... I was leaving, but I turned around, came back, and took the other one as well... Thus, it is true that in some people lust can be generated by the very act of crime! I'll go further, and say that it is therefore the case that crime alone arouses and precipitates it, and that there is not a single pleasure in the world that it does not inflame and increase...'

'Oh, Monsieur, how shocking!'

'Could I not have committed an even greater crime? I very nearly did, I admit, but I suspected that you were already at death's door, and this thought satisfied me and so I left you alone. But let us say no more on this subject, Thérèse. Let us come to the matter that made me wish to see you.

'The incredible taste I have for both of a little girl's maidenheads has not left me, Thérèse,' continued Saint-Florent. 'It is the case here as with all the other perversions of libertinism. The older one is, the stronger such urges become. New desires arise from old crimes, and new crimes spring from these desires. None of this would matter at all, my dear, were it not for the fact that the means one employs to succeed are themselves most sinful. But as the thirst for evil is the chief motive of our whims, the more criminal our urges are, the more we are aroused. Once we get to that point, the more mediocre our methods, the less pleased we are; the more horrible they are, the

keener our pleasure, and so we sink further and further into the mire
without the least desire to pull ourselves out.

'That is my history, Thérèse. Each day two young children are
required for my sacrifices. If I have climaxed, not only do I not see
the objects of my desires again, but it even becomes essential for the
complete satisfaction of my fantasies that these objects immediately
leave the town! I should not enjoy the next day's pleasures if I
imagined that the previous day's victims still breathed the same air as
I, and it is easy to get rid of them. Would you believe it, Thérèse? It
is my debauchery that fills the Languedoc and Provence with the
great many victims of libertinism found there.[1] One hour after these
little girls have served my needs, dependable emissaries ship them off
and sell them to the matchmakers of Nîmes, Montpellier, Toulouse,
Aix, and Marseilles. This commerce, from which I receive two-thirds
of the profits, recompenses me amply for what the girls have cost me,
and in this way I satisfy two of my dearest passions, my lust and my
cupidity, but the identification and seduction of victims are far from
easy! What is more, the nature of the subjects is extremely important
for my lubricity. I want them all to be snatched from those refuges of
misery where the need to stay alive and the impossibility of doing so
use up all of one's courage, pride, delicacy, and eventually threatens
to destroy the very soul, to the point of determining the subject to try
anything that seems likely to preserve it in the hope of securing an
indispensable means of subsistence. I have all these hovels merci-
lessly searched, and you cannot imagine what I uncover there. I'll go
further, Thérèse: some activity and industriousness, and just a little
easing of circumstances, would help them to resist my bribes and
would deprive me of the greater number of my subjects. Against
these risks is the credit that I enjoy in this town, the waves I make in
its commerce, leading to higher prices in goods which, multiplying
the numbers of the poor, by on the one hand taking job opportunities
away from them, and making it difficult to stay alive on the other,
increase in equal number the sum of subjects that misery delivers
into my hands. It's a well-known ploy, Thérèse: those shortages of

[1] This must not be considered fictitious. This dreadful person actually existed in
Lyons itself. The description here of his machinations is an accurate one: he dishonoured fifteen or twenty thousand little wretches. Once he had done the deed, they were
shipped off on the Rhone, and the towns in question were filled with the objects of his
debauchery for thirty years, all of them this villain's victims. The only fictitious detail in
this episode is his name.

wood, of corn, and of other foodstuffs that have been the scourge of
Paris for so many years had no other objects but those that promote
my interests. Avarice, libertinism, these are the passions that, issuing
from gilded mansions, cast a thousand nets over the humble roofs of
the poor. But whatever skill I employ to exert pressure on the one
hand, if adroit hands do not swiftly abduct the girls on the other I get
nothing for my pains, and the system works just as badly as if I were
not drawing upon every resource or calling in every credit I could
think of. I therefore need a quick, young, intelligent woman who,
having herself gone down the thorny pathways of misery, knows better than anyone else how to debauch those girls who are there, a
woman whose penetrating gaze can spot adversity in the darkest of
garrets, and whose evil mind can identify the victims to rescue from
oppression by the means I make available, in short, a witty woman,
without scruples or pity, who will use any means to succeed, to the
extent even of cutting off those few resources that, in keeping hope
alive in these unfortunates, prevents them from bringing themselves
to accept her offers. I had an excellent and dependable woman who
has just died. You cannot imagine how far this intelligent creature
carried her effrontery. Not only did she isolate these wretches to the
point of forcing them to come and beg help on their knees, but if
these methods did not succeed quickly enough to accelerate their fall,
the wicked woman would go so far as to rob them. She was a treasure.
I need only two subjects a day, but she would have given me ten if I
had wanted them. The result was that I made better choices, and that
the overabundance of the raw materials needed for my operations
compensated me for the fees she demanded. This is the woman that
you must replace, my dear. You will have four women at your command and two thousand écus salary. As I say, I need an answer,
Thérèse, and above all, don't allow fantasies to prevent you from
accepting happiness when chance and my hand offer it to you.'

'Oh, Monsieur!' I said to this dishonest man, trembling at his
words, 'how can you conceive of such lusts and how can you dare
suggest that I should facilitate them! What horrors you have just
forced me to listen to! Cruel man, if you were unhappy for just two
days you would soon see this philosophy wither in your heart. It is
prosperity that blinds you and hardens your heart. You have become
indifferent to the spectacle of ills from which you think yourself to be
safe, and because you hope never to experience them, you suppose

that you have the right to inflict them. May I never get close to being
happy if it can corrupt me to such a degree! Oh, dear Heaven, not to
be content with exploiting misfortune but to take audacity and ferocity so far as to increase it, to prolong it, for the sole satisfaction of
one's desires! What cruelty, Monsieur! The most ferocious beasts do
not behave so barbarically!'

'You are mistaken, Thérèse. There are no tricks that the wolf does
not invent to lure the lamb into its traps. These ruses are in Nature,
and benevolence is not. It is merely a characteristic of weakness pro-
moted by the slave to move his master to pity and dispose him to treat
him more gently. It is only ever found in Man in two cases: either if
he is the weakest, or if he is afraid of becoming so. The proof that this
alleged virtue is not found in Nature is that it is unknown by men
who are closest to it. The savage is contemptuous of it because he
kills his fellow man without pity, either out of revenge or greed...
would he not respect this virtue if it were inscribed in his heart? But
it has never appeared there, and will never be found anywhere where
men are equal. By weeding out certain individuals, by dividing men
into classes and ranks, by making the poor visible to the rich, and
making the latter fear a change of status that could plunge them into
the abyss of poverty, civilization immediately put into their head the
desire to relieve misfortune in order to be relieved in their turn if
they should lose their wealth. It was this that gave birth to benevolence, fruit of both civilization and fear. It is therefore nothing but a
virtue of circumstance, but in no way a sentiment of Nature, which
has never placed in us any other desire but that of self-satisfaction at
whatever cost. It is by thus confusing all feelings while never analys-
ing anything that one becomes blinded to everything and that one
deprives oneself of all sensual pleasures.'

'Oh, Monsieur,' I interjected with feeling, 'can there be anything
sweeter than the relief of misfortune! Leaving aside the fear of suffering oneself, is there any greater sense of satisfaction than that which
comes from obliging another?... The joy of seeing tears of gratitude,
of sharing the well-being that one has just spread among those unfortunates who, though like you, nevertheless lacked the barest essen-
tials, of hearing them sing your praises and call you their father, of
restoring serenity to brows darkened by debt, abandonment, and
despair? No, Monsieur, no, there is not a pleasure in the world to
match it. It belongs to the gods themselves, and the happiness that it

promises to those who have served it on earth will be only the beginning, since they will be able to see or make others happy in Heaven.
All the virtues spring from this, Monsieur. One is a better father, a
better son, a better spouse, when one knows the charms that come
from relieving misfortune. One might say that, like the rays of the
sun, the presence of a charitable man spreads fertility, sweetness, and
joy all around, and the miracle of Nature that derives from this source
of celestial light is that honest, delicate, and sensitive soul whose
supreme happiness comes from making others equally happy.'

'That's all Phoebus nonsense,* Thérèse. Man's pleasures are
determined by the kind of faculties he has received from Nature.
Those of the weak individual, and consequently of all women, must
necessarily lead to moral pleasures that are more strongly experienced by such people than pleasures of a physical nature would be,
given a constitution entirely devoid of energy. The opposite is the
case for those strong souls who, being far more delighted by vigorous
shocks given to those around them than they would be by the delicate
impressions felt by those same individuals, in view of their constitution inevitably prefer that pain felt by these others to any more gentle
contact. Such is the only difference between the cruel and the good-
natured. Both are endowed with sensitivity, but each after their own
fashion. I don't deny that both groups experience pleasure, but I
maintain, no doubt with many philosophers, that that of the individual who is more vigorously constituted will undeniably be more
intense than that of his opposite. Once we accept these differences,
there can and must be a category of men who find as much pleasure
in all that cruelty inspires as others experience in benefaction, but the
latter will be mild pleasure while the former will be extremely intense.
There is no doubt that the last category will be more real, more true,
since it represents the leanings of all men when still in the cradle of
Nature, and of children themselves before they have experienced the
constraints of our civilization. The other category will simply be the
product of this civilization and, consequently, subject to dubious
pleasures totally lacking in piquancy. In any case, my child, as we are
here less to philosophize than to reach an agreement, please be good
enough to give me your final answer... Do you accept or not the
proposal I am making to you?'

'I categorically refuse, Monsieur,' I replied, getting to my feet.
'I am very poor... oh, yes, very poor, Monsieur, but richer in the

feelings of my heart than in all the gifts of fortune, and I will never sacrifice the former to possess the latter. I shall die in poverty, but I shall never betray virtue.'

'Be gone!' cried the detestable man coldly. 'And see to it that I never have to fear your indiscretion, or else you will soon be put into a place where I would no longer have to fear it.'

Nothing encourages virtue as much as the fear of vice. Much less timid than I would have thought, having promised him that he would have nothing to fear from me, I dared to remind him of the money he had stolen from me in the forest of Bondy, and to impress upon him that, in the circumstances in which I found myself, I absolutely needed that money. The monster then sternly replied that it was simply up to me to earn some, and that I refused to do so.

'No, Monsieur,' I responded firmly, 'no, I repeat, I would rather die a thousand deaths than save my life at such a cost.'

'For my part,' said Saint-Florent, 'there is nothing I would not rather suffer than the vexation of giving away my money when it has not been earned. Despite your having the insolence to reject my offer, I am still happy to spend another quarter of an hour with you. Let us go into this boudoir where a few moments of obedience will put your finances into better shape.'

'I have no more desire to serve your debauchery in one respect than in another, Monsieur,' I answered with pride. 'It is not your charity I am asking for, cruel man, no, I would not give you that pleasure. It is only what you stole from me in the most shameful fashion. Keep it, then, you cruel man, keep it if that's what you want. Look upon my tears without pity. Listen, if you can, without compassion, to the sad voice of need, but remember that, if you commit this new infamy, my loss will buy me the right to despise you forever.'

Saint-Florent ordered me to leave, and from his awful expression I could see that, were it not for the things he had confided in me, and the exposure of which he feared, I would perhaps have paid for the boldness of speaking out to him too truthfully with some brutal treatment at his hands, and so I turned to leave. At that same moment one of those unfortunate victims of the debauched man's sordid vice was being taken to him. One of the women whose horrible duties he was proposing I share was bringing to him a poor little girl of about nine years old, and whose every feature was listless and wretched. She scarcely seemed to have the strength to support herself. 'Oh, Heaven!'

I thought when I saw her, 'how can such creatures inspire any other feelings but those of pity! Woe betide the depraved person who can imagine deriving pleasure from a body consumed by want. Who could wish to steal kisses from a mouth ravaged by hunger, a mouth that opens only to curse him!'

My tears flowed. I would have loved to rescue this victim from the tiger that awaited her, but I dared not. Could I have done so? I quickly returned to my inn, as humiliated by an ill luck that attracted such propositions to me as I was revolted by the wealth that dared to make them.

I left Lyons the next day to take the road to the Dauphiné, still filled with the insane hope that a little happiness awaited me in this province. I was scarcely two leagues away from Lyons, on foot as usual, with a couple of shirts and a few handkerchiefs in my pockets, when I met an old woman who came up to me with a pained expression and begged me to give her alms. Far removed now from the hardness of heart whose cruel instances I had just witnessed, and knowing no other joy in the world but that of obliging the unfortunate, I immediately took out my purse, intending to find an écu and give it to this woman. However, although I had at first judged her to be old and infirm, the shameful creature was much quicker than me. She swiftly seized hold of my purse, knocked me over with a vigorous punch in the stomach, and was a hundred feet away before I was able to catch sight of her again, and surrounded by four villains who threatened me if I dared to approach.

'Dear Lord!' I cried out with bitterness, 'so it is not possible for my heart to open up to any virtuous impulse without my being instantly punished in the harshest of ways!' At that fateful moment, all of my courage abandoned me. Today I most sincerely ask Heaven for forgiveness, but I was blinded by despair. I felt on the point of quitting a path that was covered with so many thorns. Two alternatives presented themselves to me: that of joining up with the rogues who had just robbed me, or that of returning to Lyons to accept Saint-Florent's proposal. With God's grace, I did not give in, and although the hope that it rekindled in me was deceptive, since so many adversities still awaited me, still I thank God for having sustained me. The fateful star that leads me, however innocent, to the scaffold, will only ever bring about my death, while other choices would have brought me infamy, and death is a far less cruel fate than this.

I resumed my journey in the direction of the town of Vienne, resolved to sell there what I had left in order to get to Grenoble. I was walking on sadly when, a quarter of a league from this town, I caught sight of two horsemen down in the plain to the right of the path, trampling a man beneath the hooves of their horses and, leaving him for dead, riding off at great speed. This awful spectacle moved me to tears. 'Alas!' I said to myself, 'there is a man more to be pitied than I. At least I still have my health and strength, I can earn a living, but if this unfortunate man is not rich what will become of him?'

However much I should have resisted these feelings of compassion, and though it might be fatal for me to give in to them, I could not overcome the strong desire I felt to approach this man and offer him assistance. I flew to his side and revived him with some smelling-salts I kept with me. He eventually opened his eyes, and his first utterances were words of gratitude. Even more anxious to be of service to him, I tore one of my shirts into pieces to bandage his wounds and staunch the flow of his blood. This was one of the only possessions I had left, and I was glad to sacrifice it for this unfortunate. Having carried out this first aid, I gave him a little wine to drink. This wretch having completely recovered his senses, I was better able to observe and study him. Though on foot and travelling light, he nevertheless did not appear impoverished, having some effects of value, rings, a watch, boxes, but all severely damaged in the incident. As soon as he can speak he asks me who the beneficent angel is who comes to his assistance in this way, and what he can do to show her his gratitude. Still being naive enough to believe that a person bound by gratitude must be forever in my debt, I think I may safely enjoy the sweet pleasure of sharing my tears with one who has just shed them in my arms. I tell him of my misfortunes, he listens with interest, and when I have finished recounting the final catastrophe that has just befallen me, the account of which reveals to him the state of misery in which I find myself, he cries: 'How happy I am at least to be able to show my gratitude for all that you have just done for me. My name is Roland,' continues this sharper, 'I possess a very beautiful castle in the mountains fifteen leagues from here, and I invite you to follow me there. So that this proposal may not injure your sensitivities, I shall explain to you straightaway how you can be of use to me. I am a bachelor, but I have a sister whom I love passionately, and who has committed herself to sharing my solitude with me. I need someone to serve her. We have just lost the girl who fulfilled these duties, and I offer you this position.'

I thanked my protector, and took the liberty of asking him by what chance a man like him risked travelling without retinue and being attacked by knaves, as had just happened to him.

'Being well-built, young, and vigorous, I have for several years been in the habit of visiting my place in Vienne in this way,' Roland said to me. 'It's good for both my health and my pocket. It's not that I need to be careful with my expenditure, as I am rich—you will soon see proof of this if you will do me the honour of coming to my home— but there is never any harm in being economical. As for the two men who have just insulted me, they are a pair of so-called gentlemen from the area. I won a hundred louis from them last week in a house in Vienne. I took them at their word, I meet them today, I ask for what's owed to me, and that's how they treat me.'

I was deploring as much as this man the double misfortune of which he was the victim when he suggested we resume our journey: 'I feel a little better, thanks to your attentions,' Roland said to me. 'Night is approaching, let us head for a house that cannot be more than a couple of leagues from here. Using the horses that we will pick up there tomorrow, we will be able to reach my place the same evening.'

Utterly resolved to take full advantage of the assistance that Heaven appeared to be sending me, I help Roland to begin walking, support- ing him on the journey, and two leagues down the road we do indeed come to the inn he had mentioned. There we share a decent supper together, and after the meal Roland recommends me to the mistress of the house. The following day we hire two mules, escorted by a valet from the inn, and in this way reach the Dauphiné frontier en route for the mountains. As the journey is too long to manage in one day, we stop off at Virieu, where I received the same care and atten- tion from my employer, and the next day we continued walking in the same direction. Around four o'clock in the evening we arrived at the foot of the mountains. There the road became almost impassable, and Roland advised the mule-driver to stay with me for fear of acci- dents, and we headed into the gorges. The path twisted and turned, rising and falling for more than four leagues, and by then we had left behind us all human habitation to such a degree, being so far off the beaten path, that I thought I was at the end of the world, and I began to feel a little anxious in spite of myself. Roland could not help noticing this, but he did not say a word, and his silence scared me even more. Eventually we saw a castle perched on a mountain-top at the edge of a terrible precipice, by which it seemed on the point of being swallowed up. No road seemed to lead there. The one we were following, used only by goats and filled with rocks on all sides, nevertheless led to this frightening lair, a place that looked more like a robbers' hideaway than the home of virtuous people.

'That is my house,' Roland said to me as soon as he knew I had caught sight of the castle. And when I expressed my astonishment at seeing that he lived in such a solitary spot, he replied brusquely: 'It suits me like this.'

This response increased my fears. In misfortune nothing escapes one's attention, a word, a greater or lesser inflection in the voice of those on whom we depend, can stifle or revive hope, but no longer being able to take a different course, I kept silent. The road twisted and turned, and suddenly this ancient, tumbledown ruin appeared ahead of us. We were a quarter of a league away at the most. Roland got down from his mule, and telling me to do likewise, he handed both over to his valet, paid him, and ordered him to turn back. I was not happy with this new turn of events, and Roland noticed my reaction.

'What's the matter, Thérèse?' he said to me, leading the way to his home, 'you are not outside France. This castle is on the borders of the Dauphiné, and is a dependancy of Grenoble.'

'Very well, Monsieur,' I replied, 'but how ever did it occur to you to take up residence in such a cut-throat place?'

'The fact is, those who live here are not very honest people,' said Roland. 'It is quite possible that you would not be very edified by their conduct.'

'Oh, Monsieur,' I said to him, trembling with fear, 'you make me shudder... Where are you taking me?'

'I am taking you to serve a gang of counterfeiters, and I am their leader,' Roland said to me, grabbing me by the arm and pushing me across a small drawbridge that was lowered as we arrived, and was immediately raised again behind us. 'Do you see this well?' he continued as soon as we had entered the castle, pointing to a big, deep grotto situated at the end of the courtyard, where four naked women in chains were turning a wheel; 'there are your companions, and that is your task. You will do ten hours work per day turning this wheel, and provided that, like these women, you satisfy all of the whims I wish you to obey, you will receive six ounces of black bread and a plate of beans a day. You must renounce all hope of freedom, because you will never achieve it. When you have died of this hard labour you will be thrown into this hole that you see next to the well, alongside sixty to eighty other wretches like yourself who await you, and you will be replaced by another girl.'

'Oh, dear Lord!' I cried, throwing myself at Roland's feet, 'be good enough to remember, Monsieur, that I saved your life, and that, moved for a moment by gratitude, you seemed to offer me happiness, and that you are now repaying my assistance by casting me into an eternal abyss of suffering. Is what you are doing just? Am I not already avenged by remorse in the depths of your heart?'

'What do you mean by this feeling of gratitude with which you imagine you have captivated me?' said Roland. 'You must reason better than that, you puny creature! What were you doing when you came to my assistance? Given the option of going on your way and that of accompanying me, did you not choose the latter on an impulse straight from the heart? In other words, you gave in to a movement of pleasure, didn't you? What the devil gives you the right to think that I am obliged to reward you for the pleasures you allow yourself? And how can it ever enter your head that a man who, like me, swims in gold and opulence, should deign to stoop low enough to be beholden to a miserable creature such as you? Even if you had saved my life, I would not owe you anything if you were acting in your own interests. To work, slave, to work! Learn that, in overturning the principles of Nature, civilization does not take away its rights. It originally created the strong and the weak, intending that the latter should always be subordinated to the former. The skills and intelligence of Man varied the position of individuals, so that it was no longer physical strength that determined status, but gold. The richest man became the strongest, the poorest became the weakest. With the exception of those factors that established power, the superiority of the strong was always determined by the laws of Nature, to whom it mattered not that the chains that bound the weak were in the hands of the richest or the strongest, and that they crushed the weakest or the poorest. But Nature is oblivious to these impulses of gratitude that you want to attribute to me, Thérèse. It was never one of her laws that the pleasure derived by a person in obliging another should become a reason for the latter to renounce his rights over the former. Do you find these feelings that you claim in animals that serve as examples to us? When I am dominant over you by dint of my wealth or my strength, is it natural that I should renounce my rights over you, either because you enjoyed obliging me, or because, being a victim of misfortune, you imagined you would gain some advantage by this means? Even if the service were done between equals, the pride of a superior individual would never let itself be cowed by gratitude. Is not the one who receives help always humiliated, and is not the humiliation he suffers adequate payment for the benefactor who, in this respect alone, finds himself to be superior to the other person? Is it not a boost to one's pride to raise oneself above one's neighbour? Does the person who obliges another need any other pleasure? And if, in humiliating the one who is in receipt of the favour, the obligation he is under becomes a burden to him, by what right should he be forced to keep it? Why should I accept being humiliated whenever the person who has done me a favour looks in my direction? Instead of being a vice, ingratitude is therefore the virtue of the proud, just as gratitude is just as surely the virtue of the weak alone. Let people do me favours as much as they want if they enjoy doing so, but they should expect nothing from me.'

At these words, to which Roland does not give me time to respond, two valets seize hold of me on his orders, strip me, and chain me up alongside my companions, whom I am forced to assist immediately, without even being allowed to rest after the exhausting journey I have just undertaken. Roland then comes up to me, brutally manhandles all those parts of my body that modesty forbids me to name, heaps sarcastic and impertinent remarks on me because of the disfiguring and undeserved brand that Rodin had imprinted on me, then arming himself with a pizzle that was permanently on hand, he applies twenty strokes to my backside.

'That's how you shall be treated, wretch,' he says to me, 'when you fail in your duties. I am not doing this for any fault already committed by you, but simply to show you how I deal with those who do commit them.'

I utter piercing cries, struggling under my chains. My contortions, my screams, my tears, the cruel expressions of my pain only serve to amuse my torturer...

'Oh, you'll have other cause to scream, whore,' says Roland, 'this is only the beginning of your suffering. I am going to acquaint you with the most barbaric refinements of misery.'

Then, he leaves me.

Six dark hovels situated beneath a cave surrounding this vast well, and which were locked like dungeons, served as our cells for the night. As the day ended shortly after I had begun working on this deadly chain-gang, they came to unfasten me and my companions, and after we had been given the portion of water, beans, and bread of which Roland had spoken, we were locked up.

I had been left alone for scarcely a minute when I was able to contemplate at leisure the horror of my situation. Is it possible, I said to myself, that there are men hard-hearted enough to stifle the feeling of gratitude within themselves? Can this virtue, to which I would succumb so gracefully if ever an honest soul put me in the position of feeling it, be unknown, then, to some individuals? Can those who stifle it with such inhumanity be anything else but monsters?

I was deep in these thoughts when all of a sudden I hear the door of my cell open—it is Roland. The villain has come to complete his insults by subjecting me to his odious whims. You can guess, Madame, that these must have been as ferocious as his behaviour, and that for such a man the pleasures of love necessarily bore the marks of his odious character. But how can I abuse your patience by recounting these fresh horrors to you? Have I not already soiled your imagination too much with these unspeakable accounts? Should I dare to tell you more?

'Yes, Thérèse,' said Monsieur de Corville, 'yes, we require these details from you. You veil them with a decency that takes the edge off all of the horror, and that which is helpful to those who wish to know Man is all that remains. One cannot imagine how much these scenes help to develop one's spirit. Perhaps it is due to the stupid reticence of those who have wished to write on these matters that we are still so ignorant in this area. Bound by absurd fears, they speak to us only of those puerile things that any fool already knows, and dare not look with courage into the human heart and open our eyes to its gross errors.'

'Well, then, Monsieur, I shall obey you,' Thérèse replied with emotion, 'and proceeding as I have done thus far, I shall attempt to present my descriptions in the least repulsive colours.'

Roland, whom I must first describe to you, was a small, stout man of thirty-five years, unbelievably strong, as hairy as a bear, with a sombre countenance and a ferocious expression, a dark complexion, manly features, a long nose, a beard up to his eyes, thick, black eyebrows, and that part of the body that differentiates men from our sex was so long and so excessively thick that not only had I never seen anything of the kind before, but assuredly Nature had never produced anything so prodigious. I could barely get both hands round it, and it was as long as my forearm. Roland combined this physique with all of the vices that can result from a fiery temperament, a great deal of imagination, and a wealth that was always too great not to have plunged him into serious bad habits. Roland had made his fortune—his father already accumulated a great deal and left him extremely rich—and with such means this young man had already lived life to the full. Blasé about run-of-the-mill pleasures, he now had recourse only to horrors which alone succeeded in reviving in him desires exhausted by too many vices. The women who served him were all employed in his secret debauches, satisfying pleasures only a little less dishonest, and in which this libertine might find the piquancy of crime that delighted him more than anything else. Roland had made his own sister his mistress, and it was with her that he requited the passions that he had already aroused with us.

He was almost naked when he came in, and his face, greatly inflamed, bore the effects of the excesses he had just indulged in at table, as well as the abominable lusts that devoured him. He considers me for a moment with a look that makes me shudder.

'Take off those clothes,' he says to me, while himself tearing off what I had taken to cover myself during the night; 'yes, take off all that and follow me. I made it clear to you just now what you risked if you gave in to idleness, but if you took it into your head to betray us, since the crime would be far greater, the punishment would have to be in proportion—come and see what form it would take.'

I was in a state that is hard to describe, but without giving my heart the time to burst, Roland instantly seizes me by the arm and drags me off. Leading me by the right hand, then by the left, he holds a small lantern that dimly lights our way. After several turns in the path, we

find ourselves at the door of a cellar. He opens it and, pushing me in
front of him, tells me to go down the steps while he closes this first
door behind us. I obey. A hundred steps down we find a second door
that opens and closes in the same way, but after that there are no
more stairs, just a small path hewn from the rock, full of twists and
turns, and dropping at an extremely steep angle. Roland does not say
a word, and his silence scares me all the more. Roland lighting our
way with his lantern, we journey like this for nearly a quarter of an
hour. The state I was in made me feel the horrible humidity of these
underground passages all the more intensely. In the end we had gone
so far down that I am not afraid of exaggerating when I say that the
place we arrived at must have been more than eight hundred feet
deep in the bowels of the earth. To the right and left of the path we
were following were several niches where I saw chests containing the
wealth accumulated by these criminals. We finally come to a door of
bronze. Roland opened it, and I nearly fell over with fright when I
realized what a dreadful place this immoral man was taking me to.
Seeing me quake, he gives me a hard push, and so, whether I want to
or not, I find myself in the middle of this awful burial-chamber in
spite of myself. Just imagine, Madame, a round cavern twenty-five
feet in diameter, whose walls draped in black were decorated with
nothing but the most baleful objects, skeletons of all sizes, skulls and
crossbones, bundles of birch-rods and whips, sabres, daggers, and
pistols. Such were the horrors one could see on the walls, lit by a
three-wick lamp suspended in one of the corners of the ceiling. In the
middle of this dungeon a long rope hung from the arch, reaching to
between eight and ten feet from the ground, and which, as you will
soon see, was there for the sole purpose of facilitating dreadful murders. To the right was a half-open coffin, out of which the spectre of
death was climbing, armed with a menacing scythe. There was a
kneeler beside it. A crucifix could be seen above it, positioned between
two black candles. To the left was the wax effigy of a naked woman,
so natural that for a long time I was fooled by it. She was attached to
a cross and lying on her stomach, so that her cruelly molested posterior parts were clearly visible. Blood appeared to flow from several
wounds and run down her thighs. She had the most beautiful hair in
the world, and her lovely face was turned towards us, seeming to beg
for mercy. One could make out all the contortions of pain imprinted
on her beautiful features, even the tears that streamed down her

cheeks. At the sight of this terrible image, I thought I would lose all my strength a second time. The far end of the cavern was filled with a vast black sofa, from which all the atrocities of this mournful place unfolded before one's eyes.

'This is where you will perish, Thérèse,' Roland said to me, 'if ever you conceive the fatal idea of leaving my house. Yes, it is here that I shall come to put you to death myself, that I will make you suffer the harshest punishments I can think of.'

Roland's face was on fire as he uttered this threat. His excitement and agitation made him like the tiger about to devour its prey. It was then that he pulled out the redoubtable member with which he was equipped. He made me touch it and asked me if I had ever seen anything like it.

'Yet this is how it must enter the narrowest part of your body, whore,' he said to me, furiously, 'even if I cleaved you in two in the process. My sister, who is much younger than you, can take it in that same part. I am never able to come differently with women, and so it must cleave you in twain too.'

And so as not to leave me in any doubt as to the place he meant, he introduced three fingers into it, armed with very long nails, saying: 'Yes, it's here, Thérèse. That's where I shall shove this member in a while. It will tear you apart, make you bleed, and I shall be drunk with pleasure.'

He foamed at the mouth as he uttered these words, which were interspersed with curses and odious blasphemies. The hand with which he caressed the temple that he seemed to wish to attack then wandered over all the adjacent parts. He scratched them, and did the same to my bosom, bruising it so much that I suffered horrible pains for a fortnight because of it. Next, he placed me on the edge of the sofa and rubbed wine spirit into that moss with which Nature decorated the altar at which our species reproduces itself. He set fire to it and burned it. His fingers seized the excrescence of flesh that crowns this same altar, he bruised it heavily, and from there introduced his fingers inside, his nails damaging the membrane lining it. Unable to contain himself any longer, he told me that, since he held me in his lair, he might just as well keep me down there, as this would save him the trouble of taking me down there again. I threw myself at his feet, daring to remind him of the favours I had done him... I realized that I was irritating him all the more by again bringing up the rights I assumed I had to his pity. He told me to be quiet, kneeing me as hard as he could in the pit of my stomach so that I fell backwards onto the floor.

'Come!' he said to me, pulling me up by my hair. 'Come! Prepare yourself! I am definitely going to sacrifice you…'

'Oh, Monsieur!'

'No, no, you must perish. I don't wish to hear any more reproaches concerning your good turns. I don't like being beholden to anyone. It's for others to be wholly in my debt… You are going to die, I tell you. Get into this coffin so that I can see whether it fits you.'*

He carries me to it, shuts me up in it, then leaves the cavern, pretending to leave me there. Never before had I thought myself to be so close to death. Alas! It was to present itself to me in a form that would be even more real. Roland comes back and takes me out of the coffin.

'You fit in there perfectly,' he said to me. 'It seems made for you, but to let you end your life quietly there would be too pleasant a death for you. I am going to acquaint you with a different kind of death, but which also has its charms. Come! Implore your God, whore, beg him to come and avenge you, if he really has the power to do so…'

I throw myself on the kneeler, and as I open up my heart out loud to the Eternal, Roland redoubles his attacks and torments more cruelly still upon those posterior parts of my body that are exposed to him. He whipped these as hard as he could with a strap armed with steel points, each blow of which made my blood shoot right up to the ceiling.

'Well, then!' he continued, blaspheming, 'he's not coming to help you, your God, he lets unfortunate virtue suffer like this, he delivers it into the hands of the wicked.* Oh, what kind of God, Thérèse, what kind of God is that! Come!' he then said to me. 'Come, whore, you must say your prayers'—and so saying, he lays me on my stomach at the edge of the sofa at the far end of the room—'I told you, Thérèse, you have to die!'

He grabs hold of my arms, ties them behind my back, then he passes around my neck a cord of black silk, the two ends of which, still held by him, can be tightened at will and so can restrict my breathing, sending me into the next world whenever it pleases him to do so.

'This torture is sweeter than you may think, Thérèse,' Roland says to me. 'Death will come to you, but with inexpressible sensations of pleasure. The constriction that this cord will produce on the mass of your nerves will set your organs of pleasure on fire. The effect is certain. If all of those who were condemned to this sentence knew what an intoxicating death it was, they would be less afraid of this punishment for their crimes and would commit them more often and with far more confidence. This delicious operation, Thérèse, which equally constricts the spot where I am going to put myself' (he adds, pursuing a criminal route to be expected of a villain such as him) 'will also redouble my pleasure.'

However, he tries in vain to get in. Despite preparing the way, he is too monstrously proportioned to succeed, and his attacks are always repulsed. Then his fury knows no bounds. His nails, his hands, his feet serve to avenge him for the resistance that Nature puts up against him. He tries again. His fiery sword slips over the edges of the neighbouring canal, and given the vigour of the thrust, penetrates it almost halfway. I utter a cry. Roland is furious at the error and pulls out in a rage. This time he knocks on the other door with so much force that the moistened dart plunges in, tearing me open as it does so. Roland takes advantage of this initial thrust, and his efforts become more violent. He gains ground, and as he advances, the deadly cord which he has passed around my neck tightens further and I let out terrible screams. The ferocious Roland is amused by these and urges me to redouble them, quite sure of their inadequacy, quite able to stop them whenever he wishes, and their shrill sounds inflame him. Nevertheless, he is on the point of being overcome with intoxication, and the compressions of the cord increase by degrees with his pleasure. Gradually, my organ enlarges, and the tightening becomes so acute that my senses weaken, nevertheless without losing their sensitivity. Roughly shaken by the enormous member with which Roland is tearing my bowels, and in spite of the dreadful state I am in, I feel myself drowned by the jets of his desire. I can still hear the cries he utters as he squirts them into me. A moment of stupor followed, I don't know what happened to me, but I soon opened my eyes and found myself to be free, untied, and my organs seemed to recover.

'Well, Thérèse,' my torturer said to me, 'I wager that, if you are willing to speak the truth, you felt nothing but pleasure?'

'Nothing but horror, Monsieur, nothing but disgust, anguish, and despair.'

'You are mistaken, I know the effects that you have just experienced, but whatever they may have been, what does it matter to me? I imagine that you must know me well enough to be quite certain that your pleasure is of infinitely less concern to me than mine in those acts I engage in with you, and this pleasure that I seek has been so intense that I'm going to experience it again. It's up to you now, Thérèse,' this arrant libertine said to me, 'your life depends on you alone.'

He then passes the rope hanging from the ceiling around my neck. As soon as it is tightly knotted, he ties a piece of string to the stool on which I am standing and which has raised me up level with him, as he holds the other end of it. He then goes and sits in an armchair opposite me. In my hands is a sharp billhook which I must use to cut the rope at the same moment when he will use the string he is holding to overturn the stool beneath my feet.

'You see, Thérèse,' he then says to me, 'if you miss your chance, I shall not miss mine. So then, I am not wrong when I tell you that your life is in your hands.'

He excites himself, and it is at the peak of his intoxication that he must pull away the stool, leaving me hanging from the ceiling. He does all he can to feign this moment. He would jump for joy if I misjudged it, but his attempts are vain, I guess correctly, the violence of his ecstasy betrays him, I see him make the fatal movement, the stool falls away, I cut the rope and, completely freed, fall to the floor. There, although more than twelve feet away from him, would you believe it, Madame, I feel my body inundated with the evidence of his frenzy and delirium.

Any other girl would have taken advantage of the weapon she held in her hands, and would no doubt have hurled herself upon this monster, but what good would this courageous action have done me? Not having the keys to these underground caverns, and having no knowledge of its twists and turns, I would have died before I was able to get out. Moreover, Roland was armed. So I got up again, leaving the weapon on the floor so that he should not harbour the slightest suspicion about me. He did not. He had savoured his pleasure as far as this was possible, and content with my docility and resignation far more perhaps than he was with my skill, he gestured to me to leave, and we went back up.

The next day I inspected my companions more closely. These four girls were aged between twenty-five and thirty. Although stupefied by misery and deformed by an excess of labour, they still retained some traces of beauty. They had lovely figures, and the youngest one, whose name was Suzanne, had charming eyes and her hair was still very beautiful. Roland had abducted her from Lyons. He had taken her virginity, and having stolen her from the bosom of her family, vowing to make her his wife, he had brought her to this dreadful castle. She had been there now for three years, and was a greater object of this monster's ferociousness than her companions. As a result of blows from the pizzle, her buttocks had become as hard and callused as cow-skin dried in the sun. She had a tumour on her left breast and an abscess in her womb that caused her unimaginable pain, and all this was the handiwork of the perfidious Roland. Each of these horrors was the fruit of his lusts.

It was she who informed me that Roland was about to go to Venice the following day, if the considerable sums he had just recently sent to Spain brought him the bills of exchange he was expecting for Italy, because he had no desire to carry his gold across the mountains. He never sent any there. He circulated his counterfeit money in a different country from the one where he intended to live. By this means, he would be rich in the place where he wished to settle, but only on the basis of banknotes from another country, and so his knavery could never be discovered. But anything could go wrong at any moment, and the retirement he was contemplating depended absolutely on this final transaction, in which the bulk of his fortune was at stake. If Cadiz accepted his counterfeit piastres, sequins, and louis, and sent him bills in exchange for all of this via Venice, Roland would be happy for the rest of his life. If the fraud were discovered the frail edifice of his fortune could come crashing down in a single day.

'Alas!' I said when I learnt of this situation. 'Providence will be just for once and will not allow such a monster to succeed. Then we shall all be avenged...'

Dear Lord! After the experiences I had had, how could I think like this!

Towards midday we were given two hours break, and we always took this opportunity to take a breather and dine separately in our bedchambers. At two o'clock we were chained up to the wheel again and made to work until night-time, without ever being permitted to enter the castle. If we were naked, it was not only because of the heat, but rather so that it was easier for our ferocious master to whip us with the pizzle from time to time. In winter we were given a vest and breeches that were stretched so tight across our skin that our bodies were no less exposed to the blows of a villain whose sole pleasure was to beat us.

A week passed without my seeing anything of Roland. The next day he appeared at our workplace, and on the pretext that Suzanne and I were turning the wheel too slowly, he gave each of us thirty strokes with the pizzle between the small of our backs and our thighs.

At midnight that same day the vile man came to find me in my cell, and aroused by the sight of the effects of his cruelty, he again introduced his terrible weapon into the dark cavern that I exposed to him in the position in which he held me, as he considered the traces left by his fury. When his passions were requited, I wanted to take advantage of the moment of calm to beg him to make my situation more comfortable. Alas! I did not know that, if in such individuals the moment of delirium makes more active the penchant they have for cruelty, they are no more inclined to the sweet virtues of an honest man when they are calmer. It is a fire that burns more or less brightly according to the foods fed to it, but one that burns nonetheless, even when beneath ashes.

'And by what right', Roland answered, 'do you demand that I loosen your chains? Is it because of the fantasies that I am willing to enjoy with you? Am I to kneel at your feet requesting favours in return for which you may beg some compensation? I ask you for nothing, I take from you, and I do not see why, because I exercise one right over you, I should refrain from demanding another one. There is no love in my argument. Love is a chivalrous sentiment which I despise above all else, and of which my heart has never felt the effects. I use a woman out of necessity, as one uses a round, hollow vessel to satisfy a different need. But never conceding anything, whether esteem or tenderness, to such individuals that my money and my authority subject to my desires, owing what I take to no one but myself, and never requiring anything from them but submission, it follows that I cannot be expected to show them any gratitude. To those who would wish to force me to show it, I ask, if a thief steals the purse of a man in a wood because he is stronger than him, does he

owe any gratitude to this man for the wrong he has just done him?
The same goes for an abuse committed against a woman—which
could be sufficient reason to do it a second time, but never to owe her
any compensation.'

'Oh, Monsieur!' I said to him. 'How wicked you are!'

'As much as it is possible to be,' replied Roland. 'There is not a
single delinquency in the world that I have not indulged in, not a
single crime that I have not committed, and not one that my principles do not excuse or legitimate. I have always felt a sort of attraction to evil that always served the interests of my pleasures. Crime
arouses my lust. The more awful it is, the more it excites me. I experience the same kind of pleasure in committing it that ordinary people only find in lubricity, and thinking of crime, committing it, or
having just committed it, I have many times found myself in the
same state as one is in the presence of a beautiful naked woman. It
aroused my senses in the same manner, and I did it to excite myself,
just as one approaches a beautiful individual with lewd intentions.'

'Oh, Monsieur, what you are saying is dreadful, but I have seen
examples of it.'

'There are thousands of them, Thérèse. You must not imagine
that it is the beauty of a woman that best arouses the senses of a
libertine, it is rather the type of crime that the laws have attributed
to possessing her. The proof of this is that the more criminal the
possession, the more one is aroused by it. There is no doubt that the
man who enjoys a woman whom he has stolen from her husband, or
a girl whom he abducts from her parents, has more fun than the husband who enjoys his wife alone; and the more respectable-seeming
are the taboos one infringes, the greater the pleasure. If it is his
mother, if it is his sister, if it is his daughter, the pleasures he experiences have an additional appeal. If one has tasted all that, one would
like the barriers to increase further so that infringing them will be
harder and offer greater charms. Now, if crime adds spice to pleasure, once separated from this pleasure, it can therefore be a pleasure
in itself, so crime alone can definitely be pleasurable, for it is impossible that that which adds spice should not be endowed with it itself.
Thus, I suppose that the abduction of a girl on one's own account
will give one a very intense pleasure, but her abduction for someone
else's benefit will give one all of the pleasure deriving from the enjoyment of this girl, enhanced by the abduction itself. The theft of a

watch or of a purse will also give pleasure, and if I have accustomed my senses to become excited by some pleasure at the abduction of a girl for the sake of the abduction alone, this same pleasure, this same excitement, will be felt at the theft of a watch, of a purse, etc., and it is this that explains the whims of so many honest people who steal without being in need. Once you accept this, nothing is simpler, so let people taste the greatest pleasures in doing anything that is criminal, and let them use their imagination in any conceivable way to make simple pleasures as criminal as it is possible to make them. In behaving in this way, all one is doing is giving these pleasures the dose of salt they lacked and which had become indispensable to the perfection of their happiness. These theories can take one a long way, I know, and perhaps I'll prove this to you, Thérèse, in a while, but what does it matter as long as one enjoys oneself. For instance, was there anything simpler and more natural, my dear girl, than for me to enjoy you? Yet you are opposed to it, you ask me not to do it. It would appear from the obligations I have towards you that I ought to grant you what you ask, however, I bow to nothing, I listen to nothing, I break all of the bonds that constrain the stupid, I subject you to my desires, and out of the simplest and most monotonous of pleasures I make one that is truly delicious. Submit yourself, then, Thérèse, submit yourself. And if you ever return to this world as a stronger character, take full advantage of your rights, and you will recognize which, of all pleasures, is the keenest and the most piquant.'

With these words, Roland went out, leaving me with thoughts which, as you can imagine, were not in his favour.

I had been in this house for six months, serving the arrant debauchery of this scoundrel from time to time, when I saw him come into my prison one evening with Suzanne.

'Come, Thérèse,' he said to me, 'it's been a long time, it seems to me, since I took you down into that cavern that frightened you so much. Follow me there, the both of you, but don't expect to come back up again. I absolutely must leave one of you down there. We shall see which one will be chosen by destiny.'

I get up, I look at my companion with alarm, and I see tears rolling down her cheeks... We follow him.

As soon as we were shut up underground, Roland inspected the two of us with a ferocious look in his eyes. He enjoyed telling us again of our sentence, and impressing on both of us that one of us would definitely be staying there.

'Come,' he said, as he sat, making us stand to attention in front of him, 'each of you must do your best to disenchant this stiff object, and woe betide the one that reinvigorates him.'

'That's not fair,' said Suzanne. 'The one who arouses you most should be the one who obtains mercy.'

'Not at all,' said Roland, 'once it is demonstrated which one of you arouses me the most, it is established that she is the one whose death will give me the most pleasure... and my sole aim is pleasure. Moreover, if I were to show mercy to the one that aroused me first, you would both proceed with such ardour that you would perhaps plunge my senses into ecstasy before the sacrifice were consummated, and that must not happen.'

'That's to want to do evil for evil's sake, Monsieur,' I said to Roland; 'the complement of your ecstasy should be the only thing you should desire, and if you can achieve this without crime, why do you want to commit one?'

'Because that's the only way I can do so deliciously, and because I only come down to this cavern to commit one. I know perfectly well that I could manage it without doing so, but I want a crime as means to this end.'

And during this dialogue, since I had been chosen to begin, I excited him with one hand from the front and with the other from behind, while he was free to touch all parts of my body, accessible to him because of my nakedness.

'It will still take quite a lot, Thérèse,' he said to me as he touched my buttocks, 'for this beautiful flesh to be in the same state of leatheriness and mortification as Suzanne's. You could burn the dear girl's buttocks and she would not feel it, but yours, Thérèse, but yours... are still roses interlaced with lilies. We'll get there, we'll get there.'

You cannot imagine, Madame, how much this threat reassured me. In issuing it, doubtless Roland was not aware of the calming effect it had on me, and yet was it not clear that, since he was planning to subject me to further cruelties, he had no desire to sacrifice me yet? As I have told you, Madame, in misfortune one is alert to everything, and from then on I felt reassured. Another piece of good luck! I was having no effect, and that enormous piece of flesh remained limply folded over itself, resisting all of my caresses. Suzanne, in the same position, was felt in the same places, but as her flesh was far rougher Roland was much less gentle with her, and yet Suzanne was younger.

'I am persuaded', said our persecutor, 'that the most terrifying whips would not now manage to extract a drop of blood from that arse.'

He had us both bend over, and as our posture offered to him the four paths to pleasure, his tongue wriggled into the two narrowest, and the horrible man spat into the others. He turned us round to face him, making us kneel between his thighs, so that our two bosoms were level with what we were exciting in him.

'Oh, when it comes to your breasts,' said Roland, 'you have to concede to Suzanne. Your titties are nowhere near as lovely. Here, just see what they're like.'

So saying, he squeezed the unfortunate girl's bosom between his fingers till it was covered in bruises. Now it was not me that excited him any more, Suzanne had taken my place. She had hardly held it in her hands when the arrow shot out of its quiver, promptly menacing all around.

'Suzanne,' said Roland, 'your success is frightening. The sentence falls on you, Suzanne, I fear,' continued this ferocious man, pinching and scratching her bosoms.

As for mine, all he did was suck and nibble at them. Finally he places Suzanne on her knees on the edge of the sofa. He bends her head forward and enjoys her in this position in that awful manner that is natural to him. Roused once again by pain, Suzanne struggles, and Roland, who is interested only in skirmishes and is content with a few strokes, comes to seek refuge in me at the same temple where he has sacrificed with my companion, whom he continues to torment and molest at the same time.

'There's a whore who excites me cruelly,' he said to me, 'I don't know what I'd like to do to her.'

'Oh, Monsieur,' I said, 'have pity on her. Her pain could not possibly be more excruciating.'

'Oh, yes, it could,' said the villain. 'It could... Ah! If I had the famous Emperor Kie here, one of the greatest rogues that China has ever seen on its throne, we would certainly do something more, truly.[1]

[1] The Chinese Emperor Kie had a wife who was just as cruel and as debauched as he was, the spilling of blood was nothing to them, and they would spill floods of it daily just for the pleasure of it. Deep within their palace they had a secret chamber where the

'He and his wife together sacrificed victims daily, and are said to have kept them alive for twenty-four hours, so that they experienced the most cruel anguish at the approach of death, and in such a state of pain that they were always ready to give up the ghost without being able to do so, as a result of the cruel attentions of these monsters who drove them from hope to despair, calling them back to the light for one moment, only to confront them with death the next... I'm too gentle, Thérèse, I don't understand any of that, I am just a schoolboy.'

Roland withdraws without terminating the sacrifice, and by this sudden withdrawal he causes me as much pain as he had done in entering me. He throws himself into the arms of Suzanne, and combining sarcasm with outrage, he says to her: 'Sweet creature, how I recall the first moments of our union with delight. No woman has ever given me more intense pleasure. I have never loved any like you... Let us embrace, Suzanne, we are going to part, perhaps for a very long time.'

'Monster,' my companion said to him, pushing him away in horror, 'be gone! I am not going to add the despair of hearing your horrible words to the torments you are inflicting on me. Requite your rage, tiger, but at least respect my misery.'

Roland grabbed hold of her and laid her on the sofa with her thighs wide apart, the workshop of generation easily within his reach.

'Oh, Temple of my former pleasures,' cried this vile man, 'oh, you who procured me such sweet pleasures when I plucked your first roses, I really must say my goodbyes to you, too...'

The villain! He introduced his nails into it, and groping around with them inside for several minutes while Suzanne screamed out loud, he pulled them out again covered in blood. Sated by these horrors, and well aware that it was no longer possible to contain himself, he said to me: 'Come, Thérèse, come, dear girl, let's end all this with a little session of the cut-the-cord game.'[1]

---

victims were sacrificed in front of their eyes while they enjoyed watching. Theo, one of this prince's successors, had a very cruel wife like him. They had invented a column of bronze which was heated up, and to which unfortunates were attached before their eyes. 'The Princess', says the historian from which we have borrowed this information, 'was greatly amused by the contortions and cries of these sad victims. She was displeased if her husband did not mount this spectacle for her regularly' (*Hist. des Conj.*, volume 7, page 43).

[1] This game, which was described earlier, was frequently in use among the Celts from whom we descend. (See *The History of the Celts* by M. Peloutier.) Nearly all of these

Such was the name of this fatal amusement which I described to you the first time I spoke to you of Roland's cavern. I climb up onto the three-legged stool, the vile man attaches the rope around my neck, and he positions himself opposite me. Suzanne, though in a dreadful state, excites him with her hands. A moment later he pulls away the stool upon which my feet are resting, but as I am armed with the sickle, the rope is immediately cut and I fall to the floor without any harm.

'Good, good,' says Roland, 'your turn, Suzanne, enough said, and I will show you mercy if you escape as skilfully.'

Suzanne is put in my place. Oh, Madame, permit me to keep the details of this dreadful scene from you... The unfortunate girl did not survive.

'Let us leave, Thérèse,' Roland said to me, 'the next time you come to this place, it will be your turn.'

'Whenever you wish, Monsieur, whenever you wish,' I replied. 'I prefer death to the awful life you force me to lead. Can life still have worth for wretches like us?'

And Roland locked me up again in my cell. The next day my companions asked me what had become of Suzanne, and I told them. They showed no surprise, all of them expected to suffer the same fate, and like me, all saw in it an end to their suffering and eagerly looked forward to it.

Two years had passed in this way, Roland indulging in his usual debauches and I in the horrible anticipation of a cruel death, when the news finally spread through the castle that not only were our master's desires satisfied, not only was he receiving the huge quantity of paper he needed for Venice, but he was even being asked for another six millions in counterfeit currency, the payment for which would be transferred to Italy whenever he wished. Surely this rogue was not making himself even wealthier? He was leaving with an income of

deviant debauches, the singular libertine passions, some of which are described in this book, and which absurdly today attract the attention of the law, were formerly either games played by our superior ancestors, or legal customs, or religious ceremonies. Now, we turn them into crimes. In how many religious ceremonies did pagans make use of flagellation? Several races employed these same torments or passions to appoint their warriors, a custom known as *Huscanaver*. (See the religious ceremonies of all the peoples of the world.) These entertainments, the greatest inconvenience of which can at the most be the death of some whore, are capital crimes now! Hurrah for the progress of civilization! How it has contributed to the happiness of Man and how much more fortunate we are than our ancestors!

more than two million, without even counting the expectations he harboured. This was the latest example to be set me by Providence. Once again, she was determined to convince me that prosperity was the lot of crime alone, and misfortune that of virtue.

This is how things were when Roland came to fetch me to go down into the cavern for a third time. I trembled when I recalled the threats he had made to me the last time we had gone down there.

'Rest assured,' he said to me, 'you have nothing to fear, the matter concerns myself alone... an extraordinary pleasure that I wish to experience and which will not involve any risks for you.'

I follow him. As soon as all the doors are closed, Roland says to me: 'Thérèse, you are the only one in the house that I dare confide in regarding this matter. I needed a very honest woman... and you are the only one I could find... I confess, I even prefer you to my sister...'

Filled with astonishment, I beg him to explain.

'Listen to me,' he says, 'my fortune is made, but however much fate has favoured me, it can abandon me at any moment. I can be spied upon, I can be seized while I am transporting my wealth, and if this misfortune befalls me, it's the rope that awaits me, Thérèse. It's the same pleasure that I enjoy subjecting women to that will be my punishment. I am as convinced as it is possible to be that this death is infinitely sweeter than it is cruel, but as the women that I have forced to experience the initial terrors have never been prepared to be honest with me, I want to find out what it feels like myself. I want to know from my own experience whether or not it is truly the case that this compression acts upon the erectile nerve of ejaculation in him who experiences it. Once I am persuaded that this death is but a game, I shall brave it far more courageously, for it is not the end of my existence that frightens me. My principles are designed to cope with that, and as I am quite persuaded that matter can never become anything else but matter, I do not fear Hell any more than I expect to enter Paradise. However, I am afraid of the torments of a cruel death. I should not like to suffer when I die. Let's try it out, then. You will do to me everything I've done to you. I shall strip myself naked, I shall climb onto the stool, you will tie the rope around me, I shall excite myself for a moment, then as soon as you see me getting hard, you will pull the stool away, and I shall be left hanging. You will leave me there until you see either the emission of my semen or symptoms of pain. In the latter case, you will immediately cut me loose. In the former case, you will let Nature take its course, and you will not cut me down until afterwards. So you see, Thérèse, I am placing my life in your hands, and your freedom and fortune will be the reward for your good conduct.'

'Oh, Monsieur,' I replied, 'your proposition is too extreme.'

'No, Thérèse, I insist on it,' he replied, taking off his clothes, 'but behave yourself. See what proof I am giving you of my trust and my esteem!'

What good would it have done to waver? Was he not master of me? Furthermore, it seemed to me that the evil I would do would immediately be compensated for by the extreme care I would take to preserve his life. I was going to be mistress of this life, but whatever his intentions might be towards me, I would only act to keep him alive.

We make ready. Roland works himself up with a few of his usual caresses. He climbs upon the stool and I attach him. He wants me to curse him as I do so, to reproach him for all the horrors of his life, and I do this. Soon his spear is threatening Heaven, he himself gestures to me to take the stool away, and I obey. Would you credit it, Madame, what Roland believed could not have been more true. His face radiated the signs of pleasure alone, and almost at that very same moment jets of semen spurted in rapid succession as far as the ceiling. When all was spent, without my helping him in any way at all, I rush to cut him down and he drops in a faint to the floor, but my first aid soon restores his senses.

'Oh, Thérèse,' he says to me, opening his eyes again, 'you cannot imagine the sensations you feel. They are beyond anything one can express. Let them now do with me whatever they wish, I shall brave the sword of Themis. You are going to find me still ungrateful, Thérèse,' Roland says to me, as he ties my hands behind my back, 'but what's to be done, my dear, I'm too old to change my ways… Dear creature, you have just brought me back to life, and I have never conspired so much against your own. You pitied Suzanne her fate, well then, you shall be reunited with her. I am going to shut you up alive in the cavern where she died.'

I need not describe to you the state I was in, Madame, you can imagine yourself: in vain did I weep and wail, I was not heeded. Roland opens the fateful cavern, he takes a lantern down into it so that I can better make out the multitude of corpses that fill it, he then passes a rope under my arms, tied, as I have told you, behind my back, and by means of this rope he lowers me to a depth of twenty feet from the bottom of this cavern and about thirty feet from where he was. I suffered horribly in this position, it felt as if my arms were being pulled out of their sockets. How gripped I was with fears of all kinds, and what sights presented themselves to me! Piles of dead bodies amongst which I was to end my days, and the smell of which was already infecting me. Armed with a knife, Roland ties the rope to a rod fixed across the hole, then I hear him exciting himself.

'Come, Thérèse,' he says to me, 'commend your soul to God, the instant of my delirium will be when I shall throw you into this sepulchre, when I shall plunge you into the eternal abyss that awaits you. Ah, ah... Thérèse, ah...' and I felt my head covered with the proofs of his ecstasy, fortunately without his having cut the rope. He pulls me up.

'Well, then,' he says to me, 'were you afraid?'

'Oh, Monsieur!'

'That's how you will die, Thérèse, you can be sure of it, and it pleased me to get you used to it.'

We went back up... Was I to complain, was I to congratulate myself? What kind of reward was this for what I had once again just done for him! But could not the monster do more than this? Could he not take my life? Oh, what a man!

Roland finally prepared to depart, and he came to see me the evening before at midnight. I throw myself at his feet, I implore him with the most earnest entreaties to set me free, and to give me just enough money to get to Grenoble.

'To Grenoble! Certainly not, Thérèse, you would denounce us there!'

'Well, Monsieur,' I said to him, drenching his lap with my tears, 'I make an oath to you never to go there, and to convince you of this, be so good as to take me with you to Venice. Perhaps I shall not find hearts there as hard as in my own country, and once you have been good enough to leave me there, I swear to you by all that is most holy never to trouble you.'

'I shall not give you any help, not a sou,' was this arrant rogue's harsh response. 'Everything that touches on pity, commiseration, and gratitude is so far from my heart that were I three times richer than I am, you would not see me give an écu to a poor man. The spectre of misfortune arouses me, it amuses me, and when I cannot do evil myself, I delight in the evil done by the hand of fate. I have principles on this matter, Thérèse, from which I shall not deviate. The poor are part of Nature's plan. In creating men of unequal strength, she has convinced us of her wish that this inequality should be preserved despite the changes our civilization would bring to her laws. It would be going against Nature's wishes to disturb the equilibrium that is the basis of her sublime organization, to work towards an equality that would be dangerous for society, to encourage indolence and sloth, to teach the poor to steal from the rich when the rich choose to refuse to help, because such assistance would have accustomed the poor to obtaining it without working.'

'Oh, Monsieur, how harsh these principles are! Would you speak in the same way if you had not always been rich?'

'That may be, Thérèse, every person sees things in their own way. This is mine, and I shall not change. People complain about all the beggars in France. If one wished, there could soon be none left. You need hang only seven or eight thousand, and this odious breed would soon disappear. The political body must have the same rules on this issue as the physical body. Would a man devoured by vermin let it live off him out of compassion? Do we not uproot the parasitical plant in our gardens that is harmful to those that are useful? Why, then, should we wish to act differently in this case?'

'But religion, Monsieur,' I cried, 'charity, humanity...'

'Are the stumbling-blocks to any pretence to happiness,' said Roland. 'If I have consolidated my own happiness, it is only on the ruins of all those vile, antiquated notions of man. It is by deriding laws both human and divine, by always sacrificing the weak when I found them in my way, by taking unfair advantage of public good faith, by ruining the poor and stealing from the rich that I have scaled the dizzy heights to the temple of the divinity that I worshipped. Why have you not done likewise? The narrow path to this temple lay before your eyes as it did mine. Have those fanciful virtues that you preferred to it consoled you for your sacrifices? Your time has come, wretch, your time is nigh, mourn your errors, suffer, and if you can, try to find amongst the phantoms you revere those things that your worship of them caused you to lose.'

With these words, the cruel Roland jumps on me and once again I am forced to serve the shameful lusts of a monster whom I abhorred for such good reason. I thought he was going to strangle me this time. When his passion was sated, he took the pizzle and struck me with it more than a hundred times all over my body, assuring me that I was fortunate, because he did not have the time for any more.

The next day, before he left, this wretched man performed for us a fresh scene of cruelty and barbarism, the like of which cannot be found in the annals of Andronicus, the Neros, Tiberius, or Wenceslaus.* Everyone in the castle thought that Roland's sister would be leaving with him, as he had got her to dress accordingly. When the time came to mount up, he brings her to us. 'Here is your station, vile creature,' he says to her, commanding her to strip naked, 'I want my comrades to remember me by leaving the woman they thought I held dearest as security, but as only a certain number are required here, and I am going on a dangerous journey for which my weapons will perhaps be useful to me, I must try out my pistols on one of these wretches.' So saying, he loads one of them, and pushes it into the chest of each one of us, finally coming back to his sister: 'Take that, whore,' he says to her, blowing her brains out, 'go tell the devil that Roland, the richest villain on earth, is the man who most insolently challenges the hand of God and his own!' The wretched girl did not expire immediately, thrashing around in her chains for a long time, a horrible spectacle that the unspeakable rogue watches cold-bloodedly, eventually tearing himself away to leave us forever.

The day after Roland's departure everything changed. His successor, a sweet and most reasonable man, had us released straightaway.

'This is not work for the weak and delicate sex,' he told us with kindness, 'it is for animals to serve this machine. The trade we follow is criminal enough without further offending the Supreme Being with gratuitous atrocities.'

He lodged us in the castle, and without demanding anything from me in return, put me in charge of the duties previously carried out by Roland's sister. The other women were put to work making coins, no doubt a much less tiring occupation, and for which they were nevertheless rewarded like me with decent rooms and excellent food.

Two months later Dalville, Roland's successor, informed us of the safe arrival of his colleague in Venice. He was settled and had made his fortune there, enjoying all the repose and happiness which he had flattered himself would be his. There was little chance that the fate of his replacement would be the same. The unfortunate Dalville practised his trade with decency, which was all that was needed for him to be quickly crushed.

One day, when all was quiet in the castle, when under the governance of this good master the work, though criminal, was carried out gaily all the same, the gates were smashed open, the ditches scaled, and before our people had time to think of defending themselves, the house was filled with more than sixty troopers of the mounted constabulary. We had to surrender, there being no other option. We were chained up like beasts, tied on horseback, and taken to Grenoble. 'Oh, Heaven!' I told myself as we entered that city, 'so the scaffold will be my fate in this town where I was mad enough to believe that I would find happiness... Oh, how misleading are man's expectations!'

The trial of the counterfeiters was soon over. All were sentenced to be hanged. When they saw the brand I bore, they almost dispensed with the trouble of questioning me, and I was about to be treated like the others when I finally attempted to obtain some mercy from the illustrious magistrate honoured by this tribunal, a judge of integrity, a cherished citizen and enlightened philosopher, whose wisdom and benevolence will ensure that his famous name shall forever be engraved in the temple of Themis. He listened to me. Convinced of my good faith and the veracity of my misfortunes, he deigned to pay a little more attention to my trial than his colleagues... Oh, great man, I owe you my homage. The gratitude of a wretched girl will not be a burden for you, and the tribute she pays you in making your kindness known to the world will ever be her sweetest pleasure!

Monsieur S—— himself became my lawyer. My case was heard, and his powerful eloquence enlightened minds. By and large, the depositions of the counterfeiters who were going to be executed supported the zeal of the man who was good enough to take an interest in me. I was found to have been seduced and declared to be innocent of all charges, completely free to do whatever I wished. In addition to these services, my protector organized a collection for me, worth more than fifty louis. I was finally seeing the dawn of happiness shine before my eyes. It seemed that my presentiments were at last coming true, and I believed that my woes were at an end, when it pleased Providence to convince me that this was still far from being the case.

On leaving prison, I had lodged at an inn opposite the Pont de l'Isère, on the suburban side, where I had been assured I would be decently accommodated. My intention, following the advice of Monsieur S——, was to stay there for a little time to try to find a position in the town, or, if I was not successful, to return to Lyons with the letters of recommendation that Monsieur S—— was good enough to give me. As was my custom I was eating in this inn at what people call the table d'hôte, when on the second day, I noticed that I was being closely observed by a substantial and very well-dressed lady who went by the title of Baroness. Scrutinizing her in my turn, I thought I recognized her, and we approached each other. We embraced like two people who have met before but who cannot recall where.

Finally, the Baroness drew me aside, saying to me: 'Thérèse, am I mistaken? Are you not the girl I saved from the Conciergerie ten years ago, and do you not remember Dubois?'

I was not exactly delighted by this encounter, nevertheless I responded politely, but I was dealing with the cleverest and most astute woman in France, and there was no escape. Dubois showered me with compliments, and told me that she had taken an interest in my fate with the rest of the town, but that, had she known that I had been involved, there were no representations she would not have made to the magistrates, several of whom, she claimed, were her friends. Weak as I always am, I let myself be taken into this woman's chamber, and I recounted my misfortunes to her.

'My dear friend,' she said to me, embracing me once more, 'if I wished to see you again in private, it was to tell you that my fortune is made, and that all I have is at your service. Look,' she said, opening boxes full of gold and diamonds, 'here are the fruits of my labours. If I had worshipped virtue like you, I would be locked up or hanged today.'

'Oh, Madame,' I said to her, 'if it's to crime that you owe all of this, Providence, which is always just in the end, will not allow you to enjoy it for long.'

'Wrong,' Dubois said to me, 'do not imagine that Providence always favours virtue. A brief moment of prosperity should not blind you to that extent. It makes no difference to the maintenance of the laws of Providence that Paul pursues evil whilst Peter does good. Nature requires an equal amount of both, and the exercise of crime rather than virtue is the thing in the world to which she is most indifferent. Listen, Thérèse, listen to me carefully,' continued this diabolical woman, taking a seat and bidding me sit beside her. 'You are not unintelligent, my child, and I should like to persuade you. It is not whether man chooses virtue or not that brings him happiness, dear girl, for virtue, like vice, is merely one way of behaving in the world. Therefore, it's not a question of following one path rather than the other. You just need to walk on the main road. He who strays from it is always wrong to do so. In a world that is entirely virtuous I would recommend virtue to you, because since rewards are associated with it, happiness would unfailingly depend upon it. In a thoroughly corrupt world I would only ever recommend vice to you. He who does not follow the same path as others inevitably perishes. He goes against all he encounters, and as he is weak, he must necessarily be broken. Our laws wish in vain to restore order and bring men back to virtue. Too unjust to achieve this, too inadequate to succeed, they will take people off the beaten track for a moment, but they will never get them to leave it. When it is in the general interest for men to be corrupt, anyone who is unwilling to become so with the rest will therefore be pushing against the general interest. Now, how can those who are perpetually acting against the interests of others expect to be happy? Will you tell me that it is vice that is not in men's interests? I would grant you that, in a world made up in equal parts of good and evil, because then the interests of one group would clearly go against those of the other, but this is no longer the case in a totally corrupt society. Therefore, my vices offend against the depraved alone, inspiring in him other vices that compensate him for them, and we are both happy. The tremors are felt by everyone. There is a multiplicity of shocks and mutual injuries whereby, each one immediately regaining what he has just lost, he constantly finds himself in a happy situation. Vice is dangerous only to that virtue which, being weak and timid, never dares to try anything out, but when it no longer exists on earth, when its fastidious reign is over, then vice that offends only the depraved will give birth to other vices, but will corrupt no more virtues. How could you not have come to grief a thousand times in your life, Thérèse, by constantly going in the opposite direction to that followed by everyone else? If you had gone with the flow, you would have safely entered port like me. Will he who tries to go up-river cover as much distance in the same day as he who goes downstream? You speak to me all the time of Providence.

Well, how do you know that this Providence loves order, and consequently virtue? Does she not ceaselessly offer you examples of its injustices and irregularities? Is it in sending men war, plague, and famine, is it in creating a world that is thoroughly depraved that she manifests her absolute love of good in your eyes? Why do you imagine that depraved individuals displease her, since she manifests herself through vice alone, since everything in her works is vice and corruption, since she wills nothing but crime and disorder? Moreover, where do we get those impulses from that draw us to evil? Is it not her hand that gives them to us? Is there a single one of our sensations that does not come from her, a single one of our desires that is not her work? Is it, then, reasonable to say that she would allow us inclinations towards something that would harm her, or would be of no use to her? Therefore, if vice serves her purpose, why would we wish to resist it? By what right would we work to destroy it, and on what basis would we stifle its voice? A little more philosophy in the world would soon restore order everywhere, and would make magistrates and legislators realize that those crimes they censure and punish with so much severity are sometimes far more useful than the virtues they preach without practising them themselves and without ever rewarding them.'

'But even if I were weak enough, Madame,' I replied, 'to embrace your dreadful theories, how would you manage to stifle the remorse that they would immediately engender in my heart?'

'Remorse is an illusion,' Dubois said to me, 'it is nothing, my dear Thérèse, but the imbecilic murmuring of the soul that is too timid to dare to suppress it.'

'Suppress it! Is that possible?'

'Nothing simpler. One repents only of those things one is not in the habit of doing. Practise more often what makes you feel remorse and you will soon be rid of it. Counter it with the flame of the passions and the powerful laws of self-interest and you will soon have dispelled it. Remorse is not proof of crime, it is merely evidence of a mind that is easy to subjugate. If some ridiculous order should be made to prevent you from leaving this chamber immediately, you would not leave it without remorse, however certain you might be that you would do no harm in doing so. So, it is not true that crime alone leads to remorse. Having convinced oneself that crime is nothing at all, and is even necessary, given Nature's overall plan, it should therefore be possible to conquer the remorse one would feel after committing it, as easily as it would be for you to stifle that which would result from your leaving this room after the illegal order you would have received to stay here. One must begin with a precise analysis of everything men call crime, in order to persuade oneself that it is nothing but the infringement of their laws and their national customs: that what one calls crime in France ceases to be such two hundred leagues away, that there is no act that is really considered as a crime all over the world, none that, debauched or criminal here, is not virtuous and praiseworthy a few miles from here, that all is a matter of opinion and of geography, and that it is therefore absurd to wish to compel oneself to practise virtues that are nothing but vices elsewhere, and to shun crimes that are excellent actions in another climate. Given these reflections, I ask you now whether I can still feel any remorse for having committed in France, whether out of pleasure or interest, a crime that is quite simply a virtue in China, and whether I should make myself most unhappy, and inconvenience myself greatly, in order to carry out in France acts that would get me burnt in Siam?* Now, if remorse is just a defensive reaction, if it arises simply from the idea of the forbidden and in no way from the action committed, is it an impulse it would be wise to allow to subsist within oneself? Is it not stupid not to suppress it at once? Let us become accustomed to regarding the action that has just given rise to remorse as indifferent, let us judge it to be so following a considered review of the manners and customs of all nations of the earth. Consequently, this action, such as it is, should be repeated as often as possible, or better still, one should commit even graver crimes than the one that's been done in order to get used to it, and habit and reason will soon destroy remorse. They will soon get rid of that gloomy feeling, sole fruit of ignorance and poor education. One will then feel that, as there is no real crime against anything, it is stupid to repent of it, and pusillanimous to dare to do only what can be useful or agreeable to us, whatever the obstacles that must be overcome to achieve it. I am forty-five years old, Thérèse, I committed my first crime at the age of fourteen. This freed me from all ties that constrained me. Since then, I have not ceased to pursue fortune in a career that has been filled with it, there is nothing that I have not done or caused to be done... and I have never known remorse. However this may be, I am nearing my goal, just a few more strokes of luck and I shall pass from the state of mediocrity in which I was going to end my days to more than fifty thousand livres income a year. I repeat, my dear, I have never felt the pricks of remorse as I have travelled this happy road. Were some awful setback to plunge me this instant from the heights into the abyss, I should not feel it any more, I should complain about others or about my own blunders, but I would still be at peace with my conscience.'

'So be it, then, Madame,' I replied, 'but let us reason for a moment according to your own principles. What gives you the right to demand that my conscience should be as harsh as your own, given that it has not been accustomed since childhood to overcome the same prejudices? By what right do you demand that my mind, which is not organized like yours, adopt the same ways of thinking? You admit that there is a balance of good and evil in Nature, and that in consequence, there is a need for a given number of individuals who do good and another who do evil. The position I adopt is therefore in Nature. Given this, how can you demand that I infringe the rules it prescribes for me? You say that you find happiness in the career that you pursue. Well, Madame, what makes you think that I would not equally find it in the one I follow? Moreover, do not imagine that the vigilance of the laws leaves those who infringe them alone for long. You've just seen a striking example of this: of the fifteen rogues I was living with, one got away and fourteen perished ignominiously...'

'And so that's what you call a misfortune?' continued Dubois. 'But what does that ignominy matter to him who no longer has any principles? When one has crossed all boundaries, when, in our eyes, honour is now simply an antiquated notion, reputation an indifferent thing, religion a myth, death complete oblivion, is it not then the same thing to die on a scaffold as in one's bed? There are two kinds of criminal in the world, Thérèse, those that a huge fortune and prodigious credit protect from this tragic end, and those who will not be able to avoid it if they are caught. The latter, born into poverty, must have only one desire if they are intelligent, to become rich whatever the cost. If they succeed, they have what they wished for and are bound to be content. If they are broken on the wheel, what regrets will they have, since they have nothing to lose? The laws are therefore impotent with regard to all villains, as long as the powerful are beyond their reach; it is impossible for the wretched to fear them, since the sword of justice is their only resource.'

'And do you believe', I replied, 'that in another world celestial justice does not await those for whom crime has no fears in this one?'

'If there were a God,' this dangerous woman responded, 'I believe there would be less evil in the world. I believe that if evil does exist here, either such disorder is ordered by this God, in which case he is a barbaric entity, or else he is unable to prevent it, and then he is a weak God. In either case, he is an abominable being, a being whose thunderbolts I am bound to defy and whose laws I must despise.* Oh, Thérèse, is not atheism better than either of these extremes? These are my beliefs, dear girl, I have had them since childhood, and I shall doubtless never abandon them as long as I live.'

'You make me tremble, Madame,' I said, rising to my feet, 'forgive me if I cannot listen any longer to your sophisms and your blasphemies.'

'One moment, Thérèse,' said Dubois, stopping me, 'if I cannot conquer your mind, at least let me capture your heart. I have need of you, don't refuse to help me. Here are a thousand louis, they are yours once the job is done.'

At this, following only my inclination to do good, I immediately asked Dubois what was involved in order to prevent, if I could, the crime that she was preparing to commit.

'There he is,' she said to me. 'Have you noticed that young merchant from Lyons who has been eating here for four or five days?'

'Who? Dubreuil!'

'Precisely.'

'Well?'

'He has told me in confidence that he is in love with you. He is very taken with your sweet and modest looks, he loves your candour and he is enchanted by your virtuousness. This romantic lover has eight hundred thousand francs in gold or in paper money in a small chest next to his bed. Let me give this man the impression that you agree to listen to him. What does it matter to you one way or the other? I will get him to propose a walk outside town with you. I will persuade him that his suit to you will be advanced during this walk. You will amuse him, and keep him outside for as long as possible. Meanwhile I will rob him, but I will not flee. I will still be in Grenoble while his valuables will be in Turin. We will employ all possible ruses to allay his suspicions; we shall appear to assist him in his investigations. Meanwhile, my departure will be announced and will not surprise him. You will follow me and the thousand louis will be paid to you when we reach the territory of Piedmont.'

'I accept, Madame,' I said to Dubois, determined to warn Dubreuil of the theft that was being planned, 'but just consider', I added, the better to deceive this villainous woman, 'that if Dubreuil is in love with me, by warning him or by giving myself to him, I can obtain far more than you are offering me to betray him.'

'Bravo,' Dubois said to me, 'that's what I call a good pupil. I am beginning to think that Heaven has given you a greater gift for crime than me. Anyway,' she continued, as she wrote, 'here is my promissory note for twenty thousand écus. Dare to refuse me now.'

'How could I do so, Madame,' I said, taking the note, 'but you should at least understand that it is because of my wretched condition that I am weak enough and culpable enough to give way to your powers of seduction.'

'I wanted to pay tribute to your intelligence,' Dubois said to me, 'but you prefer me to blame your misfortune. As you wish. Serve me without fail and you will be content.'

Everything was arranged. I began to be a little more receptive to Dubreuil's attentions, and I did indeed realize that he had some feelings for me. My situation was extremely awkward. Certainly, I was far from wanting anything to do with the proposed crime, even if there had been ten thousand times more gold on offer, but to denounce this woman was another problem for me. The idea of imperilling the life of a creature to whom I had owed my freedom ten years earlier was extremely repugnant to me. I would have liked to find a way to prevent the crime without having it punished, and with any other person than a consummate criminal like Dubois I would have managed to do so. This, then, was what I resolved to do, unaware that this horrible woman's secret scheming would not only upset the entire edifice of my well-meaning plans, but would even punish me for having conceived them.

On the appointed day of the planned walk, Dubois invites the two of us to dine in her chamber. We accept, and when the meal is over Dubreuil and I go down to hasten the carriage that was being made ready for us. As Dubois had not accompanied us, I found myself alone for a moment with Dubreuil before we left.

'Monsieur,' I said to him in haste, 'listen to me carefully, don't create a stir, and above all, observe strictly what I am going to tell you to do. Do you have a friend you can depend on in this inn?'

'Yes, I have a young associate that I can count on as much as myself.'

'Well, Monsieur, go quickly and instruct him not to leave your chamber for one minute all the time that we will be on our walk.'

'But I have the key to the room, what's the point of such excessive precaution?'

'It is more essential than you think, Monsieur, avail yourself of it, I beg you, or I shall not go out with you. The woman we dined with is a villain, she has arranged the outing for the two of us just so that she can rob you more easily in the meantime. Hurry, Monsieur, she is watching us, she is dangerous. Give your key to your friend so that he may go and wait in your room, and tell him not to budge until we have returned. I will explain all the rest to you as soon as we are in the carriage.'

Dubreuil hears what I say and squeezes my hand to thank me. He hurries to instruct his friend accordingly, returns, and we set off. On the way I explain the whole affair to him, recount my own adventures to him, and inform him of the unfortunate circumstances of my life that have led to my making the acquaintance of such a woman. This honest and sensitive young man shows me the warmest gratitude for the service that I wish to do him, he is interested in my misfortunes, and proposes to alleviate them a little with the gift of his hand in marriage.

'I am more than happy to be able to repair the wrongs that fortune has done you, Mademoiselle,' he said to me. 'I am my own master, I am answerable to no one. I am going to Geneva to make a considerable investment of sums that your good advice has prevented me from losing, and you must follow me there. When we have arrived I shall become your husband, and you will appear in Lyons in this position alone, or if you prefer, Mademoiselle, if I do not have your complete trust, I shall give you my name in my native land.'

I was too flattered by such an offer to dare to refuse, but neither did I feel it appropriate to accept without making Dubreuil aware of all the reasons why he might come to regret making it. He was grateful to me for my sensitivity, and pressed me all the more insistently... Wretched creature that I was! Must happiness offer itself to me, only to penetrate me more deeply with the sorrow of never being able to seize hold of it! Must it, then, be so that no virtue could take root in my heart without preparing torments for me!

Our conversation had already taken us two leagues from town, and we were about to get out to enjoy the cool air in avenues bordering the Isère where we planned to walk, when suddenly Dubreuil told me that he felt ill... He gets out and is seized with a dreadful fit of vomiting. I immediately have him put back in the carriage, and we make haste to drive back into town. Dubreuil is so ill that he has to be carried up to his bedchamber. His associate, whom we find there, and who, as ordered, has not left the room, is astonished by his condition. A physician arrives. Dear Heaven! Dubreuil has been poisoned! Scarcely have I heard this fateful news than I run to Dubois's apartment. The wretched woman! She's gone. I go to my room, my cupboard has been forced open, and the little money and clothing I possess has been taken. Dubois, I am assured, has been heading in the direction of Turin for the last three hours. There was no doubt that she was the author of all these crimes. She has called on Dubreuil. Annoyed to find someone with him, she had avenged herself on me, and had poisoned Dubreuil during dinner, so that subsequently, when she had succeeded in robbing him, the unfortunate young man would be more concerned with staying alive than with chasing after the woman who had stolen his fortune, and would let her safely escape. The event of his death happening in my arms, so to speak, I might more readily be suspected of it than her. There was nothing to confirm her machinations, but how could they possibly have been any different?

I hurry back to Dubreuil's chamber. I am no longer allowed near him. I complain about this denial and am informed of the reason. The unfortunate man is expiring and his only concern henceforth is the Lord. However, he has declared me free of all blame. I am innocent, he assures them. He expressly forbids that I be charged. He dies. Scarcely has he closed his eyes than his associate makes haste to come with news for me, begging me to calm down. Alas! How could I do so? How could I not weep bitter tears over the loss of a man who had so generously offered to drag me from the gutter? How could I not deplore a theft that plunged me back into the misery which I had only just left behind? 'Frightful creature!' I cried, 'if this is where your principles have brought you, is it any wonder that they are abhorred, and that honest people punish them!' But I was reasoning as the injured party, and Dubois, who saw only her own happiness and her own interests in what she had undertaken, doubtless reached quite different conclusions.

I confided everything in Dubreuil's associate, whose name was Valbois, both what had been plotted against the friend he had lost and what had happened to me. He pitied me, sincerely regretted the loss of Dubreuil, and blamed the excess of delicacy that had prevented me from going to the authorities as soon as I had learnt of Dubois's plans. We agreed that this monster, who required only four hours to reach safety in another land, would get there before we could arrange for her to be pursued, that it would cost us a lot of money, that the master of the inn, who would be deeply compromised in any suit we might bring and who would defend himself impressively, would perhaps end up destroying me... I who seemed to breathe easily in Grenoble, having barely escaped the gallows. These reasons convinced me and even frightened me so much that I resolved to leave this town without taking leave of Monsieur S——, my protector. Dubreuil's friend approved of this plan. He did not hide from me that if this whole episode came to light, the depositions he would be obliged to make would compromise me, whatever precautions he might take, as much because of my intimacy with Dubois as because of my last walk with his friend; that he therefore advised me accordingly to leave immediately without seeing anyone, in the safe knowledge that, for his part, he would never take action against me, believing me to be innocent, and being unable to accuse me of anything but weakness in all that had just taken place.

Thinking about Valbois's advice, I recognized that it was all the more sound in that it seemed just as certain that I appeared guilty as it did that I was not, that the only thing that spoke in my favour—the advice given to Dubreuil during the walk, and which, I had been told, was not clearly expressed by him at the moment of death—would not be such overwhelming proof that I could count upon it. In view of all this, I quickly made up my mind and told Valbois.

'I would have liked my friend to have given me favourable instructions about you,' he said to me, 'I should have carried them out with the greatest of pleasure. I would even have liked him to tell me that it was you who advised him to stay in his room, but he did none of this. I am therefore obliged to restrict myself to executing his orders alone. The misfortunes that you have experienced for his sake would determine me to do something for you myself if I could, but I am young, with a limited fortune, and I am obliged to deliver Dubreuil's accounts to his family without delay. Permit me, therefore, to limit

myself to this one small favour which I beg you to accept. Here are
five louis, and there is an honest merchant-woman from Chalon-sur-
Saône, my homeland. She is returning there after a twenty-four-hour
stay in Lyons, where she was called on business. I am putting you in
her hands.' 'Madame Bertrand,' continued Valbois, taking me to this
woman, 'this is the young person I spoke to you about. I commend
her to you. She wishes to find a position. I beg you as earnestly as if
she were my own sister to do all you can to find something for her in
our city, in keeping with her person, her origins, and her upbringing,
and that until that time she should not have to pay anything, and I
will account to you for everything when next I see you. Adieu,
Mademoiselle,' continued Valbois, asking my permission to embrace
me. 'Madame Bertrand is leaving tomorrow at dawn. Go with her,
and may a little more happiness follow you to a town where I shall
perhaps have the satisfaction of seeing you again soon.'

The honesty of this young man, who at bottom owed me nothing,
made me weep. Courteous behaviour is sweetest when you have
experienced odious conduct for so long. I accepted his favours,
swearing to him that I was going to devote all my efforts to making
myself able to repay them one day. 'Alas!' I thought as I retired, 'if
the exercise of a new virtue has just plunged me into misfortune, at
least for the first time in my life the hope of consolation presents
itself in this horrific abyss of evils into which virtue plunges me once
again.'

It was early in the morning. The need to breathe fresh air made me
go down to the banks of the Isère with a view to walking there for a
few moments, and as often happens in such cases, my reveries took
me a long way along the path. Finding myself in an isolated spot, I sat
down there to think at greater leisure. Meanwhile, night came on
without my thinking of retiring to bed, when suddenly I felt myself
seized by three men. One places his hand over my mouth, and the
other two hurriedly bundle me into a carriage, getting in after me,
and we drive like the wind for a good three hours without any of
these brigands deigning either to say a single word to me or to respond
to any of my questions. The shutters were down and I could not see
anything. The carriage arrives near a house, gates open to let it in and
close again immediately. My abductors carry me inside and through
a number of dimly lit apartments, leaving me eventually in one of
them, next to which is a room from which I can see a light shining.

'Stay here,' one of my abductors says to me, going off with his companions; 'you will soon see people you know.'

And they disappear, locking all the doors carefully behind them. At almost the same time the door of the chamber where I could see candlelight opens, and from it I see emerge, a candle in her hand... Oh, Madame, guess who this might be... Dubois... none other than Dubois, that horrible monster, eaten away no doubt by the most ardent desire for revenge.

'Come here, charming girl,' she says to me arrogantly, 'come and receive the reward for the virtues you indulged yourself in at my expense...', and angrily squeezing my hand... 'Oh, you villain, I'll teach you to betray me!'

'No, no, Madame,' I quickly said to her, 'no, I have not betrayed you. Make enquiries, I have not made the slightest complaint that could give you concern, I have not said the least word that might compromise you.'

'But were you not opposed to the crime that I was planning? Did you not prevent it, shameful creature? You must be punished for it...'

And as we were going inside, she did not have time to say any more about it. The apartment that I was shown into was as sumptuous as it was magnificently lit. At the far end, on an ottoman, was a man of about forty in a dressing-gown of flowing taffeta, whom I shall describe to you shortly.

'Monseigneur,' said Dubois, presenting me to him, 'here is the young person that you requested, the girl that all Grenoble is interested in... the famous Thérèse, in short, sentenced to be hanged with counterfeiters, and then released because of her innocence and her virtue. See how skilful I am in serving you, Monseigneur. Four days ago you told me of your keen desire to sacrifice her to your passions, and I am delivering her to you today. Perhaps you will prefer her to that pretty boarder in the Benedictine monastery in Lyons that you also wanted, and who is due to arrive at any moment. That girl's physical and moral virtue is still intact, whereas this one only remains virtuous in her sentiments, but virtue is a part of her existence, and nowhere will you find a creature of greater candour and honesty. Both girls are yours, Monseigneur. You can either dispatch both this evening, or one today and the other tomorrow. As for me, I am leaving you now. The kindness you have shown me obliges me to tell you about my experiences in Grenoble. A man dead, Monseigneur, a man dead, and I must flee.'

'Oh, no, no, charming woman,' cried the master of the house, 'no, stay, and you need fear nothing under my protection! You are the soul of my pleasures. You alone possess the skill to arouse and satisfy them, and the more you multiply your crimes, the more you set my passions alight... But she's pretty, this Thérèse...', and addressing me, 'How old are you, my child?'

'Twenty-six, Monseigneur,' I replied, 'and full of woe.'

'Yes, woe, misfortune. I know all that, it's what amuses me, it's what I wanted. We shall put all this to rights, and put an end to your reverses. I assure you that in twenty-four hours you will no longer be unhappy...', and with bursts of horrendous laughter, 'Is it not the case, Dubois, that I have a sure means of ending a girl's misfortunes?'

'Assuredly,' said this odious creature, 'and if Thérèse were not one of my friends, I should not have brought her to you, but it is only fair that I reward her for what she has done for me. You could never imagine, Monseigneur, how much this dear creature has been useful to me in my latest enterprise in Grenoble. You have offered to pay my debt of gratitude for me, and I beg you to acquit this debt in full.'

The obscurity of these remarks, the observations that Dubois had made to me when we came in, the type of man I was dealing with, this young girl who was yet to arrive, all this instantly filled my imagination with an anxiety that it would be hard to describe to you. A cold sweat exhales from my pores, and I am on the point of fainting. This is the moment when I finally understand what this man is about. He calls me to him, he begins with two or three kisses, forcing our mouths together. He takes my tongue, he sucks it, and shoves his own down my throat, seeming to pump up my very breath. He pushes my head onto his chest, and lifting my hair, carefully examines the nape of my neck.

'Oh, it's delicious,' he cries, squeezing hard this part of my body, 'I've never seen anything so well attached. How divine it would be to sever it.'

This last remark removed all my doubts. I clearly saw that I was again at the house of one of those libertines with cruel passions, whose dearest pleasures consisted in the enjoyment of the pain or the

death of the unfortunate victims procured for them with money, and
that I ran the risk of losing my life there.

At that moment there was a knock at the door. Dubois went out
and immediately brought back the young girl from Lyons of whom
she had just spoken.

Let us try now to describe to you the two new characters you are
going to see me with. The Monseigneur, whose name or position I
never knew, was, as I have told you, a man of forty years, thin and
scrawny but vigorously constituted. Muscles that were almost always
bulging stuck out of arms that were covered in coarse, black hairs,
proclaiming both good health and strength. His face was a fiery red,
his eyes small, black, and mean, he had fine teeth, and there was spirit
in all his features. His well-shaped figure was well above the average,
and his love-stick, which I had only too often the occasion to see and
feel, was a foot in length with a circumference of more than eight
inches. This instrument, lean and sinewy, constantly foaming, and
upon which could be seen thick veins, making it even more redoubtable, was erect for the entire five or six hours that this session lasted,
without going limp for a single minute. I had never before come
across such a hairy man—he resembled those fauns that fable
describes to us. His dry, callused hands ended in fingers that gripped
like a vice. As for his temperament, it seemed harsh, abrupt, and
cruel to me, tending to a type of sarcasm or teasing intended to
increase the misery that one clearly had to expect from such a man.

Eulalie was the name of the young girl from Lyons. You only had
to see her to realize how virtuous and well-bred she was. She was the
daughter of one of the best families in the town, from which Dubois's
female criminals had abducted her, on the pretext of reuniting her
with a lover she idolized. In addition to an enchanting naivety and
candour, she possessed one of the most delicious physiognomies that
it is possible to imagine. Scarcely sixteen years old, Eulalie had a real
look of the Virgin. Her innocence and modesty matched her features
and embellished them. She had little colour, but this made her all the
more fetching, and the lustre of her lovely dark eyes gave her pretty
countenance all the fire of which her pallor seemed at first to deprive
her. Her mouth, a little on the large side, was furnished with the
most beautiful teeth, and her bosom, which was already well formed,
seemed even whiter than her complexion. She was as pretty as a
picture, but none of this was at the expense of a generous and

well-rounded figure, with firm, but soft, plump, and dimpled flesh all over. Dubois claimed that it was impossible to see a lovelier arse. Being little acquainted with this part of the body, you will permit me to remain uncommitted on this point. A faint moss covered the front, and magnificent blonde hair hung loosely over all these charms, making them all the more piquant. To complete her masterpiece, Nature, which seemed to have taken pleasure in sculpting it, had endowed her with the sweetest and most amiable of characters. Tender and delicate flower, you were born to adorn the earth for no more than an instant before immediately withering!

'Oh, Madame,' she said to Dubois, recognizing her, 'is this how you betray me!... Dear Heaven! Where have you brought me?'

'You shall see, my child,' the master of the house said to her, roughly pulling her towards him and already starting to kiss her, while I aroused him with one hand as instructed by him.

Eulalie tried to defend herself, but Dubois was pushing her onto this libertine, making it impossible for her to extricate herself. The session was a long one. The fresher the flower, the more this foul hornet enjoyed pumping it. This repeated sucking was followed by the inspection of her neck, and as I squeezed it, I felt the member I was stimulating become even more energized.

'Come,' said Monseigneur, 'here are two victims I will really enjoy. You shall be well paid, Dubois, for I am well served. Let's go into my boudoir. Follow us, dear woman, follow us,' he continued, taking us with him. 'You shall leave tonight, but I have need of you for this evening.'

Dubois agrees, and we move to the libertine's pleasure-chamber, where we are made to strip naked.

Oh, Madame, I shall not undertake to describe to you the infamies of which I was both witness and victim. The pleasures of this monster were those of an executioner. His sole delight consisted in cutting off heads. My unfortunate companion... Oh! no, Madame... Oh no, don't make me go on... I was to suffer the same fate. Encouraged by Dubois, the monster was determined to make my suffering even more horrible, when the need to restore their strength required the two of them to sit down to eat... What debauchery! But how can I complain about this since it saved my life. Having consumed excessive quantities of wine and food, both of them collapsed dead drunk among the remains of their supper. No sooner do I see them in this state than I grab a petticoat and cloak that Dubois has just taken off to make her even more immodest in her boss's eyes, I take a candle, and dash towards the stairs. The house, having few servants, offers no opposition to my flight. I speak to the only one I come across, who has the terrified look of someone racing to the side of her dying master, and I reach the front door without encountering any further resistance. I did not know the roads, as I had not been allowed to see them, and so I take the first one I come across... it is the road to Grenoble. All goes well when fortune deigns to smile upon us for a while. People were still sleeping in the inn, and I enter unseen and run as fast as I can to Valbois's chamber. I knock, Valbois awakes, and scarcely recognizes me in the state I am in. He asks me what has happened to me, and I tell him of all the horrors of which I have just been both victim and witness.

'You can have Dubois arrested,' I said to him, 'she is not far from here, perhaps it will be possible for me to give directions... In addition to all her crimes, the wretched woman has also taken my old clothes and the five louis that you gave me.'

'Oh, Thérèse,' Valbois said to me, 'you are assuredly the most unfortunate girl in the world, and yet, as you can see, honest creature, in the midst of all the ills that befall you, the hand of the Lord protects you. This should be one more reason for you to continue to be virtuous. Good actions do not go unrewarded. We shall not prosecute Dubois. My reasons for leaving her alone are the same as those I outlined to you yesterday. Let us just make up for the wrongs she has done you. First, here is the money she took from you.'

One hour later a dressmaker brought me two sets of clothing and some linen.

'But you must leave, Thérèse,' Valbois said to me, 'you must leave this very day, Madame Bertrand is expecting you. I have persuaded her to delay her departure on your account by a few hours. Go and join her.'

'Oh, virtuous young man,' I cried, falling into the arms of my benefactor, 'may Heaven one day return all the acts of kindness you do me.'

'Come, Thérèse,' Valbois replied, embracing me, 'I already possess the happiness you wish for me, since it is my task to make you happy... Farewell.'

This is how I came to leave Grenoble, Madame, and if I did not find in this town all the felicity that I had expected to find there, in no other town, at least, have I met in a single place so many honest people to pity and soothe my pain.

My driver and I were in a little covered waggon pulled by one horse which we guided from the rear of this vehicle. In it were also Madame Bertrand's merchandise and a little girl of fifteen months that she was still suckling, and for whom, to my misfortune, I quickly developed as close an affection as she who gave birth to her could have done.

In any case, that Bertrand was a really nasty, suspicious, gossipy, annoying woman of limited intellect. We would regularly take all her belongings into the inn each evening, and we slept in the same room. All went very well until we reached Lyons, but during the course of the three days this woman needed for her business, I came upon someone in this town whom I was far from expecting to meet.

I was walking in the afternoon along the Quai du Rhone with one of the girls from the inn whom I had asked to accompany me, when I suddenly caught sight of the Reverend Father Antonin from Sainte-Marie-des-Bois, now Father Superior of the house of his order in this city. This monk approaches me, and having in a low voice bitterly reproached me for having fled, and having given me to understand that I was running serious risks of being recaptured should he warn the monastery of Burgundy, he added in gentler tones that he would say nothing if I agreed that very instant to come and see him in his new home with the girl who was with me, and who seemed to him a legitimate prize. Then, making the same proposal aloud to this creature: 'We will pay you both well,' said the monster, 'there are ten of us in our house, and I promise each of you at least one louis if your acquiescence is unlimited.' I blushed profusely at this proposition. I try to convince the monk that he is mistaken, but having no success, I try to restrain him with gestures, but nothing manages to fend off this insolent man, and his solicitations grow still more animated. As we have repeatedly refused to follow him, he eventually reduces his demands to asking insistently for our address. In order to get rid of him I give him a false one, he writes it in his pocket-book, and takes leave of us, assuring us that he will see us again soon.

While we were returning to the inn I explained as best I could the story of this unfortunate acquaintance to the girl who was with me, but either what I said to her did not satisfy her, or perhaps such an act of virtue on my part made her very angry, as it deprived her of an adventure from which she would have earned so much, because she did not keep silent. This was made only too clear to me by remarks of Bertrand's on the occasion of the dreadful catastrophe that I shall soon recount to you. However, the monk did not reappear, and we left.

Having left Lyons late in the day, we were obliged to spend the first night at Villefranche, and it was there, Madame, that I experienced the awful misfortune that led to my appearing before you today as a criminal, without my being any more responsible for this unhappy circumstance of my life than for any of those in which you have seen me so unjustly buffeted by the blows of fate, and without anything plunging me into the abyss but the goodness of my heart and the wickedness of men.

Having arrived in Villefranche at around six o'clock in the evening, we had lost no time in having supper and retiring in order to undertake a more strenuous journey the next day. We had been resting for no more than a couple of hours when we were awoken by terrifying smoke. Persuaded that there is fire close by, we leave our beds in a hurry. Dear Heaven! The fire had already spread to a frightening extent. We open our door half-naked, and all we can hear around us is the crashing sound of walls collapsing, the noise of timber cracking, and the horrific screams of people falling into the flames. Surrounded by these all-consuming flames, we are already unable to find a way out. In order to escape their intensity we plunge into their very source, and are soon caught up in the crowd of unfortunates who, like us, are searching for a way to safety. I remember that it did not occur to my guide, who was then more concerned about herself than about her daughter, to save her life. Without telling her, I run to our room through the flames that are close enough to burn me in several places. I grab hold of the poor little creature. I hurry to take her back to her mother, supporting myself on a beam that is half-consumed by the fire. I miss my footing, and my initial reaction is to put my hands out in front of me. This natural instinct forces me to let go of the precious burden I am holding... It slips from my grasp, and the poor child falls into the fire before her mother's very eyes... I am dragged away. Too upset to make anything out, I can't tell whether I am surrounded by friends or foes, but to my misfortune I am all too quickly enlightened on this question when, thrown into a post-chaise, I find myself sitting beside Dubois, who, placing a pistol against my temple, threatens to blow my brains out if I utter a word...

'Oh, you villain,' she says to me, 'I've got you now for what you did, and this time you shall not escape.'

'Oh, Madame, what are you doing here!' I cried.

'Everything that has just happened was my work,' the monster replied. 'It was thanks to a fire that I saved your life, and that's how you're going to lose it. I would have pursued you into the fires of Hell if necessary to get you back. Monseigneur was furious when he learnt of your escape. I get two hundred louis for each girl I obtain for him, and not only did he not want to pay me for Eulalie, but he threatened to bring the full force of his anger down on my head if I did not bring you back. I found out where you were and I missed you in Lyons by two hours. Yesterday I arrived in Villefranche one hour after you, and I had henchmen that I always have in my pay set fire to the inn. If I could not have you, I wanted to burn you to death. Now that I have you, I am taking you back to a house that your flight threw into chaos and anxiety, and I am bringing you back there, Thérèse, to be cruelly treated. Monseigneur has sworn that there would be no torture terrifying enough for you, and we will be at his house the moment we leave this coach. Well, Thérèse, what do you think now of virtue?'

'Oh, Madame! That it is often the victim of crime, that it is happy when it triumphs, but that if man's heinous crimes succeed in crushing it on earth, it will surely be the sole object of divine reward in Heaven.'

'It won't be long, Thérèse, before you find out whether there really is a God who punishes or rewards the actions of men... Oh! If, in the eternal nothingness which you are about to enter, you were allowed to think, how you would regret the fruitless sacrifices that your stubbornness has forced you to make to phantoms that have only ever repaid you with misfortune... Thérèse, there is still time. I can save you if you agree to be my accomplice. I cannot bear to see you constantly coming to grief on the dangerous roads to virtue. What! Are you not yet punished enough for your good conduct and your false principles? How many more misfortunes do you need to change your ways? How many more examples are required to convince you that the course you are taking is the worst one of all, and that, as I have

told you a thousand times, you can expect nothing but setbacks
when you go against the grain and try to be the only virtuous one in
a society that is completely corrupt? You're counting on an avenging
deity. Undeceive yourself, Thérèse, undeceive yourself, the God
that you have invented for yourself is nothing but an illusion, the
stupid existence of which was only ever to be found in the minds of
madmen. It is a phantom invented by the wickedness of men, the aim
of which is to deceive others, or to arm one group against another.
The most valuable service that one could have done them would have
been immediately to cut the throat of the first imposter who took it
into his head to speak to them of a God! How much blood just one
murder would have spared the world! Come, come, Thérèse, a
Nature that is constantly active, constantly in motion, has no need of
a master to direct it. And even if this master did indeed exist, after all
the faults with which he has filled his works, would he deserve anything from us but insults and contempt? Oh, if he does exist, your
God, how much I detest him, Thérèse, how much I abhor him! Yes,
if he really did exist, I admit, the sole pleasure of perpetually annoying such a being would become the most precious recompense for the
need I would then have to concede a measure of belief in him... Once
more I ask, Thérèse, will you become my accomplice? A superb
opportunity presents itself, and we will execute it with courage. If
you undertake it, I will save your life. The lord whose house we are
visiting, and whom you know, lives alone in the country residence
where he holds his parties. You know that the kind of parties they are
requires this. One servant only accompanies him, when he goes there
for his pleasures. The man who runs ahead of this chaise, and you
and me, dear girl, that makes three against two. When this libertine
is hot with lust, I shall seize the sabre with which he ends the lives of
his victims, you will hold him, we will kill him, and meanwhile my
man will knock out his valet. There is money hidden in that house,
more than eight hundred thousand francs, Thérèse, I'm sure of it,
the job is well worth it... Choose, wise creature, choose to die or to
serve me. If you betray me, if you tell him about my plans, I shall
accuse you alone, and be in no doubt that I shall prevail, given the
trust he has always had in me... Think carefully before giving me
your answer. This man is a rogue, and so in killing him we are merely
serving the laws whose rigour he has deserved. There is not a single
day, Thérèse, when this rascal does not murder a girl, and therefore,

in punishing crime, how can we be outraging virtue? How can the very reasonable proposal I am making you offend against your strict principles?'

'I have no doubt whatever, Madame,' I replied, 'that it is not in order to punish crime that you are suggesting this act to me, it is with the sole purpose of committing one yourself. To do what you are suggesting can therefore be nothing but a very great evil, with no semblance of legitimacy. In any case, even if your aim were to avenge humanity for this man's horrors, you would still be doing evil in undertaking it, this task being no concern of yours. The laws are made to punish the guilty, and we should leave it to them to do their job. The Supreme Being has not entrusted their sword into our feeble hands. We would not use it without offending against them ourselves.'

'Well, then, you shall die, disgraceful creature,' replied Dubois angrily, 'you shall die, so you should not entertain any further hopes of escaping your fate.'

'What does it matter to me,' I calmly replied. 'I shall be delivered from all my woes. Death holds no terrors for me, it is life's last sleep, the repose of the unfortunate...'

And with these words, the ferocious beast hurled herself at me so that I thought she would strangle me. She struck me several times on the breast, but let go of me as soon as I cried out, for fear that the postilion might hear me.

In the meantime we were making good progress. The man who ran ahead was preparing fresh horses for us, and we did not stop at any staging-post. As the horses were being changed, Dubois again took her weapon and held it against my heart... What was I to do?... In truth, I was in such low spirits as a result of my weakness and the situation I was in that I preferred death to the difficult measures necessary to save myself from it.

We were just about to enter the Dauphiné when six men on horseback, galloping up at full speed behind our carriage, reached it and, sabres in hand, forced our postilion to stop. Thirty feet from the road was a cottage where these riders, whom we soon recognized as being from the mounted constabulary, ordered the driver to take the coach. Once it is there, they make us get out and we all enter the peasant's home. Dubois, with unimaginable effrontery in a woman steeped in crimes and who finds herself under arrest, asked these troopers in a haughty voice if they knew who she was, and what gave them the right to treat a lady of her rank in such a fashion.

'We do not have the honour of your acquaintance, Madame,' said the officer in charge, 'but we are sure that you have in your carriage a wretched girl who yesterday set fire to the main inn in Villefranche.' Then, looking me up and down, 'she fits her description, Madame, we are not mistaken. Have the goodness to hand her over to us, and to inform us how a person as respectable as you appear to be can have taken charge of such a woman?'

'The explanation is a perfectly simple one,' replied Dubois, more impudent than ever, 'and I would neither wish to conceal this girl from you, nor to take her part, if it is certain that she is guilty of the dreadful crime you speak of. Like her, I was lodging yesterday at this inn in Villefranche. I left in the midst of the commotion, and as I was getting into the carriage this girl ran to me to implore my compassion, saying that she had just lost everything in the fire, that she begged me to take her with me as far as Lyons, where she hoped to find a position. Listening less to my reason than my heart, I agreed to her requests. Once in my carriage, she offered to serve me. Once again imprudently, I agreed to everything, and I was taking her to the Dauphiné where my property and family are. Most certainly I have learnt a lesson here, and I now recognize all too clearly the drawbacks of pity. I shall not repeat this mistake. There she is, Messieurs, there she is. Heaven forfend that I should be involved with such a monster. I deliver her to the full force of the law, and I beg you to take no account at all of my unfortunate willingness to believe her for a single moment.'

I tried to defend myself, I tried to denounce the real guilty party, but my pleadings were treated as slanderous recriminations against which Dubois defended herself with naught but a scornful smile. Oh, baneful consequences of misery and prejudice, of wealth and impudence! Was it possible that a woman who called herself Madame la Baronne de Fulconis, who paraded her wealth, who claimed to possess lands, a family tree, how could such a woman be guilty of a crime in which she did not appear to have the least financial interest? On the other hand, did not everything condemn me? I was without protection, I was poor, it was obvious that I was guilty.

The officer in charge read me Bertrand's accusations. She it was who had accused me. According to her, I had set fire to the inn the more easily to rob her, and she had lost every single penny. I had thrown her child into the fire so that the despair into which this event would plunge her would blind her to all else and prevent her from being aware of my machinations. Moreover, Bertrand had added, I was a loose woman, one who had escaped the gallows in Grenoble, and whom she had stupidly taken on out of an excess of kindness for a young man from her region, doubtless my lover. I had publicly and in broad daylight accosted monks in Lyons. In short, there was nothing that this shameful creature would not have exploited to condemn me, nothing that her calumny, embittered by despair, would not have invented to vilify me. At this woman's behest, a judicial hearing had been held at the scene. The fire had started in a hayloft, which several persons had sworn I had entered on the evening of that grim day, and this was true. Looking for a water-closet, I had been given the wrong directions by a servant I had asked, and had gone into that loft, without finding the place I was searching for, and had stayed there for long enough to be suspected of the crime of which I was accused, or at least to suggest that this was probable, and as we know, in our century, this is as good as proof positive.* There was therefore no point in defending myself, and the officer's sole response was to prepare to clap me in irons. 'But, Monsieur,' I said again before allowing them to put me in chains, 'if I had robbed my travelling companion in Villefranche, the money should still be on my person. Let them search me.'

This artless defence just made them laugh. They were in no doubt that I was not alone, they were sure I had accomplices to whom I had passed on the stolen money as I fled. Then the wicked Dubois, who knew about the brand I had had the misfortune to receive long ago when I was at Rodin's, pretended to take pity on me for a moment.

'Monsieur,' she said to the officer, 'so many mistakes are made each day in these matters, so you will forgive me if I make a suggestion. If this girl is guilty of the action she is accused of, it will probably not be her first offence. People don't get to commit crimes of this nature in one day. Examine this girl, I beg you, Monsieur... if by chance you were to find on her wretched body... but if you find no reason to suspect her, allow me to defend and protect her.'

The officer agreed to the examination, which was about to be carried out...

'One moment, Monsieur,' I said, resisting, 'there's no point in examining me, Madame knows full well that I bear this dreadful brand. She also knows full well what caused it. This subterfuge on her part is just one more horror that will be exposed along with everything else in the temple of Themis itself. Take me there, Messieurs, here are my hands, bind them in chains. Only crime blushes to bear them, wretched virtue groans beneath them and is not afraid.'

'In truth, I would never have thought', said Dubois, 'that my idea would be so successful, but as this creature rewards me for the kindnesses I have shown her with insidious accusations, I am prepared to return with her if necessary.'

'There is absolutely no point in doing so, Madame la Baronne,' said the officer, 'our investigations are concerned only with this girl. Her confessions, the brand she bears, everything condemns her. We have no need of anyone but her, and we ask a thousand pardons for having taken up so much of your time.'

I was immediately chained and pulled up behind one of these troopers. Dubois departed, with the final insult of the gift of a few écus to my guards, out of commiseration for my situation in the sad place I would be living in while awaiting my new quarters.

'O Virtue!' I cried, when I saw myself so dreadfully humiliated, 'could you be any more stingingly insulted than this! How was it possible for crime to dare confront and defeat you with so much insolence and impunity!'

We soon arrived in Lyons, and immediately on arrival I was thrown into the criminals' dungeon, and was committed there as an arsonist, fallen woman, child-murderer, and thief.

Seven persons had been burnt alive in the inn. I had thought I would be one of them myself. I had tried to save a child. I was going to die, but she who was the cause of this horror was escaping the vigilance of the laws and heavenly justice. She was triumphant, going on to commit new crimes while, innocent and wretched, I could look forward only to dishonour, branding, and death.

For so long accustomed to calumnies, injustice, and misfortune, used since childhood to embracing sentiments of virtue only to be certain of encountering thorns, my pain was more numb than heart-rending, and I wept less than I would have imagined. However, as it is natural for the suffering creature to seek all possible means to extract itself from the abyss into which its misfortune has plunged it, Father Antonin came to my mind. However feeble the help I might hope to get from him, I would not deny myself the wish to see him. I asked for him, and he appeared. He had not been told who had requested his presence, and he affected not to recognize me, so I told the concierge that it was indeed possible that he did not remember me, having acted as my spiritual adviser when I was very young, but that, by virtue of our past acquaintance, I would like to meet with him in private. This was agreed to on both sides. As soon as I was alone with this cleric I threw myself at his feet and bathed them with my tears, imploring him to save me from the cruel situation in which I found myself. I demonstrated my innocence to him. I did not conceal from him that the indecent proposals he had made to me a few days earlier had set against me the person to whom I was recommended, and who now was my accuser. The monk listened very carefully to me.

'Thérèse,' he then said to me, 'don't flare up as you usually do, as soon as your accursed prejudices are infringed. You can see where they have led you, and you must now readily acknowledge that it is a hundred times better to be a happy rogue than a well-behaved wretch. Your situation is as bad as it can be, dear girl, there is no point in disguising it from you. This Dubois you've told me about, having the greatest interest in your downfall, will most certainly be working secretly to achieve it. The Bertrand woman will pursue her own interests, all appearances are against you, and nowadays appearance is all that is needed for a death sentence. So, you're doomed, that's obvious. There is only one course of action that can save you. I have the ear of the bailiff, and he has much influence over the judges of this town. I shall tell him that you are my niece and claim custody of you on this basis, and he will annul the entire proceedings against you. I will ask that you be sent back to my family. I will have you carried off, but this will be in order to shut you away in our monastery, from which you will not get out alive... and once there, I won't hide it from you Thérèse, you will be the slave of my whims and will satisfy them all without a moment's thought. You will indulge those of my fellow monks in the same way. In short, you will be the most submissive of all my victims... do you hear? It's a harsh prospect. You know what the passions of libertines of our sort are like. Make up your mind, then, and don't keep me waiting for your answer.'

'Oh no, Father,' I replied in horror, 'oh, no, you're a monster to dare take such cruel advantage of my situation, to place me between death and infamy. I shall die if I must, but at least I shall do so without remorse.'

'As you wish,' this cruel man said to me, making to leave. 'I have never tried to force people to be happy... Virtue has worked so well for you up to now, Thérèse, that you are right to worship at its altars... Farewell, and never take it into your head to ask for me again.'

He was on his way out when some instinct stronger than me made me throw myself at his feet once more.

'Tiger,' I cried in tears, 'open up your heart of stone to my dreadful setbacks, and don't impose conditions for putting an end to them that are more frightful to me than death...'

The violence of my gestures had disturbed the veils that covered my bosom. It was naked, bathed in my tears, my dishevelled hair falling upon it. This arouses the rude man's desires... desires that he instantly wishes to satisfy. He dares to show me just how much he is excited by the state I am in. He dares to think of pleasure when I am chained up beneath the blade that is about strike me... I am on my knees... he pushes me over and jumps on me, with just the straw for my bed. I want to cry out, but in a rage he stuffs a handkerchief into my mouth. He ties my arms together. Now having complete control of me, the vile man inspects me all over... everything falls prey to his gaze, his touching, and his perfidious caresses. Finally, he satisfies his desires.

'Listen,' he says to me, as he unties me and adjusts his clothing, 'if you don't want me to help you out, that's up to you! I'll leave you alone. I shall neither serve nor harm you, but if you take it into your head to utter a single word about what has just happened, I shall accuse you of the most heinous crimes and immediately remove from you all means of being able to defend yourself. Think carefully before speaking out. I am regarded as your father confessor... do you hear? We are permitted to reveal all where a criminal is concerned, so listen well to what I am about to say to the keeper, or I shall immediately finish you off.'

He knocks and the jailer appears:

'Monsieur,' the villain says to him, 'the dear girl is mistaken. She was thinking of a Father Antonin who is in Bordeaux. I do not know her in the slightest and have never even seen her before. She asked if I would hear her confession, which I have done. I bid you both farewell. I shall always be happy to give evidence, should my ministry be considered of importance.'

With these words Antonin went out, leaving me as confused by his trickery as I was revolted by his heartlessness and his libertinism.

In any event, my position was too horrible not to consider all options. I remembered Monsieur de Saint-Florent. I found it impossible to believe that this man could hold me in low esteem, in view of my behaviour towards him. I had in the past done him quite an important favour, whereas he had treated me in quite a cruel manner, so it was hard to imagine that he would refuse in such crucial circumstances, either to make up for the wrongs he had done me, or at least to acknowledge, as best he were able, how generously I had behaved towards him. He may have been blinded by the fire of passion on both of the occasions I had known him, but in this case he could not, in my view, be prevented by any such feelings from assisting me... Would he repeat the propositions he made to me on the last occasion? Would he make the horrible services he had described to me the price for the help that I was about to request from him? Well, then, I would accept and, once free, I would easily find a means of extricating myself from the abominable way of life to which he would have had the baseness to commit me. My head full of these thoughts, I write to him, I describe my misfortunes to him, I beg him to come and see me. But I had not thought carefully enough about the soul of this man, which I had imagined was capable of being filled with benevolence. I had not remembered his horrible maxims well enough, or else, since it was my unfortunate weakness to be drawn to judge others according to my own heart, I had wrongly supposed that this man must behave towards me as I had certainly done towards him.

He arrives, and as I have asked to see him alone, he is shown into my chamber and left there. It was easy for me to see from the marks of respect he had been accorded that he was a pre-eminent figure in Lyons.

'What the...! It's you!' he said to me, looking at me contemptuously. 'I was deceived by the letter. I thought it came from a more honest woman than you, one that I would have served with all my heart. But what do you expect me to do for an imbecile like you? You... you're guilty of a hundred crimes, each more dreadful than the previous one, and when a means of earning your living in an

honest fashion is proposed to you, you obstinately reject it. No one
has ever been more stupid.'

'Oh, Monsieur,' I cried, 'I am not guilty.'

'What must one do to be guilty, then?' replied this hard-hearted
man in bitter tones. 'The first time in my life I see you, you're in the
midst of a gang of thieves who want to kill me. Now you're in the
prisons of this town, accused of three or four new crimes, and, it is
said, bearing on your shoulders the certain brand of the old ones. If
that's what you call being honest, I'd like to know what you have to
do not to be!'

'Heaven, Monsieur!' I replied, 'how can you reproach me for the
period of my life when I met you? Do I not rather have more reason
to make you blush for those times? As you know full well, Monsieur,
I was forced to be a part of the gang of robbers who attacked you.
They wanted to take your life and I saved you by allowing you to flee.
And once we had both escaped, cruel man, what did you do to thank
me for the service I had done you? Can you possibly recall what you
did without horror? You tried to kill me. You beat me unconscious
with terrible blows, and taking advantage of the state you put me in,
you took from me what I held dearest. By an unparalleled refinement
of cruelty, you stole from me the little money I possessed, as if you
wanted to finish off your victim with humiliation and misery! Well,
you barbarian, you have succeeded. No doubt at all, your success is
complete. You are the one that plunged me into misery, you are the
one who opened up the abyss into which I have kept falling ever since
that unfortunate moment. Nevertheless, I can forget everything,
Monsieur, yes, all this has disappeared from my memory. I even ask
your pardon for daring to reproach you for it, but how can you pretend that I am not deserving of some amends, some gratitude on your
part? Oh, please do not close your heart to me, when the veil of death
hangs over my sad life. It is not death that I fear, it is ignominy. Save
me from the horror of dying a criminal. All I require from you is this
one favour, do not refuse me, and both Heaven and my heart will
reward you for it one day.'

I was in tears, kneeling before this ferocious man, and far from
reading in his expression the effect I might have expected from my
efforts to move him, all I could make out was an alteration of the
muscles caused by the kind of lust that is born of cruelty. Saint-
Florent was seated before me, his wicked black eyes staring at me in

a frightful way, and I could see his hand touching his body in a manner that proved that the effect I was inspiring in him was anything but pity. Nevertheless, he disguised this well.

'Listen,' he said to me, getting to his feet, 'your case here is wholly in the hands of Monsieur de Cardoville. I do not need to tell you how important his position is. All you need to know is that your fate depends on him alone. He has been my close friend since childhood. I shall speak to him. If he agrees to certain arrangements you will be taken from here at nightfall, so that he may see you either at his place or at mine. Such an interrogation in secret will make it much easier for him to turn everything in your favour than he could do here. If this favour can be obtained for you, defend yourself when you see him, prove to him your innocence in a manner that persuades him. This is all I can do for you. Farewell, Thérèse, be prepared for all eventualities, and above all, do not make me take such steps for nothing.'

Saint-Florent went out. Nothing could equal my perplexity. There was so little resemblance between this man's offer, the sort of man I knew he was, and his present conduct that I still feared some trap or other. But try to understand me, Madame, how could I waver in the cruel position I was in, and ought I not to waste no time in grasping any semblance of help? I therefore determined to follow those who came to take me. Should I be required to prostitute myself, I would defend myself as best I could. If it meant my death, then so be it, at least it would not be ignominious, and I would be relieved of all my suffering. The clock strikes nine, the jailer appears, and I tremble.

'Follow me,' this ill-tempered guard tells me, 'I am here on behalf of Monsieur de Saint-Florent and Monsieur de Cardoville. Make sure you take full advantage of the opportunity Heaven is offering you. We have many here who would like to be given such a chance and who will never get it.'

Having improved my appearance as best I could, I follow the keeper, who hands me over to a couple of huge rascals whose ferocious looks greatly increase my anxiety. They say not a word to me. The coach drives on, and we arrive at a vast mansion which I soon recognize to be Saint-Florent's. The apparent solitude of the whole place only serves further to increase my fears. Meanwhile my guides take me by the arm, and we go up to the fourth floor where small rooms are located that seem to me to be as sumptuous as they are mysterious. As we advanced, all of the doors closed behind us, and in this way we reached a drawing-room in which I could not see a single window. There were Saint-Florent and the man I was told was Monsieur de Cardoville, upon whom my affair depended. This large, stout person of saturnine and ferocious appearance was maybe about fifty years of age, and although he was in *déshabillé*, it was easy to see that he was a lawyer. His entire presence seemed cloaked with a very stern air, and he exploited this to intimidate me. It is, then, a cruel injustice of Providence that crime can frighten virtue. The two men who had brought me there, and whom I was better able to make out in the light of the candles that illuminated this room, were not more than between twenty-five and thirty years old. The first, whom they called La Rose, was a handsome, dark-complexioned young man, built like Hercules. He appeared to me to be the elder of the two. His junior had more feminine features, the most beautiful chestnut-coloured hair, and very large black eyes. He was at least five foot six inches tall, as handsome as any portrait, and with the loveliest complexion in the world. His name was Julien. As for Saint-Florent, you know him already. There was as much roughness in his features as in his character, and yet he did have some attractive characteristics.

'Are all the doors locked?' said Saint-Florent to Julien.

'Yes, Monsieur,' replied the young man, 'your people are engaged in debauchery by your orders, and the porter is the only one keeping watch and will be careful not to open up to anyone at all.'

These few words enlightened me and I trembled, but what could I have done against four men!

'Take a seat over there, my friends,' said Cardoville, kissing the two young men, 'we shall call upon you when necessary.'

'Thérèse,' Saint-Florent then said to me, pointing to Cardoville, 'this is our judge, this is the man on whom your fate depends. We have discussed your affair, but it seems to me that your crimes are of such a nature as to make any accommodation quite difficult.'

'She has forty-two witnesses against her,' said Cardoville, who was sitting on Julien's knees, kissing him on the mouth, and allowing his fingers to caress this young man in the most immodest fashion, 'it has been some time since we sentenced anyone to death whose crimes were more firmly established!'

'My crimes are firmly established?'

'Established or not,' said Cardoville, getting up and with effront-ery, speaking to me defiantly, 'you'll be burnt pissing yourself, unless out of blind obedience you are willing to resign yourself completely and instantly to all that we are going to require of you.'

'Yet more horrors,' I cried. 'Oh well, then, it will only be by yield-ing to infamies that innocence will be able to survive the traps laid for it by evil men!'

'That is the way of things,' replied Saint-Florent, 'the weak must give in to the desires of the strongest, or else fall victim to their wick-edness. Therefore, Thérèse, it is your lot to obey.'

So saying, this libertine quickly lost no time in lifting my skirts. I recoiled, pushing him away in horror, but as I did so I fell into the arms of Cardoville, who grabbed hold of my hands, rendering me defenceless against his colleague's assaults. The ribbons of my skirts were cut, my corset, neckerchief, and shirt were ripped, and in a flash I found myself exposed to the gaze of these monsters, as naked as when I arrived in the world.

'She's resisting,' they both said as they proceeded to strip me... 'she's resisting... the whore imagines she can resist us...', and as each piece of my clothing was torn off, the villains struck me a few blows.

As soon as I was in the state they desired, both sat on curved arm-chairs which were positioned next to each other, trapping between them any unfortunate individual who was placed there, and exam-ined me at leisure. Whilst one inspected my front, the other surveyed my behind, then they changed places, and then changed round again. In this way, I was leered at, manhandled, and kissed for more than half an hour, during which time no lubricious episode was neglected in the course of their examination, and I realized that, as far as pre-liminaries were concerned, both men had more or less the same fan-tasies.

'Well, then,' said Saint-Florent to his friend, 'did I not tell you that she had a beautiful arse!'

'Yes, indeed! Her behind is sublime,' said the lawyer who was kiss-ing it then, 'I have seen very few bottoms as shapely as this one. It's so firm and fresh!... How is that possible given the dissipated life she's led?'

'It's because she's never given herself willingly. I told you, this girl's adventures are truly amusing! She's only ever been taken by

force'—and with this, he sticks all five fingers together into the peri-
style of the temple of Love—'but she's been had... unfortunately,
it's much too wide for me. Being accustomed to first fruits, I could
never enjoy that.'

Then, turning me round, he subjected my behind to the same
ceremony and found it to suffer from the same disadvantage.

'Oh, well!' said Cardoville, 'you know the secret.'

'And therefore, I shall make use of it,' replied Saint-Florent, 'and
since you have no need of this same resource, and are content with an
unnatural act which, however painful it may be for a woman, makes
a man's pleasure just as perfect, you will not take her until I have, I
hope?'

'That's fair,' said Cardoville, 'I shall watch you and occupy myself
with those preludes that are such a sweet part of my enjoyment. I
shall play the girl with Julien and La Rose, while you play the male
part with Thérèse, and the one is as good as the other, I think.'

'A thousand times better, without a doubt. I am so sick of women!
Can you imagine that I could possibly come with those whores, if it
weren't for the scenes that whet both our appetites so much?'

With these words, this lewd couple, having made me realize that
their state required more vigorous pleasures, rose and placed me
upright on a wide armchair, with my elbows resting on the back of
the seat, my knees on the arms, and the whole of my behind thrust
out towards them. I was no sooner in position than they removed
their pants, rolled up their shirt, and so were perfectly naked below
the waist except for their shoes. They displayed themselves to me in
this state, walking to and fro several times in front of me, affecting to
show me their arses, and assuring me that what they had was quite
different from anything I could offer them. Both were indeed formed
like women in that area. Cardoville's, especially, was pale and plump,
as well as shapely and elegant. They defiled each other for a while in
front of me, but without emission. There was nothing very special
about Cardoville's, but Saint-Florent's was a monster, and I trembled when I thought that this was the dart that had pierced me. Oh,
dear Heaven, how could a man of this size need first fruits? Could
such fantasies be driven by anything other than ferocity? Alas! What
new weapons were about to present themselves to me? Julien and La
Rose, who were no doubt aroused by all this and had also removed
their breeches, now advanced, pike in hand... Oh, Madame, I had

never seen anything so foul before, and however shocking my previous accounts have been, this surpassed anything I have so far described, in the same way that the imperious eagle surpasses the dove. Our two libertines quickly grabbed hold of these menacing spears. They caress them, they defile them, they put their mouths upon them, and the combat soon becomes rather serious. Saint-Florent bends over the armchair I'm in, so that the parted cheeks of my buttocks are exactly level with his mouth. He kisses them, sticking his tongue into both temples. Cardoville penetrates him, offering himself to La Rose for the latter's pleasure, whose frightening member immediately disappears into the nook presented to him, and Julien, positioned beneath Florent, seizes hold of his hips and excites him with his mouth, in rhythm with Cardoville's thrusts, while the latter, treating his friend with unparalleled roughness, does not stop until his incense has moistened this sanctuary. There was nothing to equal Cardoville's transports when this climax took hold of his senses. Abandoning himself limply to the boy that served as his husband, but forcefully pummelling the one that he was treating as his wife, this vile libertine would then utter atrocious blasphemies, together with a rattle in the throat like that of a dying man. As for Saint-Florent, he contained himself, and the scene broke up without his making any contribution to it.

'Really and truly,' said Cardoville to his friend, 'you still give me as much pleasure as when you were only fifteen years old... It's also true,' he continued, turning around and kissing La Rose, 'that this lovely boy knows just how to excite me... Didn't you find me rather wide today, dear angel?... would you believe it, Saint-Florent, it's the umpteenth time I've had it today... it really is time I came. It's up to you, dear friend,' the abominable man continued, placing himself in Julien's mouth, his nose thrust into my behind, while his own was offered to Saint-Florent, 'over to you for one more go.'

Saint-Florent comes with Cardoville, La Rose with Saint-Florent, and the latter, after a short spell, burns the same incense with his friend as he has received. If Saint-Florent's ecstasy was more concentrated, it was no less lively or noisy or criminal than Cardoville's. The one screamed out every word that came into his mouth, while the other contained his climax without its being any the less active. He selected his words, but for all that they were only filthier and more foul. In short, rage and frenzy seemed to be the characteristics of Cardoville's delirium, while meanness and ferocity were the traits of Saint-Florent's.

'Come, Thérèse, put some life back into us,' said Cardoville. 'You see these extinguished torches? They need to be lit again.'

While Julien set about pleasuring Cardoville, and La Rose Saint-Florent, the two libertines leaned over me, alternately placing their blunted blades into my mouth. As I pumped one of them, I had to shake and defile the other with my hands, and then, with the aid of a spirit liquor that I had been given, I had to moisten both the member itself and all adjacent parts. But my role was not limited to sucking, I also had to lick around the heads with my tongue and bite them with my teeth at the same time as I squeezed them with my lips. Meanwhile, our two patients were vigorously shaken. Julien and La Rose kept changing places in order to multiply the sensations produced by the frequency of entries and exits. When two or three homages had finally flowed into these foul temples, I noticed some hardening. Although the older one of the two, Cardoville was the first to show signs of it. He rewarded me by slapping me on one of my breasts with his hand as hard as he could. He was quickly followed by Saint-Florent. The reward for my pains was to have one of my ears nearly ripped off. They paused to recover, and soon after I was warned to prepare myself to be treated as I deserved. From the horrific language used by these libertines, I clearly saw that torments were about to rain down upon me. To implore them for mercy in the state they had just got into would only have served to inflame them all the more. They therefore placed me, naked as I was, in the middle of a circle, formed by the four of them sitting around me. I was obliged to pass from one to the other in turn and to receive from each of them the penance it pleased him to impose on me. The youngsters were no more compassionate than the old men, but Cardoville in particular distinguished himself with a more refined brand of teasing that Saint-Florent, as cruel as he was, could scarcely get close to.

A brief respite followed these cruel orgies, and I was allowed to breathe for a few moments. I was black and blue, but what surprised me was that they healed my wounds in less time than they had taken to inflict them, and not the least trace of them remained. The orgies recommenced.

There were moments when all of their blows seemed to be just a single one, and when Saint-Florent, lover and mistress, generously received what Cardoville gave only grudgingly. The next moment, though no longer active, he accommodated himself in every way, his mouth and his arse serving as altars to receive their dreadful homages. Cardoville cannot contain himself, watching so many libertine scenes. Seeing his friend already erect, he comes over and offers himself to his lusts. Saint-Florent enjoys him. I sharpen the arrows, and present them at the locations which they must penetrate, and my exposed buttocks serve as a visual stimulus to the excitement of some and as a target for the cruelty of others. Finally, calmed down by their need to recover, our two libertines emerge without any loss, and in a state fit to frighten me more than ever.

'Come, La Rose,' said Saint-Florent, 'take this tramp and close her up for me.'

I did not understand this expression, but experience soon cruelly taught me what it meant. La Rose seized hold of me and laid me on my back onto a stool that was no bigger than a foot in diameter. There, with no other means of support, my legs dangled on one side, my head and arms on the other. My four limbs were attached to the floor as wide apart as possible. The torturer who is going to narrow the passages arms himself with a long needle, at the end of which is a waxed thread, and without any regard for the blood he is going to spill, or for the pain he is about to cause me, the monster sews up the entrance to the temple of Love, in full view of his two friends, whom this spectacle amuses. He turns me around as soon as he has finished, so that my stomach is flat on the stool, my limbs dangling, and they are tied to the floor as before, then the indecent altar of Sodom is barricaded in the same manner. I need not describe my pain to you, Madame, you can imagine it, I was close to fainting.*

'That's how I need it,' said Saint-Florent, when I had been replaced on my back and he could see the fortress he wished to invade to be well within his reach. 'As I am accustomed only to gathering first fruits, how could I derive any pleasure from this creature without this ceremony?'

Saint-Florent had the most violent erection, which was being slapped to maintain it. He advances, pike in hand. To excite him all the more, Julien is pleasuring himself with Cardoville before his eyes. Saint-Florent attacks me, and inflamed by the resistance he encounters, he pushes with incredible force, the threads break, and all the torments of Hell cannot equal my own. The sharper my pain, the more exquisite my persecutor's pleasure appears to be. Eventually, everything yields to his efforts, I am ripped, the gleaming spear has touched the end, but Saint-Florent wants to pace himself and holds himself back. They turn me around, the obstacles are the same, the cruel man studies them as he frigs himself, and his ferocious hands molest the surroundings the better to attack their target. He is in position, the natural narrowness of the passage renders the attacks much more painful, and my redoubtable conqueror has soon breached all obstacles. I am bathed in blood, but what does this matter to the victor? With two vigorous thrusts of his thighs he has entered the sanctuary, and there the villain consummates a dreadful sacrifice, the pain of which I could not have borne for a moment longer.

'Give her to me,' says Cardoville, untying me, 'I shall not sew the dear girl up, but I shall place her on a camp-bed that will restore to her all the warmth and elasticity that her temperament or her virtue refuses us.'

La Rose immediately gets a diagonal cross of very thorny wood out of a large cupboard. This vile libertine wants to put me on this, but how is he going to improve his cruel climax? Before tying me onto it, Cardoville himself inserts a silver ball the size of an egg into my behind, and pushes it in with the aid of pomade. It disappears. It is scarcely inside my body than I feel it swell and start to burn me. No heed is paid to my moans, and I am brutally bound on this sharply pointed rack. Pressing himself next to me, Cardoville penetrates me. He presses my back and bottom onto the points that are supporting them. Julien similarly puts himself inside him. Forced to bear the weight of these two bodies all on my own, and having no other support but those accursed knots that are dislocating me, you can easily imagine my pains. The more I push against the bodies that are pressing down on me, the more they push me back onto the bumps that are lacerating me. Meanwhile, the terrible ball has gone far up into my bowels and is contracting, burning and ripping them. I scream out loud. There are no words in this world that can describe what I am feeling. Meanwhile, my torturer orgasms, his mouth glued to mine seeming to breathe in my pain in order to increase his pleasure. You cannot imagine his intoxication, but following his friend's example, feeling his strength about to go, he wants to taste everything before it abandons him. I am turned over, the ball that they force back out of me is going to cause the same fire in my vagina as it has ignited in the place it has left. It goes in and burns its way into the depths of my womb. I am tied on my stomach onto the perfidious cross, and far more delicate parts of me are about to be abused on the bonds that hold them. Cardoville penetrates the forbidden path, perforating it, while he is similarly enjoyed. Finally, delirium overcomes my persecutor, his awful cries announcing the culmination of his crime. I am inundated. They untie me.

'Come, my friends,' Cardoville says to the two young men, 'take hold of this whore, and enjoy her as you wish. She's yours, we leave her to you.'

The two libertines seize hold of me. While one enjoys himself from the front, the other thrusts himself into my behind. They keep changing around. I was more seriously torn by their prodigious size than I was by Saint-Florent's artful barricades, and he and Cardoville enjoy the two young men while they occupy themselves with me. Saint-Florent sodomizes La Rose, who treats me in the same manner, and Cardoville does likewise with Julien, who excites himself in a more decent place with me. I am the centre of these abominable orgies, I am their focus and mainspring. La Rose and Julien have worshipped at my altars, while Cardoville and Saint-Florent, less vigorous or more weakened, pay homage to those of my lovers alone—it is time for the last one, and I am on the point of fainting.

'My friend has hurt you, Thérèse,' Julien says to me, 'and I am going to make it all better.'

Armed with a flask of oil, he rubs me with it a number of times, and all trace of my torturers' atrocities disappear. However, nothing alleviates my pains, which are greater than any I have ever experienced before.

'With the art we possess to make all traces of our cruelties disappear, any girl who wanted to lodge a complaint against us would be wasting her time, wouldn't she, Thérèse?' Cardoville said to me. 'What proof could they offer to support their allegations?'*

'Oh!' said Saint-Florent, 'our charming Thérèse is in no position to make complaints. Given her imminent death sentence, it's prayers and not accusations that we might expect from her.'

'She should not think of doing either of these,' replied Cardoville. 'If she tried to incriminate us, no one would listen to her. Given the great respect and consideration accorded to us in this town, people would pay no heed to complaints that would always get back to us, and which we would always be able to suppress. Her suffering would just be longer and more cruel as a result. Thérèse must realize that we have had fun with her for the pure and simple reason that the strong are drawn to abuse the weak. She must realize that she cannot escape her sentence, that it has to be carried out, that she will endure it, that there would be no point in revealing that she left prison tonight, no one would believe her, since the jailer is one of us and would immediately deny it. Therefore, this lovely, sweet girl, so full of the grandeur of Providence, must offer it with humility everything that she has just suffered and everything that awaits her still. These things will be like so many expiations for the dreadful crimes that have subjected her to our laws. Pick up your clothes, Thérèse, it is not yet daylight and the two men who brought you here will take you back to your prison.'

I wanted to say something, I wanted to throw myself at the feet of these ogres, either to move them to pity or to ask them to end my life. However, I am dragged off and thrown into a coach, which my two guides also jump into, locking the doors behind them. Scarcely have they done so than they are again inflamed with outrageous, unspeakable desires.

'Hold her for me,' says Julien to La Rose, 'I must sodomize her. I have never seen a behind in which I was squeezed more deliciously. I'll do the same favour for you.'

The plan is carried out, I try to defend myself in vain, Julien triumphs, and it is not without terrible pain that I must suffer this fresh assault. The excessive size of the assailant, the tearing of this part of my body, the burning sensations with which that accursed ball has eaten into my intestines, all of these things contribute to make me suffer torments, renewed by La Rose as soon as his friend has finished. Before I arrived I therefore fell victim once again to the criminal libertinism of these shameful valets, and we finally entered the prison. The jailer received us, he was alone, it was still night-time, and no one saw me return.

'Go to bed, Thérèse,' he said to me, taking me back to my chamber, 'and if you ever took it into your head to tell anyone that you have left prison tonight, remember that I would deny it, and that such a pointless accusation would not get you out of trouble...'

'And to think that I would regret leaving this world!' I said to myself, as soon as I was alone. 'To think that I would fear leaving behind me a universe composed of such monsters! Oh, may the hand of God take me away from it all this very instant in whatever way it sees fit, and I shall complain no longer. The only consolation that can be left to the wretch born among so many ferocious beasts is the hope of quitting them soon.'

The following day I received no news, and, resolved to abandon myself to Providence, I became comatose, wishing to take no food. The day after, Cardoville came to interrogate me. I could not help trembling when I saw how cold-bloodedly this villain came to exercise justice, he, the most wicked of men, he who, against all the rights of this justice which he claimed to represent, had just so cruelly abused both my innocence and my misfortune. I pleaded my cause in vain, this dishonest man was artful enough to make all my defences into crimes. When all the charges of my case were well established according to the iniquitous judge, he had the impudence to ask me if I knew Monsieur de Saint-Florent. I replied that I did know him.

'Good,' said Cardoville, 'that's all I need to know. This Monsieur de Saint-Florent, whom you admit to knowing, also knows you very well. He has given evidence that he saw you in a gang of thieves, where you were the first to rob him of his money and pocket-book. Your comrades wished to spare his life, but you were for killing him. He nevertheless managed to flee. This same Monsieur de Saint-Florent adds that, some years later, having recognized you in Lyons, he had, at your insistence, permitted you to come to pay him a visit at his residence. Though you had given your word that you were now on your best behaviour, while he was preaching to you there, urging you to continue to pursue the path of virtue, you had carried insolence and crime so far as to choose these moments of his benevolence to steal from him a watch and one hundred louis which he had left on his mantelpiece...'

And making the most of the anger and resentment that such atrocious calumnies drove me to, Cardoville ordered the clerk of the court to write that I confessed to these accusations by my silence and my facial expressions.

I hurl myself on the floor, the rafters echo with my cries, I hit my head against the tiles with the intention of seeking death more quickly, and unable to find words adequate enough to express my rage, I cry: 'Villain! I commend myself to that just God who will avenge me of your crimes. He will recognize innocence, and will make you repent of the shameless manner in which you abuse your authority!' Cardoville rings the bell, and tells the jailer to take me back to my cell, in view of the fact that, troubled by my despair and my remorse, I am in no state to submit to an interrogation, and in any case the interrogation is complete since I have confessed to all of my crimes. And the villain leaves peacefully! And he is not struck down by a thunderbolt!

The case went well, driven by hatred, vengeance, and lust, and I was promptly found guilty and taken to Paris for my sentence to be confirmed. It was in the course of this fateful journey, during which, though innocent, I was treated as the worst of criminals, that my heart was finally torn apart by the bitterest and most painful reflections! I must have been born under such a fatal star, I said to myself, since it is impossible for me to conceive a single honest sentiment that does not instantly plunge me into an ocean of misfortunes! And how can it be that this enlightened Providence, whose justice I like to admire, while punishing me for my virtues at the same time shows me those who have crushed me with their crimes at the pinnacle of success!

In my childhood a usurer tries to force me to commit a theft, I refuse, and he grows rich. I fall among a band of thieves, from whom I escape with a man whose life I save. He rewards me by raping me. I arrive at the house of a debauched lord who sets his dogs on me for not wanting to poison his aunt. From there, I go to the house of an incestuous and murderous surgeon whom I try to prevent from committing a horrible act. The torturer brands me as a criminal. He doubtless commits his crimes, and makes his fortune, while I am obliged to beg for my bread. I wish to take the sacraments, I wish fervently to implore the Supreme Being for help, despite His sending me so many ills, and the august tribunal where I hope to purify myself in one of our most sacred mysteries becomes the bloody theatre of my ignominy. The monster who abuses and defiles me is elevated to the greatest honours of his order, and I am again plunged into the dreadful abyss of misery. I try to save a woman from her husband's fury, and the cruel man tries to put me to death by causing me to lose blood one drop at a time. I try to help a poor man and he robs me. I assist a man who has fainted, and the ungrateful wretch makes me turn a wheel like an animal. He hangs me for his own amusement. He is favoured by fate at every turn, and I am about to die on the scaffold for my forced labour at his hands. A shameless woman decides to seduce me into committing another crime, and for the second time I lose the few goods I possess when I try to prevent the theft of her victim's treasures. A sensitive man wants to make up for all my ills by offering me his hand in marriage, and he expires in my arms before he can do so. I expose myself to danger in a fire in order to save from the flames a child that does not belong to me. The mother of this child makes an accusation and brings a criminal action against me. I fall into the hands of my most mortal enemy, who wants to take me back by force to a man whose passion it is to cut off heads. If I manage to escape this villain's sword, it is to fall under the sword of Themis. I implore a man whose life and fortune I have saved to protect me, I dare to expect some gratitude from him, he lures me into his house and subjects me to horrors. There, I am confronted with the iniquitous judge on whom my case depends, both men abuse me, both insult me, both hasten my doom. Fortune showers them with favours, while I face an imminent death.

This is what men have done to me. This is what I have learnt from the dangers of associating with them. Is it surprising that, embittered by misfortune and revolted by outrages and injustices, I should in my heart aspire only to avoid all contact with them in the future?

'A thousand excuses, Madame,' said this unfortunate girl as she ended the account of her adventures, 'a thousand pardons for having sullied your spirit with so many obscenities, for having, in short, abused your patience for so long. Perhaps I have offended against Heaven with my foul tales, I have reopened my wounds and I have disturbed your rest. Farewell, Madame, farewell, the sun is coming up, my guards are calling me, let me go to meet my fate, I fear it no longer, it will put an end to my torments. This final moment in the life of man is terrifying only for that fortunate person whose days have been cloudless. But the wretched creature who has breathed in nothing but the venom of vipers, whose faltering steps have walked on nothing but thorns, who has seen the light of day only as the traveller who has lost his way trembles to see lightning fork across the sky, she whose cruel setbacks have taken away parents, friends, fortune, help, and protection, she who has nothing left in the world but tribulations to eat and tears to drink, such a girl, I say, sees death approach without fear, and even welcomes it as a safe port where she will once again find peace in the bosom of a God too just not to allow innocence, defiled on earth, to find recompense in another world for so many woes.'

The good Monsieur de Corville had not heard this story without being profoundly moved by it. As for Madame de Lorsange, in whom, as we have said, the monstrous errors of her youth had not extinguished all sensitivity, she was on the point of fainting.

'Mademoiselle,' she said to Justine, 'it is difficult to hear what you say without taking the keenest interest in you, but I must admit that an inexplicable feeling, one far tenderer than I can describe, irresistibly draws me to you and makes your woes my own. You have disguised your name and concealed your origins from me, and I beg you to confess your secrets to me. Do not imagine that I am compelled to speak to you like this out of vain curiosity... Good Lord! Could my suspicions be true?... Oh, Thérèse! Could it be that you are Justine?... Could it be that you are my sister!'

'Justine! Madame, what a name!'

'She would be around your age today...'

'Juliette! Can it be you?' said the unfortunate prisoner, throwing herself into Madame de Lorsange's arms, 'you... my sister!... Oh, I shall die far less unhappy, now that I have been able to embrace you one more time!...'

And the two sisters, their arms wrapped tightly around each other, could communicate only in sobs and express themselves only in tears.* Monsieur de Corville could not help weeping himself. Feeling that it is impossible not to take the greatest interest in this affair, he goes into another chamber, writes to the Chancellor, describing in vivid detail the horror of the fate of poor Justine, whom we shall continue to call Thérèse. He answers for her innocence, asking that, until all can be cleared up at the trial, the accused shall have no other prison but his chateau, and undertaking to represent her when this sovereign head of justice commands it. He introduces himself to Thérèse's two guards, entrusting his letters to them, and accepting all responsibility for the prisoner. They agree, and Thérèse is entrusted to his keeping. A carriage approaches.

'Come, wretched creature,' says Monsieur de Corville to Madame de Lorsange's fetching sister, 'come with us, and everything is going to change for you. It will not be said that your virtues have never been rewarded, and that the beautiful spirit you have received from

Nature has only ever encountered hearts of stone. Follow us, and your fate will henceforth depend on me alone.'

And Monsieur de Corville briefly explains what he has just done.

'My dear, decent man,' says Madame de Lorsange, throwing herself at her lover's feet, 'that's the finest thing you've done in your life. It is for him who truly knows the heart of man and the spirit of the law to avenge oppressed innocence. There she is, Monsieur, there is your prisoner. Go, Thérèse, go, run immediately and throw yourself at the feet of your just protector, who will not abandon you like the others. Oh, Monsieur, if the bonds of my love for you were already dear to me, how much more will they be, strengthened by the tenderest estimation...'

And these two women in turn embraced the knees of such a generous friend, bathing them with their tears.

A few hours later they arrived at the chateau. There, Monsieur de Corville and Madame de Lorsange vied with each other to transport Thérèse from an excess of misfortune to the height of luxury. They delighted in feeding her with the most succulent dishes, they gave her the best beds to sleep in, they wanted her to be in charge in their home. In short, they invested their attentions with all the delicacy that it was possible to expect from two sensitive souls. For several days they plied her with remedies, they bathed her, they adorned her with jewels, they beautified her, she was the idol of the two lovers. It was a matter of which of the two would make her forget her woes the soonest. An excellent surgeon undertook treatment to remove that ignominious brand, the cruel fruit of Rodin's wickedness. All of Thérèse's ills responded well to the care and attention lavished on her by her benefactors. The traces of her misfortunes quickly disappeared from the countenance of this amiable girl, and the Graces soon re-established their empire in her features. The livid hues of her cheeks of alabaster, that so much woe had made pale and gaunt, were replaced by the roses of youth. The laughter banished from her lips for so many years finally reappeared there, fanned by pleasure's wings. The best news had just arrived from the Court. Monsieur de Corville had set the whole of France in motion, he had inspired Monsieur S—— with renewed zeal, so that the latter had joined him to describe Thérèse's misfortunes, and to restore to her the peace and tranquillity that was so clearly due to her. Eventually letters arrived from the King, purging Thérèse of all legal actions unjustly brought against her, restoring to her the status of honest citizen, forever silencing all the tribunals of the kingdom where men had sought to defame her, and awarding her one thousand écus pension from the gold seized in the workshops of the counterfeiters of the Dauphiné. The authorities had attempted to arrest Cardoville and Saint-Florent, but following that fateful star that governed all of Thérèse's persecutors, one, Cardoville, before his crimes were brought to light, had just been appointed to the Administration of ——, the other to the General Administration of Colonial Trade. Each one had already arrived at his destination, and the arrest warrants came up against powerful families who soon found the means to quieten the storm, and, safe in the bosom of good fortune, the crimes of these monsters were soon forgotten.[1]

As regards Thérèse, as soon as she learnt of so many agreeable prospects in store for her, she almost expired with joy. For several days in a row, in the bosom of her protectors, she wept tears of happiness, when suddenly her mood changed without its being possible to work out why. She became sombre, anxious, and dreamy, occasionally crying in the midst of her friends without herself being able to explain the reasons for her anguish.

'I was not born for so much happiness,' she would say to Madame de Lorsange... 'Oh, my dear sister, it cannot last long.'

They tried in vain to assure her that all her problems were over, that she need worry no longer; nothing could calm her. One might have said that this creature, uniquely destined for misfortune, and feeling the hand of ill luck still hovering over her head, was already foreseeing the final blows that were about to crush her.

Monsieur de Corville was still living in the countryside. Summer was almost over, and it seemed that the approach of a frightful storm might threaten a walk they had planned. The excessive heat had obliged them to leave all of the windows open. The lightning flashes, the hailstones fall, the winds hiss, the clouds are stirred by the fire of Heaven, sweeping them along in a horrible manner. It seemed that Nature, bored with her works, was determined to mix up all the elements to reshape them anew. A fearful Madame de Lorsange begs her sister to close up all the windows and doors as quickly as she can. Eager to calm her sister, Thérèse rushes to the windows, which are

[1] As for the monks of Sainte-Marie-des-Bois, the suppression of religious orders will expose the atrocious crimes of this dreadful brood.*

already shattering. For a few moments she struggles in vain against the wind but is driven back, and then a flash of lightning throws her back into the middle of the drawing-room.

Madame de Lorsange utters a piercing scream and faints. Monsieur de Corville calls for help, all lend a hand, Madame de Lorsange is brought round, but the unfortunate Thérèse is struck in such a manner that there can be no hope for her. The thunderbolt has entered her right breast. Having destroyed her chest and her face, it has come out through the middle of her stomach. The miserable creature was horrific to look at. Monsieur de Corville ordered her to be carried away...

'No,' said Madame de Lorsange, rising with great calm to her feet, 'no, leave her here in front of me, Monsieur, I need to contemplate her so that I may remain firm in the resolutions I have just made. Listen to me, Corville, and above all, do not oppose the decision I have made. Nothing in this world could distract me from my intentions now. The unique misfortunes experienced by this wretched girl, despite her having always observed her duties, are too extraordinary not to open my eyes to myself. Do not imagine that I am blinded by those false rays of happiness that we have seen the villains enjoy who sullied Thérèse in the course of her adventures. Those whims of Heaven are enigmas that are not ours to divine, but they should never seduce us. Oh, my friend! The prosperity of crime is but a trial that Providence wishes virtue to undergo. It is like the thunderbolt whose deceptive fires embellish the skies for an instant, merely to plunge the wretch they have dazzled into the chasms of death. The example of this lies before our eyes. The unbelievable calamities, the terrifying and repeated setbacks endured by this charming girl, are a warning from the Eternal to listen to the voice of my conscience and at last to throw myself into His arms. What punishments must I fear from Him, I, whose libertinism, irreligion, and abandonment of all principles have marked every moment of my life! What am I to expect, when a girl who had not one single fault to be reproached for in the whole of her life is treated like this? Let us part, Corville, it's time, no ties bind us, forget me, and approve of my decision to renounce the infamies with which I have besmirched my name, and to repent of them forever at the feet of the Supreme Being. This dreadful blow was necessary for my conversion in this life, and also for the happiness I dare to hope for in the next.

Farewell, Monsieur. The last mark I expect of your friendship is that you will not conduct searches of any kind to discover what has happened to me. Oh, Corville! I shall wait for you in a better world where your virtues must surely take you. May the mortification in which, to expiate my crimes, I intend to spend the unhappy years that I have left, permit me to see you again there one day.'

Madame de Lorsange immediately leaves the house. She takes some money with her, jumps into a carriage, leaving to Monsieur de Corville the remainder of her property with instructions for charitable legacies, and hastens to Paris where she enters the Carmelite Order, where, within a very few years, she becomes a shining example and lesson to all, as much by her great piety as by the wisdom of her thought and the steadfastness of her morals.

Deserving to attain the highest office in his homeland, Monsieur de Corville was successful, and only used this honour to work in equal measure for the happiness of his people, the glory of his master, whom he served well, *even though the latter was a minister*,* and the fortune of his friends.

Oh, you who have shed tears over the misfortunes of virtue, you who have pitied the wretched Justine, while forgiving the perhaps rather strong colours which we have felt obliged to use, may you at least derive the same benefit from it as Madame de Lorsange! May you be convinced like her that true happiness is found in the bosom of virtue alone, and that if, for reasons which it is not ours to divine, God allows it to be persecuted on Earth, it is to make up for it in Heaven with the sweetest rewards.

EXPLANATORY NOTES

3 *Yes, Constance . . . this work*: Sade dedicates his novel to Marie-Constance
Renelle (Madame Quesnet) who was his mistress from August 1790. This
relationship would last until his death in 1814. Marie-Constance was an
actress, familiarly known as '*Sensible*' ('Sensitive').

Tartuffe was put on trial by bigots: Sade is referring to the five-year ban on
Molière's comedy about a religious hypocrite. *Le Tartuffe*, premiered in
1664, was immediately attacked in the *Gazette de France* as 'extremely
harmful to religion and likely to have a most dangerous effect'. Despite
Molière's defence that he was actually ridiculing the falsely pious, many
other clerics launched similar attacks against the author and his play, cul-
minating in the Archbishop of Paris's threat of excommunication of any of
the faithful who saw it.

5 *If, filled with respect for our social conventions...*: in the first version of the
Justine narrative, 'The Misfortunes of Virtue' of 1787, this sentence is
composed in more neutral tones: 'speaking of our social conventions'. In
the third and final version, *The New Justine* of 1797, Sade's narrator is
considerably less circumspect, contemptuously dismissing the pieties of a
religious society, 'filled with a vain, ridiculous and superstitious attitude
towards our absurd social conventions'.

With greater knowledge . . . of doing good?: in spite of its subtitle, Voltaire's
short story, *Zadig, ou la destinée*, which first appeared under a different
title in 1747, is really about Providence, and poses the same question as
Justine: is virtue rewarded by happiness? After many reversals of fortune,
the young hero, Zadig, comes to realize that not only is virtue seldom
rewarded, but that human beings are more often bad than good. The out-
of-context quotation of the angel Jesrad's words to Zadig at the end of the
tale and the conclusion which Sade's narrator draws that doing evil is just
another way of doing good are both disingenuous and tongue-in-cheek,
since Jesrad is not allowed to have the last word, Zadig's interjection of the
single word, 'But...', suggesting the hero's, the author's, and no doubt the
reader's lack of conviction. Furthermore, this well-known tenet of
Leibnitzian optimism—that partial evils are simply part of the universal
good, as Alexander Pope put it in his *Essay on Man* of 1732–4—will be
more openly satirized in Voltaire's *Candide, ou l'optimisme* (1759), where
the hero's teacher, the ridiculous Pangloss, glibly dismisses all evil events
and actions with a piece of pure sophistry: 'All is for the best in the best of
all possible worlds.' This reference to Voltaire's satirical fiction is equally
an attempt by Sade both to place himself in the respected tradition of the
conte philosophique, or philosophical narrative, that Voltaire initiated, and
to demonstrate his own literary knowledge, which was indeed vast and
comprehensive. Allusions of this kind pepper all of Sade's writings.

6 *Cythera*: in ancient Greek mythology, Cythera, one of the seven Ionian islands, was considered to be the island of Aphrodite, goddess of love. By the time Sade was writing, the island had become synonymous with sexual licence.

12 *tax-farmers*: under the *ancien régime*, the 'ferme générale' was an outsourced customs and excise operation which collected land duties on behalf of the king. The 'fermiers généraux', or tax-farmers, were the major tax-collectors in this system. In the seventeenth and eighteenth centuries these officials became extremely rich, and so for Sade would be prime examples of a corrupt bureaucracy from which he and his landowning relatives would undoubtedly have suffered.

15 *the Supreme Being*: this was the phrase sanctioned by Robespierre during the Revolution to denote God, the latter term being too closely associated with the *ancien régime* and the corrupt Catholic Church. At the height of the Terror in 1794 Robespierre ordained that a Feast of the Supreme Being should be held. Given Justine's words, it is perhaps a delicious irony that three years after Sade had published this novel the term became the watchword of a man guilty of the most appalling abuses in French history.

22 *Clothes . . . with a feather-duster*: the name and avaricious nature of Monsieur Harpin are a clear echo of Harpagon in Molière's *The Miser* (*L'Avare*), who similarly instructs his servants 'not to polish the furniture too hard for fear of wearing it out'. Sade is an inveterate plagiarist, both at the literary and philosophical level, and, as here, is frequently not above lifting whole sentences from their earlier source.

25 *unjust imprisonment . . . did commit it*: there are clear echoes in these lines of Sade's own deep sense of unjust treatment at the hands of the law under the *ancien régime*, leading to years of imprisonment without proper trial.

such infamy and horrors!: given that *Justine* was first published at the height of the revolutionary period, the author's note here, in similar fashion to the paragraph to which it is appended, reads as a transparent condemnation of the rough justice meted out, this time under the Terror, to those without wealth or influence to buy their freedom—a condition with which, as a penniless former aristocrat, struggling to stay alive at a time when so many of his peers were being summarily imprisoned and guillotined, the ex-marquis was only too familiar.

the Conciergerie: part of a larger judicial complex and a former royal palace, this was a prison in Paris, from which hundreds of prisoners were taken during the Revolution to be guillotined at a number of locations around Paris.

33 *La Fontaine*: Jean de La Fontaine (1621–95), French poet, best known for his *Fables* (1668–94), a collection of tales containing a moral lesson, and his *Contes* (1665–74), a series of witty and improper tales in verse. The allusion here may be to 'The Wolf and the Lamb' (I. 10), with its moral: 'La raison du plus fort est toujours la meilleure' ('The reason of the

strongest is always the best'), though in fact, many of his fables show that apparently weak creatures like the gnat can prove to be less vulnerable than the strong, like the lion: see 'The Lion and the Gnat' (II. 9). It would seem unlikely that Sade was not aware of this, and so we might here be tempted to infer a hint of ridicule of the pompous Ironheart, whose sweeping claim that, for La Fontaine, force always triumphs is clearly a questionable one.

37 *Can they truly be happy . . . to preserve the rest?*: there is an implicit reference here to Jean-Jacques Rousseau's notion of the social contract. According to this theory, citizens gain civil rights in return for accepting the obligation to respect and defend the rights of others, giving up some individual freedoms in the process. The social contract is associated with the notion of the general will, expounded in Rousseau's *Discours sur l'économie politique* (*Discourse on Political Economics*) and referring to the desire or interest of a people as a whole. The phrase occurs in Article 6 of the *Déclaration des droits de l'homme et du citoyen* (*Declaration of the Rights of Man and the Citizen*), composed during the Revolution. Voicing the author's own contempt for Rousseau's political ideas, which he considered naive and unworkable, Ironheart will shortly rebut them.

40 *he outrages Nature only by resisting it*: Ironheart's argument is clearly rooted in eighteenth-century materialism, here following Rousseau's conception of Nature as a sure guide to Man. However, he pushes Rousseau's reasoning to a logical extreme in proposing a 'bad' Mother Nature to match Rousseau's 'good' Mother, suggesting that we should obey her promptings either way.

41 *Aesop's dog*: a reference to the fable of the dog who, having found a bone and jealously held on to it, happened to catch sight of his own reflection in a stream. Thinking it was another dog with a bigger bone, he growled at the reflection which, of course, growled back. Opening his jaws to bite his adversary, the dog immediately lost his own bone, which dropped out of sight into the water. This warning against forsaking the real for the illusory is generally attributed to the Greek storyteller, Aesop (*c*.620–564 BC).

42 *'So don't be concerned . . . close of their existence'*: Ironheart is clearly a mouthpiece for Sade's atheism in this speech. In a godless universe, Nature is neither good nor bad, but simply indifferent to Man's behaviour.

payable on demand on the capital: Saint-Florent has promissory notes, which are negotiable instruments wherein one party (the maker or issuer) makes an unconditional promise in writing to pay a determinate sum of money to the other (the payee), either at a fixed or determinable future time or on demand of the payee, under specific terms. Such notes were a rudimentary system of paper money, substituting for large amounts of metal coin that would not have been so easily transportable in the eighteenth century.

45 *six leagues away*: a league was considered to be approximately the distance a man could walk in one hour.

50 *Themis*: in Greek mythology Themis was the personification of law and order.

55 *the altars at which our Celadons worship*: Celadon is a lover who is more absorbed with the sentiments of love than the acts of love, after the hero of the romance, *L'Astrée* by Honoré d'Urfe, published 1606–26. The meaning of the reference in this context is not entirely clear, but is probably 'our lovers' in the emotional as well as physical sense.

57 *a leprous Jew . . . born of a whore and a soldier*: Sade here is alluding to early claims (e.g. of the 2nd-century pagan philosopher Celsus) that Jesus's father was a Roman centurion called Panthera.

58 *weak, cruel, ignorant, and fanatical emperor*: presumably a reference to Constantine, the first Christian Roman emperor.

59 *When atheism . . . my blood is ready*: in an age when atheists were executed for their convictions, the notion of martyrdom is no exaggeration. While the question of an authorial voice behind the libertines' discourse is not always a settled one, there is no doubt that Sade shares the view Bressac expresses here.

61 *When I have been convinced . . . injurious to its plans*: Bressac here voices an argument which Sade develops at greater length in *The 120 Days of Sodom* and *Juliette*, that is, that since nothing is created or destroyed in Nature but merely changes its form, murder cannot be viewed as a crime. On the contrary, the murderer merely serves Nature's laws in serving the process of metamorphosis. Such a view, according to which Nature's determinism is paramount, pushes atheistic materialism to its logical extreme. There is no room in this argument for a humanistic (and Darwinian) conception of society as dependent on solidarity based on natural fellow-feeling.

67 *'lettre de cachet'*: this was an order under the king's private seal, widely used under the *ancien régime* to keep unfortunates who had fallen foul of the powerful with influence at court locked up for indefinite periods without trial. Sade himself was held under a *lettre de cachet* for thirteen years at the instigation of his mother-in-law, the Présidente de Montreuil, embittered by the effect of Donatien's libertine behaviour. At the age of thirty, and while married to the elder daughter, Renée-Pélagie, he had seduced her seventeen-year-old daughter, Anne-Prospère de Launay, and absconded with her to Italy. The whole affair had not ended well. Anne-Prospère spent the rest of her days in a convent, where she succumbed to smallpox at the young age of twenty-nine. Sade was finally released from prison in the Revolution with all other prisoners held under this iniquitous system.

68 *'perjury is a virtue . . . threat of crime'*: the quotation is from Act V, Scene 9 of *Le Siège de Calais* by Pierre-Laurent Buirette de Belloy (1765). Belloy's tragedy was extremely popular, marking the rise of French patriotism following France's humiliating defeat by the English in the Seven Years War (1756–63).

85 *Receiving less . . . those who do it*: Rodin is here a mouthpiece for the author's contempt for Rousseau's social contract. See note to p. 37.

91 *The Persians . . . the Greeks*: Rodin again acts as the author's mouthpiece in another display of authorial erudition. The speech that follows abounds with geographical, historical, and cultural references. It is certainly true that infanticide has been practised on every continent throughout history, including all those mentioned here. Most of the specific examples Rodin gives are accurate, or at least likely. Lycurgus was the legendary lawgiver of Sparta, who established the military-oriented reformation of Spartan society in accordance with the Oracle of Apollo at Delphi. All his reforms were directed towards the three Spartan virtues: equality (among citizens), military fitness, and austerity. The myth of the founding of Rome by Romulus and Remus has the two brothers thrown into the river Tiber by their father in a failed attempt to murder them. According to the Laws of the Twelve Tables, the earliest attempt by the Romans to create a code of law in 450 BC, a badly deformed child was to be quickly killed. Both Plato and Aristotle recommended infanticide as legitimate state policy in ancient Greece. Child sacrifice was common among the ancient Gauls. The Pentateuch, which consists of the first five books of the Old Testament, certainly contains many examples of child murder, though these are not always positively represented. Mary Hamilton, the mistress of Tsar Peter the Great, was decapitated for infanticide in St Petersburg on 14 March 1719. On the other hand, there is no clear evidence that the Parthians practised infanticide, the first Christian emperor of Rome, Constantine, enacted measures to prevent it, and the Stoics believed that the newborn baby had a prima-facie right to life.

92 *Cook . . . South Seas*: reference to James Cook, the eighteenth-century British explorer, whose accounts of his discoveries are classics that Sade would undoubtedly have read.

93 *Chilperic*: Chilperic I was the sixth-century king of Neustria (or Soissons) from 561 to his death. He was one of the sons of the Frankish King Clotaire 1 and Queen Aregund. Having married a number of times and arranged for at least one of his wives to be murdered in order that he might take another bride, Chilperic has a bloodthirsty reputation in the early history of France.

The Jesuits in Fine Fettle: this libertine and highly blasphemous tale (*Les Jésuites en belle humeur*) is part of a larger volume entitled *The Jesuits and Monks in Fine Fettle* (*Les Jésuites et les moines en belle humeur*). It was first published anonymously in 1675 and reprinted in numerous editions well into the eighteenth century. The work is a biting satire of the Jesuits in particular and monastic orders in general, which it represents as thoroughly corrupt and abusive of women. It contains many explicit scenes of perverse sexual acts. Sade no doubt had a well-thumbed copy in his library.

97 *the Dauphiné*: a former province in south-eastern France, whose area

roughly corresponded to that of the present departments of Isère, Drôme, and Hautes-Alpes. In addition to many other locations in the south-east of the country, Justine visits the Dauphiné's historical capital Grenoble, and one of its major towns, Vienne. The distance from Paris to Grenoble is 575 km, or roughly five-and-a-half hours' driving time. In the eighteenth century to cover such a distance on foot would have taken several weeks. Justine's travels through France are many and varied, but tend to include those cities and areas best known to the author, such as this region, and of course, Paris, while there are also references throughout the text to Languedoc and Provence, Sade's stomping ground. *Justine* is on one important level a picaresque novel or *Bildungsroman*, in which a naive young person is seen to learn (or in this case, perhaps, fail to learn) from the experiences he or she undergoes on his or her travels. In true picaresque tradition, Sade's heroine must certainly have covered thousands of kilometres by the end of her journeying, most of this on foot.

108 '*I want the hen to lay . . . how soft it is!*': Clement's penchant is for coprophagy, or the act of eating faeces for sexual arousal. Sade dwells on this activity in his unfinished prison work, *Les Cent-Vingt Journées de Sodome* (*The 120 Days of Sodom*).

112 *The monks drink and replenish their energies*: see note to p. 170.

123 '*Without a doubt, there are certain sponges . . .*': sponges were in use in Europe by eighteenth-century prostitutes and were dipped in various solutions, including vinegar, lemon, and other astringents. Such solutions were intended as a primitive attempt to kill sperm, while the sponges were thought to increase the method's success.

124 *the infamous Maréchal de Retz*: the reference is to Gilles de Montmorency-Laval, Baron de Rais, also known as Gilles de Retz (1404–40), a Breton knight and companion-in-arms of Joan of Arc. He bears the reputation of being one of history's most ruthless child-rapists and murderers. He was accused by the Inquisition of the rape and murder of numerous children and executed for these crimes, although it has been suggested that he was framed for political reasons. He may have been the inspiration for the 1697 fairy-tale *Bluebeard* by Charles Perrault.

Dom Lobineau: *The History of Brittany* by Guy Alexis Lobineau (1666–1727), better known as Dom Lobineau, a Breton historian and Benedictine monk. He is best known for his *Histoire de Bretagne* (*History of Brittany*) of 1707. The book contains a lurid description of the deeds of Gilles de Retz (see previous note).

137 *It is in the mother's womb . . . nature of our tastes*: Sade frequently, as here, appears to prefigure certain concepts of Freudian psychoanalysis. On a philosophical level this is also a deterministic view of human nature, allied to atheistic materialism, according to which behaviour is predetermined from an early age and therefore worthy of neither praise nor blame.

143 *The wolf that devours the lamb . . . his lubricity*: Sade here joins earlier

eighteenth-century philosophers, notably Voltaire, in attacking philosophical optimism, a doctrine that held Nature to be fundamentally good: cf. note to p. 5.

153 *Yet, who can define the soul of a libertine?*: this sentence is an almost verbatim copy of a line in Choderlos de Laclos's epistolary novel, *Les Liaisons dangereuses* (Letter 9 from Madame de Volanges to the Présidente de Tourvel), another instance of Sade's penchant for plagiarism. In this masterful study of libertine psychology, published nearly a decade earlier, in 1782, the Vicomte de Valmont and the Marquise de Merteuil vie with each other to debauch pious young men and women. The 1999 film *Cruel Intentions* (dir. Roger Kumble) offers a rather good modern reworking of Laclos's novel.

170 *They served two soups . . . and ten cups of coffee*: food and drink play an indispensable role in the Sadean orgy, both as restorative in the case of the libertine and as means of 'fattening up' the victim. Eating and drinking are frequently carried to impossible and occasionally laughable extremes. The giant Gernande's hunger for his wife's blood is matched only by the food and drink he consumes daily. The long list of dishes and wines he gets through at dinner recalls the exaggerated abundance of fairy-tales and ends on a particularly humorous note, which is more suggestive of extraordinary over-indulgence than of an ogre's gruesome diet.

176 *Euripides*: the ancient Greek dramatist (*c*.484–407 BC) was in fact bitterly criticized for the sympathy he showed to slaves, beggars, and women characters like Medea. His plays depict many other complex suffering female figures, including Andromache, Electra, Iphigenia, Helen, and Phaedra.

177 *the Council of Mâcon*: this reference owes less to fact than to a persistent legend, according to which bishops of the Catholic Church are said to have seriously debated the existence of a soul in women. One version of the legend has it that this debate took place at the Council of Trent in 1545, while another version insists that it was held in the sixth century at the second Council of Mâcon. There is no reliable historical evidence that any such debate ever took place. Many other examples cited here of the little worth accorded to women in different cultures are of equally dubious veracity, as is Sade's rather vague location of Eskimos in America.

Cato the Wise: Marcus Porcius Cato (234–149 BC), known as Cato the Wise or Cato the Elder, was reputed to have a particularly low opinion of women.

180 *'But there is no need . . . of my own heart'*: Sade is attempting to demonstrate his erudition again here, but these many historical, cultural, and geographical references mix fact with fiction, although Sade probably believed them all to be accurate. The sacrifice of widows on the banks of the Ganges is certainly factual. An ancient Hindu practice, named *sati*, ordained that the widow of a deceased Hindu should throw herself, either voluntarily or forcibly, onto her husband's funeral pyre. The practice was

outlawed by the British in 1829. The reference to Captain Cook's recent discoveries in the New World is sufficiently vague to be unobjectionable.

190 *Phoebus nonsense*: in Greek mythology Phoebus was literally 'the radiant one', and the name was an epithet of Apollo because of his connection with the sun. The Romans venerated him as Phoebus Apollo. Saint-Florent is referring to Justine's comparison of the charitable man with the sun as source of 'celestial light'.

202 *You are going to die . . . whether it fits you*: this is a good example of Sade's fondness for a black humour that may be related to a certain contempt on his part for the more laughable aspects of Gothic fiction: see John Phillips, 'Circles of Influence: Lewis, Sade, Artaud', *Comparative Critical Studies*, 9: 1 (2012), 61–82.

Well, then! . . . into the hands of the wicked: Roland appears to be ironically echoing the taunting of Christ on the cross.

217 *in the annals of Andronicus, the Neros, Tiberius, or Wenceslaus*: Andronicus is probably a reference to Shakespeare's eponymous anti-hero. Shakespeare's play *Titus Andronicus* tells the fictional story of Titus, a general in the Roman army, who is engaged in a cycle of revenge with Tamora, Queen of the Goths. It is the bard's bloodiest and most violent work. The Roman emperors Nero and Tiberius are examples of extremely cruel monarchs from history. Saint Wenceslaus, ruler of Bohemia in the tenth century, was murdered by his brother Boleslav I, or the Cruel (with whom Sade may have confused him), who then occupied the throne from 935 until his death in 972.

222 *Given these reflections . . . burnt in Siam*: Dubois here extrapolates from Montesquieu's doctrine of the relativity of laws, expounded in the 1748 work *De l'Esprit des lois* (*On the Spirit of the Laws*), to reach the illogical conclusion that there are no universals in human culture, and that therefore no act can ever be considered a crime.

224 *If there were a God . . . I must despise*: for Voltaire, whom Sade here echoes, God is either omnipotent or benevolent but cannot be both, given the existence of physical and moral evil in the world: see Voltaire's *Poem on the Disaster of Lisbon* (1756) and *Candide* (1759).

241 *Looking for a water-closet . . . proof positive*: one can hear a bitter reference here to the author's own experiences during what came to be known as 'the Marseilles affair'. In 1772 the young marquis was accused of attempting to murder a prostitute and, on evidence that subsequently proved false, sentenced to death by the court at Aix.

253 *I did not understand this expression . . . I was close to fainting*: this episode prefigures the rather more serious fate of Eugénie's mother in *Philosophy in the Boudoir* (1795), whereby the young heroine sews up her mother's vagina to prevent her from 'giving her any more little brothers and sisters'.

255 *'What proof could they offer to support their allegations?'*: there are echoes

here of Sade's own brushes with the law. On at least one occasion a prostitute had lodged a complaint against him on grounds of physical cruelty and sacrilege, accusations for which there proved to be no material evidence: see the Introduction, p. x.

260 *And the two sisters . . . only in tears*: there is a hint of parody here of the *conte larmoyant* or sentimental tale, popular in the period. The principal characteristic of such tales was their extreme exaggeration in the expression of human emotions, especially joy and sadness, both of which frequently give rise to floods of tears. The fashion for such stories was probably begun by Johann Wolfgang von Goethe's hugely popular *The Sufferings of Young Werther* (*Die Leiden des Jungen Werthers*) of 1774.

262 *this dreadful brood*: Sade refers to the period following the French Revolution in 1789, when the Benedictine Order, along with all other religious orders, was formally abolished. Sade became a successful orator and eventually rose to the position of magistrate during the Revolution, and would have been well acquainted with—and, as an atheist, wholly approving of—the suppression of monastic orders.

264 *even though the latter was a minister*: the stress placed on these words suggests that it is surprising for ministers of state to serve anyone well except themselves. This is simply another instance of Sade's cynicism about the corruption of politicians, or indeed any powerful figure under the *ancien régime*.

The Oxford World's Classics Website

www.worldsclassics.co.uk

- Browse the full range of Oxford World's Classics online

- Sign up for our monthly e-alert to receive information on new titles

- Read extracts from the Introductions

- Listen to our editors and translators talk about the world's greatest literature with our Oxford World's Classics audio guides

- Join the conversation, follow us on Twitter at OWC_Oxford

- Teachers and lecturers can order inspection copies quickly and simply via our website

www.worldsclassics.co.uk